A DAUGHTER'S RETURN

Florence Stanville is a woman with a past.
When she moves to Guisethorpe on the east
coast of England, the townsfolk are intrigued
by this glamorous and mysterious stranger
with her flame-red hair and abrupt manners.
Florence doesn't care about the gossips —
she's drawn to the peaceful seaside town by
the pull of her childhood. The riddle of those
days remains, and now she can only snatch at
half-remembered memories and shadowy figures in her dreams. As Florence is reluctantly
drawn into the lives of her new neighbours, the
layers of her own life are revealed. Far from
finding peace, Florence has found instead turmoil and secrets. Can she put the pieces of her
past together, or will it remain a closed book
forever . . . ?

JOSEPHINE COX
with GILLY MIDDLETON

———————◆———————

A
DAUGHTER'S
RETURN

Complete and Unabridged

CHARNWOOD
Leicester

First published in Great Britain in 2021 by
HarperCollins*Publishers*
London

First Charnwood Edition
published 2021
by arrangement with
HarperCollins*Publishers*
London

Gilly Middleton is acknowledged as the
co-author of this work

*A catalogue record for this book is available
from the British Library.*

ISBN 978–1–4448–4751–2

Published by
Ulverscroft Limited
Anstey, Leicestershire

Printed and bound in Great Britain by
TJ Books Ltd., Padstow, Cornwall

This book is printed on acid-free paper

In loving memory of Josephine Cox

Prologue

'Wait for me. Wait . . . ' Little Flo calls. It starts as a game. She's happy, full of fun, keen to play. 'You'll never catch me,' whispers a voice in the air around her, and the other, taller girl is smiling her dazzling smile over her shoulder. She flicks her head round, her red hair swinging across her narrow back in a bright curtain, and forges ahead down the long straight corridor.

The walls are papered with an old-fashioned floral design, pretty but very faded with age. There are no pictures and the ceiling is high. Many rooms lie to either side but all the doors are closed and the passage is as dim as twilight, though it is not clear what the source of even this meagre light is. Little Flo doesn't know where this corridor leads, only that it stretches far, far ahead.

The other girl's legs are longer than Flo's and the distance between the two children is soon doubled, then tripled . . . And still they run and run, endlessly, the beautiful red-headed child getting further and further away, Little Flo tiring and panting, beginning to panic that the other girl is leaving her behind. She's frightened now. This is no longer a game. It is imperative that the older girl is caught, that she stays, that she is safe — Little Flo will keep her safe — and yet she keeps running away into the unknown, to some unnamed peril.

'Wait, please wait . . . ' pleads Little Flo, her

arms extended beseechingly.

Eventually she has to stop to catch her breath and as she pauses she sees the flash of red hair as the other girl, way, way in the distance now, reaches the end at last, takes a turn to the left and disappears.

Little Flo resumes her pursuit. All will be well if only the two are together again. She knows this instinctively. She *has* to catch up.

When she reaches the end there is no left turn, just blank wall. Not even a door that can be opened. She is just a little girl all alone, in the semi-dark, and there is nowhere to go and no one to go with. She feels tears rise in her eyes and her throat is tight as she turns the only way she can: back where she came from, her legs so weary, her breath tight with all the running, her heart stricken with fear.

The long corridor stretches out ahead and Little Flo starts back down it on heavy legs. But every step takes her further from the girl, who looks so like herself: older, taller, but the same skinny, coltish legs and beacon-bright hair.

Eventually, far ahead she sees a tall figure, a woman who also has red hair, hers coiled up at the nape of her neck, and wearing a long straight frock. The woman has her hands to her face and she's crying hard, her shoulders heaving.

'Mummy!' screams Little Flo.

$\star$ $\star$ $\star$

Florence wakes with a gasp, her heart pounding. The not-yet-familiar room is dark and silent but

2

for the quiet tick of her bedside clock. The memory of the nightmare quickly recedes, in the way of all dreams, its sharp edges of fear and grief softened in a minute or two, but leaving her with a hollow feeling of loss.

They have all gone now — the father she cannot even envisage at all, the child she pursued in the dream, and now her mother, too. Only Florence remains.

1

'I think,' said Mildred Yateman to her husband, Jim, 'that I might just pop over to Paradise.' Better than going to hell, thought Jim, but resisted the temptation to say it. 'So what's happening at Paradise?'

'That's what I mean to find out. Doreen's been asking since the 'Sold' sign went up and I know she and Mary will be wanting to know who the new owner is. I saw a woman there earlier; went up the lane for a few minutes with a dog. Funny-looking little thing — the dog, not her. *She* looked quite smart. Nice little jacket — red, would you believe, and so is her hair. I didn't like to visit when her furniture was being moved in, but the van came and left yesterday and I think it's time I went over to say hello. I've been keeping a lookout and she's back now so this could be my chance.'

'Quite right, love,' said Jim, determinedly not looking through the front windows towards Paradise Cottage, over the lane. 'You've a duty to Guisethorpe to find out everything you can and report back in full. No time to lose. In fact, I think you should make a list of questions to ask her, so's you don't overlook anything. Take a notebook and pen with you, why don't you?'

Mildred gave him a long look. 'Are you being funny, Jim?'

'Never.'

'Well, I still think I ought to go and introduce

5

myself; welcome her to the village.'

'It's not your village to welcome her to, Mil. You know, you could leave it until you just happen to meet her in the street instead of bothering the poor woman. She probably hasn't even got her boxes unpacked yet.'

'I suppose so.' Mildred stood on tiptoe, craning her neck and peering short-sightedly over her own front garden, trying to see into the windows of the pretty cottage opposite. 'But Doreen said — '

'Doreen Potter and Mary Davis can wait. Mary, at least, is a good sensible sort and I can't think that she'd want you to be intruding on the new-comer.'

'Mm . . . maybe.' Mildred was secretly a little in awe of Mary Davis, who was a retired headmistress and whom Mildred considered 'refined'.

'Leave it, love. The chance will come to meet the woman, never fear, and when it does I have every confidence you'll take full advantage of it.'

'Thank you, Jim,' said Mildred, as if her husband had paid her a compliment.

She gave Paradise Cottage a last careful inspection, so far as she could see it without blatantly putting on her glasses, then reluctantly gave up her vigil and went to make lunch.

After Jim and Mildred had eaten, Jim decided he'd better work off the vast helping of steak and kidney pudding he'd consumed by weeding his vegetable plot, which was a very large part of the long back garden, beyond his shed. He donned his gardening togs and collected from the shed his tools and a large chip basket for the ripe produce, wondering how he'd even be able to look at any

6

vegetables that afternoon, so full did his stomach feel. Still, at least it would be peaceful down there. Mildred considered vegetable-growing to be man's work and she'd made the front garden her own domain.

Mildred went to sit in her armchair by the front window, her favourite spot to watch if anyone was passing in the quiet lane, but this afternoon her attention was solely on Paradise Cottage and its briefly glimpsed new owner. She put on her glasses and, safe from Jim's censure, stood on the chair seat, holding on to the high back, craning her neck to see if she could make out anyone or anything happening at the cottage.

There was no doubt that it was a very pretty little house — almost picture-perfect, in fact — with blowsy pink roses growing up the criss-crossed wooden trellis that made up the sides of the porch, a white clapboard front giving it the characteristic 'seaside' look of many Guisethorpe cottages, and two little upstairs windows, which, right up under the eaves, gave the impression of eyes in a friendly face. The garden was overgrown, since the cottage had been unoccupied for several months, but even that was attractive, with roses and dahlias blooming brightly among poppies and other tall weeds. It looked somehow . . . carefree. Yes, that was the word, Mildred decided. Not to her own taste really — she glanced proudly at the serried rows of French marigolds edging her straight front path — but it certainly had charm, if you didn't mind disorder and wildness.

There was no sign of the new owner, though, or the little dog.

7

After a while Mildred's ankles started to swell with her balancing on the cushioned armchair seat, and she carefully lowered her feet to the floor one at a time, sat down, changed her distance glasses for reading ones, and decided to catch up on the latest *Woman's Own*, while still keeping vigilant for activity at the cottage. Soon, however, the heaviness of her lunch overcame her, her eyes closed and the magazine slipped off her lap as she dozed.

★　★　★

Florence Stanville had just finished washing out the last of the kitchen cupboards when the bell in the narrow hallway jangled and Scamper gave a little bark.

Not the best moment to have a visitor, and who could possibly want to see her anyway? Crossly, Florence pulled at her wet rubber gloves, which stretched and snapped around her hot hands but would not be removed. The bell jangled again and Scamper was now at the door, fussing and letting the visitor, whoever it was, know she was there.

'All right, all right, I'm coming,' Florence huffed. 'Scamper, out of my way.'

She opened the front door and there was an overweight grey-haired man, wearing a moth-eaten sleeveless pullover and shapeless grubby trousers. He was smiling and holding out a twine-tied bundle of slender runner beans. She'd never seen him before, of course, and he didn't look like a greengrocer, so why was he here handing out beans?

'Yes?' she asked, snapping the yellow rubber fingers, again to no effect.

The man's smile slipped a little but he was passing her the beans before she could refuse them.

'I'm Jim Yateman. I live over there, Sea View, with my wife, Mildred.'

'Yes?'

'We saw you'd moved in and I just came to say hello. Thought you might like some runners. I've a load to spare and, frankly, you'd be doing me a favour if you took them off my hands.' The man looked embarrassed, as if he knew he was gabbling foolishly. 'Is there anything you need?' He glanced at the yellow gloves. 'I take it you've managed to light the range, Mrs . . . ?'

Florence put the beans on the floor and started to peel off one of the gloves from the wrist end; her hands were very clammy now.

'Hello, Mr Yateman. Thanks for the beans. Yes, thank you, I did *manage* to light the range and I've plenty of hot water. In fact, I was up to my elbows in it when you rang the doorbell,' she added pointedly.

Jim Yateman looked cowed. 'I'm sorry if it's not a good time.'

'It isn't.'

'Oh . . . oh, well, maybe I should be off then, Mrs . . . ?'

Florence continued working on the removal of the gloves, turning each inside out as she peeled it off her hand. Jim dithered, evidently waiting for her to say something else.

'So you grew these beans yourself?' she asked poor Jim eventually.

9

'Yes, of course . . . in my garden, Mrs . . . ?'

'Clever . . . Thank you. Good of you to call. Goodbye, Mr Yateman.' And she picked up the vegetables, gave him a brief smile and gently closed the door.

'Nosy busybody,' she muttered. At least the runner beans would do for dinner tonight. Beans on toast, sort of . . . She was grateful for that, but it didn't mean she was prepared to part with any information about herself in exchange, certainly not until she knew who was who and what was what. She hadn't asked Jim Yateman to come round and she wasn't going to play up to his expectations or by his rules, or anybody else's. She'd start as she meant to go on: on her own terms. If folk wanted to visit when it wasn't convenient, pressing home-grown veg on her, then she'd say thank you, but that was all she'd say.

'We're not in a hurry to get to know folk, are we, love? Better it's just you and me for the moment, eh, Scamper, till we're settled in?' She reached down and patted the little dog's curly head, and Scamper gave an answering wag of her tail and gazed at her mistress adoringly, as if she knew they were everything to each other and in this together.

Florence went to shut Scamper in the sitting room, where she'd put the dog basket. Then she went back to the kitchen and put the beans on a shelf in the recently cleaned pantry.

Reluctantly she donned the sweaty rubber gloves again, ran a fresh bucket of hot water, added ammonia, dunked her mop in and began vigorously cleaning the floor.

At least there was endless hot water today . . . Oh,

10

but that range had been a bugger, filthy dirty on top, the ovens caked in grease and a disgusting layer of ash left in the firebox. Luckily there was plenty of coal in the little shed at the side of the house, though that was festooned with black spider webs and it looked as if mice had been gnawing the door. She'd had no kindling and had had to improvise with pages ripped from a book. She felt bad about that but not once had she even considered going to the house opposite to ask for help. That would have been falling at the very first fence. No, independence was the rule in this new life, in this old place, and she meant to stick to it.

★ ★ ★

Jim, cleaning his gardening tools in a bucket under the outside tap, decided not to tell Mildred about his encounter with the impatient new resident of Paradise Cottage. He hadn't meant to be nosy or interfering, just neighbourly. He hadn't even meant to visit until the ludicrous excess of runner beans in today's harvest had made him think his neighbour opposite might not have any, while he could easily spare any amount. It had been a spur-of-the-moment idea, but a bad one, as it turned out.

Jim tried not to feel hurt or petty about his reception. He hadn't intended to patronise her, asking about the range, but she'd obviously taken it the wrong way. Or maybe she was just tired after the house move and was busy trying to get straight. That would be it . . . No doubt when they met the next time she'd apologise and they'd both

11

laugh it off and become friends. After all, he got on all right with most people . . .

She hadn't even told him her name, though he'd given her a cue. Thrice, in fact. Perhaps she was shy . . . Certainly, with that soft-vowelled northern way of speaking, she wasn't local to the east coast: Lancashire, he thought. A pretty woman, too: not young, but a lot younger than Mildred and him. Slim, and very striking with all that red hair coiled up. None of that permed style Mildred went in for. Jim laughed. The little brown dog was cute and had a permed look about its coat. There must be an element of poodle in there somewhere, along with some kind of terrier, perhaps.

Back in his shed, Jim tied up several more bundles of runner beans with garden twine and placed them in an orange box with the usual sign: '3d a bunch. Money in tin, please.' He took the box and the tin down to the table in the lane beside the front gate and left it there without much hope. Many of the keen vegetable gardeners of Guisethorpe grew runners, and there must be enough beans in the village to feed everyone, and probably most of Fleming St Clair further down the coast, too, though they were likely swamped with their own beans, of course.

As he turned to go back inside he noticed, at the far side of Paradise Cottage, a car, parked on the little bit of rough ground there. So, the rude woman — and there really was no other way to describe her — was not only competent at lighting her range but she was a driver, too. Of course, the car — which he saw was a green Morris Minor very much in need of a clean, as if it had just been driven a long way — might belong to her husband. Yet there'd been no sign of any man at the cottage. Jim tried to think whether the woman had worn a wedding ring but all he could remember of her hands was a pair of bright yellow rubber gloves. He did remember her eyes, though: blue, a proper dark blue — unusual with such red hair — and with a very direct look in them, when she could be bothered to give him her attention. Jim surprised himself with this thought. He had enough self-knowledge to know he didn't usually notice the colour of a woman's eyes.

No, he would definitely not be mentioning his foolish excursion over the road to Mildred. He'd told her it would be a mistake to go, and then he'd gone himself and proved it. And, after all, he had nothing to say about the visit anyway. He knew no more about the woman at Paradise Cottage than he had before he went.

★　★　★

Florence had eaten the beans on toast — far better than toast by itself; the beans had been delicious and very tender — and decided to take advantage of the light summer evening to take Scamper for a walk. The dog had been bored while Florence cleaned the kitchen, and then overexcited when she'd started to unpack some of the tea chests in the sitting room.

They went down the lane this time, towards where it joined the road that, from there, ran parallel to the beach. Florence pointedly did not even glance at the windows of the house opposite, set higher up than her cottage. Beside the gate labelled 'Sea View' — Florence rolled her eyes at the name, which managed to be both predictable and inappropriate — was a small spindly table, now empty, but the purpose of which she guessed at once. Jim Yateman was probably almost giving away his glut of beans. She thought about that as she walked, Scamper pulling a little on her lead, keen to explore all the new scents along the way.

As they approached the sea and the lane broadened, the breeze blowing in from the east could be felt, even on this warm summer evening; with it, stronger with every step Florence took, came the glorious seaside smell, and then the insistent *shushing* wash of waves on the shore. Next the view of the beach, stretching away south as far as she could see in a long ribbon of pebbly sand. There was no one else close by as Florence stopped to take in the scene, watching the roll of the waves between the groynes, seeing the last of the children packing up to go home, abandoning ambitious sandcastles, which would be gone by morning, leaving pristine sand to be dug again tomorrow. Once, she had been such a child. The tired walk home on sandy feet, with a red-painted spade, a decorated tin bucket and a heart full of happiness had been her end to the day.

She closed her eyes and inhaled deeply. This special mixture of salt and fresh air, the clean-but-dirty beach smell, the tang of seaweed, with the background sounds of the call of herring gulls and the whisper of the waves was a perfect evocation of the best of her childhood. Her stomach did a little flip as the memory of herself and her mother, just the two of them together, surrounding each other with love on such a summer's day, on this beach, by this village, with this same soft evening light, the same gently buffeting breeze, and all these sounds and smells, came rushing back in a moment. So complete was the sudden surge of her recall that Florence was filled with a longing that left her breathless.

'Oh, Mum, my darling mum . . . ' she whispered, and her free hand flew to the locket on the fine silver chain around her neck. Briefly she gripped it tightly; if only she could hold her mother again as she was holding the locket she had given her, containing a photograph of each of them: 'Lily' and 'Little Flo' pencilled on the backs.

Lily had been dead for seven months now and, at unexpected moments, Florence still felt the sudden weight of her grief assaulting her heart. It was as Lily lay dying that something she had said had called Florence's mind back to this beautiful place and a time that, to Florence, was for ever full of love and happiness.

'Guisethorpe,' Lily had whispered, 'so lovely . . . the perfect place to start again.'

'Oh, Mum, yes, Guisethorpe! It was wonderful. You made life there so happy for me. When I think of it I always remember sunshine, that golden beach and the sea. You were so brave, making that new life for us.'

Lily had given a sigh. 'Not brave, love . . . running away. I just couldn't forgive . . . '

'Forgive, Mum? Forgive what? Who?' Florence questioned quietly, gently smoothing back her mother's faded hair. Lily's mind tended to wander

15

and Florence knew not to pick up on everything she said. This, however, might be some worry Florence could explain away.

'So many widows in those days . . . what was one more? Didn't matter what the truth was. Too late now . . .'

Lily was so very weak; this was not the time to bombard her with questions and risk any upset. Even so: 'The truth, Mum?' Florence ventured, but Lily had her eyes closed now. 'Mum . . . ?'

'Too late now . . .' Lily murmured again faintly. 'So long ago. Oh, such a beautiful seaside . . .'

In the weeks after Lily's death the idea of the 'beautiful seaside' of that idyllic time had played on Florence's mind. So, in a bid to push aside her misery and rediscover hope and happiness, she had come to Guisethorpe, found Paradise Cottage and bought it without hesitation. And now she was here, settling into her new life, hoping to heal her grief. Her mother's words on her death-bed settled at the back of her mind: maybe she would find out eventually what Lily had meant — if, indeed she had meant anything — and here, at least, was the place to do it.

Scamper, puzzled and excluded, was beginning to fuss now. Florence opened her eyes, surprised to feel tears threatening — ridiculous when Lily had been dead for all these months — and pleased to see she and Scamper were still alone.

Two deep breaths, then: 'Come on, lass, the beach is all ours,' she said determinedly, and strode out along the pavement beside the seafront road, then took the first set of steep steps down onto the sand, Scamper bouncing ahead on the

16

long lead, then turning with a little bark to make sure her mistress was keeping up.

* * *

Anthony Bird stood at the large bay window of his flat above the café he owned on the seafront. From up here he had an uninterrupted view of the sea and of most of the beach across the road. He loved this time of the evening, when the beach cleared of visitors and their noise and picnic mess, and he could just stand here and relax, and do nothing but drink his beer or his Scotch and think about not very much. During the high season these quiet times were doubly precious. Thank goodness the summer holidays would soon be over, the visitors would go home, and life in Guisethorpe would return to its habitual sleepy pace.

He noticed a woman walking her dog along the beach, right down by the water's edge. The occasional rogue wave swept in around their feet and sent the woman skittering back, laughing, while the little dog splashed in the shallows. Anthony didn't recognise her, so she must be a visitor, but she certainly hadn't been in the café. He'd have remembered that red hair, doubly striking with the scarlet jacket she wore. She was tall, he could tell, even though she was by herself, and very slim, and the jacket was tailored perfectly to her figure. He watched her for several minutes, knowing he was unseen up here, until she turned for home, the dog trotting obediently to heel beside her.

The doorbell rang. For a moment Anthony considered not answering it, but it might be Trudie, though she didn't usually come round on a Tuesday. Still, an evening lying on the sofa with Trudie in his arms would be perfect after the stress-filled day he'd had, and she might even cook dinner for them both . . . if there was anything in the fridge.

It wasn't Trudie waiting on the step. It was Margaret McGee, carrying a briefcase and wearing a tightly buttoned two-piece and a severe expression.

'Good evening, Mr Bird,' she said. 'I hope you haven't forgotten our appointment.'

'Er, no, Miss McGee. Come on up.' With a sinking heart he dismissed any thought of Trudie and dinner as he led the accountant up the stairs to the flat.

'Would you like a cup of tea, Miss McGee, before we get started?'

'No, thank you, Mr Bird. We've got a lot to go through so let's begin straight away, shall we?' She put her briefcase down in a large squashy armchair, unbuckled the flap and extracted a sheaf of typed papers, including columns of figures. Then she went to sit at the dining table and officiously pulled out a chair beside hers for Anthony. 'Come along, Mr Bird, we've no time to lose,' she ordered him, 'though looking at these figures I can only think you must have money to lose.'

Anthony, who had been about to bring his glass of beer over, decided he'd better sit soberly and hear the worst. Margaret McGee was absolutely terrifying but she knew what she was talking about and wasn't given to exaggeration, which was worrying, given what she had implied.

It turned out that it would have been difficult to

exaggerate quite how bad the figures for the café business were.

'I suppose I could always cut Violet's wages,' Anthony offered meekly when they had gone through everything and he saw how bleak the prospects of continuing in business were.

'Frankly, Mr Bird, I'm amazed she's prepared to work for such a paltry sum as it is. It's not over-paying your cook that's got you in this mess, or your waitress either.'

'Maybe I could get rid of Carmen altogether,' Anthony suggested.

'A café without a waitress?' said Miss McGee. She raised one eyebrow and Anthony looked down at the table of figures in front of him, feeling silly.

'I'm sorry to have to tell you this,' Margaret McGee said, 'but the reason this business is failing is because of you. It's *you* that is drawing out a wage far greater than the business can support, and — if I may speak quite frankly, Mr Bird — what is it actually for? What do you *do*?'

'Well, it is my business . . .'

'Yes, and your father's and your grandfather's before you, as I am well aware, but Mr Bird senior was also a client of Blackett and McGee, and I had the pleasure of dealing with him in his later years. He cooked the food most days and your mother worked tirelessly to serve it. They both paid themselves only as much as the business could afford, which in the winter was not a lot, and in summer they worked all hours to make Bird's a special place for visitors to Guisethorpe. I think, Mr Bird, you might have been trading on your father's reputation, but if you use the café

19

as if it were your private bank account instead of a business that requires upkeep and investment, then I'm very much afraid that before the end of the year you'll be 'over-drawn', by which I mean bankrupt.'

'Surely not?'

'Mr Bird, you have seen the figures, you know what your turnover is and you know what your expenses are, and one of the main withdrawals from the business is what you pay yourself. I cannot make it plainer: you must either pay yourself less or work harder and increase profit. It's as simple as that.'

Anthony slumped back in his chair, scowling. The woman was like some strict and bossy schoolteacher, telling him off. He'd a good mind to sack *her*. Heaven knew, Blackett and McGee were well enough paid for delivering bad news every quarter.

'So what do you suggest I do?' he asked, aware that he sounded both clueless and desperate.

'I have told you,' Miss McGee said patiently. 'You must take less out of the business for yourself.'

'But — '

'Economise! Live more cheaply! And get in more customers — though, goodness knows, the season's nearly finished and there isn't much opportunity to make a difference by the end of August.'

'But — '

'I cannot tell you how to run your café, Mr Bird. That is not the job of an accountant. But I have shown you the gap between what you pay yourself and what the business can afford to pay you, and you need to close that gap, and quickly.' She glanced around the large, stuffy and untidy room with its magnificent sea view. 'You own this whole building — have you considered renting out the flat?'

'But it's my home . . . '

'Mr Bird, I only make a suggestion. You have the figures and if I were you I'd give them some very serious consideration.'

She left him a duplicate copy of the accounts and stood up, shaking his hand, which he offered auto-matically, still shell-shocked at the very thought of having to leave the flat.

'Goodbye, Mr Bird. I shall see myself out,' Miss McGee said. She picked up her briefcase and left.

Anthony heard her tread on the stairs and then the thud of the front door being closed firmly behind her.

He exhaled loudly and, muttering curses, went to sit in the armchair. What remained of the glass of beer from earlier was flat and warm. He lit a cigarette and, head back on the cushion, blew a smoke ring. What on earth was he to do? This beautiful flat was his home — how could he possibly rent it to someone and go to live somewhere else? How could he give up that view? Inhaling sharply, he went to stand at the window. The beach was now deserted and twilight was setting in. The streetlamps along the quiet road were linked by strings of pretty coloured lights, modest and tasteful, in keeping with Guisethorpe's reputation as a seaside village that appealed to the elderly and to respectable families with small children, who didn't want the rowdi-ness of more popular resorts like Brighton and Blackpool. It was a pretty, old-fashioned place where people came to do nothing for a week or so in summer, as Anthony Bird himself had been doing nothing for most of his life.

He thought about telephoning Trudie, but it was too late for her to come round now. And even if she did, she'd only make a fuss if he tried to persuade her to cook his dinner, and he'd had enough upset to cope with for one evening.

He tore himself away from the beautiful dusky panorama and went to the kitchen to look in his fridge. Far from yielding the makings of a dinner, it was empty but for a half-empty box of Dairylea triangles. He thought about going down to the café to see what he could take from Violet's pantry, well stocked for the week, but even the trip downstairs and through the linking door at the back seemed too much effort. In the end he poured himself a large glass of whisky and sat down morosely before the window.

While his mind played on the disaster of his business accounts, he took up a soft-leaded pencil and, grabbing a piece of paper and a magazine to rest on, quickly sketched the severe, ample-chinned features of Miss Margaret McGee. Her nose grew more prominent than in real life, and her eyes bulged slightly as if with indignation. Her neatly waved hair took on the appearance of ripples set in concrete. It was a very satisfactory cartoon likeness and Anthony was congratulating himself on having achieved something today when he saw he'd drawn Miss McGee on the back of a sheet of the quarterly figures she'd prepared for him.

With a sudden flood of anger at the unfairness of his lot, he stabbed Miss McGee in the eye with his pencil and then crossed through her features with such force that he ripped through the paper. Scrunching it into a ball, he hurled the cartoon into the corner of the room.

Sinking back into the cushions, he breathed deeply, his eyes closed, until his angry pulse slowed and his rage passed.

After he'd replenished his glass from the bottle on the sideboard and resumed his chair, looking out over the darkened beach, his thoughts wandered to the woman with the little dog he had seen earlier. With her bright hair and brighter jacket, her air of confidence and independence, alone with just her dog, she seemed to Anthony to embody drama and style. What was a woman like that doing in sleepy little Guisethorpe? Who was she? It shouldn't take much effort for him to find out.

2

So much achieved already, Florence commended herself, putting the last of her cookery books onto the shelf in the sitting room. A slacker was no use to anyone, and she had barely sat down to eat today. Her hunger was like a private badge of honour; she would cook something delicious later and sit outside to eat it in the evening sunshine as a well-deserved reward for her hard work. Not that there was much here to eat anyway. She needed to get to the shops before closing time. But at least the sitting room was dust free, swept and vacuumed, the bedrooms were aired and pristine, the bathroom and kitchen were spotless.

Time to take Scamper for a long walk, buy some food and take a proper look at the Guisethorpe of 1957.

Florence had vague memories from her childhood of there being a butcher's shop with strings of sausages hung up, and a greengrocer's with baskets of shiny red apples arranged outside on the pavement, but that was all. Those shops might well be long gone now, nearly forty years later.

'Come along, love . . . ' She fastened Scamper's lead to her collar, took up her shopping basket from the hall floor and locked the door behind them.

As she swung the front gate shut, Florence noticed Jim Yateman's table, on the other side of the lane, was well stocked with vegetables. And there was the man himself, coming through the garden gate of Sea View, holding a box of tomatoes.

Hearing Florence's gate creaking shut, he looked up and gave a small nervous smile.

'Afternoon,' he murmured, placing the punnets of tomatoes on the table and labelling them with the price, handwritten on what looked to Florence like a square of cardboard cut from a cornflakes packet.

'Good afternoon, Mr Yateman,' said Florence. While she'd cleaned the cottage she'd had time to consider her reception of the man the previous day and thought she might have been a little bit abrupt. Maybe he really had thought nothing more than that she'd like some runner beans. But that still didn't mean she was prepared to surrender any information to fuel gossip, or strike up friendships that she might well regret later.

'I enjoyed those runners last night, Mr Yateman. Thanks for bringing them over.'

The man looked relieved, as if he'd expected a different opening. 'You're welcome, Mrs . . . ' he said.

'You've some grand stuff there, Mr Yateman.'

'Thank you. It's my hobby, really, growing veg, but there's only me and Mildred, and we soon end up with more than we can eat ourselves.'

'Do you sell much?' Florence asked, genuinely interested.

'Not many folk pass up Nightingale Lane, 'cept to walk dogs,' Jim said, eyeing Scamper. 'We're not central enough to catch the attention of visitors. The soil's good round here so a lot of folk with time on their hands — old, like me — enjoy growing vegetables. You can't sell to those that already have, though, can you?'

'No,' said Florence slowly. 'Quite right, Mr Yateman. So what happens to what you don't eat yourselves or sell here?'

'Well, it mostly just gets chucked on the compost heap in the end. Seems a waste, but we have what we need and that's really all I grow it for — that and the pleasure of doing it.'

Florence smiled and nodded. 'Well . . . must get on. Good day, Mr Yateman,' and she turned away with a wave of her hand and was off, cheerily striding down the lane towards the sea.

'Bye, Mrs . . . ' she thought she heard Jim saying, but she was on her way and didn't turn back.

When Florence got to where the shops were, on the seafront road, she saw they were partially familiar. The butcher's had the same big window, the same blue-tiled shopfront that she remembered, sawdust on the floor and pig carcasses hanging from massive hooks at the back. At the sight of these now, she recalled instantly that such carcasses had repelled her infant self, and that sometimes there had been rabbits, too, hung up by the back legs, still furry, like pets, but bigger. Fascinating but awful. Once, the pitiful sight of these poor dead creatures had overwhelmed her, and her mother had sent her out to wait on the pavement and dry her tears while the shopping was done.

Florence tied up Scamper outside, went in and bought a lamb chop, two sausages, and a bone.

While the young man in the striped apron

weighed and wrapped her purchases, Florence looked round to see if there was anything tasty to accompany the sausages. She couldn't see anything.

'Do you have any mustard or pickles, please?' she asked.

'No, I'm sorry, madam. You could try the grocer's at the end of the street. I think he has Branston,' said the butcher, and smilingly handed over Florence's shopping wrapped in brown paper, which she put in her basket.

The greengrocer's shop was, she thought, on the same premises as it had been all those years ago, too, but it looked quite different, with all the stock inside instead of a display on the pavement. She was about to go in when she thought about Mr Yateman's table of excess vegetables. It seemed unlikely he'd have sold the lot by the time she got back, and his would be fresher and cheaper.

The shop next door sold mainly sweets in tall glass jars, but just inside the door, on the floor, there were also boxes of buckets and spades, a smaller box of paper windmills and another of little red and blue patterned flags glued to thin wooden sticks, to top sandcastles. Florence thought she would have remembered this delightful combination of sweets and beach toys from her childhood, but was sure she had never seen it before. Maybe it dated from more recently.

Further up, a striped awning over the wide pavement sheltered a couple of café tables. 'Bird's Café' was embossed in slightly peeling but cheerful curly lettering on the window. A man sat smoking at one of the tables, an empty teacup in front of him. Florence peered inside and saw that the place looked clean but shabby, and that the majority of the tables were either occupied, or hadn't been cleared of used crockery. She fancied a cup of tea but she couldn't go in with Scamper; there was a sign on the door: 'No Dogs'.

'Sit here, if you like,' said the man. He got up, stubbed out his cigarette in a cheap tin ashtray and pulled out a seat at the other table for her.

'Thanks,' said Florence. Scamper tucked herself neatly under the table and lay down; she knew how to behave in public.

'What can I get for you?' asked the man. 'Would you care to see the menu?'

'No, thank you,' said Florence, surprised, hoping he wasn't going to crowd her. She hadn't realised he was anything to do with the café — he'd appeared to be a customer, sitting there with his empty cup, smoking and doing nothing — but now he was looking at her in an interested manner. 'A pot of tea for one, please.'

'Anything else? Cake, or a maybe a toasted teacake? We do sandwiches, if you would — '

'No, thank you, just the tea,' said Florence firmly, and looked away to gaze over the sea, dismissing the man with a slight turn of her shoulder. Really, was it possible to order a pot of tea without some creepy fella trying to press food on her? She might have considered a teacake if he hadn't been so pushy but she wasn't going to order one now. She'd drink the tea, pay for it and then go.

Perhaps he had got the message because the tea was brought out by a very young waitress. The girl was about fifteen, plump and tired-looking, with untidy fair hair escaping from a stubby plait.

'Your tea, madam . . .' She carefully and slightly nervously unloaded the crockery onto the metal table, almost spilling the milk. 'And what about your little dog? Shall I bring out a bowl of water?'

'Thank you . . . kind of you,' said Florence, and the girl bustled away and returned moments later with a shallow bowl of water, which she managed to slop over onto the pavement in her eagerness to please.

'Oh, sorry!'

'It's all right. No harm done.'

The girl put down the bowl, smiled shyly and then left Florence and Scamper in peace.

Florence sat gazing at the relentless breaking of the waves and inhaling the wonderful beach smell. The sun was warm but there was a pleasant breeze to take off the heat. Young families and elderly couples were sitting on the beach, some in deckchairs, and a few people were strolling along the street, glancing in the shops, but Guisethorpe on a sunny August day was far from crowded. In Florence's opinion it was just lovely.

She tried to remember what other shops had been in the little row all those years ago, when she was here with her mother, but drew a blank. She also struggled to bring to mind the house where they'd lived. She knew only that it wasn't opposite the beach — they had had to walk to the seaside — and it wasn't in Nightingale Lane, where she lived now, either. Maybe it would all come back to her in time, as that sudden rush of recall about the rabbits had in the butcher's shop. And, after all, there would be plenty of opportunity to revisit old memories, with no deadline. This wasn't a summer holiday, it was her new life. It might even be better not to go looking for the house. It could turn out to be mean and poky when once, to a child, it had seemed big and full of exciting places to play. Florence had a vague idea that there had been a lot of stairs, big rooms, but that was all. Disappointment was always a risk although, Guisethorpe being the size it was, it seemed inevitable that she'd come across her former home sooner or later. Perhaps she'd meet someone who had known her mother and could throw light on those mysterious things Lily had said at the end, about running away, not being able to forgive, and it being 'too late now'.

But it was the seaside — *this* seaside — that she had come here for — the sight of it, the scents and the sounds, and all their happy attendant associations — and those remained unchanged and unchanging.

Paradise Cottage was nice enough: pretty, in a quiet lane, not too near the main road end, yet just a short walk from the beach, but it was that beautiful beach and the quietness of the village that had clinched her decision to sell up in Lancashire and move here. She'd made up her mind quickly: she had only herself to please now and it was the right thing to do.

She drank her tea and, keen to finish her shopping, looked through the café window to catch the eye of the waitress and request the bill. Or should she go inside to pay? She was taking out her purse when the man from earlier came out.

'Did you enjoy your tea?' he asked, smiling

broadly and rubbing his hands together in an annoying fashion.

'Yes, it was fine, thank you.' Florence didn't smile. *It was tea, for goodness' sake — how enjoyable could it be?* 'Do I pay you here or at the counter?'

'I'll get you the bill.' He disappeared inside again and Florence waited impatiently, hoping he wouldn't try to engage her in conversation while she paid.

Suddenly from inside the café came a very loud crash, the unmistakable sound of a considerable amount of crockery shattering, followed by a loud wail. Florence guessed at once that it was the lament of the clumsy young waitress. The wailing grew louder until Florence decided she could hardly sit here as if nothing was happening. She got up and went inside the café, hitching Scamper's lead to a chair-back at an empty table and leaving her basket on the chair seat. Never mind 'No Dogs'!

The other customers were looking either askance or embarrassed, but all remained where they were. The man and the girl were not in sight but the girl's cries were rising in pitch and volume from behind a closed door beyond the counter.

Florence went round and opened it. There were three people in the café kitchen: the man, the girl, who was sitting on a chair, red-faced, flapping her hands and crying loudly, and a large woman at least ten years older than Florence, who was trying to calm the girl while keeping one eye on something toasting under a grill. A lot of broken cups and plates lay on the floor in front of the sink at the rear of the kitchen.

'Can I help?' Florence asked anyone. 'Are you hurt?' she asked the girl.

'Carmen's had *another* little mishap with the washing-up,' said the man angrily. 'Please don't concern yourself.'

Carmen's wails increased and she blurted out something incomprehensible.

'Is she hurt?' asked Florence again.

'I don't think so,' said the woman. 'She's just upset. It was an accident, you see.' She half addressed this pointedly to the man.

Just at that moment the smell of well-browned toast wafted from the grill and she shot back to her duties, dishing the toast onto a plate, simultaneously filling a teapot with boiling water from a gigantic tea urn. Then she put a teacake under the grill with one hand while pouring milk into a little jug with the other. Cups and saucers, lined up on the side, went on a tray next, then she loaded the tray with the toast and tea, then butter and jam, using alternate hands and moving at lightning speed. Distracted, Florence watched in fascination.

'Now, Mr Bird, perhaps you could take that out while I see about this teacake and Carmen,' said the woman.

'Yes, Violet,' the man muttered, but hovered instead of going.

Florence gathered the situation immediately. That useless man was the café owner, the efficient woman, Violet, was his cook, and the accident-prone child, Carmen, was his waitress, who had probably already been threatened with the sack if she broke any more crockery.

'Right,' said Florence, addressing the cook as clearly the only sensible person there, 'I know nowt about cafés but I can clean a floor. Why don't I clear up the mess and you can get back to the food?'

Violent hesitated for only a fraction of a second. 'Oh, that would be marvellous,' she said, 'if you're sure . . . ?'

'Come along — Carmen, is it? — and you can show me where the broom and the mop are kept. Dry your eyes and we'll do this together.'

Florence did not bother to address the café owner as clearly a waste of time, and after a few more seconds' hovering he picked up the tray Violet had prepared and took it through to the café.

Carmen's wails had decreased in the presence of the customer from outside. She gulped and sniffed into a sodden hankie, then got up and skirted the mayhem on the floor to show Florence the cleaning cupboard.

'I didn't mean to,' she said tearfully. 'It was just there was so much to wash up and I'd got behind, what with all the tables to serve and clean down earlier and — '

'Never mind that, love,' said Florence. 'I'll sweep and you can bring that bin over. There's only one place this little lot is going. Now don't start that again because it won't make matters any better.'

'But Mr Bird said — '

'It was an accident, Carmen. They happen all the time. It's kind of expected . . . almost,' Florence assured the girl, though looking at the volume of shattered crockery, Florence did wonder how she'd managed to break quite so much all in one go.

Soon the smashed pots were in the bin and Florence mopped the floor while Carmen took the full dustbin out through the back door to empty it. All the while Violet filled teapots and milk jugs, whacked bread and teacakes under the grill, shimmied omelettes in little frying pans and set trays, which she directed the proprietor, Mr Bird, to take out every time he reappeared.

'All done,' Florence declared eventually. 'Right, I'd better let you get on, Mrs . . . ?'

'Peasall. Violet Peasall,' said the cook, breaking off from her work long enough to offer Florence her hot hand.

'Florence Stanville.'

They shook hands and exchanged smiles, recognising the same strong work ethic in each other.

'Thank you, love,' said Violet. 'A ministering angel, just when we needed one.'

'Yes, thank you, Mrs Stanville,' said Carmen, shyly.

The café owner came in just in time to hear Florence's name. 'Yes, thank you, Mrs Stanville. Please . . . ' He held the door open with an awkwardly flamboyant gesture.

Florence smiled again at the staff and stepped out into the café, careful not to let the wide skirt of her dress brush against the man.

She went to retrieve her basket and Scamper.

'Now, where were we? I was just about to pay for my tea,' Florence said, finding her purse where she'd hidden it under her shopping.

'Oh, no charge,' said Mr Bird, as if he was conferring a huge favour on her. Really, the man's manner was very unfortunate for someone who catered to the public. 'Least I can do when you got us all organised,'

he added, a touch flintily, indicating he thought Florence had overstepped the mark as a stranger and a customer.

'I think the least you can do,' said Florence quietly, 'is to go and tell Carmen that she still has a job here. She's only young and she's clearly trying very hard to please. I reckon she's anxious about breaking things and that makes her clumsier, would you agree?'

'Very perceptive of you, Mrs Stanville. I'm sure you're right. Is there anything else you'd like to tell me about my staff? Or how to run my business? Because I'm sure I could benefit from your vast knowledge and experience.'

Florence raised an eyebrow, looked him square in the face and said lightly, 'No, nowt to add, Mr Bird. Thank you for the tea.'

She looped Scamper's lead over her hand, took up her basket and left.

'Woo, touched a nerve there, didn't I, love?' she laughed. 'What a horrible man. I'm not sure Bird's Café will be on our round again, though I did take to Violet Peasall . . . ' She glanced at her watch. 'Just time to get to the grocer's and then home to see what Jim Yateman's got left on his table, eh?'

★ ★ ★

Florence sat in the overgrown back garden of Paradise Cottage. She had discovered she'd bought some elaborate old wrought-iron garden chairs and a table along with the cottage. These had, inevitably, required a good clean — and would get a much-needed coat of paint eventually — but it was grand sitting out, sheltered from the breeze by the tall, shapeless hedge at the sea end of the little garden. Hollyhocks bloomed beside the back door and Scamper was sitting beneath them, noisily enjoying her bone.

Having eaten her dinner of sausages, some beautiful French beans and freshly dug potatoes bought from Jim Yateman's table, and a rather disappointing spoonful of piccalilli from the grocer's, Florence was mentally reviewing her day and physically making a list of what needed doing tomorrow. She wanted to find a job — she had inherited enough money to live on for life, though who wanted to live a life without a sense of purpose or achievement? — but her conversations with Jim Yateman and the grocer in the village, Mr Blake, had got her thinking of some exciting possibilities. She'd need to do some research and think it all through thoroughly, and also introduce herself properly to her neighbour opposite . . . Avoiding introducing herself was beginning to be a game, and a rather silly one at that. They were neighbours and bound to meet occasionally. What harm could there be in the old man, anyway?

When she'd made her list she went inside. The sun was sinking and the temperature dropping with it. Leaving the door open for Scamper to come in when she was ready, Florence went into her sitting room and sat down with a sheet of fine paper from her writing box. It was time to tell Lucille her news.

Paradise Cottage
Nightingale Lane
Guisethorpe
21 August 1957

Dear Lucy,

Well, Scamper and I are here, I've cleaned the place and it's looking a bit like home already. I'm getting a telephone installed on Friday and I'll let you know the number so you can ring me from work if you need to in an emergency.

It was lovely to see you and Denis so happy before I left. I'm glad to have you settled and married, if marriage is what suits you. I know I gave it a few tries, and not always success- fully. What suits one doesn't necessarily work for another. But it's what you and Denis want and it's my dearest wish that you be happy.

I've got great plans but I won't say what just yet in case they don't work out. But tomorrow I'm going to look for a job. No hurry, but I need to make a start. I think something part-time will be useful, if I can get it, allowing me the rest of the week free to get on with my own plans. Wish me luck!

I must tell you what happened this afternoon in a little café on the seafront. It was quite funny really, though I don't think the café proprietor thought so. He was really cross about the loss of his crockery and maybe that's what made him so rude after I'd helped him out, but honestly, love, the man was worse than useless . . .

When Florence had finished her letter, she folded the sheets of crisp paper, slid them into an envelope and addressed it in her big bold hand. She'd post that tomorrow in Fleming St Clair, where she thought she would see what employment was available. The little town was the big sister to Guisethorpe, busier and with more facilities for visitors, though it wasn't seasonal work that Florence was looking for and, anyway, the holiday season was nearly over. It was with a happy feeling of anticipation that she went to round up Scamper and lock the doors and windows.

'Come on in, Scamper, love. Was that a nice old bone, then? *Good* girl. You know, I reckon we've done all right today. It's looking pretty good here so far — what do you say?'

Scamper gave a little woof of agreement and then allowed Florence to give her face a much-needed wash.

★ ★ ★

The next morning Florence rose early and took Scamper up the lane at a brisk trot. They ate their breakfasts and then Florence changed into a cotton frock in a bold geometric print with matching jacket, and wound her hair up elegantly: it was as well to be prepared to impress a prospective employer, should she be fortunate enough to meet one. She did her makeup carefully, finishing with a smart red lipstick, then looked out her good shoes with the heels, and the nice handbag that nearly matched that had been her mother's. She imagined it would bring her luck, invoking her mother's presence like a kind of talisman, along with the little silver locket containing the pictures of herself and her mother. She put on a little hat, but not too dressy. After all, she might end up being interviewed for any kind of job, and provided she thought she could do it well and would enjoy it, she didn't really mind if it was lowly. She wouldn't want anyone to think she was too grand for whatever employment they might be offering.

They got in the car — Scamper on a rug on the back seat — and Florence drove off down the lane, onto the main road and then south towards Fleming St Clair.

Standing at a bus stop on the seafront were Violet Peasall, from the café, and the waitress, Carmen.

Florence drew up, leaned over and wound down the window.

'Hello, Mrs Peasall. I'm going to Fleming. Do you and Carmen want a lift?'

'Mrs Stanville! You're out very early. Yes, please.'

Carmen moved the front seat and climbed into the back, then Violet sat in the passenger seat.

'Just shove Scamper's rug along, love,' said Florence over her shoulder. 'She won't mind.'

'We're off to the dentist. Carmen's got a check-up and I thought I might change my library book while she's there. The café doesn't open until ten so we've got time if we get a shift on,' Violet told her. 'It doesn't take me long to get the urn going and prep for the lunches.'

'Oh, I didn't realise you and Carmen are . . . family?'

'Yes, Carmen's my granddaughter.' Violet lowered her voice. 'Lost her dad, my son, in the war and her mother a few years ago now . . . *cancer*,' she whispered, a word to be spoken with dread, 'so I've Carmen and my old mum with me now. Mum and I are widows so we're a house of women, aren't we, love?'

'We certainly are, Grandma,' beamed Carmen, making a fuss of Scamper.

'Was everything all right at the café after I left?' Florence ventured. 'No unpleasant repercussions, I hope.'

'You were a godsend, Mrs Stanville. There was a sticky moment after you'd gone,' said Violet, rolling her eyes and making Florence smile, 'but we weathered the storm, didn't we, Carmen?'

'Thing is,' Carmen informed Florence seriously from the back seat, 'Mr Bird is so lazy that he'd rather do nothing than almost anything else at all. I'm always having mishaps because there's so much to see to and it's such hard work, but if he sacked me he'd have to find someone else prepared to do all that work. And Grandma wouldn't stand for it and she'd leave then, anyway, so he'd have to find *two* new people. He's never going to raise the energy to do that. I thought for a minute he might yesterday, but I wasn't thinking straight. It was the shock of breaking all those plates, I think. It addled my brain.'

Florence caught Violet's eye as she winked at her and she burst out laughing.

'Sounds like you've got Mr Bird summed up,'

she said. 'Why does he have the café if he makes so little effort with it?'

'It was his father's and his grandfather's,' Violet explained. 'I can remember Mr Bird's father, Albert, was a fine gentleman who put his heart and soul into the business. But Anthony just isn't interested. He's inherited the café but it's like a weight around his neck . . .'

'An albatross,' said Carmen heavily.

'He's living on his inheritance, and the flat over the café is his now, too, so he's got a home. I reckon he was spoilt: the café business gave him whatever he wanted when he was younger and now he refuses to see that he can't live like that for ever without putting something back into it, at least in terms of effort. I worry the business is going to the wall, but what can I do? I'm paid only to cook the food, not run the place.'

'What will you do if the café goes under?' Florence asked. 'Mr Bird will find it hard to keep such a place ticking over in the winter, I reckon.'

'I'll just have to find something else.'

'Grandma's a brilliant cook. She can do much nicer food than is on the café menu. Mr Bird doesn't know how lucky he is to have her,' said Carmen.

'Oh, I reckon he does, love,' said Violet ironically.

'How do you like Guisethorpe, Mrs Stanville? You don't look like you're here for a holiday.'

'You're right about that, Carmen. I've been here only since Monday, so it's hard to be sure, but I seem to be liking it very well, thank you.'

'Good. I hope Scamper does, too.'

'If you ask her I'm sure she'll let you know,' smiled Florence.

'But what brought you here, love? I can tell you're not local, if you don't mind me saying.'

'Not at all, Mrs Peasall. I'm from Lancashire. That is, I've lived much of my life in Lancashire, most lately in the countryside, north of Blackburn. It can be a bit bleak up there, but it's very pretty. Once, when I was a little girl, I lived . . . on this coast. I loved it so much that I decided to come back. It's easy when you have nowt to consider but yourself.'

'I hope you'll be happy here,' said Violet.

'So do I,' Carmen added wholeheartedly.

They passed a sign announcing Fleming St Clair, decked around with geraniums. The lamp-posts all along the street supported gigantic hanging baskets, and bunting fluttered across and back the whole length.

'Goodness, it's very cheery,' said Florence.

'It is,' agreed Violet. 'I wish Guisethorpe would do something similar but we're only a little village and don't have the resources. Never mind, we can't have it both ways: we don't have the visitors, either, which is why we're the same as we have been for decades.'

'Since William the Conqueror,' nodded Carmen.

'Probably, love. Unspoilt, we are, and I think most folk who live there like it like that. It has its own appeal.'

'Yes,' Florence said. 'I'd have been disappointed to find Guisethorpe had changed.'

'Turn left here, love, and you can go round

to the parking behind the shops, if it's the shops you're heading for?'

Florence drove into a rather uneven area that was signposted as a car park and was undoubtedly an old bomb site, and parked in the shade of a buddleia bush. They all got out and Florence opened the little window at the front to give Scamper some fresh air.

'I'd offer you a lift back, Mrs Peasall, but I don't know how long I'm going to be.'

'Oh, please call me Violet. We're grateful for the lift and we haven't long so we'll be rushing back soon. Thanks again, Mrs Stanville — '

'Florence.'

'Florence — thank you, love — and we'll maybe see you in the café . . . ?'

Florence laughed. 'Mebbe.'

'Oh, do please come and rescue me again, Mrs Stanville. I'm always breaking things,' smiled Carmen, and with a wave the grandmother and granddaughter disappeared quickly towards the main street and the dentist's surgery.

Florence followed more slowly, posting her letter to Lucy at the first postbox she saw. She'd made a plan, which was to find a newsagent's that had a notice board advertising jobs and requesting services. There might be something worth considering there.

This turned out to be a disappointment, but there was a pile of a slim publication called the *Fleming and Guisethorpe Courier*: 'Your truly local newspaper, published every Thursday', so she bought a copy. Then she walked up one side of the main street and back down the other, looking in the shop windows to see if any job vacancies were advertised.

There was one office, Blackett and McGee, Accountants, that had the front window onto a small reception area, with a typed notice discreetly in one corner, asking for a typist with a speed of fifty words per minute, and offering a very small wage. Good heavens, thought Florence, some people want a lot for a little. She supposed that's why they were accountants: they were good at minding money. Florence could type well — though admittedly not as fast as the advert mentioned — but she didn't fancy being shackled to a desk going hell for leather at some ancient Remington all day for a pittance.

Further down was a bakery advertising for a 'Saturday girl', but Florence wasn't a 'girl' and wanted to work more than just Saturdays.

When she got to the end of the main street, she crossed over onto the side of the road that bordered the sea and found an empty bench where she could sit and read her newspaper.

The *Fleming and Guisethorpe Courier* lived up to its boast as 'truly local'. It mentioned a lot of people as if the reader would know them personally, or at least know exactly who they were. 'Mrs Rendle, whose floristry has delighted us ...' 'Miss Margaret McGee, captain of the ladies' bowls team ...' Florence smiled to herself, remembering the name on the accountants' office, and wondered if Margaret McGee was also the bowls club treasurer.

She leafed through to find the job vacancies. Some were the same dismal short-term seasonal jobs that she'd seen on the newsagent's notice board. Others required skills that she didn't have, such as hair-dressing and chiropody.

Then, towards the bottom of one column of personal advertisements she read a modest little notice.

Person required to read aloud. Hours nego-tiable. Pay negotiable. Friendly and pleasant environment. Telephone Fleming 242 for details.

What kind of place could this be? To read what? The advert was unclear, but Florence supposed if she phoned the number she'd find out whether it was worth pursuing.

She folded the newspaper and went back towards her car, deciding to wait to make the call. By this time tomorrow she'd have her own tele-phone installed at Paradise Cottage.

Scamper was, as always, overjoyed to see her mistress, as if Florence had left her for days, and Florence drove them both home with a light heart.

Really, there was no rush to secure a job. She'd find the right part-time occupation soon enough. It was the plans she'd made yesterday and in the small hours of this morning that really excited her.

3

Florence had a pile of cookery books open on her table and was making lists and notes from the recipes. The best of the books was the one her mother had compiled herself and passed on to her daughter. Florence treasured the dog-eared old exercise book, the sugar-paper covers worn thin and shiny with age and use. Some recipes were written straight onto the lined pages in her mother's neat old-fashioned handwriting — which had become less neat as she'd got older — and others were cut out of magazines and glued in. In places the glue had dried and failed, so the notebook now contained many loose yellowed newsprint cuttings, lying askew on the page, annotated and occasionally stained with little cooking splashes.

From her sitting-room window Florence could see over to the lane and, through the gap in the paling fence where her little iron front gate was, Mr Yateman's vegetable table. And there was Mr Yateman, just coming out to collect up the unsold produce. In a moment Florence was on her feet, had put her purse in her dress pocket and was out through her door.

'Good afternoon, Mr Yateman,' she said, approaching nonchalantly now, with a smile.

'Hello, Mrs . . . ?'

'Stanville. Florence Stanville.'

Jim Yateman looked relieved to learn her name at last. 'I'm pleased to meet you,' he said magnanimously, as if they were meeting for only the first time now, offering a rather soil-encrusted hand, which Florence took without hesitation.

'My fault we got off on the wrong foot, Mr Yateman,' she said.

'Think nothing of it. Now's now and we are where we are.'

Florence smiled. 'Quite right — thank you. Doesn't look like you've had many takers for your vegetables today.'

'Or most days, Mrs Stanville.'

'Shame to put it on the compost when it's as good as this, though. You must have a very big garden to grow so much.'

'Not especially. It's just that so much gets ready at once and overwhelms me and Mildred. It's no use leaving them on the plants because they just grow coarse and inedible. Come and look . . . if you'd like to?'

'Yes, please, I would,' said Florence. 'Shall I take one of those boxes?'

'Thanks.' Jim handed her the lighter of two orange boxes into which he had placed the unsold vegetables, and took the other himself.

The Yatemans' front garden was neat but drearily unimaginative, Florence noticed, following Jim up the arrow-straight front path, the bedding plants on either side all exactly the same size and distance apart. Jim led her round to the side, past the kitchen door and into the back garden, which looked altogether more interesting. Beyond a patch of mown grass edged by pretty shrubs, a path led between the trees of a tiny orchard to a big shed and then to a beautifully laid-out vegetable garden

47

beyond.

'I thought you said it wasn't big,' Florence said. 'It's enormous!'

'Well, round here there are farms and market gardens selling to vegetable markets all over the country,' Jim said. 'My garden's tiny compared to those.'

He proudly showed Florence round and she admired the quality and variety of his plants.

'I've in mind a recipe I was reading this afternoon,'

she said when she'd seen what there was. 'Do you think I could buy what I need from you now?'

'Oh, I'll give it to you, Mrs Stanville, and be glad to be shot of it. Help yourself if there's anything in those boxes from earlier and tell me what else you'd like.'

'No, Mr Yateman, that wouldn't be fair. If you give me owt I won't feel able to ask for what I need another time, will I? I'll pay and then we'll both know where we are and there'll be no awkwardness.'

The old man looked at her with interest and then he smiled. 'Right you are, Mrs Stanville. And, please, call me Jim.'

'In that case, Jim, I'd love a cauliflower, if you can spare one, please? And I think I told you, my name's Florence.'

In the end Florence borrowed an orange box to take home the vegetables she'd bought. Jim was just showing her to the gate when his wife appeared from the lane, carrying a bag of shopping. Jim introduced Florence.

'Hello,' his wife said, offering her hand. 'I'm

48

Mildred Yateman. Are you settling in all right?'

'Yes, thank you.' Florence took her hand.

'Looks like you've bought some of my Jim's lovely veg.'

As this was indisputable, Florence said nothing.

'Now, if there's anything you'd like to know about Guisethorpe, or to be introduced to some people, then you only have to ask,' said Mildred. 'I know everyone, and it'll be a pleasure to take you round and show you . . . '

She prattled on and Florence tuned out, thinking about all the beautiful vegetables she'd been shown in Jim's garden and their possibilities in her plans, until the woman drew breath, her face expectant.

Oh dear, she was waiting for an answer to something she'd said. Well, never mind, she wouldn't be getting one. Florence beamed at Mildred, assured her it was lovely to meet her, and then turned back to Jim.

'Thanks for these, Jim. I'll return the box to the table, shall I?'

'That'd be fine. Enjoy your veg, Florence.'

They said goodbye and Florence went over the lane, not looking back.

★ ★ ★

'*Florence? Jim?* Good gracious, Jim, you seem to be getting on well with our mysterious new neighbour. That was quick work,' said Mildred as she unpacked her shopping onto the kitchen table. She sounded miffed.

'She just came to buy some veg, Mil. There was

49

no *quick work* about anything.' Jim started putting packets in the cupboards.

'So tell me, what did she say? Where's she from — not from round here, I think, the way she talks — and has she got a family? Is there a Mr Stanville, did she tell you that, or did the pair of you just move straight to first-name terms and talking about veg?'

'*The pair of us* — really, Mildred, you don't half talk nonsense sometimes. She's called Florence Stanville and that's all I know about her.'

'Well, that's not much help, is it? You could at least have found out what her husband does. I wonder how much they paid for the cottage . . .'

I wonder when you'll shut up . . . 'I haven't a clue, I won't be asking her and I hope you won't either.'

'I'm just curious, that's all. No need to snap.' Mildred looked sulky. 'I saw Doreen in the grocer's and she was asking. I felt foolish, not having anything to tell her and the cottage occupied since Monday.'

'Well, never mind about Doreen. The lady didn't tell me anything but her name, she admired the garden and bought a few vegetables, that's all.'

'She likes my garden?'

'No, she likes the vegetable garden.'

'She came round the back? You invited her over? Did you offer her tea? I wish you had: it would have been a chance to find out a bit more about her, get chatting . . .'

'I think,' said Jim, after a few moments' careful consideration, 'that Florence Stanville is not one for chatting.'

'That's a shame,' said Mildred, filling the kettle.

'Maybe she's just shy. She'll soon find out we're a likeable lot in Guisethorpe. Still, now I know her name I can address her by it and no doubt we'll soon be friends.'

'If you say so, Mil,' Jim replied doubtfully.

★ ★ ★

Lucille Walden picked Florence's letter off the doormat on Friday morning as she left for work. She put it in her handbag and looked forward to reading it during her brief lunchtime break at the shop.

Denis had gone out early, as he did every morning. He was a self-employed painter and decorator and put in long hours. Thinking about Denis — with his twinkly blue eyes, untidy blond hair and paint-splattered overalls — Lucy smiled to herself and her heart did a little flutter. They'd been married since May and, oh, what a lovely man he was! She'd enjoy sharing the news of Mum's new house at the seaside with her darling husband this evening.

'You're looking pleased with life, Lucy,' said Judy, when the young woman arrived at the shoe shop where she was Judy's only assistant.

'I am indeed, and why not? It's not raining and I've got a letter from Mum. I can't wait to learn how she's getting on.'

'Well, I hope she's settling in nicely, Lucy. But I'm afraid you'll have to wait to find out. The van's just pulled up at the back and we've a load of new stock to take in. You get the kettle on, I'll deal with the delivery man and then we'll shift the boxes,

51

unpack and get the best of those autumn lines in the window sharpish. The sandals can go on the sale rack and we'll move the old boxes to the side in the stockroom and then stow the new stuff in its place, all right?'

'Right-oh,' Lucy nodded.

Judy was a good employer. She didn't expect Lucy to do all the hard work and she led from the front so that Lucy always knew what was expected of her. The shop was just off King William Street in the centre of Blackburn and specialised in the kind of comfortable shoes that fitted, in Lucy's words, 'old feet'. Judy was in her mid-thirties, Lucy ten years younger, but the pair made the buying of arch supports and wide fittings a little bit of fun for their elderly customers, adding a touch of glamour to the experience so far as they were able. Judy was a good saleswoman, too, and knew how to butter up 'her ladies' with a sympathetic chat and a restorative cup of tea, which often helped secure a sale. She even had an arrangement with her cousin, who was a chiropodist, to pass on his business card to women with painful foot problems, while Cousin Edwin kept a pile of flyers advertising Ruby Slipper, the improbable but aspirational name of Judy's shop.

The two women set to work and the morning seemed to pass quickly, what with the new stock to organise and customers to serve. By lunchtime Judy had sold several pairs of the new-season shoes.

'It's nice to have cool feet, and of course we always sell some to the more optimistic customers, but I don't really think our ladies have quite the assets to show off a summer sandal,' sighed Lucy, as — during the afternoon, in a rare quiet moment — she was arranging the old stock on the sale rack.

Judy was astonishingly glamorous and had sported high wedges and immaculate stockings all summer long. With a well-pressed short-sleeved blouse, a smart pencil skirt, and her cardigan hanging prettily from her shoulders whenever she left the shop, she was going for the Grace Kelly look. Lucy had raised her game in the glamour stakes since coming to work for Judy a few years before, and Denis had said he was the proudest man in Blackburn to have such a gorgeous new wife. Neither Judy nor Lucy had Grace Kelly's budget, of course, but they were both clever at putting together a look on a shoestring and the customers often remarked how smart they appeared.

'But everyone likes to have a choice,' Judy reminded Lucy. 'Just 'cos you're getting on in life and your feet hurt, doesn't mean you can't admire stylish shoes and search out the nicest you can find that fit. At Ruby Slipper we just have to work with what we've got but we still do our best. Now, tell me how your mum's getting on. Seems such a big life change to up and leave and go to live in a place where she doesn't know anyone. I'm not sure I could do it.'

'Mum's very independent,' Lucy said, 'but even I was a bit surprised by the speed of it. You'll remember my grandma died in January . . . ?'

'Course I do, love.'

'Well, when Mum inherited her house I thought she was going to stay there and that was that. After all, they'd lived together for quite a few years, since Mum parted from Frank, and I thought she was settled. Of course, I hadn't been there for a while, living at my friend Betty's so I was near to here, and then I got distracted with the wedding and all, but next thing I know, Denis and I are back from our honeymoon and settled down in our new home, and suddenly Mum's selling Grandma's house and buying a place at the seaside. She says she remembers how happy she was there, when she was little and it was just her and Grandma, and she wants to feel like that again. She misses Grandma terribly, I know. But I do worry that, without Grandma, and now Mum is grown up . . . and all she's lived through . . . well, it won't be the same; that she's gone looking for summat that's never going to come back to her.'

'But it's working out all right so far, I hope?'

'Sounds it, Judy, though she's only been there since Monday. She's getting a telephone put in today, apparently, which I reckon is a good idea. She's thinking of getting a job, too.'

'Well, she's not old, is she? She'll want summat to occupy her time. A great doer, is your mum. What kind of job is she looking for? She's got all kinds of skills, hasn't she? Didn't you tell me she used to be a secretary at one time?'

'She did, and she turned her hand to lots of practical things during the war. When she was young she was a house model in a smart shop and used to walk about showing off the dresses. That's how she met my father. She can do all sorts. I expect she'll end up organising summat or someone. She's very good at organising.'

'Well, I'm all for that,' said Judy. 'Now, why don't you organise us a pot of tea and I'll price up those sale sandals? I don't want to give them away, but if they don't sell soon they won't be selling at all.'

Just then the shop doorbell rang and a very old lady shuffled her way into Ruby Slipper, a net bag of vegetables in one hand and her walking stick in the other.

'Mrs Metcalfe, how lovely to see you,' beamed Judy. 'Take a seat, love. Lucy was just going to put the kettle on. Now, make yourself comfy and you can tell me how your grandson is doing . . .'

By the time she'd heard all about young Ian Metcalfe's exam results and his hopes for an apprenticeship, and given Mrs Metcalfe a nice cup of tea with one sugar, just the way she liked it, it was pretty much a certainty that when, eventually, the talk got on to shoes and the new-season stock, Judy would be making a sale.

★ ★ ★

It was mid-morning when a green GPO van drew up in Nightingale Lane in front of Paradise Cottage and two men got out. The older man rang the doorbell while his junior colleague started to unload cables and tool boxes.

Scamper was delighted to welcome the workmen and Florence was keen for them to get on with installing the telephone and leave so she could begin using it. She made a pot of tea for them, told them where she wanted the telephone — 'No, I really do want it in the sitting room, not the hallway, please. You can bring the wire in through the front wall and it won't be any extra work for you,' she insisted — and let them get on. She'd already perused the *Fleming and Guisethorpe Courier* again, and found a couple more advertisements for jobs to follow up as soon as the telephone was installed.

Eventually a black telephone sat on a little table that had belonged to Florence's mother. A round white label in the centre of the dial said 'Fleming 865', and a long plaited flex went into a box set low down on the wall. The older workman checked the installation was working correctly and at last Florence was able to show the two men the door.

It was time to follow up those adverts. She dialled the first number, for a job as a part-time cook at a guesthouse, but the position had already been filled.

'Missed that one, Scamper,' said Florence, having put the phone down. 'Never mind, it was not to be.'

She hadn't set her heart on the job and wasn't really disappointed.

The next vacancy was an office job requiring filing and typing skills but no shorthand. Florence thought it sounded manageable. She could type well, and anyone could file, she thought. It was just a case of being organised. The advert named a solicitor's office in Fleming St Clair.

When she dialled the number the phone rang for a long time. She was about to give up when a man she thought at first sounded ill or half-asleep answered.

'Neshbish and Harrishon,' he slurred.

56

'Good afternoon, I'm enquiring about the vacancy advertised in the *Courier*.'

'Vacanshy . . . ?'

'Part-time: typing and filing.'

'Oh . . . Mish Shymons . . . she's left . . . '

By now Florence had the picture. 'I'm not surprised she's left,' she snapped. 'And I'll leave you to sober up. Good afternoon to you,' and she put the phone down.

'Different place, same folk, Scamper,' she said. People everywhere had the same failings and weaknesses. It was disappointing to find such a man encroaching even on the edge of her bright new life already, but she supposed it was just human nature. Frank Stanville would be quite at home at Nesbit and Harrison, if that's the way they work, she thought, pulling the newspaper towards her to check the number in the last advertisement, the mysterious one she'd noticed the day before.

She dialled the number. The phone rang for a full minute. She had almost given up when an elderly-sounding woman answered, confirming the number.

'Good afternoon. I'm telephoning about the reading job advertised in the *Courier*,' Florence said. 'I'm interested but I'm afraid it's not entirely clear what is required.'

'Just someone to read aloud,' said the woman, evidently wondering what was puzzling her caller.

'But what is the nature of your business?'

'Oh, we're not a business,' said the woman, but kindly. 'My sister and I are very fond of novels. We like a strong story. We don't go in for poetry

much, and we're not bothered about the newspapers because we can get the news on the
wireless if we want it.'

'And you want these . . . novels read aloud to
you . . . and your sister?'

'Yes, that's right,' said the woman. 'That's all
there is to it. There are no catches,' she added
gently.

Florence thought the woman sounded unworldly
and kind, but the job was still a strange one. Why
couldn't the lady and her sister read to themselves
if they were so fond of books?

There had been a pause in the conversation
while Florence was wondering about all this and
the woman ended it by saying hopefully: 'You
have an interesting voice — do you think you'd
like to give it a go?'

'I could come to see you and have a try-out,
if you like; see if we're all suited?' That gave
Florence a way out of it if she needed one.

'Good idea. Can you come on Monday morning? We're in Fleming, but set back behind the
town. I'll give you the address . . . '

They talked details, which Florence wrote in
her diary, and then she gave the lady, whose name
was Miss Kendal, her telephone number, wished
her a good weekend and rang off.

'She sounded nice, Scamper, but I still don't
quite get it. Never mind, I'll just have to see what
happens on Monday. Right, a *walk*, Scamper, and
a bit of shopping.'

Florence went to fetch her basket and Scamper's lead and they set off to the grocer's to buy
some vinegar, sugar and, with luck, the particular

spices Florence needed. What was left of the day when she got back from the shop would be spent cooking and she was eager to get started.

★ ★ ★

Several sealed jars of gloriously yellow piccalilli stood on the table in Florence's kitchen. She could hardly wait to taste the result of her afternoon's work, but it wouldn't be ready to eat for a month. That was the problem with pickles: you had to be patient, let them mature. The commercial jar she'd bought earlier in the week looked lurid in colour and mean of content compared to her own, yet it was the only one Mr Blake, the grocer in the village, sold. She'd asked him about local producers in a roundabout way, not wanting to reveal her plans until she was quite ready, and he had said he didn't stock any, just the well-known brand. Jim had told her there were a lot of vegetables grown in Guisethorpe, so it was likely that other people were trying to preserve them. Florence knew she had to get on with her plans before any rival cooks thought to move in on a gap in the market, and she also had to make the best. The second she was reasonably confident about, having cooked this recipe of her mother's many times before; the first partly depended on other folk, and that's where the best-laid plans often fell down. So frustrating . . .

So was the presence of the aroma of vinegar that always hung about a kitchen. Her mouth tasted of it, the whole cottage probably smelled of it, and certainly her hair and clothes did.

Scamper and Florence went for a last quick walk up the lane — even the dog smelled of piccalilli, and yes, the whole cottage certainly did, she noticed when they came back in from the fresh air outside — and then Florence locked up and settled Scamper in her basket. Then she went up to bed with her favourite novel, *Rebecca*, and spent twenty minutes practising reading aloud. Whether or not she decided to take the job, she wanted to be properly prepared.

★ ★ ★

It was a little later than usual when Lucy left the shop to walk home, bone weary with all the shifting of boxes and unpacking of stock. Even Judy's well-made-up face looked drawn by the time she locked up and the two of them wished each other a good night.

'It's home with a fish supper for me,' said Judy, 'and I might even eat it lying in a bubble bath.'

Lucy smiled and waved goodbye. She didn't think she'd be eating fish and chips in a bubble bath this evening — or any other.

She opened the door to an empty house. Denis was late again. Never mind, if she got a move on she could have his tea on the table ready for him, and he could tell her about his day while they ate. He often had an amusing story to relate, or a tale of some drama they could laugh over together. Denis had a young assistant called Tim, who was willing but daft, and who spent his working days having 'adventures' from which he needed rescuing, either by Denis or, occasionally, the

60

emergency services. Luckily for Tim, Denis was very easy-going and kept the lad on, though a stricter boss might have given him his marching orders months ago.

The meat pie she'd heated was drying up and the boiled potatoes were starting to fall apart by the time Lucy heard Denis's key in the front door.

'Hello, love. You're late. Tea's ready when you are.'

'Hello, Luce.' Denis came through into the kitchen, kissing her briefly as he passed. 'I'll just have a quick wash and be there.'

The bathroom was downstairs at the back of the terraced house, in what had once been the scullery. It meant traipsing through the kitchen but that was nothing to grumble about compared to having to wash in the scullery. At least they didn't have to share any facilities with the houses on either side, and they both knew how fortunate they were to have this arrangement in their new home.

When he emerged, his hair standing up adorably in peaks at the front where he'd got it wet, Lucy turned off the oven, dished up the over-browned pie and crumbling potatoes with a spoonful of tinned peas she'd heated while Denis was washing, and took the food through to the dining table, to one side of the sitting room.

'You look tired, Den,' she said, setting down the plates and then almost flopping into her chair. Her stomach was rumbling with hunger by now.

'Yes . . . long day. Do we have any ketchup, love?'

'Oh, sorry — forgot. I'll get it.' Her back was

beginning to stiffen now; nevertheless she pushed herself off her chair and headed for the kitchen. 'Never mind, it's Saturday tomorrow and you can have a lie-in.' She came back with the tomato ketchup, shaking it violently and upending it in a mug she'd thought to bring. 'Here you are, Den. I'd give it a minute or two to slide down or it'll never come out.'

'Thanks, Luce.' He looked over the table. 'Did you forget the salt, too?'

'I did. Sorry, love.' Once more she headed off to fetch the salt and pepper pots, placing them in front of him on the table. 'I must be a bit tired. It was hard work at the shop today. We had a load of new shoes to unpack. I was bending and kneeling, then up and down the ladder in the stockroom . . . '

'That Judy works you too hard. She should try doing more of it herself.'

'That's not true, Den. She works just as hard as I do *and* she has to take all the decisions about the business.'

'Mm, you're too nice about her. She seems to have plenty of time for getting herself dolled up like some . . . film star or summat. I reckon she can sometimes be a bit over the top with her makeup and her hair all fancy.'

'Judy always looks lovely, and it's part of the job, as you well know. She wants to make shopping at Ruby Slipper a good experience for women who might otherwise not have a lot of glamour in their lives. Anyway, you said you liked me looking smart and I take my cue from Judy. It's Judy who's honed the business's image.'

'*Honed the business's image*? Hark at you!'

Lucy smiled at herself and shrugged. 'It's just shop talk, love. But I'll not hear a word against Judy.'

'Aye, all right.' He changed the subject. 'This pie's a bit dry, though, isn't it? Could have done with some gravy.' He reached for the ketchup and splattered a generous dollop directly onto the pie.

'It's a bought pie and it didn't come with gravy,' said Lucy. 'I covered it in the oven, but you were a bit later than I thought you'd be.'

'Ah, I'm sorry about that, Luce. I sent Tim off to get some more emulsion and he was gone an age, then came back with magnolia when we needed white.'

'Write it down for him next time. You know he's a half-wit,' Lucy said.

'I would, but I'm not sure he can read,' said Denis.

They both laughed and the tension between two very weary people evaporated.

'Sorry I was late,' said Denis.

'Sorry about the pie,' Lucy answered, and reached out to squeeze his hand.

'I've asked Mum to come for tea tomorrow,' he announced then.

'Oh . . . all right. But it won't have to be owt special. I'm at the shop until gone midday, remember? When did you see your mother? I thought you told me you were working late?'

'No, Lucy, I told you I have had a *long day*. I'm telling you now that I popped in to see Mum. We are working close to hers and it wasn't out of my way. Just thought I'd see how she was. You wouldn't expect me to pass right by her house and not stop, would you?'

'Course not, love.'

''Cos that's what it sounded like.'

'Well, it wasn't what I meant, Den. Your mother's very welcome, as you know. But as I said, I'll be at the shop in the morning, so mebbe I can get in some tinned salmon and a bit of salad; a nice cake or some tinned fruit for after. Would that be all right?'

'Aye, you see what's left, love. I don't want you going to a lot of trouble and Mum wouldn't either, what with you and Judy being so busy *honing the business's image.*'

'Give over, Den . . . ' Lucy smiled tiredly.

She tried not to mind that Mrs Walden was coming round the following day, but she had looked forward to a lazy afternoon, maybe resting her back . . . and her poor feet. She'd be in need of shoes from Ruby Slipper herself if her feet hurt any more than they did this evening. And Mrs Walden wasn't what Lucy would call easy company. She could be a bit . . . undermining. Lucy would rather not spend a Saturday afternoon with someone quite so draining. Still, she was Denis's mum, so Lucy would just have to make the best of her.

'Tell you what,' said Denis, finishing off every last crumb of his pie, 'you do the washing-up and I'll make us a pot of tea. How about that, love? Then it's off to bed,' he winked.

'Or you could dry if I wash and we'll be done a lot quicker,' said Lucy. 'After all, it may only be at a shop, but I do work too, you know. And it's you who has a lie-in on a Saturday. I shall be up and out by half-past eight.'

'Yes, all right, don't go on, Luce. It's not a competition,' said Denis, knowing he was, if not bettered, at least equally matched.

It wasn't until Lucy was lying beside Denis, who was snoring gently, in the half-dark of the late summer evening, that she remembered her mother's letter. She had meant to tell Denis all Mum's news and had completely forgotten to mention any of it.

She lay thinking about her mother, the bright smile that lit up her whole face and beamed through her blue eyes, her beautiful hair that turned people's heads in the street, her fierceness and fearlessness, even when everything was against her. Like when Grandma had died and Mum's heart broke because Grandma had been her true constant, her only parent for most of her life. So what had she done but sold the house and decided to start all over again. And like, a few years before that, when she'd thrown Frank Stanville out, and her heart had been rather less broken but scarred nonetheless because she said she thought she had loved Frank once, and the tragedy was that she loved him no longer and had wasted two years of her life with him, which was his fault entirely. And she'd just moved back in with Grandma and never spoken to him again, so far as Lucy knew.

That was the thing about Mum: she wasn't quite like other people — or no one that Lucy had met, anyway.

She missed her. She hoped that Mum and darling little Scamper were cosy and happy in Paradise Cottage tonight.

4

Florence had another strange dream that night, and she woke on Saturday morning feeling unsettled and anxious. She tried to remember what it was that had entered her mind in the depth of the night so she could face it down in the bright light of a summer's day, but all she could recall was her mother weeping pitifully, though Florence didn't know why.

There was also a recollection of the red-headed child again, very like her young self, yet not her, running, always out of reach, receding into the distance in a dim corridor until she disappeared, leaving a pervading atmosphere of sadness. Florence knew that little girl; did not have to explore the dream more carefully to identify her, though her face was an uncertain image now, like an out-of-focus photograph. It was an innate knowledge that conjured her, but the idea of her rather than her features. Florence had not thought about her for years before the dreams started and, as she dressed and brushed her hair, she wondered why the child had come to her in the middle of the night. She hoped she would not visit again. There was no place for her and all her attendant sadness here. Florence had come to Guisethorpe to start a new and happy life, though her mother's words as she was dying had embedded themselves in Florence's mind. What had Lily meant about running away, and it not mattering what the truth was?

Did it matter now? Yet would Lily have spoken out in her last hours if it didn't? And who or what couldn't she forgive? Florence suspected that Lily's words had triggered the unsettling dreams, that they were nudging her conscience. She ought to try to find out what it all meant yet she felt a little resentful at having her peace of mind disturbed.

Florence went downstairs and turned on the wireless, playing the Light Programme too loudly, galvanising herself to be up and doing, bustling around tidying up and crashing pans as she made breakfast, getting Scamper a little overexcited with her forced cheerfulness. A walk was what they both needed to work off their hectic energy.

That morning Florence and Scamper strolled briskly along the beach all the way to Fleming St Clair and back. By the time they returned, both were happy and hungry and calm, and Florence's disturbing dream was almost forgotten.

★　★　★

The new week heralded the last of the summer holidays. Already there were fewer visitors in Guisethorpe, Florence noticed, as she and Scamper enjoyed the quiet beach, and the cooler weather would soon send home the rest. It was early in the day and the breeze off the North Sea was chilly with a hint of autumn in it.

Two figures approached and Florence recognised Violet Peasall and her granddaughter, both wearing coats.

'Hello, Mrs Stanville. Hello, Scamper,' called

Carmen.

'Carmen, Violet, it's good to see you,' Florence greeted them as they stopped to talk. 'It'll be quieter at the café after this week, I reckon.'

'You're not wrong, love. We had a busy day on Saturday. It won't be like that again until next summer,' said Violet. 'I must have cooked dozens of lunches and brewed many more pots of tea.'

'*Hundreds*, Grandma. I kept looking out for you, Mrs Stanville. I didn't want anyone else to sit at that outside table in case you and Scamper came by and wanted it.'

'That's nice of you, Carmen, but I don't know as Mr Bird would be so keen to see me after last time.'

'Ah, ignore him, love. I do. I doubt he'd notice, that's if he even puts in an appearance today,' Violet confided. 'If you did want to stop by, you'd be made very welcome by our top waitress.'

'Grandma would give you the fruitiest teacake, too, when I told her it was for you,' Carmen smiled.

'I'm pleased to find I've got friends in the right places,' said Florence. 'Maybe I'll see you later then.' She didn't know if she really meant it, though.

'Good-oh. Now I'm sorry, Florence, I'm afraid I've got to go and open up. Anthony's girlfriend, Trudie, telephoned me quite early. Himself has got a *headache*,' Violet gave Florence a meaningful look, 'and is feeling too delicate to come downstairs to do it, so would I mind coming in a bit earlier than usual? Course, I said I'd be there.'

'Then I'd better not hold you up,' said Florence. 'I hope your extra effort is appreciated.'

Violet pursed her lips but said nothing. With a wave of farewell she and Carmen crunched their way up the sand and shingle towards the steps to the road and the café on the far side, while Florence and Scamper turned for home.

Back at Paradise Cottage, Florence made up her face carefully, changed into a clean dress, brushed her jacket and tidied her hair, then gave Scamper a couple of biscuits and promised to be back as soon as she could.

She drove to Fleming St Clair feeling excited and just a tiny bit nervous; she had no idea what to expect of this job interview with Miss Kendal.

The house was easy to find, following Miss Kendal's very specific directions, set high up behind the little town and down a leafy road, Long Barrow Lane, which had become more of a track by the time Florence reached the last house, number fifty-three, with just a field beyond.

The gates were open and she drove in and parked on a gravelled drive in front of a very old-fashioned and interesting-looking red-brick house, all gables and angles, with windows seemingly placed at random in its front rather than equally spaced. Before she was out of the car the front door was opened and a tall woman, possibly in her early seventies, white-haired and wearing glasses, stood smiling on the doorstep.

'Mrs Stanville, welcome. Perfect timing.'

'Hello, Miss Kendal.' They shook hands.

'Come in and meet my sister, and let us explain what we have in mind.'

She stood aside to let Florence pass. The inside of the hall was painted white but the colours from the stained glass above and to the sides of the front door were reflected onto the white floorboards, making a pattern in jewel colours. The newel post was carved like an owl, the stair banister was wide and solid-looking, the doors leading off the hall very tall, with big brass handles, yet the whiteness of every surface created an air of lightness and space.

Florence gazed around with interest.

'Completely out of fashion these days — no one would build a place like this now — but we don't care,' said Miss Kendal. 'This was our parents' house, and built for them.'

'It's beautiful. It feels warm and welcoming.'

'That's because it knows it's loved,' said Miss Kendal, unembarrassed at sounding fanciful. 'Now . . . ' she opened a door on the right and led the way inside, 'here's my sister. She's also Miss Kendal. We're twins.'

Florence shook hands. The second Miss Kendal was a little plumper than her sister, and had grey hair, but otherwise they did look very alike.

'I'm Miss Jane,' said the second lady, 'and my sister is Miss Beatrice. Better call us by those names, otherwise we'll be Kendalled to death before we're through.'

Florence smiled, thinking she would probably get on with the sisters, but still unclear about the job. 'And I'm Mrs Florence Stanville, Miss Jane. I'm sorry, I still don't know quite what it is you want me to do,' she said.

'Just read to us, Mrs Stanville, that's all. Please sit down. Would you like coffee?' Jane passed Florence a cup of coffee from a tray set out for three.

70

'Help yourself to milk and sugar.'

Florence rarely drank coffee, not liking it made from the fine dry powder that most people used, but this smelled rich and delicious. She poured a little milk into it, thinking it might be too strong without.

Beatrice explained, 'We like to read — or *did* like to, until our eyes started to fail. We both wear glasses, as you see, but for reading the glasses we need these days are huge and heavy . . .'

'. . . and it takes away all the pleasure, having those great things resting on one's nose. They are so uncomfortable after a while that we simply can't bear them,' said Jane. 'We've tried listening to the wireless, but the music on the Light Programme . . .'

'. . . it's intended for factories, we're certain, trying to make everyone work faster. It gets on our nerves after a bit . . .'

'. . . so that it's a relief to switch it off. The Third Programme is better, but then we miss the conversation, and the music can be rather serious. And we don't care for the Home Service all the time: all those men with voices like headmasters or doctors, talking at you and bombarding you with facts. But then we're left with silence, and after a while we get bored with that. We don't want to talk to each other, necessarily . . .'

'. . . because we don't need to communicate in words so much as people who aren't twins and haven't lived together all their lives, so we had the idea of asking someone to read to us so we can revisit our favourite books, maybe for one last time in our lives.'

They both looked enquiringly at Florence over their raised coffee cups and she realised it was her turn to speak.

'What a grand idea!' The words were out before she had time even to think that she was committing herself to the job. 'I understand exactly now you've explained. How often would you need a reader? I was thinking it would mebbe be a part-time job from your advertisement.'

'Oh, yes, only a few hours a week . . . ' said Jane.

'. . . so that it would be a treat and a variation rather than the same every day . . . ' Beatrice added.

'. . . and we could vary the days to suit us all,' finished Jane.

'We wouldn't be difficult, or impose awkward restric-tions on your time, Mrs Stanville,' Beatrice assured her in her gentle manner.

In unison the sisters looked at Florence again and waited for her response.

'I think I'd better read summat to you and you can see if I'll do,' she said, glad she'd been practising over the weekend. It was surprisingly difficult to read aloud fluently when you weren't used to doing it, and since Friday she'd put in several hours of preparation for her audition.

'Yes, have a go and see whether you like it,' said Jane, which Florence thought was a generous way of putting it.

'What would you like me to read to you?' asked Florence.

'Come through to the library and you can choose,' said Beatrice, getting up and leading the way out to the hall and into the room behind.

The walls were lined with white bookcases, and

plain blinds were down over the windows to keep the northern light off the books.

Jane hoisted up one of the blinds so that Florence could see better. 'Daylight is death to books,' she said, 'so we keep the windows covered when we're not in here. Have a look and see if anything is familiar to you.'

Florence realised this was a test. She wondered what kind of novels the sisters liked and quickly scanned the nearest bookcase. On some shelves were children's books, the bindings a little dog-eared and bent. These were clearly well read. No one would keep their children's books for their whole lives unless they meant a great deal to them, and Florence remembered that Beatrice had said they wanted to 'revisit our favourite books' again. Florence, as much as anyone, understood the power of happy memories from childhood.

'How about *Treasure Island*?' she said.

Beatrice and Jane both clasped their hands before them. 'Yes, *please*.'

All three sat down, the sisters leaning back in armchairs in happy anticipation and Florence choosing to sit in a more upright chair at a table with the book before her. She began to read . . .

★ ★ ★

Florence drove home feeling very pleased with her morning so far. The Kendal sisters were a little bit odd, but in an interesting way, and very kind, too. They had praised her reading of *Treasure Island* rather more than Florence herself felt it warranted, but their being happy with her effort was entirely the point. The pay for the part-time reading job was a few shillings an hour but Florence knew she couldn't expect more, and the hours were very flexible. It was an ideal part-time job to fill in between other occupations.

As she was saying goodbye to them, Jane had looked at her carefully in an enquiring way and then said, 'You know, Mrs Stanville, you do remind me of someone.'

'Yes,' agreed Beatrice. 'It's not just the beautiful colour of your hair but a look about your face that is vaguely familiar. I can't think of who, though.'

'Do you have family hereabouts?' asked Jane.

'How strange that you should ask,' Florence replied. 'I don't, but many years ago, when I was quite a small child, I lived near here with my mother, who was a widow. She also had red hair, but it's a long time ago now, and I can't think that you would have known her.'

'Oh, but we might . . . '

'. . . as we've lived here all our lives . . . '

'. . . or at least we may have met her.'

'What was your mother's name, Mrs Stanville?'

'She was called Lily Townsend.'

'Mm . . . I don't remember the name . . . '

'. . . but yet . . . We'll put our minds to it, won't we, Jane, dear?'

Jane had replied with a smile, and the Kendal sisters had waited to see Florence safely turn her car in the drive and then waved her off into the lane.

Scamper was overjoyed to see her mistress when Florence opened the door of Paradise Cottage. Florence noted down in her diary when the next agreed reading was scheduled, then prepared some cheese on toast, which she ate with some pickled radishes she'd made the previous day. While she ate, she wrote another letter to Lucy, letting her know the telephone number and telling her about the unusual part-time job she'd secured.

The fresh pickles were another of her mother's recipes, and had the advantage of being ready to eat almost immediately. Jim had been pleased to sell the cucumbers and radishes. Now they looked very pretty sitting in jars of clear vinegar and spices: pale green in two jars and pink in two others. Florence held them up to the light and the colours were luminous. Surely people would be pleased to buy these . . . ?

There was the rattle of the letterbox and she went to see what had been posted through. The parish magazine — a little folded-over newsletter comprising two typed and rotary duplicated sheets of paper — lay on the doormat. Florence took it up before Scamper could start chewing it and looked through without real interest — she wasn't a churchgoer — but then saw there was a list headed 'Events'. Along with various village activities was, 'Produce Market, 4th Wednesday of the month, St Jude's Hall. Next market: 28 August, 10 a.m.—12 noon. Contact Mary Davis, Fleming 843.'

When Florence rang the number, the efficient-sounding Mrs Davis answered straight away.

'No, there's no charge for a table, Mrs Stanville, but I must ask what it is you're selling. You see, we need to have some variety for the event to be worth holding. It would be no use, for instance,

75

if we had six tables of runner beans and nothing else.'

'Yes, Mrs Davis, I understand. I've made some jars of pickles.'

Florence thought she heard Mary Davis quietly sighing. 'I'm afraid we've already got two stalls entirely devoted to pickles and preserves, and some of the growers have a few jars alongside their produce at this time of year, too. It's the glut of fresh vegetables that does it, you see.'

'Oh . . . ' It was what she had feared, but she had hoped to be ahead of the other pickle makers. Why had Mr Blake at the grocer's not said when she'd asked him about local producers?

Because you didn't ask him the right question. He just said he sold only the big brand. He doesn't have to sell any other because everyone is already making their own!

Florence had been guarding her business idea too carefully and now she realised she hadn't done her research, just made assumptions: a basic mistake and a bad one.

'I'm sorry to disappoint,' said Mary Davis, reading Florence's silence correctly, 'but if you'd like to come along on Wednesday, make yourself known to me and I'll be pleased to show you round. Perhaps you'll find a gap in the market you can fill.'

'Thank you, Mrs Davis. I might well do that. Goodbye.'

Florence put the receiver down and sank into her chair.

Idiot! Thinking to strike out on your own without getting to know the lie of the land first.

Scamper came over to see what the matter was.

'Your mum's a fool, sweetheart,' said Florence. 'Still, I've got enough pickles to keep me going for a while . . .'

Her cheerful triumph of earlier eclipsed by this setback, she decided to take Scamper along the beach again and think about what she could do next. It was all her own fault, but it was a lesson learned and she wouldn't get caught out that way another time.

The wind was whipping up now and she put on a pair of trousers and a jumper, then wrapped a pretty cotton scarf over her hair and around her neck, tucking the ends into her red jacket. She'd walk for a bit, remember to post the letter to Lucy, and then maybe drop in at Bird's Café, which would please Carmen. The thought of that unpleasant man, Anthony Bird, was an inducement to stay away, but he had been nursing a raging hangover this morning, if what Violet had implied was correct, and he might not be there; might still be in bed even now, from what his two put-upon employees had confided about his idleness.

There were very few people on the beach, just a hardy-looking couple with a toddler in a knitted bathing costume, the youngster sporting blue flesh but loudly refusing to get dressed. Two or three wind-breaks valiantly battled with the strong gusts, old people wearing coats and huddled in deckchairs behind them. Florence didn't care about the cold: the only bad weather was that for which you had dressed inappropriately, she thought.

Still, she'd make her way up to the café and order a warming pot of tea to celebrate her new job and comfort her for her failure with the pickles idea before the walk home.

The outside table she'd occupied the first time was empty and she sat down, Scamper tucking herself underneath, as before. Florence looked through the window and was relieved not to see Mr Bird. Carmen, bustling about inside, spotted her straight away, though.

'Hello, Mrs Stanville,' she beamed. 'What can I get for you?'

'Just a pot of tea for one, please, Carmen.'

'Yes, of course. And I'll bring a bowl of water for Scamper.' Carmen hurried back inside, slightly tripping over the doorstep in her eagerness to please.

She brought out the tea things in record time, spilling only a little on the tray, then returned with Scamper's drink.

Florence sat back in her seat as the awning overhead flapped in the wind. The light over the sea was amazing. She'd never get tired of looking at the massive east-coast sky . . .

'Hello, Florence.'

She snapped out of her thoughts to see Jim, wearing an ancient blazer and carrying a plaid shopping bag.

'Jim! Shopping?'

'Yes, Mildred's sent me on a mission. She says I need the exercise and she needs some more Bisto, so here I am.'

'Have you time for a cuppa, Jim, my treat?'

'Well, I don't want to disturb — '

'Oh, please do. I've done summat daft and I'm trying to think of a way forward instead of going round in circles. It'll be nice to put it aside for a bit.'

'Well, if you're sure . . . ?'

'I said so. And here's Carmen already.'

'Hello, Mr Yateman. I didn't know you knew Mrs Stanville.'

'We live opposite each other, love,' Jim explained.

'Oh . . . ' Carmen took in this information while he decided he'd have tea to drink. 'That pretty cottage with the roses? I know it.'

'Mm . . . ' Florence nodded vaguely. 'So, tea for Mr Yateman, please . . . and a teacake, Jim?'

'Oh, go on then, twist my arm. Thank you, Florence.'

Carmen disappeared with the order and the two sat in companionable silence for a moment. Then Jim bent down to pat Scamper, saying, 'I can't think what 'daft' thing you've done that is so very foolish, Florence, but sometimes it helps just to run it past someone else; gives you a different perspective. I'm a good listener, if you think I can help.'

Florence liked to be independent, especially of men and especially these days, but Jim was kind and might even have a wise viewpoint to offer, and her mistake was not so silly that she'd look completely ridiculous.

'It isn't the daftest thing I've ever done — not by a long chalk — but it means rethinking my plans, and I'm one who likes to move forward once I've got an idea . . . ' She told Jim about all the pickles she'd made. 'Seems the whole of Guisethorpe is

79

ahead of me, from what Mrs Davis at St Jude's Hall said. I had thought of making all kinds and selling them, mebbe even to Mr Blake, the grocer. I'd made plans, done some costings, and was going to ask you to be my supplier of veg. I was dreaming of — literally — a cottage industry.'

They paused while Carmen brought out Jim's order, managing not to spill anything but nearly treading on Scamper as she turned to go back inside the café.

'Mary Davis is a straight-up kind of person and she wouldn't tell you different from the truth,' said Jim. 'And it's not much of a setback if you've made only a dozen jars so far. Why not come along on Wednesday? You never know, you might think of a new idea; see where there's an opening. I shall be there with my veg. And I tell you what, I could take some jars of your fresh pickles to sell on the side, if you like? No one would think I was setting myself up as a rival, and Mary doesn't mind if we have a little sideline, so to speak, provided we stick mainly to what we're there for. What do you say?'

'Doesn't Mrs Yateman make pickles, though?'

'She does not. Doesn't like the smell of vinegar hanging round the house, she says.'

'Well, that's very kind of you, Jim. I'll take you up on that.' Florence extended her hand and they shook on the plan.

'All's not lost, Florence,' said Jim kindly, finishing the gigantic teacake Violet had sent out for him. 'Thanks for the tea. I'll see you on Wednesday, if not before. I usually get to the hall about nine o'clock to set up the tables and help get the place arranged.'

'Then I'll give you a lift and I can lend a hand, too, if you like,' said Florence.

'Thank you. I generally wheel it all down in the barrow, but I'd rather ride than walk.'

They said goodbye and Jim set off slowly for home. Florence watched him go, thinking what a gentle old man he was, and rather kinder than some of the men she'd met in her life before now. The afternoon had not been a total write-off after all.

She was pouring herself a second cup of tea when Carmen came out again.

'We're closing in a few minutes, Mrs Stanville.'

'All right, I'll just finish this tea and bring the things in with me when I come to pay, if you like?'

'Oh, no. Thank you, but you're a customer and it's my job.'

'It's no trouble, Carmen, honestly. I can see you've plenty to do.'

Through the window she saw a few tables were still to clear.

'Thank you,' said Carmen with a smile, and shot inside to tidy up.

Florence finished her tea, reached for a tray from a table just inside the door and piled the crockery onto it. Then she went to deposit it on the counter in the now empty café, leaving Scamper's lead looped around the chair outside.

'You again!' said Anthony Bird furiously, appearing through the door from the back like the villain in a pantomime. 'Are you making a habit of interfering in my business, Mrs Stanville? Because I don't think I employ *you* to clear tables, do I? What exactly is your game?'

Florence had been unaware the proprietor was even there that afternoon — he'd certainly been keeping a low profile while Carmen rushed in and out of the kitchen with laden trays — but she rapidly recovered from her surprise.

'Good afternoon, Mr Bird. I have simply come inside to pay my bill.'

'And I asked you what your game is, pretending you work here, trying to take over where you're not wanted.'

Florence felt she could not ignore his accusations now. '*Take over? Pretending to work here*, simply by bringing in a tray of used pots, just to help out? Don't talk daft.'

'It's not me that's *daft*,' he said, shortening the vowel, giving a blunt impression of some kind of catch-all northern accent. 'It's not your place to *help out* — get it? I don't need your help, Mrs Stanville, and I certainly didn't ask for it. So keep your nose out of my business.'

By now, Florence could see, the kitchen door was ajar behind Anthony Bird, and Violet and Carmen were peeping out, both looking shocked. Violet's eyes were wide and Carmen had her hand over her mouth.

Florence drew herself up to her full height, which meant she was looking Anthony Bird straight in the eye, and she made him wait for her answer, giving herself time to contain her rising temper. Eventually: 'Mr Bird, *you* are not getting my help,' she said quietly. 'The only thing I'm prepared to give you is the money for two pots of tea for one and a toasted teacake. Now, may I have my bill, please?'

Flustered and looking ill, Florence now noticed, as well as ill-tempered, Anthony searched the counter for the bill but couldn't find it. Florence thought it might still be in the pocket of Carmen's apron, but she didn't say anything, refusing to help him. Instead she stood waiting in silence, watching his growing discomfort while he picked up things at random and put them down again in his search. Violet and Carmen stepped back into the kitchen and let the door swing silently shut.

Eventually Anthony had to admit he hadn't got the bill. 'What was it again, Mrs Stanville?'

'Two pots of tea for one and a toasted teacake.'

'*Two* pots of tea for one?'

'Correct.'

'But only *one* toasted teacake?'

'Yes.'

'Oh, for goodness' sake,' said Violet, bursting out of the kitchen, where, Florence thought, she must have been listening, 'here you are!' And she slapped a sheet from Carmen's order pad down on the counter in front of her employer and disappeared again.

Florence offered only a raised eyebrow in response.

'Er, that's one and six, please,' said Anthony quietly, not quite looking at her.

Florence handed over the money and a tip. 'That's for Carmen, if you wouldn't mind giving it to her, please. She was very welcoming,' she said. 'And please give my regards to Violet,' she couldn't resist adding, deliberately winding him up. 'Good afternoon, Mr Bird.'

She turned and walked out without waiting for an answer, gathering Scamper's lead up as she passed.

Good grief, what on earth was the matter with the man? Rude, yes; hungover, almost certainly; paranoid, without a doubt. So angry, and for no reason that Florence could see.

She walked home, thinking about Anthony Bird. Poor Violet and Carmen! Not only did it seem that he left them to run the café pretty much unaided, but also that he had been really unnerved by Florence's presence, so that he came across as bad-mannered and insecure.

Perhaps his laziness had become a way of avoiding facing up to reality — pretending all was well, especially if he had never been interested in the business he'd inherited from his father, and which he might have felt obliged to take on whether he wanted to or not — but now, at the end of this holiday season, reality could no longer be avoided. Clearly the business was in difficulties, and this had just happened to coincide with her own arrival in Guisethorpe. From his point of view, a stranger suddenly appearing and offering help in the troubled café might well be seen to be interfering; he might even feel she was gloating over its failings.

And I don't know why you're trying to make excuses for him, Flo, because the man is an oaf and doesn't deserve your sympathy.

Whatever the reason for his rudeness and his anger, Florence wished she could rescue Violet and her sweet-natured young granddaughter from the café. They deserved better but she was powerless to help.

★ ★ ★

84

Anthony Bird paced his sitting room, lighting a new cigarette from the stub of the last. He stopped to pour himself a glass of whisky from the half-empty bottle on the sideboard, then resumed his pacing, Scotch in one hand, smoke in the other.

He could not settle this evening, and it was all the fault of that arrogant Stanville woman. Twice now — *twice* — she had been in the café, interfering and seeking to tell his staff what to do. It was almost as if she'd seen those quarterly figures that Miss McGee had given him — on the very day that he'd first seen Florence Stanville, too — and she was playing some cruel game with him, mocking his efforts now the business was looking shaky. Could it really be a coincidence that she had arrived just as it became clear that the café was in serious trouble?

Where was she from, anyway, and why was she here? No one knew anything about her, from what he'd gathered from listening to his customers. She'd got a plain-spoken northern kind of voice, yet she looked . . . special, eye-catching, with her bright clothes and bright hair. Like she knew people would notice her and she didn't mind. Like she wasn't going to put her head down and shut up.

She certainly hadn't been sent by the gods to help him, that was for certain. No, she wasn't a kind woman, a womanly woman, with her assured manner, her confidence in herself. And then there was the fact that she always looked him straight in the eye because she was so tall and could do so, instead of deferring to him. Clearing tables, indeed!

He stopped pacing long enough to replenish his glass, then slouched over to the window to look out at the beautiful evening light softening over the grey sea.

Eventually he sank into the armchair in front of the window and reached for his drawing pad and a pencil. Quickly he sketched Florence Stanville, making her a beautiful witch. Her height became freakish, her hair a nest of snakes, her straight nose lengthened to poke into other people's business, her narrow feet also hugely elongated. Beside her was a small dog with — and Anthony was rather pleased with the likeness — a mock-innocent look on its evil little face.

Vile woman!

The doorbell rang and Anthony screwed up the cartoon and chucked it carelessly in the direction of the wastepaper basket, missing his target, then went down to see who it was.

Trudie Symons was on the doorstep, looking very pretty in a dress and jacket get-up.

'Tony, you haven't forgotten, have you?' she said, looking at him, crumpled and unwashed, tired and angry. 'Oh, you have. We were supposed to be going to that tennis club do in Fleming.'

Anthony cursed loudly.

'It's all right, darling. Still feeling a bit fragile after last night? Doesn't really matter. I don't suppose it would be heaps of fun, anyway,' she said with a regretful sigh. 'I just thought . . . oh, never mind. Are you going to let me in?'

'Yes, of course.' He led the way upstairs to the flat.

'What's up?' Trudie asked, taking off her jacket.

'Oh, just an awful afternoon in the café, and this woman came in — I've seen her before — and it's . . . her whole attitude . . . '

'Well, you kind of expect some customers to be awkward, Tony. They're not all easy to please. I used to hear all sorts at Nesbit and Harrison and that was supposed to be a respectable solicitors' practice. Though I think you might expect that some people who want a solicitor would be in a bit of trouble and not at their best . . . Anyway, never mind, I'm here now. Are you sure you can't face the social? It might take you out of yourself.'

'I've said I don't want to go,' he snapped.

'You didn't actually, Tony. You just swore a bit . . . '

'And so would you if you'd had the day I've had,'he said, his voice getting louder.

Trudie took a deep breath and decided to back off. Anthony could be moody and prone to outbursts of temper, especially just lately.

'It's all right, darling. Let's think of something else to do with the evening. It's the mobile chippy tonight. How about we take a stroll and get some chips and eat them on the beach with a beer? Nothing too demanding when you're feeling tired.'

'S'pose we could.'

'It's a bit cold but I'll borrow one of your coats. You'll soon feel better for some food. Go and get your jacket and a coat for me and we can do that now.'

Anthony went to do as Trudie suggested, leaving her hoping she'd saved the evening. Honestly, it was like pandering to a three-year-old sometimes . . .

She looked around the dusty and untidy room. Could he not make a little more effort? There was a ball of paper right next to the wastepaper basket. She bent to retrieve it and flattened it out to see what he'd drawn. Anthony was always sketching the people of Guisethorpe. Some of the cartoons were just funny, but he had been known to be unkind, too.

This one was of a very tall, very thin woman with a witch's pointy nose and snakes for hair. Trudie guessed immediately it must be the customer from the café who had annoyed Anthony earlier. And, good heavens, how she must have annoyed him to deserve such a cruel portrait. It wasn't that he'd made her ugly — far from it; she was evidently rather impressive — but he'd made her evil: the snakes, the malevolent look in her large eyes, those long feet prepared to trample anyone in her way . . .

Trudie felt a pang of misgiving at the venom of the cartoon. Before she had thought through what she was doing she had flattened it out, folded it up and put it in her handbag.

'Ready, Tony? OK, let's go . . . '

5

Mondays tended to be quiet at Ruby Slipper.

The shop didn't open to customers until the afternoon, though Judy went in earlier to clean and tidy, and get organised for the week ahead with administrative jobs and stock-checking.

Lucy arrived mid-morning, just as Judy was making a pot of tea, ringing the doorbell outside so that Judy would let her in.

'I wasn't expecting you for a couple of hours yet,'

said Judy. She looked at Lucy's face. 'What's the matter, love?'

'Oh, Judy, I just thought I'd prefer to be here doing summat useful than at home by myself brooding. I've had such a horrible weekend.'

'Tell me,' said Judy, hanging up Lucy's jacket for her.

'Mrs Walden,' said Lucy succinctly, sinking into a chair on the end of a row. 'You remember I told you Denis invited her for tea on Saturday? As I didn't know until I got home on Friday there wasn't time to get in owt special. Well, I did my best with a tin of salmon — which I always think is a treat — and some salad, but I couldn't get a fresh loaf so it was a case of what we already had. It wasn't nasty or owt but, oh, did she make me pay for that! It was all: 'How long have you had this bread, Lucille, love?' and, 'I'm never sure how fresh the fish is that goes into tins,' and, 'I never touch cucumber, thank you, love. It doesn't agree with me.' Sorry, Judy, I'm going on, I know. I shouldn't grumble about Denis's mother but she really gets my goat.'

'I'm not surprised, Lucy. Rude woman. But how come she ruined the weekend? She must have taken herself off home eventually?' Judy handed Lucy a cup of tea.

'She did, and I've never been so pleased to see the back of her. It felt like the longest evening of my life. She didn't even offer to lend a hand with the siding up afterwards. Not that I'd have let her help, of course, but she could have offered. Anyway, I didn't say owt 'cos I wasn't going to be rude, even if she is. But when she'd gone Denis took up complaining where she'd left off. I reckon he'd never have said owt if she hadn't started, but I'd hardly sat down and he was on about me making no effort. He said it was like I couldn't be bothered to make owt nice for his mum and she might think she wasn't welcome.'

'Well, that's hardly fair. It was he who asked her to tea when he knows you work on Saturdays, and he could have gone and done a bit of shopping himself, couldn't he? What was he doing when you were here working?'

'I don't know. I left him in bed. He gets up so early during the week, he's that tired by Saturday he needs to have a lie-in.'

Judy sniffed. 'Only ill people *need* to stay in bed, Lucy,' she said severely. 'Why don't you tell him his mother is very welcome, but the next time he invites her on a day that you're working he can get the shopping in and make the tea, too?'

Lucy looked askance: this was revolutionary.

'I bet his mother won't make a fuss about owt she's given to eat if she knows her precious boy has prepared it,' Judy added, offering an open packet of Garibaldis.

'She'd think I was hopeless,' Lucy said, taking a biscuit and looking tearful. 'She'd think I couldn't even make a simple meal, or that I didn't want to make the effort for her. She'd go on about that instead, I know she would. I can't seem to do owt right for her.'

'Now listen, Lucy,' said Judy, sitting down in the seat next to hers, 'there's a type of woman — and she's often a widow, like Mrs Walden — who thinks no one is good enough for her precious boy, especially if that boy is her *only* boy. It doesn't matter how hard you try to please, you'll never get it right. It's impossible to win her approval, love, because she is the one who has raised that little god, and she can allow no rivals to her position as number one woman in his life. Never mind that you're married to him and that you chose each other, the mother must be for ever top in his affections.'

Lucy nodded. 'That does sound like Mrs Walden.'

'Trust me, love, I know her sort. So what happened then?'

'Well, when Denis started on about how I'd made no effort for his mother, I was so cross I told him he shouldn't have invited her without giving me more notice, and he said, so she's not welcome in her own son's home, then? She has to make an appointment weeks in advance? And

I said . . . oh, Judy, I said, no she wasn't welcome if she was going to pick holes in what I'd done for her. And then he said he'd never thought he'd hear the day, and I was difficult and moody and his mother deserved better, and it just got worse after that, and then he slept in the armchair on Saturday night and went out all day yesterday — I reckon he was at her house — and only came home for his tea and would hardly speak to me then, though I said I was sorry.'

'Crikey! That's a bit of an overreaction.'

'How was I to know she doesn't like tinned salmon and cucumber gives her indigestion?' Lucy whispered tearfully.

'But I told you, Lucy, it wasn't really about that, was it? It was about Mrs W wanting to put you in your place, that place being rather lower than her own.'

'I s'pose. But what can I do about her? I've always been nice to her and she still doesn't like me.'

'But it's not *you* she doesn't like, Lucy. It would be the same for anyone married to her son. If Denis was married to Doris Day you can bet Mrs W'd be telling her all that singing was giving her a headache!'

Lucy smiled through her tears. 'But what can I do? I'm never going to win at this rate.'

'It's not about winning, Lucy, it's about managing, I'm afraid: self-preservation, damage limitation, keeping the peace while keeping your sanity.'

'That doesn't sound very easy. What do you suggest?'

'I reckon you just have to disarm her, Lucy. She throws you a barbed comment or a snide criticism, you smile nicely and tell her you're sure she's right. She insults your cake, you ask for her own recipe. She doesn't like the food you've served her, ask her what she'd prefer next time. She's never going to help side up or make any effort to be pleasant, so if you recognise that from the start at least you won't be disappointed.'

'Yes, I think you're right, Judy.'

'I know I am. Remember that man who used to call for me after work last year? Gerry his name was — very good-looking, charming, generous with flowers and evenings out. Well, nearest I've ever been to falling in love. I was beginning to think he was the one . . . but then I met his mother.' Judy rolled her eyes drama tically and Lucy couldn't help giggling. 'Oh, Lucy, I tried, I really did. Luckily I saw the light in time and got out while the going was good.'

Lucy looked stricken then. 'But it's too late for me! I'm married to Denis!'

'And that's what you want, isn't it? You and Denis are properly in love — anyone can see that by just looking at the pair of you — but Mrs W is a part of his life that isn't going to fade into the background, and, as I say, you have to manage her. It's either that or you and Denis move right away and get her out of the picture.'

'I don't think that's likely to happen, what with Denis's business established round here,' said Lucy mournfully.

'Mm. And I'd be right sorry to lose you from the shop. No, Lucy, I'm afraid you're stuck with

Mrs Walden so you're just going to have to make the best of it. But cheer up, love . . . she can't live for ever.'

For a moment Lucy was shocked and then she saw Judy's face and they both burst out laughing.

★ ★ ★

Florence drove to St Jude's Hall with Jim beside her. The boot was full of vegetables for the produce market, and there were jars of fresh pickles rattling cheerfully in a cardboard box on the back seat, with a huge bunch of the tall, unruly flowers that grew in Florence's garden, wrapped in newspaper, lying on top.

'It's good of you to offer to take the jars on your table,' said Florence, 'but I've got an idea of how I might be able to show them off without taking up space that you need for your veg.'

'I'll make room for you, Florence, don't you worry . . . Take this next one on the right and the hall's at the top of the road beside the church. You can park round the back.'

Florence parked as Jim directed, then helped him out of the car.

'We need to set the place up before we move the produce in,' Jim said. 'Come and meet the others.'

He led the way through the back door, past a kitchen in which there was an urn already heating up, and into the hall itself. There were several people there, unstacking chairs and moving trestle tables into rows along three sides of the big room.

There was a chorus of 'Good morning, Jim', and Jim went round the room with Florence, introducing her to the others.

Florence wasn't sure she'd remember all the names, but she didn't think the people, who were being very industrious with their furniture shifting, would remember hers either. She made a point of shaking Mary Davis by the hand, though.

'We spoke on the phone,' said Florence.

'Oh, yes, I remember. Pickles!'

'Jim has offered to have a few of mine alongside his veg. He reckons we won't be putting anyone's nose out of joint if we keep a low profile,' said Florence, remembering Mrs Davis had mentioned this arrangement was all right.

'That's fine. Doreen Potter — she's not here yet — and Derek Clough are our pickle and preserve makers. Any rivalry here is always of the friendliest nature but it's an unwritten rule not to tread on anyone else's feet.' Mary smiled. 'Have a look and see what they've got, once we're all set up. You never know, there might be room for you, too, another month.'

'Thank you, Mrs Davis,' said Florence. 'Now, shall I grab the other end of this table? Where do you want this one . . . ?'

When the tables and chairs were in place, Florence and Jim went back out to the car and began to bring through the vegetables, jars and Florence's flowers.

'I'll just put these under the table until we've got your veg in place, Jim,' said Florence, pushing her box out of the way with her foot.

'I generally just heap it up with the price in front,' said Jim, producing from his cardigan pocket a little pile of cardboard labels written in

Biro, the ones he used on his table at the garden gate.

Florence already had an idea. 'Would you mind if I have a go at a bit of an arrangement?'

'You can do as you want, love. I told you, I'm grateful for the help.'

Florence took a look at what Jim had got and then started arranging the vegetables. She mixed them up, creating height at the back with the boxes they'd been packed in, cascading carrot and beetroot tops over the sides like waterfalls, alternating different types of lettuce to contrast in shape and colour, placing little punnets of tomatoes between, piling onions high next to radishes, adding width to the picture with bundles of beans and cucumbers.

'It looks like a harvest festival,' said Jim approvingly, when he saw what she was creating.

'That's exactly what it is, Jim. A celebration of your harvest. Now, I'll just see if I can find a vase for the flowers.' She went off to the hall's kitchen, where Mary Davis was drawing water from the urn into some large pots to make tea for the stallholders. Predictably, there was a whole shelf of tall and not very clean vases.

'I wanted to borrow a vase for my flowers,' Florence told her as she selected the most attractive one.

'Flowers?' Mary asked. 'I don't think anyone else sells flowers. Perhaps you've found your gap in the market already, Mrs Stanville.'

'Oh, no, they're not for sale — unless someone wants to make an offer for them,' said Florence. 'Just summat I picked to make Jim's table look nice. I wasn't even going to use them if there wasn't room, but I think they may have a place.'

Mary followed Florence back to Jim's table to look. Florence unwrapped the poppies, ox-eye daisies and bits of greenery she'd brought with her. She trailed some ivy around the sides of the boxes and over the front of the table, then placed the vase slightly to one side of centre and fanned out her flowers.

'Lovely,' said Mary. 'Very eye-catching.'

'It's certainly an improvement on what I usually do, Florence,' Jim said. 'It looks proper dandy with everything all mixed up. But what about your jars? You haven't left any room for them.'

'Ah, but I have,' said Florence. She turned and pointed to the high windowsill behind the table and chairs. 'That's going to be my bit of space. If I stand on this chair, would you pass 'em up, please, Jim?'

He did so, and when Florence had arranged her fresh pickles in a row with the light shining through them, he could see why that was the perfect place to show them off.

'It's just like stained glass,' he said.

'That's exactly what I hoped,' said Florence, remembering the jewel colours shining onto the floor from the glass around the Kendal sisters' front door.

'You've got a very good eye, Mrs Stanville. Hasn't she, Mavis?' Mary asked the woman on the table next to Jim's. Mavis Farlowe was selling cakes and had them set out in rows like in a high-street cake shop.

'It looks lovely, dear,' said Mavis. 'Maybe you

97

could help me with mine next month.'

Florence smiled her thanks but didn't say she'd do so.

'Looks amazing, Jim. Bet you can't do that without the lady's help,' called the man standing behind a table of jars on the other side of the room. This must be Derek Clough, whom Mary had mentioned.

'We open in a few minutes, so I've just got time to make sure everyone's got everything they need and take round the cups of tea. I could do with a hand with that, if Jim can spare you, please, Mrs Stanville,' said Mary.

'Of course.'

Florence wound her way around the room, offering tea and also seeing what was for sale.

Derek Clough's table held seasonal chutney and jam. He had a huge variety to sell, but he used old jam jars of all different sizes, the labels stuck on untidily, the shaky writing sloping and uneven, and the lids of different styles, so that the overall effect was not the smart hand-made look that Florence sought to achieve with hers, but rather an amateurish home-made appearance. Florence thought she'd buy some goose-berry jam later. The jam itself looked good, when you could see past the poor presentation.

Doreen Potter had her table next to the door where the customers would come in. It was the last one Florence got to with her tea order. Mrs Potter had not quite finished setting up yet, having arrived late.

'Hello. I'm helping Mrs Davis with teas this morning. How do you like yours?' Florence said, casually assessing the woman's preserves.

Mrs Potter looked up from behind her table, where she was kneeling on the floor surrounded by cardboard boxes and crumpled newspaper.

'Oh, hello. I'm Doreen Potter.' She stood up stiffly and offered her hand. 'And you, I believe, are Florence Stanville, is that right?'

'It is.' Florence took her hand out of courtesy, wondering how the woman knew her name. Of course, any news travelled fast in a small community, but there was something about Doreen Potter's eager, inquisitive face that Florence did not want to encourage. Anything said to her would be passed on, whether it was interesting or not, Florence felt sure. She hoped Doreen Potter wasn't the kind to embellish and speculate as well, but she rather feared she knew the type.

'Milk and one sugar?' she said, as if to remind herself.

'Oh, er, weak, milk, no sugar, thank you.'

Florence quickly went off to get the tea before Mrs Potter had a chance to speak again, choosing the exact moment Doreen Potter was tidying up under her table to leave her tea for her. Florence then moved away to hand out tea to the elderly couple selling tea cosies on the next table.

The tea cosies were in bold colours and knitted in garter stitch, like winter hats, with a pompom on top of each and vents on opposite sides for the teapot spout and handle. Florence noticed one patterned with blue and white stripes. Suddenly a vision flew into her head of her mother pouring tea from a pot with just such a cosy on it. It was in a huge kitchen with a table in the middle of the red-brown tiled floor, an echoey room with sun-light shafting through high windows. Her mother, tall and straight, was wearing a dark frock in a slack style and an apron with a bib, her long red hair folded in at the back in a loose bun.

Where was that house? I'd forgotten that kitchen until now . . .

'You all right, Mrs Stanville?' It was Mary. 'Only you looked a bit . . . gone.'

'I'm fine, thank you,' said Florence. She did not want to say anything at all about her sudden rush of childhood memory, like a stray piece found on the floor from a long-forgotten jigsaw puzzle. She'd not come here to rake over her past with people she'd only just met.

'I ought to go and help Jim now we've finished doing the teas,' she said.

'He looks quite busy,' said Mary. 'I think his table is attracting the attention of some of the holidaymakers.'

Florence thought it odd that people on holiday should want to buy vegetables, but maybe they were city folk, just about to return home, and Jim's were rather fresher than they were used to.

But when she got to his table, he was reaching down a jar of her pickled radishes, one of only two left.

'Let me get that for you, Jim,' Florence said, moving the chair to climb on it.

'They look grand,' said the woman who was purchasing. 'I'll take both of them, if I may?'

'Course,' said Florence. 'Thank you.' She handed them to the woman. 'They're ready to eat now.'

'Lovely. I'll tell my daughters. They'll make nice presents for them from my holiday,' the woman explained. 'They are so pretty I couldn't resist.'

Florence took the money and thanked her again, then helped Jim with his vegetables. They got a system going, with Jim handling the veg and Florence taking the money. It was fun and they did a brisk trade. Soon the display was partially dismantled and beginning to look sparse.

Mavis Farlowe, the cake maker on the next table, came to buy some beetroot while her trade was slack.

'I've never seen Jim so busy,' she told Florence. 'You've got an eye for a pretty display and it's made a difference. Really, Mrs Stanville, I did mean what I said. If you could help me with my table next month, I'm sure I would sell more.'

'But don't folk from Guisethorpe know the quality of your baking, however you display it?' Florence asked, hoping to get out of helping in case it proved to need more diplomacy than she could readily summon up.

'Oh, we always attract customers from the other villages, not just Guisethorpe,' said Mavis. 'The monthly market is a bit of an event. You've seen for yourself that we've holidaymakers and all sorts here today. There's people from Long Barrow, Fleming and even further afield.'

'Well, it's nice of you to ask. I'll have to see,' said Florence, vaguely. 'But I'll have a piece of that ground rice tart, please.'

'Thank you. And I really would appreciate the help,' said Mavis. 'Jim'll tell you where I am if you'd like to get in touch before next time.'

Oh Lord, I can see you only have to raise your nose above the windowsill in this place and before you know it there are folk trying to commit you to doing stuff you'd rather not be bothered with, thought Florence. Jim and I are getting on just fine but I don't want to be roped into owt everyone else is doing.

Florence paid for her cake and escaped back behind Jim's table. And oh, no, there was Mildred Yateman, talking to Doreen Potter. The two of them kept glancing in Jim and Florence's direction. Florence busied herself tidying the remaining vegetables into a smaller display.

'We're nearly sold out and ready to go home, Jim,'

she said.

'Aye, Florence, I'll not be taking much back with me this month, thanks to your work on the table. Proper caught the attention, it did. I've never sold so much before. Thank you.'

'It was just an idea I thought might work. And I've sold my jars, too, so we've both had a good morning.'

'A shame I can't really take a lot more of yours, Florence, but we have to agree the rules for the event to work.'

'I know that. But I've come away with plenty of ideas. I'm not downhearted.'

'I should think not,' said Jim. 'And there's Mildred talking to Doreen. I wouldn't be surprised if you're not the subject of that conversation. Like an interesting new subject, they do.' Jim lowered his voice. 'I wouldn't say anything to Doreen that you don't want the whole of Guisethorpe to know about. Just a friendly bit of advice, Florence, love.'

She nodded. 'Thanks, Jim.'

Mildred came over. 'You've done well, Jim. Not much to take home. Shall I fetch the barrow?'

'I didn't bring it, Mil. Florence gave me a lift down in her car.'

'I didn't know that,' Mildred said. She sounded cross. 'When was this arranged?'

'Just the other day,' said Jim. He hadn't told Mildred he'd met Florence in the village and had tea with her at Bird's Café, and it seemed unwise to mention it now.

'Well, I wish you'd told me.'

'I never thought anything of it,' said Jim.

Florence felt sorry for Jim. Mildred was clearly feeling left out, though Florence knew she took little interest in her husband's vegetable garden. Nor had she been here to lend a hand earlier.

'I've offered to take Jim back home, too, of course, Mrs Yateman. Would you like a lift?'

'Yes, please.' She jumped at the chance.

I bet you would. But you won't learn owt interesting on the way. It isn't only Doreen Potter who likes a gossip, I'll be bound.

★ ★ ★

Florence helped Jim and Mildred to unload their things beside Sea View's garden gate.

As she drove the few yards further down to park beside Paradise Cottage, Jim waved his thanks, but Mildred was already going up the path and round to the kitchen door.

Jim put the orange box of his unsold veg on

the table by the gate, pulled from his pocket the appropriate price labels, which he weighed down with pebbles, and then took the empty boxes round to his shed.

When he appeared in the kitchen, Mildred was very pointedly busying herself at the sink, peeling potatoes for lunch. She didn't look round.

'Best sale I've ever had, this morning,' said Jim. 'Sold quite a bit to visitors as well as those from the villages that always come to buy.'

'Mm . . . ' said Mildred.

'Florence did a splendid job with the table display.

Pity you didn't come earlier and you'd have seen it in all its glory. It made all the difference. I said, 'Why, it's like a harvest festival.' And she said — '

'So when did you plan all that, the pair of you? Was it when you were having tea at Bird's Café?'

'How did you know about that?' said Jim, then realised he sounded exactly as if he'd been caught doing something behind his wife's back.

'Found you out, haven't I?' said Mildred nastily, turning to look at him, a potato and the peeler dripping in her hands.

Jim gathered himself. 'Don't be silly, Mil. There's nothing to find out about. Florence Stanville and her dog were sitting outside the café on Monday as I was going past with the Bisto and she asked me if I'd like a cup of tea.'

'She just asked you to have tea with her as you were passing, and you almost a stranger? That was very forward of her. I shouldn't wonder if that young woman is up to no good, offering tea to men in the street. Was it *just tea* the hussy was

104

offering?'

'Mildred, that was quite uncalled for. I can guess it was that mischievous old gossip Doreen that saw me drinking tea at the café on the sea-front, in public, in the middle of the afternoon, with Florence Stanville. As I was. I won't deny it because there's nothing to hide. It never occurred to me to mention it, that's all. And as for being a stranger, the lady lives opposite, as you are well aware, since you were practically falling over yourself to go round and interrogate her before she'd even unpacked her things. Also, she's neither a hussy nor particularly young. So you're wrong on all counts!'

Mildred looked taken aback. Jim didn't usually go in for long speeches.

'So what did she want, drinking tea with you?'

'I think she just wanted to be nice. Which is more than you're being. She's moved here, she was by herself, perhaps she merely wanted a person to drink tea with, instead of drinking it alone.'

'So she is by herself? There's no Mr Stanville, then?'

'I don't know, Mildred, I haven't asked her. It seemed a bit rude to be poking my nose in, not minding my own business. If she'd wanted me to know, she'd have told me herself.'

'So what did she say while you were drinking tea, the pair of you?'

'Will you stop linking us as a 'pair', please, Mildred? We are two people who happen to live opposite each other and had a cup of tea together in public. We talked about pickles.'

'Pickles?'

Nothing wrong with your hearing then, just your brain. 'Yes, pickles. She'd made some pickles, wanted to sell them at the produce sale and Mary had told her Derek and Doreen were already doing that.'

'So what was that to do with you?'

Jim sighed heavily. He'd had a long morning, having got up at dawn to pick the vegetables for his table; he'd had an enjoyable time in the company of Florence — and a successful one, too, partly down to her flair — and he really was getting very weary of Mildred's nonsense.

'Nothing. Now I'm going to weed those lettuces. There's just time before we eat.' And he went out into the garden.

When he got to his shed, instead of tending the lettuces, he went inside and sat down in an ancient and rather damp armchair he kept there, surrounded by pristine gardening tools and stacks of tiny plant pots.

What on earth was the matter with Mildred that she had to be mean and nasty about Florence? Florence had been in Guisethorpe little more than a week and already Doreen bloomin' Potter was making mischief about her. Oh, but that Doreen could be a vicious mischief-maker and she probably saw Florence as a rival, what with Florence being new to the produce market, and her jars selling in no time. As if there wasn't room for everyone! Perhaps Doreen thought she'd lead Mildred into asking him not to offer Florence room on his table another time. Good grief, she'd only brought about ten jars. They did look good, though . . .

It had been a lovely morning. Florence was hard-working, quick and funny, and she knew when to speak and when to listen, which was nice. And she'd got such a good eye for making the most of what they had to work with. Who'd have thought you could make a church-window effect from a jar of pickled radishes? Or a display like some priceless still-life painting from a table full of vegetables?

No, Florence Stanville was quite an unusual woman and Jim was a man who spoke as he found. Far from giving up on her, this was a friendship he meant to cultivate.

* * *

Kathleen Walden sat down heavily in her armchair and eased her feet out of her rather worn slippers. She glanced at the mantelpiece clock: only three more hours and it would be time to set off to see Denis. He'd dropped in this morning on his way to work to bring her her newspaper, and Kathleen had said she really hoped she'd be seeing him later. Mebbe if she could just pop round, about teatime . . . Course, her boy would be only too pleased to see his mum so soon. They had spent Sunday together, true, and it had been just like old times, even though Denis had been a bit quiet. Kathleen was knitting him some gloves for when the cold set in and she'd bring them over, see if they would fit while Lucille made the tea . . .

It was a good job someone was looking after him properly. That Lucille was a bit of a flighty piece: spent a little too much time on her appearance and rather less than she should on looking after Denis in his home, in Kathleen's opinion. Denis had not chosen wisely when he decided to marry Lucille. A working man needed the full attention of his wife, not a woman who divided her time between her man and a job in a shoe shop. And a widow who lived by herself needed to know she could count on her only son to keep an eye on her, make sure she was all right and didn't have to cook her own tea and eat it alone every evening. Or any evening, come to that. Denis and his mother had been everything to each other for years, and just because he was married to a slip of a girl, it didn't mean that they weren't everything to each other still. Lucille needed to know her place, an outsider to this long-established relationship of mother and son. It was she who was the newcomer, the one who had to learn how things were and how they'd always been, and the sooner she recognised that the better it would be. For everyone.

6

Florence was enjoying her new life in Guisethorpe. Of course, not everything was completely perfect She missed her mother terribly, but most folk outlived their parents. It was a common enough experience and she would just have to cope with it, the same as everyone else. It was a question of summoning inner strength and backbone, the very qualities that had got everyone through the war. She'd coped then and she would manage now. But that sensible resolution, so clear and so decisive during the day, could not prevent her strange dreams at night.

Every few nights she would wake suddenly in the dead hours of darkness, often crying out at a fast-fading dream, in which her mother had stood weeping. In the dreams Florence was sometimes Little Flo, sometimes herself now, but the haunting feeling of an old sorrow never healed, of a secret wanting to break through from the past, like someone buried before their time and trying to push a limb through to the light, was always the same. The other red-headed child often appeared in the dreams, sometimes half glimpsed in the distance, sometimes running away, always out of reach.

Occasionally now Florence would almost see that child in the mirror when she went to brush her hair or put on her makeup: just for a fraction of a second, a tiny moment that flipped her stomach over. She told herself not to be ridiculous but those brief feelings of that presence were always unnerving.

Florence began to wonder if Paradise Cottage was haunted, but if it was, she could make no sense of why it should be haunted by that ghost. She was certain she herself had never set eyes on the place before she had come to view it that once when she had decided to buy it. And anyway, the cottage had a warm and friendly feeling, the rooms were calm and entirely without strange atmospheres. And she was happy here . . . almost.

What could all this strangeness mean? Florence felt the dreams were trying to tell her something but she didn't know how to find out what that was. During the daytime, all she could do was deliberately shrug off her unease from the night before and instead embrace the life she had chosen. But her mother's words about running away, not being able to forgive and a hidden truth began to nag at her conscience. If Florence could find out what Lily had meant, then maybe the dreams would cease. The trouble was, she didn't know where or how to begin.

In the meantime, Florence and Lucy exchanged letters regularly, and eagerly looked forward to hearing each other's news. Florence was pleased to be able to tell Lucy that she'd found a very smart grocer in the inland village of Burton Barrow, a pretty place with unusually expensive shops, who had agreed to take her pickles.

I'd nearly given up finding anyone interested —
I'd driven for miles with Scamper in the car with
me and a boxful of jars of pickles clinking in the

boot, but nowhere could I find anyone willing to buy even a few jars — but then someone mentioned this 'fancy grocer', Nicolson & Filbert, and I thought I'd got nothing to lose by seeing if they were interested. I was just a tiny a bit over-awed when I first went in — it's like Aladdin's cave, but with wine and chocolate and all kinds of special food wrapped up like presents — but I soon pulled myself together, remembering the kinds of shops I used to go to in London when I was married to your father. Harry Nicolson is a bit standoffish, but Sandra Filbert is very down to earth and I reckon we'll see eye to eye. I've had some business cards printed with my name and telephone number and I'm calling my produce 'Florence Lily', which I hope you think properly honours your grandma, the source of so many recipes.

Anyway — great news! — after keeping me on tenterhooks for a week and more, Nicolson & Filbert put in a large order, so I'm hard at it with the pickling . . .

Lucy's letters, in return, were full of news about the shop and Judy's plans for it over the coming months, but Florence detected an element of discord at home beginning to show occasionally, too, due to the increasing presence of Denis's mother.

Florence had met Kathleen Walden at Lucy and Denis's wedding, of course, and had dismissed her privately as a selfish old woman, although she wasn't a great many years older than Florence herself. Nonetheless, she had decided not to waste time cultivating a friendship there; she neither needed nor wanted to get to know Mrs Walden. She didn't know what Mrs Walden thought of her and she didn't care. The important thing was that Denis was so obviously madly in love with Lucy that Florence expected the mummy's boy would cut the apron strings and give all his attention to his equally devoted new wife. Now, however, it looked as if Kathleen Walden was trying to establish a central role in the newlyweds' lives. This was confirmed in Lucy's next letter.

'Denis's mum does come round quite a lot these days,' Lucy disclosed.

She can be difficult to please and I've noticed when I've made an effort to make things nice for her she'll change her mind and put me in the wrong. I honestly think she does it on purpose because it happens so often, but I can't confront her every time or we'd end up at war. Sometimes I begin to doubt myself, though I've never thought I was careless about other folk's comfort before. Maybe I'm just a bit tired, what with the shop and all the cooking and housework, but I really do want Denis's mum to be glad Denis has married me . . .

Florence sighed and put Lucy's letter to one side while she measured the ingredients for her next batch of spiced vinegar. She'd write this evening and tell Lucy that if she didn't want to confront Mrs Walden — which would have been Florence's own preferred option — she'd just have to do her best to get along with her, and maybe enlist Denis's help so as not to make a difficult situation

112

worse. Surely the woman wasn't round at Lucy and Denis's that often? She wasn't suddenly going to turn into a kind, helpful mother-in-law, or disappear off the scene, so unfortunately getting on with her was a rather difficult life lesson that Lucy would have to try to manage. Florence wished she lived closer, or that Lucy was on the telephone so she could try to suggest something more specific to ease Lucy's problem, but there was nothing to be done about that. She would, however, suggest that Denis could be asked to make more effort in their home. After all, they both worked, so why should Lucy have to do all the chores as well as cope with his demanding mother?

★ ★ ★

As the days grew colder and autumn set in, Florence felt it was a shame she couldn't sit outside Bird's Café with Scamper and order a warming pot of tea after their walks along the beach when once she might have liked to do so. Anthony Bird had so far presented himself to her as ill-mannered and unreasonable, and although she felt well able to deal with his animosity, she didn't actively seek confrontation and wanted to avoid embarrassment to Violet, Carmen and any customers of the café. However, each time she happened to pass the place she noticed that customers were increasingly few and far between. But who needed encounters of the kind she'd had with Anthony Bird so far? She knew he was lazy, bad-tempered and a poor employer because Violet and Carmen inevitably met Florence in the street or on the beach some days, and as their friendship grew with every encounter, Violet and Carmen felt they owed Anthony no discretion with their complaints.

Florence happened to meet them just as the café was closing one afternoon in September.

'Scamper and I are off in the direction of Fleming, if you've time to walk along with us,' said Florence.

'Yes, I'd like that,' said Violet. 'Stretch my legs.'

'Mine, too,' said Carmen. 'They've hardly been stretched at all today, standing around waiting for someone to come in. Only good thing about it was that I didn't spill anything . . . there being nothing to spill.'

'What, no customers *at all*?'

'Not a soul,' said Violet.

'Desolate,' said Carmen sadly.

'That's bad news.'

'Mm . . . ' Violet frowned, then changed the subject. 'So, Florence, how are things with you this week? Have you heard from your daughter?'

'I have indeed, thank you for asking. She's well but she's got a difficult mother-in-law and I think she's finding it hard to be as polite as she wants to be while still keeping the wretched woman from overstepping the mark.'

'Awkward,' nodded Carmen.

'It's a shame you're so far away,' said Violet, then added: 'Excuse me for asking, but is Mr Stanville still alive and able to advise his daughter, or are you a widow, like me?'

Florence couldn't help laughing. 'Sorry, Violet,' she said then, recovering, 'but I am not Mr

Stanville's widow. So far as I know he's very much alive and probably at the races losing money or drinking it away in the pub.'

'Oh dear, so that was why you parted company?' ventured Violet.

'Let's just say that no good advice would ever come from Frank Stanville, and fortunately Lucy is not his daughter anyway, so neither of us has the slightest connection with that old reprobate any more.'

'*Reprobate,*' whispered Carmen, trying out the new word.

'Gosh, I'm sorry, I just assumed — '

'It's all right, Violet. That's understandable. No, I've long since lost touch with Lucy's father, my first husband, and I'm certain she has never tried to contact him either. He wasn't at all interested in his daughter and, because she never really knew him, she's not interested in him either. She doesn't need him.'

'That sounds sad, love.'

'I was sad at the time. I had thought he was glamorous and romantic and special.'

'Was he *very* handsome?' asked Carmen gently, her eyes wide.

'He was.'

'Well, handsome is as handsome does,' said Violet, giving Carmen a look.

'Quite,' agreed Florence. 'I was a silly impressionable girl, and if he'd had a squint and a hunched back I wouldn't have fallen for him. I'd have seen him for what he was.'

'Like Richard the Third,' said Carmen, which made Florence and Violet both look at her askance for a moment before laughing loudly.

'Oh, it's good to have a bit of a laugh,' said Violet as she and Carmen turned up towards the road and their home. 'I hope your daughter is OK. We'll see you again soon . . . '

Florence and Scamper walked on a bit and then they, too, headed for home. The cottage would be welcoming and cosy after a bracing walk in the easterly breeze off the sea. Florence had made a big effort to refurbish Paradise Cottage to her own taste, and earlier that month she had painted it throughout inside and made some pretty new cushion covers and curtains from brightly patterned fabric.

The garden needed some attention next, and she thought she'd ask Jim's advice about that.

After the produce market at the end of August, Florence had got the impression that Mildred Yateman was not being very friendly towards her, but then she had not cultivated a friendship with Mildred, either. Florence only minded because she had really taken to Jim, with his kindness and his gentle, straightforward attitude, his talent for gardening, about which he was so modest, and his generosity in giving her an opening for selling her pickles, small scale though it was. But his wife's frostiness — a crisp 'Good morning' and a cold look if an encounter could not be avoided altogether — appeared to make no difference to Jim, who either didn't notice or, more likely, ignored it. Like Violet and Carmen, he was becoming a good friend.

The part-time reading job with the Kendal sisters suited Florence well, too. She looked forward more than she could ever have imagined to visiting the twins two or three times a week to read to them. The days and the hours were flexible, the next reading always arranged in advance but not set in stone. Occasionally one of the sisters would telephone.

'Mrs Stanville, we are *desperate* to find out what happens when . . .' and she would allude to some exciting turn of plot. 'I know we said Thursday, but we wondered if you would mind — and please do say if you're busy — but are you free to come tomorrow morning and read us some more?'

The twins were like children begging for just one more chapter of a bedtime story. Florence liked to oblige them but sometimes she would say no, just because she preferred to manage her time as she wanted and she didn't want the reading gradually to grow into a bigger part of her life. It was a nice little sideline and that's how it would stay.

At first, when the weather was fine, they had sometimes sat outside, Beatrice and Jane wrapped in coats with fur collars, and with blankets over their knees, despite it being only the end of summer, and they would enquire at intervals, 'Are you quite warm enough, Mrs Stanville?' They were always thoughtful.

Florence discovered that they had 'a girl' called Becca, who moved silently and almost invisibly about the house, tidying, cooking and cleaning, and it was she who made the welcoming coffee or hot chocolate. Florence wasn't sure whether Becca lived at the house or not, but she was quite obviously devoted to Beatrice and Jane.

One day, as Florence was putting on her coat

to leave after a morning's reading, Beatrice said, 'You know, Mrs Stanville, we've been racking our brains to think if we knew your mother, Lily Townsend, and we really can't think that we did.'

'And yet we can't help this feeling that we must have done. It's the only reason we can imagine why you should look familiar to us,' said Jane.

'Did your mother live in Fleming, dear?'

'No, we lived in Guisethorpe, but it's so long ago that I can't remember where, or what the place was like at all, except that there were lots of rooms and corridors. Would you have known a lady living up the coast?'

'Well, we might. We used to get out a lot more once upon a time,' smiled Jane.

'The thing is,' said Florence, prepared to impart some information, deciding that the sisters' memories, however vague, might hold some clues she could find helpful, 'I have a rather confused idea of my childhood in Guisethorpe. Oh, it was lovely and that's why I came back to live here, but I would dearly like to know about the things I've forgotten, or didn't know or understand because I was so little.'

'Make a more complete picture of that time, you mean?' said Beatrice.

'An entirely complete picture eventually, if I can, Miss Bea,' Florence said.

'And when was this?' asked Jane.

'Not long after the Great War, Miss Jane. My father and sister had died in the Spanish flu pandemic and my mother brought me to this seaside to start a new life, to put all the sadness behind us both.'

'Oh, that was a terrible time. So many people affected . . . '

'Yes. One day we were a family of four and the next there were just the two of us. That's all I remember. My mother died earlier this year and I foolishly didn't ask her about it, and now it's too late.'

'I'm sorry to hear that, Mrs Stanville. I can see, now you live here again, why it's important to you to know all about your childhood.'

'Yes,' said Florence. 'I'd like to know the truth . . . ' She smiled at the sisters. 'So, please, if you do remember anything about a young widow called Lily Townsend, who had a red-haired child of about seven and lived in Guisethorpe, I'll be very interested to know it.'

'We'll see what we can do, dear,' said Jane.

'And, after all, two heads are better than one,' added Beatrice.

★ ★ ★

A second order from Nicolson & Filbert was going to keep Florence very busy, and she wondered if she had pushed her luck. She had left a sample of blackberry jelly with Harry Nicolson the first time she went there and now he wanted as many jars as she could supply. Jim grew only a few cultivated brambles in his garden so he hadn't much fruit, but she knew just where she could get a huge amount. It meant a lot of work, though, and she'd need some help. She was contem-plating this as she took Scamper for her walk by the sea, the perfect place to work through one's problems.

119

As if she had conjured him up, there was Jim on the beach, walking towards her.

'Jim, hello! I don't often see you down here.'

'Hello, Florence. No, but I felt like a stroll this afternoon. Mildred has got her crochet group round and I thought I'd make myself scarce. They seem to fill the place and they make a lot of noise.'

'You couldn't get away from them in your garden?'

'I'd rather get right away. They drink a lot of tea, too, and if I'm around it becomes my job to make it. Then they patronise me while I'm handing round the cups, as if I were a performing monkey or something.'

'Oh dear. Well, your escape is lucky for me, Jim, because you're the very person I want to see.'

'Oh, yes?'

'I thought I'd go blackberrying tomorrow. Would you like to come and help me?'

'Oh, I don't know . . . Mildred might not be happy about it.'

'Why ever not? Two people standing in a hedge, picking blackberries, protected against the thorns from head to toe. She can come too if she wants.' This invitation was a risk because Florence didn't want Mildred there. Jim was quiet and undemanding, and they would pick a lot of fruit, which was the whole point of going, and the conversation, what there was of it, would be easy. 'What were you going to do if not come blackberrying with me?'

'Oh, just some tidying around the vegetables.'

'Will it wait?'

Jim smiled. 'I believe it will. Where are you

120

thinking of going?'

'Ah, now, there's a place above Fleming. It's private land but I know the owners and I've asked their permission. Come over about ten o'clock. I'll pack us a picnic in case we make a day of it. If Mildred wants to come, remind her to wear trousers or she'll ladder her stockings.'

Jim nodded and said goodbye. He walked on, looking happier.

Flo, that was naughty. You know full well Mildred Yateman is highly unlikely to own a pair of trousers. She definitely won't be joining us now.

Sure enough, there was no sign of Mildred when Jim came across the lane to Paradise Cottage the next morning, wearing an ancient coat and carrying a few tubs for the harvest and a walking stick with a crooked handle.

'Mildred not coming?' Florence asked innocently, handing Jim a picnic basket and picking up Scamper's lead and a large Thermos flask.

'No, though I told her you'd kindly asked her. I've to bring back a punnet for her to make a pie, she says.'

'How was the crochet group when you got home?'

'Gone,' he grinned.

Florence locked up and led Jim round the side to the car. She stowed his tubs in the boot, where there were already stacks of punnets.

'Good heavens, Florence, do you mean to pick a ton?'

'With your help, Jim.'

On the drive to Fleming St Clair, Florence confided about the fancy grocer's in Burton Barrow, and that they had ordered some of her special blackberry jelly from her mother's recipe, so it was now or never.

'You've done well, Florence, and yes, we need to get on with the picking. If you leave it after the end of September, the devil will have . . . well, he'll have peed on the berries.'

'I've never heard that before, Jim. Luckily we're far enough ahead that there's no danger of meeting him.'

'I should hope not!' Jim sounded as though he really believed the folk tale.

Florence drove along the seafront.

'The café, Bird's,' said Jim as they passed it. He lowered his voice, though it was just the two of them and Scamper in the car. 'I hear it's in trouble.'

'I'm not surprised. I gather they have hardly any customers now the season is over,' Flo murmured.

'It'd be a shame for the staff if it had to close. Carmen is a sweet child, though rather young for her age. I don't know how easily she'd find another job that would let her be herself. And Violet Peasall — do you know her, the cook? — is getting on a bit to be looking for a new job.'

'Yes, I do know Violet. It must be worrying for her,' said Florence slowly. When Violet had told her how useless Anthony Bird was as the owner and manager, and then more recently that there were so few customers, Violet had not dwelt on what that might mean for herself and her granddaughter, and Florence had somehow not quite joined the dots to realise that Violet and Carmen would obviously lose their jobs if the café failed. A true friend would have been properly concerned, without having to have it spelled out, Florence chided herself. Surely she could think of something to help them, even if it was only a suggestion . . .

She turned inland at Fleming St Clair, through the little town and up towards Long Barrow Lane.

'All the years I've lived in Guisethorpe and I don't think I've ever been up here before,' said Jim, looking around interestedly.

Florence explained about her part-time job reading to the Kendal sisters. 'It's they who own the field where the lane peters out,' she finished. 'And here we are.' She turned in at the gate to number fifty-three and parked.

Jane had the door open before Florence could knock, Beatrice standing beside her.

Florence introduced everyone.

'But who is this?' asked Jane, looking at Scamper, so Florence introduced her little dog, who raised a front paw to shake, which delighted the twins.

'Mr Yateman, we're so glad Mrs Stanville has some help . . . '

'. . . and today is such a fine day for the job. Not too chilly . . . '

'. . . and don't forget you promised us a punnet before you go,' Beatrice smiled.

'Becca makes the most delicious crumble,' Jane added.

'I would never forget my promise,' said Florence. 'It's little enough to repay your kindness.'

Florence and Jim gathered their things and set off into the lane and then the few yards to the field gate at the end, Scamper on her lead until

Florence had surveyed the empty, weedy field and found it safe enough to let her explore by herself.

The morning passed in quiet and gentle industry. Florence and Jim seldom spoke while they worked, although Florence did mention she needed help tidying her garden. Disappointingly, Jim said it would be too much for him in addition to his own, but he'd let her know if he could think of anyone else who might be interested.

After a couple of hours they stopped to eat the picnic and assess their crop.

'That's a lot of blackberry jelly,' said Jim, looking at the row of punnets they'd lined up where they wouldn't tread on them.

'It is. I can stop worrying about picking enough and start fretting about using them all before they go mouldy,' Florence said, though she wasn't really worried. It was just a matter of hard work and being organised.

'I'll take some on my table at St Jude's, of course, if you have any jars to spare,' he ventured.

Florence smiled. 'I'll be happy to fill the windowsill behind.'

'Speaking of St Jude's, the produce sale is next week. Mavis Farlowe, with the cakes, really would appreciate your help with her setting up, you know.'

Florence remembered the lady with the nice cakes boringly set out in rows.

'She's a good sort,' Jim added, looking hard at Florence. 'Minds her own business and lets you mind yours, if you know what I mean?'

Florence understood what Jim was saying. 'Because I'm new here I have to go carefully. I need to know who I can trust,' she said. 'Some folk . . . in the past . . . well, they turned out not to be how I thought they would be.'

Jim sighed. 'We've probably all had a bit of that, Florence, and disappointment in a person can be hard to take, but I'm sorry that you've had it bad.'

Florence stared out across the field where a pheasant was calling as the autumn afternoon air grew cooler. She turned to look at Jim, with his open round face and thinning hair.

'I think I'll be all right with you, Jim,' she said.

'I intend that you should, Florence. You know, now your pickle-making is taking off, we're going to need to stick together, you and I. I'll admit it's been a help financially, you buying so much of the veg this past month.'

'Couldn't have done without it, Jim,' she answered, and they juggled sandwiches and handshakes, laughing at their blackberry-stained hands, then toasted their alliance with tea from the Thermos.

It was well into the afternoon before they carefully carried the punnets to the boot of Florence's car, rounded up Scamper, whose coat was tangled with leaves and whose paws were muddy, and then went to present several punnets of blackberries to the Kendal sisters with thanks.

'I'm very grateful you let us pick them. I'm going to be busy, I can see,' said Florence.

'But not too busy to come tomorrow as arranged, Mrs Stanville?' asked Beatrice, looking a little anxious.

'Of course. I shall be here mid-morning,' Florence assured the sisters.

125

She drove home, stopping outside Sea View to help Jim unload what he wanted of the fruit for Mildred's pie.

'Thanks for your help, Jim,' she said as she went round to get in and drive the few yards onto her parking space.

'Pleasure, Florence, love. A good day.'

And it had been — mostly — but it had also presented her with a lot to think about, Florence decided as she carried the berries into the kitchen. Would Nicolson & Filbert keep up their orders, and would she be able to meet them if they did? Where would she get help with the fast-over-growing garden, with Jim too busy to tackle it? What would happen to Violet and Carmen if the café closed? And would Violet still want to be her friend if she knew what a fool she'd been in her past and the bad thing she had done?

7

Kathleen Walden unpacked her little bit of shopping and put it away in her larder. She didn't think she needed to buy much now; she was working on being at Denis's most days for her tea. It hadn't taken long to establish a frequent invitation — from her son, of course, not from that silly girl he was married to. Well, if Lucille thought to keep Denis's mother out of their married life, she could think again. As if Denis would just turn his entire attention to his new wife and leave out in the cold the one person who had always meant so much to him.

Kathleen thought about the little terraced house Denis had bought. Apparently Lucille had put some money into it, too — or more likely her mother had done that for her. It wouldn't be likely Lucille had much saved up from her little job at a shoe shop. Florence Stanville, though, she seemed to live quite a comfortable life doing exactly what she wanted and with no husband to keep her. Quite how she managed that, Kathleen had no idea. She wouldn't be surprised if there wasn't something a bit out of the ordinary going on there and she would dearly like to learn what it was.

Denis had decorated his new house and made it smart and bright, though Lucille was quite untidy and couldn't seem to keep up with the housework. Kathleen looked around her own shabby and old-fashioned sitting room. In here could do with a coat of paint; maybe Denis would do it for her one Sunday. She'd invite him round and make him his dinner. It would be like old times, just the two of them. He could even stay over, let his lonely old mother enjoy his company for the whole evening, just the two of them, and he'd be nearer to where he was currently working next morning, too. If Lucille didn't like it, well, she'd have to lump it. She knew nothing of the bond between a widowed mother and her only son.

On the other hand, Kathleen thought, it would be even better if Denis gave her a key to his nice little house. That way she'd always have his company when she wanted it and there'd be hot food cooked for her every evening, too. He'd want to see his mother looked after properly now she lived by herself. It wouldn't be difficult to persuade him to give her a key so she could let herself in before Lucille was back from the shoe shop. After all, her boy wouldn't want his mother standing outside in the rain waiting for someone to come home. Once she could come and go as she wished, Denis would soon be used to her being there, just like when they'd lived together before Lucille arrived on the scene. It would simply be like things had been, very agreeably, for years, and that would suit both Kathleen *and* her son, of that she was sure. Lucille would soon realise where she fitted in and come to know her place . . .

Kathleen had been working hard to make sure Lucille did indeed know her place. The girl was only a beginner at cooking and sometimes, if Kathleen was round at Denis's house, as she was increasingly, Lucille would ask her mother-in-law's advice

128

on how to prepare something. Kathleen was only too glad to tell her, though never the same way twice.

'Are you sure? I thought I'd mebbe added the milk later last time,' said Lucille, puzzling at Kathleen's instructions.

'Well, do as you want if you know best,' Kathleen would reply. 'What are you asking me for if you know it all already?'

'I'm sorry, I didn't mean to argue,' said Lucille. 'I just thought . . . oh, never mind.'

That, and the fact that Lucille was always losing her things — her magazine (which Kathleen had tidied away into the coal scuttle with the old newspapers), her purse (which turned up in her coat pocket, although she always carried it in her handbag), and her keys, the loss of which caused a major emergency at the little house one evening so that even Denis became exasperated with his careless wife, who, it seemed, had inexplicably dropped them into the toe of one of her shoes.

Kathleen rather thought Denis was beginning to miss the peace and quiet of the old days, the evenings with his mother, a gentle chat and no arguing or panics about lost articles. And that suited her very well.

★ ★ ★

Florence was pleased with the speed at which the jars of blackberry jelly were mounting up in her pantry but she also thought she'd be glad to see the end of all that fruit. It was a race against time to cook it all while it was still at its best.

One afternoon she could stand the sight of blackberries no more, never mind the rush to finish. A change of scene was required and she decided to take Scamper down to the café and, she hoped, meet Violet and Carmen as they left for the day and walk with them some of their way home. It was a mild afternoon and the light over the sea would be amazing as the sun moved round and the sea shone like mercury.

Right on time, Violet and Carmen emerged through the café door, on which the sign was turned to 'Closed', and onto the pavement. Violet pulled the door to behind her rather unnecessarily firmly, Florence noticed.

'Heavens, Carmen, whatever is the matter?' she asked, coming across the road to see Carmen mopping tears from her eyes.

'Oh, just a horrid day,' sniffed Carmen, bending down to cuddle Scamper for comfort. 'Anthony was shouty from the start and I couldn't seem to do anything right for him.'

'What happened to make him angry?'

'Nothing, so far as we could see,' said Violet. 'I reckon he just got out of bed the wrong side. Then he went upstairs mid-morning — to make a couple of telephone calls, he said — and came back down in a worse temper than before, and,' she lowered her voice, 'I think he'd had a drink or two. I fear he's had more bad news about the finances of the café but it's not fair to take it out on me and Carmen.'

'On you as well?'

'Oh, he's got a bad temper for everyone some days. I don't know why Trudie puts up with him.

I'm pretty certain he's nastier with her than any of us . . . things I've noticed . . . '

Florence pursed her lips. Poor Trudie. She hadn't met the girl but Violet spoke of her in a friendly way, and no one deserved to be the brunt of a drunken temper, never mind any kind of violence, which is what she understood Violet was hinting at.

'He's hardly going to attract customers if he's in a rage, is he?'

'I wouldn't go in,' said Carmen. 'Not if I didn't work there.'

'Maybe it'll all have blown over by tomorrow,' said Violet unconvincingly.

They strolled away from the front of the café.

'So were there any customers today?' asked Florence, remembering their conversation the last time they'd met after work.

'A few, but the atmosphere wasn't pleasant so no one lingered, what with Anthony scowling and shouting about in the kitchen, though Carmen did her best to put a brave face on out front.'

Carmen nodded. 'I tried.'

They crossed the road and went down the steps to the beach.

'Bit of a cure-all, this,' said Florence, breathing deeply and gazing out to sea, the waves breaking calmly against the shore with a gentle *shushing* sound. 'Though I don't think it'll do more than soothe your worries for the moment. I wish there was summat I could do to help.'

Violet looked taken aback. 'I don't think Anthony would appreciate that. He wilfully misunderstood last time and was very ungrateful the time before.'

'I didn't mean Anthony,' said Florence. 'I don't care about him. I mean you and Carmen. What will you do if the café closes? I hope you don't mind me asking, but will you need to get another job, Violet?'

'I certainly will. I've got my mother to support and three of us can't live on a bit from the government and any wages that Carmen might earn, even supposing she could find another job. And anyway, I like working. I've been cooking all my life and now I can't imagine not doing it.'

'Mm . . . I'll have a think.' Florence had the beginnings of an idea but it was far too early to air it. 'Why don't you look in the *Courier*?' she suggested, anxious to say anything to help. 'You never know, Violet, you might just see summat that appeals.'

'I always do look, Florence, but so much of it is seasonal at the seaside. Still, new hope every week, eh?' She smiled bleakly.

'Carmen!' a girlish voice called, and a child of Carmen's age, wearing school uniform, ran towards them, waving.

'Sheila, hello,' said Carmen, looking cheered to see her friend.

Sheila, a very confident girl, came up to greet Violet and pat Scamper, who performed her little greeting, offering her paw to be shaken and enchanting everyone.

'This is my friend Mrs Stanville,' said Carmen importantly.

'How do you do, Mrs Stanville? I came hoping to find Carmen because there's the most amazing thing happening on the beach further up. You must come and look.'

'What?' said Carmen, round-eyed.

'A film being made. There's cameras and everything, and a couple of actors — though no one I recognise — and a man telling them all what to do.'

'Heavens,' said Violet. 'Well, off you go, Carmen, love, but don't get in anyone's way. Thanks for fetching her, Sheila.'

The two girls ran off up the beach towards Fleming.

'Shall we go and look, too?' said Violet, determined to shrug off her bad day. 'But at a slower pace.'

'Why not? It would be a shame to miss it.'

Florence and Violet set off southwards, the sun shining into their faces so they had to shade their eyes.

Soon they saw a group of people on the sand, a small wooden rowing boat beached at the water's edge and a pretty girl with very stiff ringlets, a woollen shawl wrapped around her shoulders, sitting in the boat, looking bored. A young man in a tricorn hat and frock coat stood, looking equally bored, slightly further up the beach. A huge film camera with a cameraman behind was set up on a temporary wooden platform, another facing the other way, both trained on the girl, and there were poles with sound equipment extending towards the actress.

A few people stood around with clipboards, boxes of props or makeup — Florence couldn't see well with the sun shining so low into her eyes — and there was a man in charge, ordering everyone about from his seat, his assistant doing a lot of running to and fro. Florence and Violet stood well back. Other observers, including Carmen and Sheila, now both holding ice-cream cones, were watching from beside the road.

'Places, everyone. Scene seven, take five. Action!'

A young man smacked shut a clapperboard chalked with numbers in front of one of the cameras and the scene was acted out. It looked very unconvincing, with the onlookers craning their necks just out of sight of the drama.

'Don't know who those two are, Violet,' whispered Florence, 'but he's rather nice.' She indicated the young actor.

'She's not much older than Carmen,' said Violet. 'And nor is he.' She raised an eyebrow at Florence and smiled.

A few more takes were done, alternating the two cameras, and then everyone started to pack up.

'Looks like that's it,' said Violet, disappointed. 'Not much excitement in the end.'

'Yes, time to head home, eh, Scamper?'

'Florence? Florence . . . Townsend? Good God, it *is* you. I *knew* it. I'd know that amazing hair anywhere.'

Florence and Violet both turned. It was the director, striding up the beach towards them. Florence shaded her eyes with her hand, trying to see who the tall thin man with the grey hair was. She thought she recognised the voice and her heart started to pound.

'Ivor?' she whispered. *It can't be, surely. Here? After all these years . . .*

'Florence, what a surprise. My goodness, but

you look amazing, but then you always did.'

'Hello, Ivor,' she said. 'And you always did know how to flatter.'

'Not still cross with me, are you, darling? It's a long time ago now.'

'Now you're flattering yourself. Violet, this is Ivor Percival. He's a film director and he was my first husband. Ivor, this is my friend Violet Peasall.'

They shook hands, Violet looking shy.

'So aren't you going to ask me what I'm doing on the bleak east coast, Flo?'

'Not necessary, Ivor. It's obvious you're making some kind of historical film. Tell me, are you filming much around these parts?'

'No, we just came for the long beach to do the boat scene, some sky and sea shots. Amazing light here. We're off to film in Whitby tomorrow.'

'Good. Then there's no chance of me bumping into you again. I'm not intending to go to Whitby.'

'Oh, don't be like that, sweetie.'

'Like what exactly?'

'Ah, you always were spirited, Flo.'

'Spirited'? You'll be calling me a 'damsel' next, Ivor. Been reading the script, have you?' Florence indicated the young actress, who had earlier emerged from the boat to show off a dress with a hooped skirt.

'Cheeky madam,' he laughed. 'But you are all right, aren't you, Florence?' He looked at her properly, giving her his full attention.

'Yes, I'm fine, thank you.'

'Seriously?'

Violet had moved away discreetly out of hearing range.

135

'Ivor, it's a long time since you left me for a more grown-up model — literally. I've got along very nicely without you. And Lucille has, too. We have our lives, you have yours, and we don't need you.'

'Lucille . . . has she still got red hair like yours? She must be, what, twenty-four?'

'She's twenty-five, married now, very happily. I don't think her husband will leave her for a more grown-up model, or any other. She's a lovely young woman.'

'So were you, Flo. That's why I married you. You were very lovely indeed . . . still are.'

'Oh, give it a rest, Ivor. Let's not revisit old graves, eh? It's far too late to resurrect the dead.'

'I know, and you're right, of course. I was an idiot and I paid for it. She went off with someone else a few years later.'

'Ha! Serves you right,' said Florence, but mildly.

There was an awkward pause.

'And who is this young fellow? Come here, let's look at you. *Good* boy.'

'*He* is a *she*, and in late middle-age in dog years. In fact, she's almost as old in dog years as you are in human ones.'

'Sorry, Flo.'

There was another pause and Florence turned to go.

'Well . . . it's good to see you, to know you're OK.'

'Yes, I've been OK for a long time now. And no, I'm not still cross with you, Ivor. We didn't really suit, I was far too young for you, and we were both too daft to realise until it was too late.

Bygones . . . '

'You take care of yourself, Flo.'

'I have every intention of doing so. Goodbye.'

'Goodbye, Florence. Here . . . take my card. Please telephone me if ever you need anything.'

He thrust a smart white card printed in black copperplate towards her. After a moment Florence took it and put it in her coat pocket without looking at it closely. She didn't thank him; she wouldn't be using it.

'Bye, Ivor.' She gave him a big smile and went to join Violet further up the shingle.

They strode back north together, Scamper leading the way.

'You all right, Florence?' Violet asked after a few minutes. 'That man hasn't upset you, has he?'

'No, not him, Violet, not now. I'm long past being upset by him.'

'I remember you saying a few weeks ago that your first husband was good-looking — and he is — but, I gather, not reliable, is that right?'

'Exactly right, Violet.'

'You do seem to have been unlucky with your husbands, Florence, and I'm sorry about that.'

'Only with two of them, Violet. The other one was a wonderful man.'

Violet looked so taken aback that Florence burst out laughing.

'Well, you've met Ivor, after a fashion, Violet, so I'll tell you about him; start at the beginning and save the best and the worst for another day.'

'I don't want to intrude, love, though I can't say I'm not curious.'

'You're not intruding, Violet. We're friends and

137

so I reckon you should know summat about me. It all started . . . oh, seems like a lifetime ago . . . '

★   ★   ★

1930

'Drink up, Flo, and I'll buy you another,' said John Dobson.

'No, thank you, John. That was delicious but one's enough. I have to keep a clear head for work tomorrow.'

'Oh, go on, Flo. Two won't do you any harm and it's early yet.'

'I said no, thank you,' said Florence. 'C'mon, Irene, time to get home.'

'I'm right with you, Flo. Night, boys.' Irene beamed a lipsticky smile at John and his friend Keith. 'Thanks for the drinks.'

'Oh, you girls are so boring,' grumbled John sulkily. 'Boring, boring, boring.'

'Limited vocabulary,' muttered Florence to Irene, who laughed.

'Call that a job, anyway?' sneered Keith. 'Parading around a shop in a borrowed frock.'

'Yes,' said Florence with a lift of her well-shaped eyebrow. 'We do. Goodnight.'

Florence and Irene got up and left the bar, then linked arms to walk home.

'You can always tell they're beaten when they resort to sneering and insults as soon as you won't do what they want,' said Florence. 'As if we're going to sit there being bought drinks and then having to pay for them later by being taken advantage of. Why can't a man just buy a woman a drink and enjoy her company without some underhand motive?'

'Because, my love,' said Irene, 'we are both far too clever for men like that, but far too pretty to avoid attracting the type. They never think we might have brains in our heads. Then when we get conversing, they're surprised we have an opinion, a single original idea, and I'm sure they'd really rather we didn't.'

'Well, I'll buy my own drinks in future,' said Florence. 'And mebbe yours.'

'Thanks, Flo. Mine's a very, very small Scotch.'

'Ooh, you emancipated woman. Scotch indeed! I think mine might be a cup of tea.'

They walked back to the flat they shared in a quiet side street not far from the centre of Southport, laughing.

They always seemed to be laughing. It was part of their job to smile and look pleasant, so that they sometimes felt they were smiling and laughing all the time; that they didn't know how to stop.

Florence and Irene were house models at an exclusive department store, Wilding's, where they would walk around the shop modelling clothes suited to the season or even the weather. Maureen Wilding, who had taken over the business from her father, could see cheap mass-produced clothes coming to the high street and putting smart stores such as hers out of business, even in well-heeled Southport. She decided she couldn't beat the cheap shops at their own game, so the only thing to do was what Wilding's had always done, but more so. Her store had to be smarter, more exclusive, more expensive. There would be no cutting of corners. It seemed to be working because women would travel to Southport from all over Lancashire and Merseyside to visit Wilding's.

Maureen adhered strictly to quality garments, and alterations for a perfect fit were included in the price of the top-of-the-range fashions. Her workroom, presided over by the fierce Geraldine O'Geraghty, 'designer' and chief seamstress, was a busy place, because Maureen also had an unpublicised arrangement with a person to whom she referred rather dismissively as 'a little man' in Vienna, who sent her high-fashion garments, which Mrs O'Geraghty took apart and copied, using different fabrics, trimmings and finishes, which lent the rip-offs some originality. When there was a rush to finish an order, Florence and Irene were sometimes asked to help Mrs O'Geraghty and her assistant, sewing on buttons and pressing the finished items.

The only part of their jobs that Florence and Irene disliked, especially when they were modelling daywear, was when they had to advertise, on cardboard discs with elastic straps worn around their wrists, the prices.

'It's humiliating,' grumbled Irene. 'I think some of the men who come in looking for an outfit for their wives — or so they say — think it's the price of me in the dress.'

'Ah, but Mrs O'Geraghty is like a mother tiger with her cubs. At least we're safe in the shop.'

But when Florence met Ivor Percival, she wasn't

sure she wanted to be safe any longer. He was several years older than her, very tall, very thin and extremely handsome, with a lot of hair that he continually swept back from his forehead. He was a theatre director, working at the time at the Liverpool Empire, and the produc-tion was due to move eventually to a theatre in London's West End. Florence could hardly believe the glamour. London was just a place one read about in the newspapers. By now she was eighteen and looking for adventure.

Lily and Florence had moved away from Gui-sethorpe, back to Lancashire, the county of Lily's birth, to a remote and pretty little village in the countryside. Florence was sad to leave Guise-thorpe, but Lily said their time there was over and she thought she'd return to Lancashire, but on her own terms.

'Not to live in a little terraced house in a sooty Blackburn street, like where I was born, but in the beautiful countryside — the best of both worlds, love.'

Eventually, Florence felt it was time for her to make her own life. Living at home, in the lovely cottage Lily had chosen, had many advantages, but pottering around the village and having little purpose didn't suit her. She had a job at the village shop but she felt she was marking time and needed a new direction.

It had seemed adventurous to apply for the house model job at Wilding's when, on a day trip to Blackpool, she had seen it advertised in a newspaper. She didn't care for the brashness and noise of Blackpool — she'd gone out of curiosity but, her curiosity satisfied, she didn't think she wanted to see it again — and she thought Southport would suit her better, but now she'd met Ivor Percival she was thinking again. Maybe life beyond Southport beckoned . . .

Ivor Percival was very gentlemanly. He didn't try to ply her with strong drinks and take advantage of her. He took her out to dinner at nice restaurants where he guided her through the menu, listened to what she said and was amused by it. He said he didn't know there were such lovely, innocent young women left in the world and he was besotted with her. She was very special.

There followed flowers being delivered to the flat, trips to the theatre, where he introduced her to interesting people — and then criticised the plays they appeared in, or had even written, behind their backs — and after just four months he asked Florence to marry him.

When the play Ivor was directing opened in London, Florence was his beautiful young wife, wearing an evening dress that he'd bought for her instead of one she was parading in for someone else to buy. She even had her photograph in the *Evening Standard*, smiling straight into the camera. The caption described her as 'a red-headed beauty in a red dress', although the photograph was in black and white, of course, so readers had to use their imaginations.

Their daughter, Lucille, was born two years later and Florence thought her life was complete: handsome husband, perfect baby girl. But she was still only twenty years old herself, and the innocence and youth that had attracted Ivor Percival in the first place was beginning to tire him. He was increasingly busy, invited to meet people in the evenings, seldom home before Florence was in bed asleep. He thought Lucille was a sweet baby but he wasn't really interested in babies, he said, and his lack of attention to his child showed this to be true.

Since she had had Lucille, Florence regularly found herself at home alone with her daughter. The kind of people she'd met since her marriage, and whom she used to consider her friends, didn't want to meet up with a woman with a baby in tow, and she was no longer invited out. She didn't really care — Lucy was her much-adored child, for whom she'd give up anything — but she did find herself a little lonely sometimes. Some days she spoke only to Mrs Hodge, her daily help.

One day Florence was wheeling Lucy in her pram along the street in Hampstead, where the Percivals lived, and she stopped to buy a newspaper from a street vendor. When she got home she glanced through it, reading the headlines and the gossip, and there was a photograph of Ivor. It had been taken at a restaurant the evening before and he was sitting very close to a beautiful dark-haired woman who looked to be in her mid-thirties — about Ivor's own age — with an amazingly slim figure shown off to perfection in a silky bias-cut gown. The caption beneath read: 'Mr Ivor Percival, the celebrated stage director, and Miss Margot Ross, fashion model.'

At once Florence knew — she just *knew* — that Margot Ross was the reason Ivor was out so very late so very often.

When Ivor got in that evening — late again — Florence, who had put Lucy to bed and had eaten her dinner alone, was waiting up, the newspaper on the table in front of her, open at the photograph in the gossip column.

'So, Ivor, how was Margot this evening?' she asked quietly.

'Margot?'

'Don't play the innocent with me, Ivor. Yes, Margot Ross — you remember? The woman you had dinner with yesterday evening? Come to think of it, you've probably only just left her — either at her door, or mebbe even in her bed. Short memory, have you?'

'Oh, Margot Ross . . . ' His eyes slanted down to the newspaper picture. 'It was just a work thing. You know the kind of people who get invited to these dinners.'

'Well, I used to, Ivor. I used to get invited, too, because I am your wife, but now we've got Lucy it looks to me as though you arrange for a different model to be your partner.'

'Flo, darling, it's not what it looks like . . . '

'And what's that, Ivor? You tell me. C'mon, I know what I *think* it looks like and I'm giving you the chance to tell me the truth.'

'Flo, please, I'm tired. Can't we just — '

'No, we 'can't just' anything, you hypocrite. Can't just pretend I haven't seen this photograph? Can't just go to bed and forget about it? Can't just carry on as if we don't both know what's going on? I'm not some stupid child, to be told, 'There, there, it's nothing to make a fuss over,' Ivor. This is our marriage I'm talking about.'

Ivor sat down heavily at the table and put his head in his hands. Even as she watched, Florence thought it was a rather affected theatrical gesture.

'I was going to tell you, Flo, but you seemed so taken up with the baby — '

'She has a name, our baby, Ivor. She's called Lucille, if you remember.'

'Lucille, yes. I'm sorry, Flo, but, yes, I did have dinner with Margot Ross, as I have done many times. Margot and I are in love and, I'm sorry — '

'How long?'

'What?'

'How long have you and Margot Ross been in love, Ivor?'

'It doesn't m — '

'It matters to me. Because I want to understand the kind of man I married. Was it before we had Lucille? Was it when I was expecting our daughter? Is that when you decided you preferred an older woman, a more worldly one, one whose waist was still tiny, one who is at least fifteen years older than me and probably *too old* to have a baby?'

'Florence, that is nasty — '

'I can be a lot nastier than that, Ivor. Because I think you've had me for a fool for months. Probably the whole of London knows about you and Margot Ross, and everyone thinks I'm a silly little idiot and . . . and . . . ' She gulped and with impatient hands swept away the tears that had started to fall. She had tried so hard not to cry.

'I don't think you're an idiot, Flo, but I do think our getting married was a mistake. You're a lovely young woman and you deserve someone younger than me, someone your own age, to have fun with.'

'Seems to me, Ivor, that you're the one having fun while I'm at home with Lucy, being the grown-up in this marriage. It's not about age, is it, it's about responsibility: you do as you like; I do the right thing. You're selfish through and through and you don't care what happens to me and Lucy, provided we don't stop you doing exactly what you want.'

Ivor heaved a sigh. 'No, you're wrong, I do care. I care about you both, but — '

'You care about yourself more? That's it, isn't it?'

Ivor stood up, sweeping his hair off his forehead. 'Probably it is, Flo. It's late and I'm tired. Can we talk about this in the morning, please?'

'You never answered my question. How long have you been in love with Margot Ross?'

'Really, Flo, it isn't important.'

'How long?' Florence grabbed his arm tightly. 'How long, Ivor?' She squeezed tighter, deliberately hurting him.

'Get off, Flo.'

'Then tell me.'

'A while . . . '

Florence looked at him very hard. Then she flung his arm away from her. 'Bastard,' she muttered.

The next morning she went to see a lawyer, Mr Lawrence Hancock, about a divorce. He was someone she had met at one of the parties she used to go to and she thought that was appropriate. At least she'd come across someone useful. She took Lucille with her in her pram, which she also thought was appropriate. She instructed Mr

146

Hancock to take Ivor Percival for every penny he could get from him in the divorce settlement, and in the meantime she leaked the love rat's tawdry private life to the press: how he had betrayed his young wife, the mother of his baby, for another woman and one, Florence soon discovered, who had a history of love affairs with other women's husbands. It wasn't that Florence needed all that money — she was going back to Lancashire to live with Lily — it was just that she thought that was the most appropriate thing of all.

★ ★ ★

'What an awful, selfish man,' said Violet. 'Oh, I am sorry you had to put up with that, and when you were so young, too.'

'Do you know, Violet, now I come to think of it all again, and at the distance of so many years, I can see that it wasn't such a bad thing after all. Most importantly, I'd got my beautiful daughter, which I haven't regretted for one single minute.'

'I can tell how much she means to you, Florence.'

'I don't think the marriage would ever have lasted — I was much too young for him and he was much too selfish to be married to anyone — so it was as well to get out early on. If it hadn't been that Margot woman, it would have been someone else. I came away with a decent amount of money to compensate for his betrayal, too, and that enabled me to have choices I'd never have had without. My time with Ivor wasn't wasted, either: I met all kinds of people and I grew braver

147

and bolder than I would ever have done had I remained the small-town girl. I suppose what I'm saying is that I grew up in those two years. That time opened the way for all that followed.'

'Still, everyone starts out hoping their love will last, don't they?' said Violet, stopping opposite the steps that would take her up to the road and the turning home. 'I was lucky with my Will: a good man. I couldn't have done better.'

'I'm glad of that, Violet. I expect he thought the same. And please don't feel sorry for me, whatever you do. I did an awful lot better the second time.'

'A wonderful man', I think you said.'

'Charlie, yes . . . but I think that little story may be for another day, possibly when you're sitting down,'

said Florence. 'It's getting cold and you need to get home to your mum, tell her about the filming.'

'I'll let Carmen do that. I won't steal the child's thunder. I'm glad she's got something to take her mind off our day at work.'

'Ah, yes, the vile Anthony. Try not to worry, Violet. There has to be summat better for you both and it *will* turn up, I'm sure of it.'

'Well, we'll have to see,' said Violet, and she gave Scamper a little pat and turned to trudge up the beach towards home.

Florence watched her go, her shoulders rounded as if she bore a burden, her steps slow and heavy.

'We've got to help her, Scamper — to help them both. We *have* to.'

8

Lucy let herself into her little house. She was looking forward to kicking off her shoes and sitting down to drink a cup of tea after a busy afternoon at the shop before it was time to start on the cooking. Denis had been getting back late for a while now. Lucy liked to have his tea ready for him to eat as soon as he got home, and the one good thing about his long days was that they gave her a little extra time to herself in the early evening. Or they had done until recently. These quiet moments alone were becoming a rarity now that Mrs Walden was coming round so frequently. It was beginning to feel like a treat for Lucy to be able to sit down after work for five minutes in her own home. The trouble was she felt so very tired that once she'd sat down it was difficult to get up again to make the effort. Often there were three people to cook for now, too, and with no help from the frequent and unwanted guest.

With the autumn days rapidly getting shorter, wet weather had set in and Judy had decided that Ruby Slipper should branch out into umbrellas, rain hats and galoshes alongside the seasonal range of stout shoes. The shop was being reorganised to accommodate the extra stock to best advantage, which meant a lot of lifting, carrying and climbing up and down the ladder. All this, while being charming with the customers and providing an efficient service. It was only Monday, Lucy's half-day, and already she felt completely whacked.

While she drank her tea she would enjoy rereading her mother's latest letter. She pulled it out of her handbag with a little lift of her spirits in anticipation. It was always a treat to hear from Florence and this morning's letter was full of good news about her preserving business. The 'fancy grocer' Florence had mentioned in a previous letter had ordered a lot of blackberry jelly made to Lucy's grandmother's recipe. It was a triumph for Florence and it honoured Lily's memory, which Lucy knew meant a huge amount to Florence. Lucy missed her grandmother but she knew her mother had been devastated by Lily's death and had found it difficult to pull herself up. Maybe this success with the old recipes was just what she needed to help her through her bereavement. Certainly it had meant a lot of hard work, but Florence had evidently put in long hours and achieved her goal of fulfilling the ambitious order.

Lucy hung up her coat, removed her court shoes, eased her aching feet and padded into the sitting room, putting her handbag and Florence's letter on the dining table.

She switched on the light, saw at once her flat indoor shoes just by the door ready to step into, and then turned for the kitchen and . . . oh, good grief, there was someone there!

Lucy's stomach lurched with shock. Almost immediately, however, she saw that it was Mrs Walden. She was sitting in the comfy armchair as if she owned the place! She appeared to be asleep. What on earth was she doing here and how had she even got in? Lucy was briefly distracted by the mental image of Mrs Walden's back view as she squeezed herself headfirst through the kitchen window . . .

'Mrs Walden?'

Denis's mother opened her eyes and sat up with a start.

'Oh, Lucille, you quite frightened me, creeping in like that. I didn't hear you at all.'

'Mrs Walden, *you* gave *me* a scare. I didn't expect anyone to be here. What are you doing?'

'Just having a little rest, that's all. No need to be alarmed, I'm quite well.'

'I meant, why here?'

Mrs Walden looked indignant. 'Denis asked me to come round, of course.'

'But how did you get in?'

'Denis gave me a key.' She adopted a slightly superior look. 'Didn't he tell you?'

'No, he did not,' said Lucy, trying to keep her temper.

'Mebbe he just forgot,' said Mrs Walden smugly, as if it was a matter her son might easily think too trivial to mention to his wife.

'Aye, mebbe he did,' muttered Lucy. 'Did he ask you to come round for owt particular or was it just for . . . a little rest?'

'I reckon he just thought I might like a bit of company . . . when I'm by myself so much. It gets a bit lonely when you're stuck at home all day, no one to chat with, and then with the evenings drawing in it can seem some days like you're the only person in the world, sat alone behind your drawn curtains. You'll learn when you're my age . . . '

151

Lucy was furious but desperately trying to compose her face. Mrs Walden knew just how to wind her up but Lucy was determined not to show the interfering old baggage how much she was annoying her. With an irrationality born of weariness, Lucy felt as if she had been ousted from her own home, that she was being treated as the one trespassing on her mother-in-law. She bit back a sharp reply and counted slowly to five — a calming measure suggested by Judy — hoping to regain some control.

'Would you like to stay and have your tea here, Mrs Walden?' she asked, taking the initiative by issuing the invitation before the woman could tell her what she expected.

'That's what Denis suggested,' Mrs Walden said, trumping Lucy straight off.

'Right...Well, I've had a busy afternoon at work so I'll just make myself a cup of tea before I begin. Would you like one, Mrs Walden?'

'No, thank you. I'll wait.' She looked at her watch but did not move from the chair.

Brew the tea and ignore her...just brew the tea and ignore her...

Lucy went into the kitchen, filled the kettle and set it on the gas, but the situation was proving too much for her and tears threatened, so she went into the bathroom, closing the door firmly. She sat down on the side of the bath to gather herself.

What on earth was going on? Why had Denis given his mother a key to their home and not even told her? Was this what her married life was to be from now on: Denis's mother turning up whenever she felt like it, coming and going exactly as she wanted and sitting there all smug, expecting to be waited on? Lucy stifled a howl of frustration, clenching her fists and battering the air with them.

After a minute or two she took some more calming breaths, got up, washed her hands in cooling water and carefully dabbed around her eyes so as not to smudge her mascara. Then, with new resolve, she straightened her back and went to make herself that much-needed pot of tea and begin on the cooking. Surely it would not be too long before Denis came home and, though Lucy might have to wait to find out what was really going on, at least he could relieve her of some of the burden of dealing with his mother.

Remembering what Judy had suggested about 'managing' Mrs Walden, Lucy thought it best to offer her a choice to eat.

'Pie or ham, Mrs Walden — which would you prefer?'

'Eh, Lucille, it's all the same to me. You know I'm not fussy.'

'Ham it is then. And would you like peas or carrots with your ham?'

'Well, if it's carrots I'd rather have the pie, Lucille, love.'

'Fine . . . pie and carrots.'

Lucy forced her mouth into the semblance of a smile and went to turn on the oven and run water to wash some potatoes, but the feeling that her mother-in-law was treating her like a maidservant overwhelmed her and she could not be calm. She went back into the sitting room with an old newspaper, a pan and the paper bag of carrots.

'Mrs Walden, would you mind just peeling a few of these while I get on, please?' she said, setting everything down on the table. She didn't wait for an answer, conscious that the woman could hardly refuse to lend a bit of a hand.

She had the pie in the oven and had just got the potatoes boiling when there was a knock at the door.

Now what?

'Someone at the door, Lucille,' said Mrs Walden, not getting up.

Lucy went to see who it was at a time when most people were settling down to cook and eat their tea after work. There on the doorstep stood her former stepfather. He looked pasty and shapeless, and the slim, straight plains of his once-handsome face were now blurred by a drinker's jowls and puffiness. His hair needed cutting and his clothes looked worn.

'Frank!'

'Hello, Lucille, love, you're looking well.'

'What do you want, Frank?'

'That's a nice welcome, isn't it, love, after all this time?'

Lucy said nothing.

'Aren't you going to ask me in?'

'I've got Mrs Walden, Denis's mother, here and I'm in the middle of cooking.'

'Oh, good, so I'm not interrupting your tea then?'

'No, but — '

'Excellent. And I could do with a cuppa, if you've got the pot hot, love.' Frank was through the front door and hovering outside the sitting room before Lucy could stop him.

'Hello, you must be Mrs Walden. I've heard a lot about you,' said Frank, going in and offering his hand to shake, then pulling out a chair at the table and sitting down to charm Denis's mother. 'Milk and two sugars, our Lucille, you remember?' he called out as Lucy reluctantly went to pour him a cup of tea. With any luck he'd drink it and be off . . . or maybe that was too much to hope? She wondered what he'd come for but decided not to ask; she just wanted him to go.

At least he could entertain Mrs Walden, though Lucy was now feeling outnumbered by unwelcome visitors.

What could Frank possibly want that she could give him? She had seen him only once — and that in the street, by accident, certainly not design — since she and Denis had married. They'd never been close. Florence had been married to him for just two years. Having given him the benefit of the doubt on numerous occasions, and forgiven him on very many more, about how freely he spent her money, when she discovered what — or rather *who* — he was spending it on, she'd given him the boot. Lucy had been eighteen by then and quite old enough to understand Frank's betrayal and her mother's anger . . .

★ ★ ★

1950

'I knew in my heart that I wasn't mistaken, and it was Frank with that woman on his arm that

155

evening you and I went to the pictures and I thought I saw them disappearing round the end of the street,' said Florence, pacing the floor of the dining room of the house in Blackburn, where she and Lucy had lived together for several years, and where Frank had come to live when he'd married Florence, two years previously. 'He's always been one for throwing the cash about, especially since it was mine, but he's been spending money like it's his last days on earth lately, and until now I had no idea what on, apart from the drinks and the bets. He always had some explanation, some story I couldn't quite follow. I've never been mean in adding to our bank account when it's getting low, but just lately I've noticed it getting low rather more often. He said he'd had a few expenses and I was not to worry. 'Just take what you need from my purse,' I said one time when he said he was short of a bit of cash, and I only found out when I went to the shops that he'd taken the lot and I never knew how that was spent either. I can guess now, but certainly I saw nothing of what it bought at the time.'

'Oh, Mum, he hasn't taken all your savings?'

Lucy was inclined to worry if anything vexed her mother. The girl wasn't by any means devoted to Frank Stanville, but she had accepted him as her stepfather because he was good fun — or he had been to start with — and Florence needed someone besides her daughter to have fun with, in Lucy's opinion. At first there had been lovely long days out and special treats at weekends, but lately these happy times had become fewer and further between. Frank seemed to be enjoying rather

156

more days out on his own or with 'the boys' — a vague crowd of friends, none of whom seemed to need to work — rather than with his wife and stepdaughter.

Florence was quick to reassure Lucy. 'No, love, please don't fret about that. But there was that day he said he was going to the races with 'the boys' and could I lend him a bit. Course, I wanted him to have a nice time so I'd no reason to refuse. Well, very odd boys, sending him home with lipstick under his ear, if you ask me. I should have thrown him out then but I allowed him to get round me. Goodness knows why I believed he'd mend his ways. I always knew he had a roving eye, but I thought I'd reined him in. And then there was that woman — and I'm sure it was the same one we saw on his arm in the street that time — who came knocking at the door as bold as Christmas and seemed surprised to find Frank's wife answering it! Her face said it all. She'd obviously got her days wrong and expected to find Frank here alone.'

'Awful . . . '

'And now I find this hidden at the back of the tallboy!' Florence kicked at a carrier bag she'd brought down from upstairs. It had the name 'Paulden's' on it, which Lucy knew by repute, though not from personal experience, was the name of a very fine department store in Manchester. Florence bent down and pulled a garment from the bag. She shook it out and held up a dress with an extravagantly wide skirt and — there was no doubt — a wide waist and top as well. 'I don't think this is meant for me, do you, Lucy?'

'Mum, it's at least four sizes too big.'

'I'd say it's more the size of that unexpected visitor I had the other week.'

'I didn't see her but, oh, Mum, I can't help but think Frank bought that frock for,' Lucy dropped her voice, 'another lady.'

'No lady, that, love.' Florence bundled the dress up and shoved it back in the bag. Then she drew herself up to her full height, which was rather taller than Frank himself, straightened her shoulders and adopted a determined expression. 'Right, that can be the first thing to go. Frank's not due back from wherever it is he said he was going — which may or may not be where he actually is — until this evening. C'mon, love, time to do what I should have done months ago. This is my house — our home, Lucy — and I'm sorry that I invited that rascal in to share it with us. He's tainted it, sullied our lovely place with his presence, and I'm that ashamed you should have had him for a stepfather. But no longer!'

Lucy's face was white with anxiety, seeing the flash of fire in her mother's dark blue eyes. Florence looked capable of anything at that moment.

'Mum, are you sure . . . ?'

'I've been sure for weeks, love, I was just trying to pretend different. I've been a fool to myself and I only wish I'd acted sooner and I'd have the price of this floozie's frock, and more, still in the bank. Second thoughts, I'll keep the dress. It's evidence: no one with eyes in their head would think he'd bought it for me. Right, now, let's gather up all his things and put them out the front for him to collect when he has the nerve to show his smarmy lying face. Come on . . . '

Florence led the way upstairs and grabbed a sheet from the linen press. She unfolded it, laid it on the landing floor, then went to gather Frank's clothes. Armful after armful were flung into a heap on the sheet. Many were new and Florence grew ever more furious, knowing that she'd paid for them all.

'Lucy, please get his things off the bathroom shelf and then look downstairs for owt that's his — shoes and his overcoat, newspapers, magazines, everything — I want the lot of it out.'

'But what will happen when he comes back?'

'He'll find his things in the gutter, where they — and he — belong. Don't worry, he'll not get in the house. You get on with filling that sheet and I'll telephone the locksmith. I'll have these locks changed before the afternoon's over and we'll not have to put up with Frank and his lies ever again.'

Lucy did as Florence asked and then Florence, who said the locksmith was on his way, bundled the sheet, the corners tied together in a knot, out of the front door, dragged it down the path, out of the gate, across the pavement and into the gutter.

The locks were changed and when Frank eventually appeared he made a fuss in the street, shouted through the letterbox and caused a disturbance. Florence and Lucy sat in the sitting room at the back and Florence put the wireless on loud to drown out Frank's protests.

Eventually she tired of his noise and telephoned the police, and Frank was escorted away with what he could manage to carry of his belongings. He did not return.

Florence had liked her house. 'But it's only a place to live, Lucy, and I don't feel the same about it now it's connected in my mind with my foolish marriage to Frank Stanville,' she said, and promptly put it up for sale. They went to live with Florence's mother, Lily, in her beautiful stone cottage in the shadow of Longridge Fell. 'Going home,' Florence called it, meaning she was going back to her beloved mother, and there followed a time of peace and contentment after the turmoil and disappointment of life with Frank.

'Frank was the biggest mistake of my life,' Florence told Lucy after the divorce was granted, 'and I'm ashamed to think I ever believed one single word he said. He married me for my money and then spent it on that outsize floozie Daphne Prescott, and possibly others of her ilk. Well, I've learned my lesson. It was a hard one and I've wasted two years of my life, so it's one I shan't forget again. Marriage and me are not always compatible, Lucy. I knew that, yet I was daft enough to give it one more go with that waster. He's dead to me now and I hope I shall never have cause to speak of him again.'

★ ★ ★

Now Frank Stanville was sitting in Lucy's little house, flirting preposterously with her mother-in-law, and Lucy, pausing to remember every detail of that afternoon when Florence finally acknowledged his betrayal of her, became instantly so incensed she was tempted for one mad moment to pick up a pan and beat him round the head with it.

160

Far from pouring him a cup of tea with milk and two sugars, she marched back into the room and stood with her hands on her hips, her face contorted with fury.

'Out!' she snarled.

Frank looked as if he wondered whether she was addressing him. 'What's the matter, Lucille, love?'

'Don't you 'Lucille, love' me, you vile man. Do you think I've forgotten what you did to my mother? Do you honestly think I'd welcome you into my home? She did, and look what happened! You spent as much of her money as you could lay your filthy, dishonest hands on, on some fat tart who wasn't fit to scrub my mother's doorstep. The only good thing to come out of that marriage is that when Mum sold the house — *her house* — we went to live with Grandma and it was lovely there. So at least I can thank you for that.'

'Now, hold on, Lucille. I've put all that behind me and I've come to make my peace with you,' said Frank, standing up to look Lucy in the eye.

'How dare you? Peace with me, indeed, after what you did? When she'd thrown you out, Mum sold her house, because the memory of you was so disgusting to her that she couldn't bear to live there any more. You'd poisoned it, with your cheating and your lying and your . . . your immoral ways.'

'Lucille, such coarseness. Please don't go on,' said Mrs Walden, sitting between them, her upturned face looking from one to the other as if following a game of tennis over her head.

'I'm telling it like it was, Mrs Walden, and if you don't like it then I suggest you go and eat your tea

161

elsewhere. I don't know why you've come here, Frank, why you invited yourself into my house and sat yourself down at my table, but I can guess. Down on your luck, are you? Thought I was a soft touch and you could come round here and extract money from me? Horses didn't come home in the right order? Or maybe it was the women.'

Mrs Walden gave a sharp intake of breath.

'Mrs Walden, be quiet,' said Lucy as she saw that woman opening her mouth to give her opinion again. 'So just go now, Frank. I can't pick you up and throw you out bodily because I'm too little, but if I have to I'll run out into the street screaming, and I promise you there's a big fella across the road who could hurl you halfway to Preston. And I'd applaud you on your way.'

Lucy paused for breath but Frank was speechless by now.

'What's the matter, Lucy? I could hear you outside.' Denis appeared at the sitting-room door, looking weary and frowning in puzzlement. 'Who's this? Why were you shouting? Hello, Mum.'

'This is Frank Stanville, a thieving, cheating black-guard who was once married to my mother, until she saw him for the miserable waster he is. I reckon he's come round to try to relieve us of our savings, probably to spend on some tart he's got in tow, and I was just showing him out,' said Lucy.

'Crikey, Luce . . .'

'So, Frank . . .' She pointed to the sitting-room door.

Frank edged round the table. No one said anything. He had to sidle awkwardly past Denis, who was a broad man, and then he shuffled silently up the little hallway, Denis and Lucy close behind him. Denis reached out and opened the door and Frank stepped outside.

'Lucille, you never listen,' he said. 'You are exactly like your mother.'

'Good!' she retorted.

He was about to add something but Denis closed the door firmly.

Then Lucy had her hands to her face and was panting. 'Oh God,' she gasped. 'Oh, Den, am I glad you turned up. If he didn't go I was going to have to make a scene in the street and I really didn't want to make a public show of myself.'

'Show of yourself!' said Mrs Walden, now standing in the sitting-room doorway. 'I'll say you did. Thank goodness you came in when you did, Denis, to see him off good and proper before Lucille became hysterical. A real hero you were, love, and no mistake.'

Denis wrapped Lucy in his strong arms and held her close until she was calmer.

'You all right, Luce?' he whispered into her hair. She nodded.

'Good girl. I'll just go and wash my hands, change out of these overalls and I'll be ready for my tea. What's it going to be?'

'Oh, good grief! The pie!' Lucy ran into the kitchen and opened the oven. The pie was blackened, smoking slightly, and the potatoes had cooked to mush, while the pan of raw carrots sat on the table where Mrs Walden had left it. 'Oh, no, it's ruined.' She started to cry.

'I always set the timer,' said Mrs Walden helpfully. 'And you've forgotten the carrots, Lucille, love.'

'Aaah!' Lucy ran screaming from the room and upstairs to fling herself on the bed. The whole evening, from the moment she'd set foot in the house, had been a disaster and there was no saving it. She might as well give in to a wholehearted bout of crying and get it over with.

Later, Denis came upstairs with some fish and chips wrapped in a newspaper. Lucy was lying on their bed, her eyes hot and swollen with weeping.

'Brought you your tea, Luce,' he said gently.

'Where's your mum?'

'Gone home. She said you'd been . . . she said she thought you weren't feeling very well and she'd come back another time.'

'She was here when I got in, asleep in a chair. Gave me a fright. She said you'd given her a key.'

'She kept asking for one, Lucy. She said she'd be able to come round and see to things for us. I thought it would help. I meant to tell you and just forgot. It's not that important, is it?'

'Denis!' said Lucy, sitting up. 'It's *our* house — you can't just give a key to your mother and not say owt. What if I gave my mum a key and she was here when you got in? How would you feel about that?'

'Well, I'd be surprised, seeing your mum's miles away at the seaside. She'd hardly be popping round, would she? Though if she did, I don't think I'd find her asleep in a chair.'

Lucy gave a lopsided smile. 'That's true. I'm sorry, I wish I was more like her and could do mountains of stuff and the house would be all lovely all the time.'

'It doesn't matter, love. And you are like your mum. Fierce. I heard you seeing off Frank Stanville and you were amazing. I was nearly scared myself. I'd better not cross you, had I, or I'll be shown the door!'

'Idiot.'

'Here, eat your chips before they're cold.'

'The bedroom will smell of fried fish.'

'Doesn't matter. C'mon, shove up and we'll eat 'em together in bed . . .'

★ ★ ★

Lucy rose early the next morning, keen to be at the shop and busy in the company of the irrepressible Judy, and to put the upset of the previous day behind her. Denis put on the clean overalls she'd washed and ironed for him, ate the eggs and bacon she cooked, gave her a kiss and left for the lockup where he kept his van, whistling and without a care in the world.

Lucy, having waved him off, finished her makeup and went to look for her handbag. She usually took it upstairs with her at night, but the events of yesterday evening had thrown her routine and she hadn't come downstairs again after rushing up in tears. She remembered putting it on the table before she turned and saw Mrs Walden asleep in the armchair. And yes, thank goodness it was where she'd left it.

But what about Florence's letter? Lucy racked her brains; hadn't she taken the letter out to reread and then never got the opportunity? So what had she done with it?

She moved her bag but the letter wasn't under or behind it. She emptied the handbag out onto the table but the white envelope addressed in black in Florence's distinctive bold handwriting wasn't inside. Lucy could feel a little flutter of panic rising and her face grew hot. Surely she hadn't lost it . . . She hardly dared to think of the obvious alternative possibility.

Increasingly frantic, she looked along the untidy mantelpiece, moving every old bill, every receipt and invitation, the clock, the horrible cat ornament Mrs Walden had bestowed on them . . . Nothing.

Think, Lucy, think!

She retraced her movements, starting in the little hallway where she thought she'd taken the letter from her handbag, then come through into the sitting room, bag and letter on the table right there . . .

Right there, just where Frank Stanville had sat himself down and ordered a cup of tea with milk and two sugars. That was, without any doubt, the last she had seen of it.

Lucy sank into a chair, going hot and cold. There was no denying what had happened: Frank had seen the letter, recognised Florence's handwriting and taken it. Her address was written out, as always, at the top of the first page. What a disaster! That lying, cheating, thieving man had Florence's precious new address in his pocket and was probably, even as Lucy sat biting her nails, planning on making a trip to Guisethorpe to settle his unfinished business with his ex-wife.

9

'Fleming 865.'

'Mum, it's me.'

'Lucy, what's the matter, love?' It must be an emergency for Lucy to be telephoning from the shop.

'Oh, Mum . . . ' Lucy was clearly struggling to hold back tears.

'Just say it, sweetheart, before I imagine the worst.'

'I think Frank knows where you live.'

Whatever Florence had been expecting to hear, it wasn't that. For a few seconds she couldn't think what to say as questions crowded into her mind. Quickly she lined her thoughts up into some kind of order.

'All right . . . Do you just *think* this, love, or do you *know* it?'

Lucy told her mother about Frank turning up the previous evening and inviting himself in, that she'd thrown him out and that she couldn't find the letter this morning.

'And you've really looked for it, Lucy?'

'As much as I was able to before I had to come to work. I'll search again this evening, but I *know* I left it on the table and it was right where Frank had sat himself down, and now it's gone.'

Florence drew in a long, slow breath.

'Thank you for phoning straight away to tell me, love. You'll let me know if it turns up, won't you?'

'Course, Mum. I'm so sorry . . . ' Lucy sounded tearful again.

'It's not your fault, love, and it's no use you worrying. If Frank has got my address then it can't be helped and at least you've warned me.'

'What do you think he might do?'

'Either he'll do nowt or he'll be paying me a visit,' said Florence. 'But he doesn't know you've warned me, so I'm ahead. But don't fret, he's probably too lazy to want to make the journey, or too poor to be able to stand the expense. He won't have gone to yours with the intention of discovering where I live, and it would have been just chance that he saw the letter and took it, if indeed he did. He's probably got other folk to bother nearer home if he's wanting money, which I expect he is.'

'I reckon you're right, Mum. He looked down at heel and I did think he'd turned up to ask for my savings, though he said summat about making his peace, whatever he meant by that. I wasn't interested in hearing.'

'Well, then, he's unlikely to be coming here. Now off you go and get on with your work, Lucy. I'm sure there are women waiting for you to ease their bunions into a new pair of wide-fitting shoes. Give my best regards to Judy, and to Denis, of course.'

'Yes, Mum. And I'm sorry again . . . '

'Go on with you. Stop worrying.'

'Bye for now, Mum.'

'Bye, love.' Florence put the phone down.

Damn.

She walked up and down her sitting room,

thinking what would be the best thing to do. In the end she decided she could do very little, and Lucy's worries might be unfounded. She'd be extra-careful to double-check the locks and windows at night and make sure the car keys were hidden out of sight, though these measures were only good sense anyway, especially for anyone living alone. It might be wise to buy some extra bolts for the front and back doors, too. She wasn't afraid of Frank Stanville, and she didn't think he was dangerous, but he would be a nuisance if he turned up and she just preferred never to have any kind of encounter with him again. It was, she thought, a matter of taste.

Scamper was watching her from her basket, aware of the change in Florence's mood. Florence went over and fondled Scamper's curly ears.

'I reckon you're not the fiercest of guard dogs, love, but you'd do your best for your mum, wouldn't you?'

The little dog grinned in reply, showing the terrier in her genes.

'Right, Scamper, busy day ahead.'

Florence marched to her desk, pulled her day book towards her and started making lists.

Many jars of savoury blackberry jelly stood in the pantry, hand-labelled with the contents, to be delivered shortly to Nicolson & Filbert. In addition to her business cards, Florence had had some simple but elegant labels printed with the Florence Lily name for all her jars. She was already discussing with Harry and Sandra at Nicolson & Filbert her ideas for Christmas preserves with festive labels and decorative finishes, suitable to be given as presents. It was going to be a lot of work, but she had had some serious thoughts about that. She'd done some costings last night and was checking them again this morning. It might just be possible . . .

Meanwhile, the jars, vinegar and dry ingredients were beginning to take over the kitchen and, though the cottage was quite big enough to be a comfortable home for herself and Scamper, she really could do with more space in which to make and store everything to do with the little business. It would eliminate the smell of vinegar that haunted the place, too, which had to be an improvement.

She thought about all her possible plans later that morning as she drove towards Fleming St Clair to read to the Kendal sisters. Having met Scamper on the blackberry-picking day, Beatrice and Jane had suggested that Florence bring her to the reading sessions. Florence hadn't mentioned her dog before then because she thought it an imposition to ask to bring her to someone else's house, but the sisters made a huge fuss of her, and Becca had found and cleaned up an old dog basket from the attic, which Florence lined with one of Scamper's blankets so she could feel quite at home.

This morning's book was *The Secret Garden*, which had been a favourite of Florence's when she was little, but which had been published long after the Kendal twins had gone beyond the age of its author's intended audience.

'But a good book is a good book for ever, don't you think, Mrs Stanville?' asked Jane.

'And it doesn't matter if you're ten, or three-score and ten, if you enjoy it,' added Beatrice.

'Quite right,' said Florence. 'It's nice to alternate a childhood favourite with a murder mystery or a romance.'

'That's exactly what Matthew said . . . '

'. . . when he was here the other day . . . '

'. . . and we told him how much we're enjoying the reading. Our nephew wasn't very keen on the idea when we first thought of it . . . '

'. . . but he can see how happy it's made us . . . '

'. . . how happy *you*'ve made us.'

'I'm glad your nephew has come round to the idea. I wouldn't want to think the reading met with anyone's disapproval,' said Florence.

Florence was rather intrigued by Matthew Kendal. He was the only son of the twins' younger brother, Wilfred, and he visited his aunts regularly, from what they said, though Florence had never met him. This wasn't surprising because he would want to avoid going round when they were being read to. He'd been injured in the war, she understood, as so many people had been, though Beatrice and Jane had mentioned this only in passing.

The rest of the morning raced by very agreeably, the wonderful story well underway by the time Becca interrupted discreetly to tell the twins that lunch was nearly ready.

'We've been racking our brains to think if we once knew your mother, Mrs Stanville . . . ' said Beatrice, showing Florence into the hall and handing her her coat.

'. . . but we're afraid the name Lily Townsend

171

doesn't ring any bells with us, which is odd when we are both so sure we remember a young woman so like you. But we do know where we think we saw her.'

'Oh, anything you can tell me might help,' said Florence. 'It's nearly forty years ago that she lived hereabouts, and I've only a small child's memory of that time, which is mostly just impressions, but with occasional sharper memories, like snapshots.'

'Well, we think we remember seeing her once or twice in Bird's Café on the seafront at Guisethorpe. I don't know if you know the café?' said Beatrice.

'Oh, yes.'

'It used to be quite famous in the old days, a Guisethorpe attraction,' said Jane. 'Anyway, we both think we remember seeing an old man and the red-haired lady having tea together a few times.'

'We got the impression she was very attentive, helpful to him, not just there to chat as a friend.'

'It's her we noticed really, because of her beauty and her distinctive hair, of course.'

'We wonder if she might have been looking after him — a nurse or paid helper, maybe, rather than a relative,' finished Beatrice.

'You don't remember the man's name, do you?' asked Florence, hopefully.

'Oh dear, no, I'm sure we never did know it . . .'

'. . . but the thing is, my dear Mrs Stanville, if this gentleman had hired your mother as a nurse or a carer or some such, he likely lived in one of the big houses in Guisethorpe . . .'

'. . . rather than one of the little cottages. You

172

could go and have a look around the roads where the bigger houses are and see if you recognise anywhere.'

'It would be a start, anyway,' smiled Jane.

'Yes . . .' said Florence. 'You're right. Thank you. That's such a help, a place to start from, and may well trigger my own memory. I'm grateful to you.'

'We'll let you know if we think of anything else,' said Jane.

'So how was the blackberry jelly?' asked Beatrice, as Florence was putting on her hat.

'I'm confident it will be a good 'un. It's too soon to eat it yet but I've a jar or two put by for you for when it is,' said Florence. 'I'm filling up my pantry fast with all the different things I've made and the cottage smells of vinegar the whole time. Even Scamper does.'

'Oh, poor darling.' Beatrice bent to make a fuss of Scamper, who lapped up the attention.

'You could always bring it to store here,' suggested Jane.

'Just what I was going to say,' said Beatrice.

'Oh, that's so kind, but won't it be in your way?'

'But we have the whole house and there's only us and Becca . . .'

'. . . and we take up hardly any space,' laughed Beatrice.

'Next time you come, we'll ask Becca to show you the storeroom and you can see if it would suit,' said Jane.

'Oh, thank you. That'd be grand,' said Florence.

She drove into the centre of Fleming St Clair thinking about the kind offer, which would solve so many of the problems that loomed ahead at the cottage if the business continued to grow, as it must in order to succeed.

★ ★ ★

Driving home along the seafront, having stopped in Fleming to buy some strong bolts for her cottage doors, Florence mentally pondered the list she'd compiled earlier in her day book. She could see that she was going to be very busy. Her part-time reading job was a change of scene and it was good to get out and into such agreeable company. Besides, she enjoyed the stories! She didn't want to have to give that up simply because she was busy making preserves, and she had already benefited hugely from the generosity of the Kendal sisters. Now they were offering storage for the finished jars at their house. She couldn't repay them by declining to read to them when she knew what a difference that made to their lives. That would be a disgraceful and was completely out of the question.

No, what she had been thinking about increasingly, and had costed up last night, was some help . . . someone who knew how to cook and didn't need the careful supervision that a novice would require, sharing this most important task and so allowing Florence more time to attend to other vital aspects of the business.

The first day of October, and the weather was mild for the autumn. The sun was behind Florence, the light catching in her rear-view mirror as she drove north. Guisethorpe, when she reached it, was very quiet, as if anticipating colder, shorter days. There was hardly anyone on the beach, although a few people were in the street outside the seafront shops. Florence recognised some of them.

There was Mavis Farlowe, the old lady who made cakes and sold them at the St Jude's Hall produce market. After Jim had mentioned it, Florence had gone to see Mavis and offered to help arrange her table if she really did want some help. They'd come up with a tea-party theme, Mavis had unearthed all kinds of pretty, old-fashioned cake stands she said she'd never thought of using, and she and Florence had made an elaborate still life featuring the delicious slices and tarts piled high, which had never looked so tempting when they'd been presented in straight rows. The September sale, the previous week, had been more successful than any before then for Mavis and she thanked Florence over and over.

Coming out of Mr Blake's grocery shop was Doreen Potter, who guarded her pickles and pre-serves table like a lioness, clearly thinking Florence a rival who would be muscling in on her territory, despite Mary Davis overseeing all arrangements.

'I wouldn't have thought it worth your while bringing those jars to clutter up Jim's windowsill,' she'd said to Florence the previous week when she'd circulated the room to make her own pur-chases. 'Derek and I have many years of experience in producing pickles and we're quite established here.'

'I know you are, Mrs Potter,' said Florence, with an easy smile. 'Don't worry, I'm quite aware of your importance at the St Jude's Hall markets. I'm no rival to you.'

'I never thought you were,' snapped Doreen, her face betraying her.

Jim caught Florence's eye and gave a little wink, and when Doreen had moved away he said quietly, 'Makes me laugh . . . She'd be speechless if she knew about that fancy grocer.'

'But none of these jars has the 'Florence Lily' label — that's strictly for the shop only — and there's no reason why anyone should make a connection, even if they did go to Nicolson & Filbert. Let Doreen Potter say what she wants; she knows nowt.'

Now Florence drove on, past Bird's Café. Funny to think of her mother having tea there, nearly forty years ago. The tables outside were empty and Florence couldn't, with the brief look she could manage, see anyone inside, either. Suddenly she knew what she should do. She looked in the rear-view mirror, saw the road was clear, braked and then quickly reversed back up the street to stop outside.

She got out of the car, leaving Scamper in the back, and rushed into the café. She didn't care whether or not she encountered Anthony Bird. He wasn't in sight, but Carmen appeared immediately.

'Mrs Stanville, is Scamper outside? Are you at your usual table?' She took up a menu ready to hand to Florence.

'Oh, Carmen, no, I've not come in for tea, just to ask if I can meet you and Violet after work today.'

'We'll be finished at three and we were only

going home after that. Mr Bird said to close early as there have been hardly any customers today and he's already taken himself off somewhere with Trudie. He's not paying us for the full day, either,' she added. 'Dismal.'

Florence looked at her watch. It was two o'clock but the café was indeed empty. She hesitated only a moment. Anthony Bird didn't deserve these women working to try to keep his café staggering on in business while he was skiving off with Trudie. He was not even paying them properly, and the café was clearly a lost cause anyway. That last thought banished any lingering hesitation.

'If you want to close now I won't tell on you,' she said. 'Go and get your grandma, and if she agrees, there's the car right outside and we'll go to my house and I'll tell you what I have in mind there.'

'Ooh . . . ' Carmen disappeared into the kitchen, already taking off her apron as she went.

Violet appeared immediately. 'Five minutes, Florence, and we'll be with you. Outside, you say? If you wait in the car we'll be quick as we can.'

★　★　★

'Pickles? Yes, I've made plenty of pickles in my time — I know all the stages — but is it really a business?' asked Violet, comfortable in an armchair in Florence's sitting room, a cup of tea at her elbow, while Carmen had chosen to sit on the floor beside Scamper's basket. 'I'm sorry, love, I know you're clever and full of ideas, but you have to sell a lot of jars to make a living and pay others

177

to help out, and many people already make their own. You know Derek Clough . . . ? And there's that Doreen Potter, too. Hers aren't as good as his, though they look all right, and of course they're both established at the hall every month. Where's the market, Florence, that's what I'm wondering.'

'Nicolson & Filbert, for a start,' said Florence, unable to resist grinning.

'What? That dear place at Burton Barrow?'

'The same. I'm their sole supplier of pickles and preserves, and I mean to persuade other fancy grocers to take my produce. That's why I need you, Violet. There's a lot to it: all the making and the running of the business. It's too much for one person. I need some help, at least with the cooking and preparation. Come and look . . . '

She led them into the kitchen and opened the pantry door. Violet went in and inspected the rows of luscious dark blackberry jelly, the jewel-coloured fresh pickles, the bottles of raspberry vinegar and the golden jars of spiced autumn chutney.

'Pretty,' said Carmen. 'They're like a rainbow.'

'Florence Lily,' read Violet. 'Is that what you call yourself?'

'It's what *we* are called if you come to work for me, Violet,' said Florence. 'I've had to start small because I've started alone and from scratch, but with you helping me I'll have time to look for new outlets. If Nicolson & Filbert want my pickles, why wouldn't other shops?'

'And what about Carmen? Have you got room for her in your plans, too? You see, Florence, Bird's Café is on its last legs and I'll be glad to come to work for you, but I can't leave Carmen there

178

by herself. She'd never cope with Anthony alone, even if it's only for a short time. If I leave, that will hasten the end of the café — Anthony is unlikely to get anyone else to work for him — but I'll not have Carmen upset by his bullying her, even for one single day.'

'I agree, it would be terrible to leave her there . . . '

'No, please don't leave me,' said Carmen plaintively.

'. . . but I reckon a good strong girl who can sterilise jars, peel vegetables and generally help on all fronts would be a real asset.'

'And I could write the labels,' said Carmen, cheering up.

'You could what?'

'Oh, yes,' said Violet proudly. 'Carmen has a real artistic flourish to her handwriting.'

'But that's grand, just what I need,' said Florence.'And what else can you do, Carmen? Have you other hidden talents?'

'I'm very good at digging,' said Carmen. 'I do the garden at home — Great-Grandma tells me what she wants me to grow — and . . . ' she sighed, looking through the kitchen window to the untidy back garden, '. . . I do think your garden needs knocking into shape.'

'Good heavens! Yes, please, help with the garden is exactly what I need. I know nowt about gardening, and it's got out of hand, with Paradise being empty for a while before I got here. I'm too busy to even attempt it, and Jim across the lane has enough to do with his own.'

'When do you want us to start?' asked Violet.

'How much notice do you have to give at the café?'

'I don't trust Anthony. If we wait until we've been paid on Saturday and then I tell him we won't be in on Monday, that'll be best. If I tell him straight away he might withhold our wages. He's exploited my good nature something terrible over the years and I feel I owe him nothing.'

'Then you can start here on Monday,' said Florence. 'How does that sound?'

'Perfect,' breathed Carmen. 'At last, something to look forward to.'

Violet and Carmen said they'd walk home and Florence went with them as far as the beach to give Scamper some exercise after her morning inside at the Kendal sisters' house.

While she and Scamper walked back home, Florence reflected on her bold move, poaching Anthony Bird's staff from the café. Bird's would definitely have to close next week unless Anthony swiftly found some replacements and it was slightly on Florence's conscience that she was knowingly bringing about the demise of the café, but then she thought of the excitement in Carmen's face and how she'd straightened her defeated-looking shoulders at the thought of her new job. 'At last, something to look forward to' — what sad words from the mouth of a fifteen-year-old. Anthony Bird had worn her down and Florence hoped that her little business would bring an element of happiness into the lives of Violet and Carmen Peasall as well as making good use of their talents.

Back at home she ate a very late lunch and then screwed the new bolts to the front and back doors.

Then she devised a shopping list of vegetables for the next batch of chutney and went over to Sea View to see what Jim could sell her.

Earlier, Florence had seen Jim putting some onions out on his table so she thought he was at home. She went up the front path and round the back, hoping to catch him in his shed or in his garden. He always asked her to 'just come through and find me'. He wasn't among the neat rows of vegetables today, however.

'Jim?' she called, tapping on the shed door, then saw it was closed from the outside, so he couldn't be in there.

'What do you want?' It was Mildred, wearing a pinafore and, disconcertingly, carrying a large kitchen knife. She neither looked nor sounded welcoming.

'Hello, Mrs Yateman. I was just looking for Jim, hoping to buy some veg and some apples.' Florence stood beside the shed, unable to get past Mildred, who now blocked the pathway out.

'Were you, indeed? You seem to be spending rather a lot of time with my Jim, Mrs Stanville.'

'I don't think we've really spent much time in each other's company, except for a couple of mornings at the hall produce market,' Florence said gently. 'And once we had tea on the seafront, and we went to pick some blackberries. I invited you to come with us, I'm sure Jim told you.'

'Yes, he did, but I don't have outdoorsy sort of clothes. And I've seen your showy set-up at the hall, Mrs Stanville, trying to make Jim into some fancy sort of greengrocer, putting on airs and graces and making out he's something that he isn't. It's quite turned his head.'

'Turned his head? Are you sure? That doesn't sound like Jim.'

'How do you know what Jim's like?' snapped Mildred. 'I've been married to him for over forty years so I think you must allow me to know when his head's turned.'

'I'm sorry, Mrs Yateman,' said Florence, wondering why Mildred was carrying the knife, but not retreating at all, 'but I don't know what you're talking about.'

'I think you do,' snarled Mildred. 'You'll never make anything of your pickles, with Doreen and Derek Clough already established at the hall sales. You've only got that dusty old windowsill behind my Jim's table, and that's because he's been kind enough to take pity on you and lend you his space.'

Ah, I detect the voice of Doreen Potter. Now I know what at least some of this is about.

'I'm quite happy with just that bit of space at the hall, Mrs Yateman, and Jim knows it. As for helping with the table display, of course I don't mind not doing it if you'd like to do it instead.'

'Well, I'll have to see . . . But my Jim is getting all kinds of hifalutin ideas now. Courgettes, aubergines — what's an aubergine when it's at home? — carrots in weird colours. If God wanted purple carrots, He wouldn't have made them orange. Jim's ordered in a great pile of seed catalogues and he spends all his time reading them and making lists. He hardly takes any notice when I speak to him — might as well talk to myself — and he's in the shed until it's too dark to see most days.

And it's all your fault.'

'My . . . ?'

'With your fancy ideas. We were all right until you came to live here. Now all I ever get out of Jim is, 'Florence this' and 'Florence that'. Seems to talk an awful lot about someone who sells half a dozen jars of chutney once a month from the windowsill behind his table, and now he's thinking of growing all this exotic stuff. I don't want his hopes raised and then dashed when you get bored of your little hobby and move onto something or someone new, leaving Jim with a load of strange veg no one wants, not even us. We've lived in this village for years and I won't have my husband made a laughing stock by some incomer with grand ideas.'

'I think, Mrs Yateman,' Florence said slowly, 'that you have nothing to fear. If there's one thing I've learned at the St Jude's Hall produce markets it's that everyone likes Jim and respects him as a good person and as a talented gardener. No one would dream of laughing at him. And he's a kind man, too, lending a helping hand and a little space to someone new to the village, who has a few jars of stuff she's made to sell. In return he allowed me to help him arrange his table in a way he thought made the best of his lovely veg. Now, if he's looking to grow summat a bit different next year, well, it's all his idea, not mine. But I hear you're a good cook and, if Jim wants to sell his exotics at the hall and folk don't know what to do with it, mebbe you can be there to tell them.'

Far from pacifying the unreasonable woman, this clearly angered her further. For a moment

Mildred looked furious, her face reddening. Florence eyed the kitchen knife and decided to risk sidling slowly towards the little orchard and the way out. But suddenly Mildred's eyes were swimming with tears and she slumped her shoulders in defeat.

'But I wouldn't know myself,' she wailed. 'Jim is off on this new track, with a load of veg going over the lane to your kitchen — though you only seem to have a bit to sell at the hall, and I'd like to know what you're doing with it all — and now he's talking about stuff I've never heard of, and . . . it's like he's growing away from me. All these years we've been on the same wavelength and now he's turning into someone different. Someone who talks about . . . I don't know . . . orange tomatoes and purple carrots!' Her voice broke and she mopped her eyes with her pinafore, then became aware of the knife in her other hand. 'Oh, good heavens, what must you think of me, coming out with this?' She put it down on the ground at her feet and held up her hands, as if she'd been disarmed and was surrendering. 'I'm sorry, Mrs Stanville, I was just preparing our tea. I hadn't meant to frighten you.'

She was genuinely contrite and Florence relaxed, though still edged round further towards the orchard and escape. She didn't want to hear any more of whatever nonsense was bothering Mildred Yateman, but Mildred was unstoppable.

'It's me who's frightened, though, and I'll tell you why.'

'Please, Mrs Yateman, I'd rather — '

'With all these new ideas in his head, I'm afraid

184

it's only a matter of time before my Jim looks at me and thinks he'd prefer someone more exciting, with new ideas of her own about how things should look, someone younger, maybe with red hair . . . '

'Mrs Yateman! I can assure you I would never — '

'I know you've got time on your hands to spend with whoever you want whenever you like, and it seems you have the money to do exactly as you please, and there doesn't seem to be a Mr Stanville in tow to keep you in check, but I won't have you seducing my husband. There, I've said it!'

Good grief, the poor woman. Never mind that she's rude and probably daft, she must be feeling very insecure. How to put her mind at rest without telling her owt of my business she can gossip about? She's certainly one for getting completely the wrong idea.

'Mrs Yateman, I can assure you that you have nowt at all to worry about on that front. Anyone can see that Jim adores you and has eyes only for you. He may have mentioned my name a couple of times to you, but he speaks of you all the time to me — what a fine cook you are and how beautifully you keep the house, what a wide circle of friends you have with the . . . the crochet group.'

'Jim said you'd even asked him if he could help with your garden. What was I to think?'

'Well, that I *wanted help with my garden*, of course. I'm sure you've noticed yourself that it needs some work. Jim said he hadn't the time and now I've found someone else to help me, so you've nowt to worry about there either.'

For a moment Mildred was distracted by the

news.

'Someone else? Who is it? He won't be a patch on my Jim.'

'Possibly not, but as I told you, Jim made it quite clear he's too busy so that's the end of the matter.'

'Oh, so it's not you who's got these ideas about strange vegetables?'

'No, I told you, Mrs Yateman. And now I'll go and let you get on with your cooking. And please, when Jim gets back, would you ask him if he can spare me some windfalls? Thank you.'

Without waiting for an answer, Florence went out round the side of the house, down the long path and out into the lane, shutting the gate to Sea View with a clang. She felt heartily sorry for Jim. His wife was not only nosy and gossipy but she was jealous, insecure and neurotic as well. Her listening to the vindictive Doreen Potter had not helped Mildred's peace of mind either, as it had been amply clear that Mildred had got herself worked up and was spouting Doreen's nonsense as well as her own.

Florence let herself into Paradise Cottage, where Scamper came to greet her with her usual doggy enthu-siasm. Florence patted Scamper in a distracted fashion, thinking over what has just happened. She valued her friendship with Jim and felt lucky, after her initial suspicion of him and, frankly, her own rudeness, that she had come to know such a good and gentle man.

What if now, because of Mildred, he felt he could no longer be in Florence's company? No more peaceful fruit-picking days out together, no more discussing the recipes and tasting the results; maybe even, if Mildred continued to listen to Doreen Potter's poison, no more mornings at St Jude's Hall, meeting the little community and enjoying their company for a few hours. Florence hoped it would not come to that: her new life restricted and compromised by that stupid woman.

She slammed across the stout new bolts on her front door, mentally drawing a line under the day that had started with that ominous telephone call from Lucy, then had blossomed as she had begun on her exciting plans and appointed her team, until this last half-hour, which she felt had been tainted by Mildred Yateman's unfounded suspicion.

'Pathetic idiotic woman with her daft ideas,' she muttered to Scamper. 'Well, if she fixes her beady eye on my front windows from Monday, minding my business for me, she shan't fail to notice that if *her Jim* comes over we have a chaperone (as if we needed one) in the formidable shape of Violet Peasall. And young Carmen, too. Mildred flippin' Yateman be damned, and Frank Stanville, too. We've far too much to do to be worrying about them. Onwards and upwards, eh, Scamper?'

10

Anthony Bird was absolutely furious. He paced up and down before the window, with its breath-taking panoramic view of the sea, in his beautiful but shabby sitting room in the flat above the café, petulantly kicking the furniture and sweeping magazines, newspapers and packets of cigarettes off the coffee table, the chair arm and the sofa and onto the floor as he went. When the ashtray hit the carpet, flipping over and coming to land face down, Trudie had had enough.

'Oh, do stop that, Tony. You'll never get rid of the smell if you tread that into the carpet.'

'Shut up, Trudie. Can't you see what a complete and utter disaster this is?'

'Course, it's not good that Violet and Carmen have both decided to leave at once and won't be turning up on Monday, but it isn't the end of the world. True, Violet was a good cook — did a smashing Welsh rarebit and her omelette was the best I've ever eaten . . . '

'You're not helping, Trudie.'

'. . . but you'll find someone else.'

'And when will that be, between now and Monday, eh? And who's going to wait on the tables, even if I do — by some miracle — find another cook?'

'I don't suppose it's that difficult a job if Carmen could do it.'

'Carmen wasn't even very good at it. She was

always breaking and spilling things.'

'Then you're well shot of her and you can look at it as a new start with a more competent waitress.'

'But where exactly am I to *find* this waitress, Trudie, now, immediately?'

'Don't be silly, Tony. It's Saturday evening; you won't find anyone now. You'll have to have a little think and then do what you've decided about the staff tomorrow.'

'And when I've had *a little think* I expect the only conclusion I can possibly reach is that there is no one in the whole of Guisethorpe who'd want to come and work at Bird's Café in the low season.'

Trudie slumped down in the comfy armchair in a swirl of stiffly gathered skirt. She'd thought they were going to the pictures in Fleming St Clair, only to find when she arrived at the flat that Anthony's staff had left, and left him in a foul mood. She'd been looking forward to the evening, too; had made an effort to look pretty and had her hair done, all platinum-blonde curls, despite being rather hard up herself since leaving the solicitors Nesbit and Harrison, where she'd been a typist and filing clerk until she became fed up with Mr Nesbit always being intoxicated and Mr Harrison never being there at all.

'So I take it we're not going to the pictures, then?'

'No we are not!' Anthony recommenced his pacing, kicking out at the things he'd swept onto the floor.

Trudie sat with a frown on her pretty face for a

minute or two and then she got up and smoothed down her skirt.

'In that case I think I'll be off home.' She put on her coat and gathered up her handbag and gloves.

'That's right, go and abandon me! Leave me to sort out this mess all by myself! What do you care if I have to close the café?'

'Close the café? You mean, for good?' Trudie slowly put her handbag back down and sat in the chair again. 'But I thought it was famous round here. Everyone's heard of Bird's Café, haven't they?'

'Might have been famous once upon a time, but no longer. At least, if people have heard of it, they don't bother coming to it any more.'

'Why's that, Tony? What's gone wrong?' Trudie reached out to Anthony as he paced by, smoking furiously. 'You always gave me the impression it was a little gold mine, that café . . . business built up by your granddad and now owned and run by you, the third generation of Birds.'

'Well, that last part is true. But since I took over when Dad died . . . well, I guess my heart hasn't really been in it.'

Trudie gave him a long look. 'Was it ever? Honest truth, Tony, I haven't seen you putting in a lot of time and effort into the cafe. Course, it's nice to have days out and all that, but you never mentioned the café was in trouble. You seemed to be . . . carefree, your time your own, money in your pocket. I thought you must be doing well. Now I'm seeing a different picture.'

Anthony sat down on the chair arm beside her, took a long drag, then looked around for the ashtray, retrieved it from the carpet and stubbed out

190

his cigarette, leaving the old ash in a toxic heap on the floor.

'It wasn't ever what I wanted to do. The whole business is a nightmare and I curse my dad every day for leaving me this burden. It was just assumed I'd take over and the café would continue to flourish as it always had done. I think I sort of believed it could go on as it had and never change, and that if I left it to itself it would do just that. Miss McGee of Blackett and McGee was round here a few weeks ago with the figures and it's bad news for Bird's and worse news for yours truly. Now, with Violet and Carmen gone, I think maybe this afternoon I closed the door on the wretched place for the last time.'

'Oh, that's really sad. I'm so sorry. So what are you going to do?'

'I don't *know*, Trudie. Will you just shut up and stop quizzing me?'

'But you've got to face this, darling. You can't just do nothing. You'll have to find another job. I've been looking and there's not much at the seaside in October, but you never know . . . '

'At least you can type; I can't do anything, well, apart from the cartoons.'

Trudie felt uncomfortable. When she'd first met Anthony she'd thought his cartoons were brilliant: funny caricatures of local people, gently exaggerating their features but always in an amusing way; nothing to cause offence. But lately the drawings had taken on an altogether darker style. She still had the one of the tall lady, the awkward customer, whom Anthony had drawn with snaky hair and witchy features, her dog like a devilish little familiar. For some vague reason Trudie felt this picture was significant, either of Anthony's view of the woman or of his life in general, and she'd kept it, but at the back of a drawer, like a guilty secret. Then there were others she'd seen here recently of people she knew: cruel, ugly, mocking, the pencil lines dark and hard, viciously scoring the paper, the figures tortured, burned, stabbed . . . They were shocking and horrible.

Anthony lowered his head into his hands, his shoulders slumped in defeat. 'Margaret McGee suggested I rent out the flat. It would mean I'd have some money to save the café but I'd also need to find somewhere else to live.'

Trudie was still trying to shrug off the images of the recent cartoons that had sullied her mind.

'What . . . ? Or you could keep the flat and rent out the café part downstairs, couldn't you? That would make more sense. Then you'd be able to continue to live here and someone else would run the café or a shop or whatever it turned into, and pay you for the use of the premises. Oh, Tony, you'd hate to have to move and not have this lovely view of the sea.'

'I would, but who would want to rent a shop on a quiet seafront in autumn? Nothing much is going to happen in Guisethorpe until Easter . . . until summer, realistically. Possibly not even then. I tell you, it's a disaster.' He got up and prowled around the room, kicking the furniture again.

Trudie was quiet for a while. She wanted to go home but she felt she couldn't just leave him to his misery.

'Well, Tony, you can't let disaster overtake you,'

she said eventually. 'You've got to put up one last fight. Then you'll feel better about . . . everything.'

'I've never put up any fight at all before now,' admitted Anthony pathetically. 'I think that's the root of the problem. I had enough to live on at first. Dad seemed to sail along with the café; I never saw him making much effort. Why should I have to do it all? It's not fair.'

'I think your dad probably worked a lot harder than you think,' suggested Trudie, quietly. 'I've heard people speaking highly of him. You should be proud of his legacy.'

I wish my dad had left me a nice little business on the seafront, she thought.

'Should I indeed, Trudie? When I want your opinion I'll ask for it, OK?'

'Fine. Well, I'll be off then,' said Trudie, gathering her things again.

'No, please. You can't go and leave me.' He grabbed her wrist, his large hand encircling it and holding her tight — too tight.

'Ow, Tony, you're hurting me,' she gasped. 'Please . . . let me go.' She tried to push his hand off with her free hand.

'You've got to help me, Trudie. You've *got* to. I'm desperate. I can't do this by myself. It's too much. Too much!' He let go of her arm, then picked up the cushion from the armchair and hurled it at the wall, knocking over a table lamp, which crashed in a heap on the floor, base, light bulb and shade all detached.

'Sit down, please, Tony, and stop smashing things,' Trudie said quietly, rubbing her wrist. 'I can't stay if you're going to hurt me and start

193

breaking things.'

'All right, all right . . . ' He subsided onto the sofa, his head in his hands.

Trudie sat, massaging her bruised wrist, wondering whether to go anyway.

'Sorry,' Anthony muttered after a minute or two. 'Didn't mean to.'

Trudie let a silence fall. Then she said, 'We must think of a plan before it's too late.'

'It's *too late* now . . . I know it is.'

She stood up, looking determined. 'No, Anthony, it isn't. We'll give it one more go, just one big effort to pull you back from the brink and get the place buzzing again. It's worth another try, isn't it? I'm sure we can do it.'

'*We?*'

'We, Tony. I'll help you. It isn't over for the café yet. I can cook, a bit. We'll rewrite the menu, keep to a few simple things I can manage, and tea and cakes. We can buy the cakes in.'

'With what? There's no money to buy in cakes or anything else. I gave Violet and Carmen the last of my money to pay them for the week and they promptly announced they wouldn't be coming back. Goodness knows where they've gone but they must have got new jobs as they've both left together.' A picture of Violet and Carmen walking on the beach with Florence Stanville flashed through his mind and he thumped the sofa arm, cursing. Could the Stanville woman have something to do with their departures?

'Just tea, then.'

'Trudie, I know you're trying to help but it's hopeless. It's a lost cause. There's nothing left.'

194

Trudie came to sit beside him on the sofa and they held each other in a hug of silent misery for a while.

Eventually she got up. 'I have to go. I'll have a think and be back tomorrow.'

'Please stay . . . '

'No, Tony. I've got some serious thinking to do and I don't want to be distracted. You clear up that mess on the carpet and I'll be back in the morning. We just need a plan, an idea. And don't go drinking that Scotch because no good ideas ever came out of a whisky bottle. I mean it.'

'All right, all right, don't go on.'

'Go and get the dustpan and brush now, otherwise I know you'll leave that ash there and the carpet will stink. It's bad enough as it is.'

'Oh, couldn't you — '

'No!'

He sloped off to get the dustpan and Trudie gathered her belongings once more and quickly went downstairs and let herself out at the street door. Really, Anthony was an idiot to have thrown away his family business through nothing more than unwillingness to bother with it, but Trudie was determined that he wouldn't sink completely in his own selfish ineptitude and become a lost cause. She just wished he could be . . . nicer when she was trying to help him. He used to be more fun, but just lately, well, he could sometimes be unkind, even a little bit frightening.

★ ★ ★

Florence was delighted to have cleared the majority of the pickles and jam out of her pantry and into the storeroom at the Kendal sisters' house.

Their storeroom turned out to be vast, cool, very clean and largely empty: perfect for Florence's needs. Florence had given Beatrice and Jane some jars as a thank you, and then read them several chapters of *The Secret Garden*, so everyone was happy.

Florence had been mulling over what Jane and Beatrice remembered of the woman who might have been her mother: they thought the elderly man they'd seen her with could have been her employer and, because he could afford some help in his old age, it was possible he had lived in one of the bigger houses in Guisethorpe.

This made perfect sense to Florence. The dreams in which her mother appeared evoked long, high corridors, and the image of an airy kitchen with high windows had flashed through her mind when she'd seen the tea cosies for sale at the hall.

Finding herself at a loose end on Sunday, she took Scamper for a long walk, but instead of their usual route along the beach, Florence turned off the seafront road after she reached the shops and decided to view the roads behind in the hope that one of the houses looked familiar.

It was a beautiful autumn day and the walk was a pleasure. The houses were a mixture of styles and ages, some behind tall privet hedges or with mature trees before them, some with pretty little cottage gardens. Florence knew she wasn't looking for a cottage. Nonetheless, she enjoyed looking at the gardens, hoping Carmen would be able to create something similar from her overgrown and weedy space at Paradise Cottage.

'Hello, Florence.'

It was Mavis Farlowe, digging in her front border, planting tiny bulbs.

'Mavis, it's good to see you again.' Her cottage, which Florence had visited when she'd helped Mavis with her table presentation, was very neat, similar in style to Florence's own, but with a garden as tidy as Florence's was overgrown. 'It's nice for me and Scamper to have a different walk.'

Mavis came over and patted Scamper. 'Lovely little dog . . . '

Florence thought she'd be silly not to enlist Mavis's help in her search, supposing she had help to offer, and Jim had said she was discreet.

'I came up here thinking I might recognise one of the houses I used to know many years ago, but I can't remember exactly where it was.'

'And you don't remember the name of the road or of the house, or the number, perhaps?'

'None of those.'

Mavis clasped her hands together, frowning slightly in thought. 'Well, you need to list what you can remember to narrow down your search. Which side of the road you think it was on when the sea is behind you, whether it was on the hill, or above where it's flatter, what the colour of the door was — you never know, that could be the same even now — brick or clapboard, big or little, long or short garden, trees or a hedge . . . you see?'

'Yes, I do. Thank you. That will help narrow it down a bit if I can remember at all. But the walk is lovely anyway. And your beautiful garden is an inspiration.'

'Thank you, Florence. Good luck with your search.'

Mavis turned away to resume her gardening, and Florence and Scamper walked on, Florence thinking hard to recall the house she could really only remember in her dreams or in sudden brief snapshots of memory. She had a very strange idea that it was a bit like a castle, but that was absurd, of course. She and her mother couldn't possibly have lived in a castle; she'd have remembered that and, besides, such a place would be a local landmark.

She stopped to think, then walked on higher up, crossing over the road, craning her neck to see if any of the houses behind the tall hedges were familiar.

At the top of the road she turned to the left, into a road that ran parallel to the sea. That seemed the right way, the right distance from the sea, somehow, but of course this might not be the correct road. She walked on anyway, making the best of the lovely autumn morning, enjoying Scamper's company as the little dog trotted along beside her, but looking carefully at every place she passed.

She had resigned herself to a fruitless search on this occasion when she saw a very tall fir tree in a garden she was approaching and she wondered if she hadn't seen that before. It would be a lot taller now than it had been forty years ago, which could be misleading, but maybe she *had* seen it before. There was certainly something familiar about it. She continued on, Scamper meandering between interesting scents along the way, but the next few houses rang no bells in her mind.

Then, a little way further on, there was a house standing well back behind a hedge, with wide wrought-iron gates set between square red-brick pillars. Florence stopped to look carefully, noticing a rather fanciful turret at one front corner of the house, like a small room in a tower. She gazed at the house, seeing a wide wooden front door and big windows. She moved a little way down the road to get a side view and saw the house was deep and spacious. Could this be the place? Certainly the big front door seemed familiar, and the turret: quite small really, but probably exciting and imposing to a seven-year-old. Perhaps that was the 'castle' element. Perhaps this was the place she'd been trying to find . . .

There was a wooden nameplate beside the front door but Florence couldn't read it from the pavement. Well, nothing for it, she'd better just go and look.

The windows were all closed, but then it was October. She couldn't see any smoke coming out of the chimneys. Why not just knock on the door and ask, if anyone came to answer? There was nothing to lose. She didn't mind if she looked a bit silly, so long as no one thought she was about some dishonest business.

She opened the gate, which was a little rusted around the handle. She didn't remember the iron gate and doubt overcame her.

Come on, Flo. You'll never know if you don't try.

She approached the house and saw the sign said 'Tempest House'.

At once she knew it was the right place and her stomach did a little flip of excitement. How wonderful if someone here had known her mother, could fill in all the gaps in Florence's knowledge and explain the meaning behind Lily's mysterious words. She stood for a few moments gazing up at the house and suddenly a distant memory of many years ago flew into her mind.

★ ★ ★

1919

A woman and a child were standing in front of the large house, their bags at their feet. The little girl looked up at the outside, seeing a huge wooden front door within a handsome porch, vast windows and, unusually, a little tower in one corner like in a fairy story: *Rapunzel, Rapunzel, let down your hair.* Rapunzel's hair wasn't red, though, and nor was Little Flo's as long as Rapunzel's. And anyway, the little girl shrugged, that had almost ended sadly, the prince saved from blindness only by Rapunzel's tears. Not a very happy story. Nevertheless, this house with the turret, and the seaside nearby, promised an exciting new life. Florence jumped up and down on the spot.

'Are we really going to live here, Mummy?'

'We are, my darling, at least to start with. Let's see how it works out, shall we?'

★ ★ ★

Feeling the presence of Lily beside her, Florence went to the door and rang the bell. Maybe she was just moments away from finding the clues that would unlock all kinds of memories and the answers she was looking for.

But the woman who answered the door knew nothing.

'I've lived here only a few years,' she said, looking at Florence at little suspiciously. 'I know nothing about the people who lived here before.'

'It was nearly forty years ago,' said Florence. 'I feel certain this was the house in which I lived with my mother and I'm trying to find out all about that time — things I can't remember.'

The woman, who looked about thirty, gave Florence a rather pitying smile, as if she was in her dotage. 'Well, it's a long time before I was even born,' she said.

'Is there anyone here who might remember?'

'No.'

Florence had hoped the woman would let her see inside but, looking at her face, Florence felt her hope of that was fading.

'I just thought there was a chance — '

'I expect you did,' said the woman rudely. 'Goodbye, and please close the gate on your way out.'

Florence was dismissed. She realised that a helpful, kind person — someone who would welcome her in, who had memories to share and would be happy to spare the time to show her around — was a fantasy she'd invented between noticing the turret and knocking on the door. It had been far too much to expect.

She sighed and exhaled heavily, surprising herself at the depth of her disappointment.

'Never mind, Scamper . . . '

Perhaps uncovering the meaning of Lily's mysterious words was also pie in the sky. Perhaps there *was* no hidden meaning; they were just the wanderings of a mind closing down. There was no mystery.

But then what about the dreams? What did *they* mean?

There were no answers, at least not here, and not today.

Florence stepped out through the gate onto the pavement when — 'Huh!' she was barged heavily in the shoulder by a man hurrying past, not stopping, not turning to see if she was all right.

Scamper was barking and straining at her lead at the broad figure retreating at speed down the hill towards the seafront.

Florence hadn't quite been knocked to the ground but her shoulder hurt from the considerable blow.

'Watch where you're going!' she called angrily, straightening and looking after the man.

It was Anthony Bird. She was sure of it.

She recalled his hostility on earlier occasions. Had he deliberately tried to knock her down or was it just a clumsy accident?

She walked home, her morning now spoiled. By the time she got back to Paradise Cottage she was convinced Anthony had run into her on purpose. Did this mean he already knew she'd offered jobs to his staff? Violet would no doubt tell her next morning. And if he didn't already know Violet and Carmen were now working for her, he was going to take it very badly when he did find out.

★ ★ ★

By Monday morning, Florence felt uncharacteristically exhausted. She had thought she was not really worried that Frank might have her address — she could surely deal with him now as ruthlessly as she'd dealt with him before — but her unconscious mind was in turmoil, giving her terrible dreams, which mixed with the recurring strange dreams about her mother, turning them into ever-more-surreal nightmares. Her encounter with Anthony Bird outside Tempest House was quite unsettling, however much she told herself that he was nothing but an idiot. And the meeting with Mildred Yateman had been oddly upsetting, too. Florence had tried to shrug her off as a ridiculous, insecure and jealous old woman, but ever since, her silly accusations had played on Florence's mind and she couldn't quite rid herself of the bizarre image of Mildred clutching that enormous kitchen knife and all but accusing Florence of trying to seduce her husband.

Early on Monday the doorbell rang and Florence found herself rushing to glance through the sitting-room window to check who was there before she went to answer it.

'You all right, Florence?' asked Jim, holding a bulging hessian sack. 'Only you look a bit tired, if you don't mind me saying.'

Florence straightened the crease from her brow and shrugged. 'Just a lot to think about, Jim, that's all. It's good of you to call early — are those the onions and apples I need this morning?'

'They are.' He handed them over. 'Exciting day, with Violet and Carmen coming to help you.'

'Mm . . . '

'What's the matter? Is it . . . it is Mildred, isn't it? She's been a bit odd for a day or two and last night she told me some daft tale about . . . well, whatever it was about, it was all her imagination, but I gather she's shared a few of her sillier ideas with you.'

'Aye, she did mention her worries. It's made me feel a bit awkward. I never thought how our friendship might look to anyone else.'

'Why, it should look the same as it is, Florence: two people with an interest in vegetables, one growing and one cooking, each to the advantage of the other. Two people who live opposite each other and who share a bit of space at the produce market, again, each to the advantage of the other. Two people who . . . well, get on together. It's called friendship, plain and simple, as you say.'

'Thank you, Jim. You're very kind and very wise.'

'I don't know about that, but why shouldn't we be friends? Heavens, you're young enough to be my daughter, I shouldn't wonder, and neither of us has anything to be ashamed of. I've told Mildred so, too. I think she might try to avoid you but it's only because she's feeling foolish and a bit ashamed of herself.'

'Jim, I am so grateful to you. I hope she understands now and I'm sorry that she was upset.'

'Not your fault, Florence. This sack is heavy —

shall I bring it through?'

Florence was about to refuse because of what Mildred had said, but Jim had cleared the air with his wife and Florence must believe that was the end of the matter. She'd try to make a point of meeting Mildred in the lane and being friendly, for Jim's sake and because, though she thought Mildred rather silly, she was Jim's wife so she was probably not really as idiotic as she presented herself.

'Thanks, Jim, I'd be grateful. Thank goodness I've got Violet to help me chop up that little lot. She'll be here before long, and Carmen, too, of course.'

'And Carmen's going to be sorting out your garden?'

'Yes. She says she looks after the garden at home but I haven't seen what that's like. I took her word for it; I don't think either Carmen or Violet would tell me owt untrue. But I have to think of summat for Carmen to do; she kind of comes with Violet, if you see what I mean.'

'Don't underestimate her, Florence. She's a good girl, and a kind one, and she's been brought up by Violet, which scores her high in my book. I don't think she'd found her place in life as a waitress, but she's moving on now, thanks to you. I think she'll turn out to be all right. What's it you say in Lancashire — a good 'un?'

'Aye, lad, a good 'un,' laughed Florence. 'And you're a right good 'un, too, Jim.'

Jim had no sooner gone but Violet and Carmen arrived on bicycles. Florence had found some gardening tools in the near-derelict little shed at the back of her garden and Carmen set to work digging out weeds while her grandmother and Florence began on a new batch of autumn chutney.

Mostly they worked in companionable silence or commented on the pickling process, but Florence was keen to know what had happened when Violet and Carmen had left their jobs the previous Saturday; that the experience hadn't been made unpleasant for them, as it was unlikely Anthony Bird would have been happy about their leaving. The previous day he'd clearly been in a furious mood; it might just have been an accident that he'd barged her in the street, but he hadn't then stopped to see if she was all right.

'I made sure he paid us what he owed and then I told him we wouldn't be in on Monday and I was afraid he'd have to find a new cook and waitress.'

'I hope he didn't make your leaving difficult for you both, Violet?'

'No, I just told him straight out. We'd a right to go and I'd sworn Carmen to secrecy about us coming to work for you because we don't want to cause you any trouble. He'll find out eventually — this is Guisethorpe, after all — but not from us. Now, I'll start on these apples, shall I . . . ?'

Florence understood that Violet was washing her hands of the café and her old boss for good, and what Anthony Bird thought about their leaving was not her concern.

At the end of the day there were far more jars of autumn chutney lined up in the pantry than Florence could ever have achieved by herself, and

Carmen had made a noticeable difference to the front garden.

'What do you want to grow, Mrs Stanville?' she asked, taking her muddy boots off at the back door and padding inside in her thick-knit socks. 'When I've got it all dug over you'll want something in place of the weeds.'

'Well, I thought some more roses at the front, and different things that flower so that I have colour all year, even in winter.'

'Bulbs,' said Carmen, nodding. 'And hellebores. Bergenia.'

'Good gracious, love, I don't even know what those are.'

'That doesn't matter,' said Carmen. 'I do.'

'And at the back I thought I'd take inspiration from Jim and have some vegetables of my own.'

'Do you need them if you've got Mr Yateman?' asked Carmen. 'It would hardly be worth having a tiny row of peas or raspberries or whatever it was. And you'd want to be able to sit out at that little table, and Scamper will want somewhere to lie in the sun in summer.'

'I reckon you're right, Carmen. Mebbe I wouldn't be making the best of the garden.'

'Herbs,' said Carmen. 'They grow well in pots so you can move them about as you like, and use them in your recipes, too. A lot of gardeners round here are men and they tend to go in for big stuff; I don't know why: the biggest marrow you've ever seen, or a prize carrot two feet long, or ten tons of beans. They don't think about the pretty little thymes or lovely rosemary in flower in summer.'

'That's a grand idea,' said Florence.

'I can bring some from home in spring and you'd soon have masses. Rosemary is really clever because it knows who grows it and always does best when there's a woman in charge.'

'In that case,' said Florence, grinning at Violet and Carmen, 'the Paradise Cottage rosemary will be three times better than anyone else's.'

⋆ ⋆ ⋆

Trudie set the tea urn to heat, then went out the back and started to unload doughnuts and iced buns from her bicycle basket. She'd asked her mother to lend her some money, got up early and cycled to one of the two bakeries in Fleming St Clair to buy them. The week before, Violet had put in the usual order for pantry and dairy goods to be delivered from the wholesaler at the start of this week, and these were waiting in boxes and crates outside the back door of the café.

'Tony, can you help bring these milk bottles in, please? . . . Please can you help me arrange these chairs around the tables? . . . Where's the salt and pepper pots? I think there should be those ready on the tables. And where do you keep the napkins? . . . Tony, will you please just pour some milk into those jugs while I spoon out this jam?'

So it went on, Trudie issuing orders while doing nearly all the tasks herself. Anthony kept escaping to skulk outside, grinning falsely at passers-by, possibly in the hope that would entice them in, and then gazing out at the sea, his mind seemingly occupied with his own, clearly angry private thoughts.

By lunchtime on that Monday they had sold three pots of tea, and one doughnut. Someone else had complained that their doughnut was apricot jam and they'd expected raspberry and weren't going to pay, and another prospective customer had asked for fresh-ground coffee and then promptly left when Anthony said they hadn't got any.

Between these people there had been stretches of time when no one came in at all. Trudie's fighting spirit was flagging and she was running out of patience with Anthony, too.

Eventually she could bear it no longer. There had been no customers for half an hour.

'No wonder the place is on its knees. You hang around outside, putting people off, we haven't got what they want, and you're in a world of your own and can't jump to it and give them what they ask for when we *have* got it.'

'I'm doing my best . . . '

'No, you're not, Anthony, you're not even trying. You don't know what it's like to make an effort. Why haven't you cleared those tables that have been used?'

'I thought it would make us look busier, like we had some customers.'

'Don't be stupid. It just looks slovenly.'

'Then come and help me, as you haven't any cooking to do.'

'I'm getting everything in the kitchen ready for when we do, *and* I've been cleaning down and tidying up in here, getting ahead. Can't you even do that little bit of table clearing?'

'I'm not used to this. Carmen did all that.'

'Well, Carmen's not here so you'd just better get used to doing it yourself. What do you think you are, Anthony, a floorwalker? Because, just in case you haven't noticed, there are no staff and no customers to supervise.'

'All right, all right, no need to get heated. I'll clear the tables and you can do whatever it is you do in the kitchen.'

He grabbed a tray from the front counter and started piling the used crockery on it. An elderly couple, smartly dressed, came in and hovered by the door.

'I'll be with you in a moment,' said Anthony, cram-ming as much crockery as he could onto the tray, tipping over a half-empty milk jug so that a trail of milk ran over the table and onto the floor. 'Damn . . . ' He went off to get a cloth to mop it up and when he came back out to the front the couple had gone. 'Hell's bells and b — '

'Mr Bird, what on earth are you doing standing there using that kind of language?'

It was Mary Davis, the headmistressy woman who ran a lot of events in Guisethorpe, including those at St Jude's Hall, and she wasn't looking at all impressed.

'I only dropped in to have a cup of tea and say hello to Violet and Carmen. Are you here by your-self?'

'They've gone,' said Anthony angrily. 'They took their pay on Saturday and said they wouldn't be back.'

'So you're coping alone? Bravo for trying. Still, if I've missed Violet . . . ' She turned to leave.

'Please stay,' said Anthony. 'Please.' Woodenly

he extended a hand to show Mrs Davis to a table. 'Please stay and have a cup of tea, even though Violet and Carmen aren't here.' He knew he sounded as if he were begging but he couldn't help it.

'No, I can see you're busy,' said Mary Davis, glancing at the pool of milk that Anthony had yet to clean up.

'No, not busy at all. A cup of tea, you said? Coming right up . . . ' He rushed into the kitchen, leaving the door open.

'Trudie, I've got Mrs Davis — you know, that bossy woman — and she wants a cup of tea.'

'Fine,' Trudie said calmly, 'then I shall make her one. Would she like anything to eat?'

'I didn't ask.'

'Then do so now, please.'

Anthony rushed back out, to find Mrs Davis had gone and the café was empty again.

'She's gone,' he reported back to Trudie. 'Can't think why she'd come in and then go.'

'Perhaps she heard you calling her 'that bossy woman', Anthony. Can't say I'm surprised she's gone. I'm thinking of going myself.'

'No, don't, please, Trudie. Don't go and leave me. Please.'

Trudie closed her eyes, breathing deeply for a few seconds. 'I think I have to, Tony. It's the only way you're ever going to take any responsibility for this mess. My sympathies are with Violet and Carmen and I'm surprised they stuck with you for so long. I'm sorry, but you're on your own. You don't listen to a word of advice or lift a finger to help yourself. You're impossible.' She took off Violet's old pinafore, which went round her almost

211

twice, and hung it on the back of the kitchen door, then put on her coat, picked up her handbag and walked out.

★ ★ ★

Anthony woke up with a raging hangover. He was lying on the sofa in his sitting room, still wearing yesterday's clothes and with his tongue feeling swollen and stuck to the roof of his mouth. His pounding head weighed a ton and the room spun alarmingly as he tried to stand. He saw then that the place was completely trashed: furniture pushed over, cushions burst, papers torn and scattered. He remembered his rage, then, and saw his hands were bruised as if he'd been in a fight. In the end he crawled to the kitchen on his hands and knees and downed several glasses of water . . .

When he woke up again he was cold and realised he'd collapsed on the kitchen floor. He peeled himself off the tiles, drank some more water and then lay back down and wondered what day it was and whether Violet had opened the café. Then he remembered that Violet no longer worked for him. Recollection of Monday, working in the café, Trudie in the kitchen, came back to him. Was that yesterday? The day before? Violet and Carmen had gone . . . Trudie had gone, left him. The café had closed for good — he vaguely remembered turning the sign on the door shortly after Trudie had walked out on him — and then he'd come up to the flat and taken his anger out on the sitting room.

The whole situation was hopeless. He could

have handled it better, but he never managed to handle anything well. It was only with hindsight that he realised his mistakes, and even then he just went on repeating them. Like all that whisky he'd drunk. What was it Trudie had said? Something about no good ideas coming out of a whisky bottle. Smart girl, Trudie. He knew that but it hadn't stopped him behaving like an idiot — again.

And she'd said something else . . . about the flat. Or was it the café? He racked his brain to remember but his ability to think had left him completely. He knew only that the café was closed . . .

When he woke up for the third time it was daylight outside and he was lying on the sofa in his sitting room. He thought of the last day in the café, Trudie trying to help him out. Was Trudie still a part of his life or had she given up on him altogether. What day was it. . .?

Then he remembered what else Trudie had said: 'You could keep the flat and rent out the café part downstairs, couldn't you?'

If only he could find someone to rent the premises downstairs he'd be able to keep the flat, to live here, on the money. He wouldn't have to worry about earning a living himself because the business premises would be earning it for him. It was the perfect solution.

Now all he had to do was find someone who wanted to start up a café in Guisethorpe in the autumn and he'd be on to a winner.

11

Florence drove to the Kendal sisters' house, happy in the knowledge that Violet was more than capable of cooking a big batch of mincemeat to perfection while she herself was out for the morning reading to Beatrice and Jane. And Scamper was quite content to be left in the company of Carmen, who had worked hard to clear the unruly front garden and was now tackling the tangle of weeds at the back of the cottage.

In the boot of Florence's car this morning were two boxes of chutney to go in Beatrice and Jane's storeroom. Since Violet had come to work for her, Florence was enjoying building up her little business all the more. It was useful to share ideas with someone wise and practical, and the volume of jars they produced was keeping pace with increased orders from Nicolson & Filbert and several other shops that Florence was now supplying. Carmen's handwriting turned out to be, just as Violet had said, very artistic indeed, and she labelled the contents of the Florence Lily jars with a far more attractive flourish than Florence could manage. With Christmas in mind, Florence had bought some reels of fine ribbon in red and green, which all three of them practised tying around the necks of the jars until they had agreed on the most pleasing presentation.

The morning at the Kendals' house passed in the intricate plot of the most delicious murder mystery, the twins enthralled by the story.

'It's funny,' said Jane, 'but however many times I've read these books I can never remember who done it.'

'And neither can I,' laughed Beatrice. 'What could be better? A book that seems new to us every time!'

When she was preparing to go home, Florence remembered the jars in the car and Becca helped her take them down to the storeroom, swapping them for a box that was ready to go to Nicolson & Filbert. When they came back out through the hall, Beatrice and Jane were welcoming a visitor.

'Ah, Matthew, you're just in time to meet Mrs Stanville, the lady who reads to us,' said Jane.

'How do you do, Mrs Stanville?' said Matthew Kendal, coming forward to shake her hand before seeing that Florence was holding a large and heavy box.

Florence set the box down on the floor and shook hands. 'How do you do, Mr Kendal?'

So this was Matthew Kendal, of whom she had heard so much. He was a few years younger than Florence, tall, very thin, and as he came over to greet her she saw he walked with a limp.

'And good morning to you, Becca,' he said.

'Hello, Mr Kendal,' she smiled, blushing slightly.

'I'm afraid Mrs Stanville is just going . . . ' said Jane.

'. . . after such a lovely time with an Agatha Christie,' added Beatrice.

'So you've spent the morning enjoying a murder, have you, Aunts?' Matthew asked, looking serious. 'What a bloodthirsty pair you are. Should

215

I be afraid to stay for my lunch?'

His aunts laughed indulgently while Becca said, 'Oh, do stay, Mr Kendal. I've made a shepherd's pie because I knew you were coming.'

'In that case I shall just help Mrs Stanville to her car with this box and be very glad to stay and eat it. Thank you, Becca.'

Becca looked away shyly and Florence thought the girl was probably a bit in love with the sisters' handsome nephew. He was certainly very dashing, with his lean, even gaunt face and military bearing, despite the limp.

He lifted the box of jars off the floor and followed Florence out with them. She saw a sporty little car, dark blue, parked next to her own, obviously his.

'Oh, thank you for that. I'll just open the boot . . . ' said Florence.

She did so and Matthew hefted the box in and then turned to her.

'Mrs Stanville, may I ask, was it your idea that you should use my aunts' storeroom for your jars?' he asked quietly.

'No, not at all. I hadn't even thought of it and then Miss Jane — or maybe Miss Bea — kindly suggested it. It is the perfect solution as I don't have much room at home.'

He nodded. 'Ah, I see. Yes . . . yes, in that case it has worked out well.'

There was a little silence in which Florence caught him looking at her speculatively.

'They thought of it and just suggested it one day?'

'Yes, they offered me the space after I said how

full of jars my cottage was getting.'

'Mm, as you say, it's the perfect solution . . . ' he added, with a slightly forced smile.

'Your aunts are always very thoughtful,' Florence said, 'and I reckon if you think about it, Mr Kendal, you'll recognise it's just the sort of generous offer they would make to help someone out.'

'Oh, yes, Mrs Stanville, I know my aunts well enough to realise that, but what I've also learned over the years, I'm afraid, is that kindness can get taken advantage of.'

'Not by me,' Florence replied promptly. 'I like Miss Jane and Miss Bea far too much ever to do such a thing. Only a scoundrel would take advantage of such good natures. Is that what you think I am, Mr Kendal? A scoundrel?'

Matthew looked taken aback at having his fears confronted in such plain terms. 'No, I wasn't suggesting that at all. It's just that not everyone has repaid my aunts' kindness with kindness in return.'

'I'm sorry to hear that, but you have nowt to fear from me on that score. And even if I wasn't very fond of your aunts and didn't love coming here to read to them, I reckon Becca would never allow me to treat those wonderful women with owt but the highest respect.'

'Yes . . . yes, of course, you're right there, Mrs Stanville. The ever-reliable Becca is like a fierce guard dog where my aunts are concerned.'

'Far better than that, Mr Kendal, she's a fine and decent woman herself,' said Florence. 'Now, I'll wish you good morning, but if you have any concerns, your aunts have my telephone number and you can put your worries directly to me. I've nowt to hide.'

'Er, yes, Mrs Stanville. I'm sorry to have offended you.'

'No offence taken, Mr Kendal. Goodbye.' She made a point of looking him in the eye and smiling.

Florence then got in her car, reversed and turned in the drive and drove away, neither hurrying nor looking back.

Well, thought Florence, that was a bit unexpected. She could hardly blame the man for looking out for his aunts, though. He had alluded to some past events when the Kendal sisters' trusting natures had been taken advantage of, and Florence resolved to keep vigilant and mindful of their safety and wellbeing. In the two months since she'd first started reading to them, she had grown to like Beatrice and Jane very much indeed.

She wondered how she had come to meet Matthew Kendal only this morning. Maybe he had finally engineered a meeting to check her out, having heard about her use of the storeroom, to make sure she wasn't abusing his aunts' kindness. She shrugged off the encounter as his dutiful assessment of her worth, which, she hoped, she had passed. She might have done something similar for her mother, she considered, had any stranger entered her life.

At the thought of her mother she felt the familiar cloud of sadness edge into her bright morning. *Oh, dear Mum. Will I ever stop missing you?*

★ ★ ★

What Jane and Beatrice had said about seeing an elderly man with the woman they thought must be Florence's mother had got Florence thinking. There *had* been an old gentleman in their lives, a person whom Florence had almost entirely forgotten about. Then there was her discovery of Tempest House; she was sure that must be where they had lived. Perhaps the house was so big that she seldom came across him — that they lived in separate parts of it — but she thought it was more likely that he liked a quiet life and she had been told not to disturb him. He had died eventually — he must have, though she could remember nothing about that — and then Lily had moved back to Lancashire and found the pretty cottage by the fell, which she lived in — sometimes with Florence, or with Florence and Lucy — for the rest of her life.

Violet had lived in Guisethorpe a long time; maybe she knew something that would help.

'How long ago was this?' asked Violet, looking up from chopping a huge pile of onions when Florence raised the subject one morning while they worked.

'Oh, nearly forty years. It wasn't long after the Great War, and my father and . . . and Rosa . . . had died of the Spanish flu.'

'Rosa?'

'My sister.'

There, she had said it, said her name and their relationship, acknowledged at last the tragic little girl whose presence infused her dreams with an anxiety of loss and a terrible weight of sadness.

Violet set down her knife and looked directly as

219

Florence as if she'd heard the tremor in her voice.

'Your sister's death must have been a big thing for you to cope with when you were so young.'

Florence, too, stopped working. 'I don't know, Violet. Strangely, it seems so now, since I came to live here. It's like the soil of memory has been turned and she's come to the surface when before she was buried deeply. I have dreams about her now that I never had before. I hadn't thought of her for years but . . . oh, I know it sounds daft, but I think there's summat I need to find out about her. Mum was very good at smoothing things over, moving on in life and making the best. She was wonderful in that way: creating a happy time and putting the bad things behind us. Now I wonder if those times really were that happy or whether she just papered over the sadness and it was all . . . a brave front. It's what she wanted, of course, to make everything all right for me, and I was too young to realise the reality was any different. But she . . . I fear she must have been so unhappy, to lose her husband and one of her children. She hardly ever spoke of Rosa, and never of my father. I think she really was trying to forget, but summat she said to me at the end of her life made me think she hadn't forgotten any of it. I reckon the past was with her always, things she'd kept to herself. With the strange dreams I've been having I feel I need to know the truth now.'

'Poor lady. Well, we each have our way of coping and who's to say your mum's way wasn't the one that worked best for her. We've all been taught to put up and shut up — it's what we do — although it's not the same as forgetting.'

'Of course, you're right. But a red-haired woman with a red-haired child of about seven, an old and frail man — I don't suppose any of this means owt to you, does it, Violet?'

'Ah, now, by the time the First War was over I was married to Will and we lived further inland. He worked on a farm and I was a cook at a hospital and then at a big house. I was a bit out of the goings-on in Guisethorpe and I didn't return to live here for several years. I'm sorry, Florence, but I don't think I can help you. If you could remember the name of the old man, you'd have a good place to start from.'

'I've been racking my brains, Violet, but it's long gone from my mind.'

'Well, you never know, you may hear the name mentioned one day and it'll all come back to you. Have you asked Jim?'

'I have, but he and Mildred came to live here some time after that.'

'Don't fret it, love. If it's meant to be, you'll find out eventually.'

'Yes, I expect you're right. I hope so. I'd dearly like to know and mebbe I won't be dreaming such strange dreams quite so often.'

'And what about your dad, Florence? Does he have a part in all this?'

Florence put down the knife she had taken up again and frowned. 'Do you know, Violet, he doesn't. I have no memory of his face now, he isn't in my dreams and, as I say, my mother, though she didn't marry again, never spoke of him.'

'Don't let it trouble you,' Violet replied, tipping a huge pile of onions into a preserving pan. 'Things are as they are now, whatever happened before.'

'Wise words, Violet. And this batch of chutney is exactly where we are now. C'mon, let's see if we can finish it by the end of the morning, and then I've got some of Mavis Farlowe's fruitcake to sustain us through the afternoon . . .'

★ ★ ★

The first Saturday in November and it was pouring with rain in Blackburn. Judy had the heavy old-fashioned radiators blasting out heat in Ruby Slipper.

'No use being mean with the heating,' she said to Lucy. 'Our ladies won't be in a spending mood if they're sitting there shivering. We want it to be nice and cosy.'

'I'm shivering a bit myself, can't think why,' said Lucy. 'It's warm enough in here but I sort of feel cold right through.'

'I'll make us a brew while you sort those boxes, Lucy.

You'll be right as rain with a cuppa inside you.' Judy laughed and grimaced as she glanced out of the window. 'Rain being the operative word.'

They both looked through the shop window at the rain teeming down, splashing up high on the pavement to wet everyone's feet twice.

'I reckon those galoshes will be flying out today,' Judy said, busy in the little kitchen area in the stockroom. 'I'm expecting the first of the Christmas stock on Monday, don't forget. We can get that sorted when you arrive in the afternoon. So much to look forward to,' she grinned. 'Oh, come

222

on, Lucy, love, you've a face like the weather. What's the matter?'

'I just feel a bit grim,' said Lucy in a small voice. 'Like my head's lagging behind my body.'

'Oh dear, I wonder if you're coming down with summat. There's a lot of colds going round — of course — and you do look a bit peaky. See if this cuppa sets you right. And mebbe take a couple of aspirins with it.' She opened up a basic first-aid box and handed Lucy a bottle of aspirin. 'Now, you sit there with your tea and I'll sort those boxes.'

The doorbell announced a customer.

'Too late! I'll leave the boxes and see to the customer; you just sit tight until those aspirins take effect.'

Judy bustled off to greet her customer by name, leaving Lucy slumped on a chair in the stockroom.

She hadn't felt well when she'd got up this morning, but thought she'd rally when she got to the shop and that Judy's cheerfulness would revive her flagging spirits.

Mebbe I'm just suffering from an overdose of Denis's mother, she thought.

Mrs Walden had been round at Lucy and Denis's house a lot lately. In fact, some weeks she spent more time there than at her own home, or so it seemed to Lucy. Since that awful evening when Frank Stanville had turned up, Mrs Walden had been, on the surface, accepting of Lucy's tiredness after work, but Lucy was still wondering why Denis had given his mother a key to the house. Several times, Lucy had returned from work to find her mother-in-law sitting in the armchair. She'd perhaps make Lucy a cup of tea then, and sometimes helped by peeling some vegetables, but she never took the initiative to do anything until Lucy arrived home. Then she ate the food Lucy had cooked and sat around until it was time for Denis to take her home.

She also dominated the conversation so that the old easy way between Lucy and Denis had been, Lucy felt, almost snuffed out over the weeks. Instead the conversation was all about Mrs Walden's ailments, her neighbours, what she wanted Denis to do for her at her house.

She had, however, been very interested in Frank Stanville and had questioned Lucy a few days after she'd sent him packing.

'So he's not your father, then, Lucille?'

'No, Mrs Walden.'

'Then he's your stepfather?'

'I think I told you, he was.'

'He's not married to your mother still?'

'No . . . Shall I find you the evening paper to read?'

'So they're *divorced*?' Mrs Walden had said the word carefully, gravely, as if saying it might give it oxygen and let it loose in the world, to be caught by innocent people, like a disease.

'Yes. He turned out not to be a good husband and so my mother threw him out and eventually they divorced. It was all his fault. That was the end of the matter,' Lucy added firmly. *And I wish you'd stop asking me about him because I don't want to have to tell you to shut up.*

'Goodness me, I knew your mother to be a woman of strong character, Lucille, but couldn't she just put up with him, same as a lot of women-folk have to put up with poor husbands?'

Lucy had become rather heated at this and let rip before she could think better of it. 'No she could not! Why should she? He wasn't good enough for her and when she faced up to how it was, she had to get rid of him.'

'Well, I never!'

Mrs Walden had seemed to be at a loss for words then. If she'd been tempted to ask for details of just what it was that Frank Stanville had done, she'd managed to resist it. Possibly the mutinous look on Lucy's face had warned her off.

Yesterday evening, however, when she'd had time to digest all this and assess the gaps in her information, she'd questioned Lucy again.

As it was a Friday, Lucy had bought some fish on the way home. Unfortunately, she hadn't been expecting to feed Mrs Walden, who had been there the previous evening, and was now facing the embarrassment of how to make two smallish pieces of haddock provide for three people. How could she not have guessed Mrs Walden would be there, sitting in the armchair, waiting to be fed?

'You look tired, Lucille. I'll put the kettle on, shall I?' Mrs Walden heaved herself out of the chair, grumbling under her breath and making a show of holding her back as if it pained her. Possibly she expected Lucy to jump to it and let her continue to sit but, if so, she was disappointed.

'Well then, this is nice,' she said, returning with cups of tea, resuming sitting in the comfy chair while Lucy perched on a dining chair, easing her tired feet. 'I've been wondering about your dad, Lucille love, now your mum's gone to live by herself, poor soul. Only it's such a terrible shame for your mum, her a widow and then her getting married to that Frank Stanville, who turned out to be a bad 'un.'

'No need to worry about Mum, Mrs Walden. She's fine as she is.'

'So what about your dad, love? It must have been awful when he died.'

'Well, not really, because as far as I know he isn't dead yet, Mrs Walden.'

'Oh . . . oh dear. I mean, not oh dear that he isn't dead but . . . what happened? Your mother didn't throw him out as well, did she?'

Her little eyes blinked expectantly in her round face, her mouth slightly open above her double chins. Lucy looked at her and it was all she could do to hide her disgust. She had had enough. She certainly wasn't going to share anything about Ivor Percival with her mother-in-law. Lucy saw his name on film posters occasionally but only his name meant anything to her. Florence had always said he was a selfish man and a poor father, and she herself had always thought of Charles Summers, Florence's second husband, as her real dad. However, knowledge of either was not Mrs Walden's business.

'I don't know, Mrs Walden. You'll have to ask her.' *And when you see her again I bet ten shillings you wouldn't dare because I happen to have noticed that you're terrified of her.*

'Aye, mebbe . . . Now is it fish for tea? Only I thought I smelled fish when you came in . . . '

Now, sitting in the stockroom in Ruby Slipper, Lucy felt she was fighting a losing battle with Denis's mother. The woman was wearing her down.

That was probably why she felt poorly today: her spirits were being eroded by Mrs Walden. Eventually Mrs Walden would move in and she, Lucy, would become her servant, with never a moment's respite from her insatiable curiosity and selfishness.

No, that would not happen. She refused to let it happen. That little house belonged to her and Denis, not his mother. Lucy told herself she had a cold coming on and it was making her feel low; that's why she was feeling overwhelmed by her mother-in-law. She swallowed down two aspirins with a gulp of tea and decided to pull herself together. What would Mum say if she could see her? Something kind but heartening; something to strengthen her backbone. Mum would not be at the beck and call of anyone in her own home. And nor would Lucy.

Lucy had tried to be discreet in her letters to her mother about the burden of Mrs Walden's visits, because she didn't want anything too obvious being said in Florence's replies, which Lucy couldn't be quite sure Mrs Walden didn't read occasionally, and which she'd lately taken to putting away safely out of sight. But she really could do with some advice and reassur-ance. Florence was a great one for dealing with difficulties head on but Lucy felt she needed more than just courage and force of character to overcome her mother-in-law or a war of attrition could well break out and spoil things between herself and Denis. Oh dear, it was all so difficult . . .

C'mon now, Lucy. Stop being so wet.

She stood up, straightened her skirt and pasted a smile on her wan face. There were customers to serve and she would not let Judy down.

By lunchtime, when the shop closed on a Saturday, Judy had sold a lot of rain hats and umbrellas and a few pairs of galoshes and shoes. The rain was still hammering against the shop window and flowing like a river in the gutter.

'Well done, Lucy. I can tell you've been struggling, so thank you for the big effort. Now you've got until Monday early afternoon to get that cold better. You go and get yourself a hot-water bottle, and ask Denis to make you a hot toddy. That and an early night will soon get you back on your feet,' said Judy.

Lucy nodded dumbly. Unusually for a Saturday Denis was working, putting in extra hours to finish a job, and he was unlikely to be in when she got home. She'd felt a little better at first after she'd taken the aspirins, but now she felt worse than ever. She looked out at the rain, at the grey sky, the grubby pavement, the shoppers hurrying by in dull, shapeless coats with black umbrellas. It would be easier not to go home at all, but just to stay here, lie down on one of the rows of seats near the radiator and sleep and sleep.

'You got your umbrella, Lucy?'

'Yes . . . ' She looked round for it and found it in the rack by the shop door, barely dry from this morning. 'Yes, thanks, Judy. I'll be all right once I get home.'

'Off you go then. Take care, Lucy. I'll see you on Monday.'

Judy let Lucy out into the rain and locked the shop door behind her. She had her office work to do now and wouldn't be going home until much later.

Lucy walked home miserably, her mackintosh flapping open so her skirt became wet, her shoes filling with water. She almost stepped into the road in front of a bus, her view obstructed by her umbrella, and a man who was passing pulled her back by the arm.

'Careful, love.'

'Oh! Thank you . . . Thanks. So silly . . . ' She stumbled on, unable to gather the strength to hurry, and eventually made it home, completely soaked.

When she opened the door of her little house, the first thing she saw was a short wide raincoat dripping from a peg in the narrow hallway and a pair of small Wellingtons. Her heart sank: Mrs Walden.

Lucy peered round the sitting-room door and, sure enough, there was Denis's mother, asleep in the comfy chair. Lucy was tempted just to go upstairs and lie down, but she wanted to use the lavatory and also dry her hair. Then she'd take Judy's advice and fill a hot-water bottle to take up with her. There was unlikely to be a hot toddy later, though.

'Ah, there you are, Lucille.' Mrs Walden opened her eyes. 'Miserable weather. I got soaked coming over even though I was wearing my mac. Put the kettle on, would you, love, and I've brought some custard creams to have with a cup of tea.'

'I'm sorry, Mrs Walden, I feel awful. I need to lie down.'

Mrs Walden looked properly at Lucy. 'You do look a bit pale. I'm sure it's nothing that a cup of tea won't sort, though.' She looked at Lucy expectantly but Lucy, suddenly dizzy, sank to the floor, dripping rainwater from her hair and shivering. 'Whatever's the matter? You're not ill, are you?' Mrs Walden stood up and retreated a step towards the door. 'It's not catching, is it?'

Lucy was beyond caring. All she wanted was to be left alone. 'Just go away,' she whispered. 'Go and leave me to die.'

★ ★ ★

'It's flu, the doctor says,' Denis told his mother. 'He says Lucy's very run down and that's why she's got it bad. He's prescribed some iron tablets and she's to take aspirins and stay in bed, drink lots of honey and lemon to ease her throat, and wait it out until she's feeling better. I've refilled her hot-water bottle and taken her up another drink.'

'Oh dear. Her being in bed is rather a nuisance, with you being so busy, working late most days, even doing extra today.'

'Mebbe I've worked too many long days, Mum. I should have been here instead, paying her a bit more attention, and then I might have seen she was getting ill.'

'She'll be all right now the doctor's seen her,' said Mrs Walden. 'You'll need to keep working if you've got the work, you and Tim. And you can't leave him unsupervised.'

'Course not. Luckily it's Sunday tomorrow and I'm at home. Mebbe Lucy will be better by Monday.'

'I doubt it,' said his mother dolefully. 'Not if it's flu. But, as you know, I've been coming over a few times recently to help her after work — why don't I stay here until she's feeling better and then she won't have to do owt? I can stay in your little spare room — I don't need luxury at my age — and be here to do your breakfast of a morning and cook a bit in the evening?'

'Oh, Mum, that'd be grand,' said Denis. 'And mebbe you could take up a warm drink for Lucy, refill her hot-water bottle and owt else she needs? I'd be that grateful, knowing she was being cared for while I'm out at work.'

'Aye, lad, I'll manage that, I expect. Now, shall I cook us summat for tea and then you take me home in the van to collect my things?'

'Thanks, Mum. I'm starving. Lucy wasn't hungry when I left her with the doctor earlier so I doubt she'll want owt.'

'Which is lucky because I've had a look in the pantry and she's not got much in.'

'I expect she just forgot, what with feeling poorly. Still, if we're all right for today we can worry about that later. Thanks, Mum. I don't know what I'd do without you.'

He went upstairs to see Lucy and tell her the good news that his mother was coming to stay.

12

Florence had given Carmen the day off. She was happy to employ the girl on a more come-and-go basis than Violet, who had quickly become essential to the business. The small kitchen at the cottage meant there was little space for three people. Carmen had mentioned that her great-grandmother had bought a lot of bulbs, which needed planting now, so she was at home gardening and keeping an eye on her great-grandma.

'It's an arrangement that suits all of us,' said Violet, stirring a pan of gently bubbling vinegar and spices. 'I'm so pleased you're easy about Carmen's days here. I think my mum was a bit lonely when Carmen and I were at the café. I used to be worried about her and it's nicer for all of us now.'

'Yes, I understand. I was always pleased to be around my mother as she got older, just to be sure she was all right. I didn't hesitate to go back to live with her when I threw out Frank Stanville and sold the house in Blackburn, and I know Lucy loved living at her grandma's, too. It was one good thing that came out of the end of my marriage to Frank. The other good thing was getting rid of Frank, of course.'

Florence had told Violet about her brief marriage to Frank, and Violet had thought Florence very unlucky after she'd had such a disastrous end to her first short marriage.

'And didn't you go back to your mum with

baby Lucy earlier, when you divorced Ivor Percival, him that we met on the beach that day?'

'Yes, and never for a moment did she suggest we couldn't live with her for ever. Mebbe I should have stayed.' Florence smiled. 'For a time we were a household a bit like yours, Violet — three generations under one roof — and it worked very nicely, but then I started wanting new horizons again.'

'So what happened, love? I thought you said your next husband was wonderful. Don't tell me it ended badly again?'

'No, Violet. I'm afraid it was me who was bad the next time, though Charlie, my husband, never knew what I'd done. I'll tell you how it started . . . '

★ ★ ★

1935

Charles Summers was a writer in his sixties. He penned detective novels, and short stories that appeared in magazines, under the pseudonym Desmond Dashwood. The books were popular with train commuters, elderly people, and even teenage children; anyone, in fact, who had a little spare time to enjoy a light, undemanding read. Charles had lived in Blackburn, or nearby, most of his life, and his fiction was always set in his beloved Lancashire. By 1935 he was living in Clitheroe, where the air was cleaner than in Blackburn, and suited him better now he had the income to exercise the choice, though he never forgot his roots.

After he had advertised in the *Northern Daily Telegraph* for a secretary, Florence applied for the

233

job. She had no references as to her typing speed, and her only real work experience, apart from being a general help in a village shop, had been as a house model in Wilding's of Southport a few years previously, but she made sure her letter of application was neatly written on good-quality stationery, and this secured her an interview at his house, from which he worked.

When Florence turned up she was quite a surprise to Charles. He had expected her to be older, yet she was only twenty-three, and with her bright hair, her height and her poise, she was striking. With her cleverness and her sense of humour she was good company.

He told her this a few months later when he had got to know her better.

Florence had read several Desmond Dashwood novels — she and Lily would swap them and discuss the plots and characters — so although the advertisement had said only that the job was 'secretary to a writer', she was, quite by chance, well prepared, enthusiastic and with good background knowledge. Her other preparation was down to clear thinking and good sense. In the few years since she and Lucy had left Ivor Percival and gone to live with Lily, Florence had thought she ought to learn to type because at least then she'd always have a job, should she want one, or in the unlikely event that she should need one. The divorce settlement Lawrence Hancock had negotiated for her was extremely generous. Lily and Florence lived modestly; they weren't born to showiness and materialism and had never wanted it, but still, Florence needed something to do in her life besides bring up her daughter. She'd bought herself a typewriter and a typing manual and learned to type fast and accurately in just a few weeks. It was, she told Lily, a skill that anyone could do if they practised; it was just a case of concentrating and putting in the hours: being organised. Teaching herself rather than going to a college to learn had given her the advantage of being able to practise — whenever she could — around bringing up Lucy, to whom she was devoted. It was time to test her new skills, and the job with Mr Charles Summers, a short car drive from her mother's cottage near Longridge Fell, was her first attempt to find secretarial work. Learning to drive had been another of the ways Florence had passed her time since her divorce, and the little Austin 7 she had bought to take herself and her mother and daughter around felt like a big and extravagant purchase. Now it enabled her to get to her job interview.

Florence easily passed the tests Charles had devised to see how proficient she was at typing. He wrote in longhand, with a fountain pen on lined paper, and it was the major part of Florence's job to type exactly what he wrote. It was as simple as that. She was also to help him with answering the many fan letters that were sent to him.

Charles worked very hard, writing for long hours in his study, with the curtains drawn against the dazzling summer light, and Florence typed in a little room just down the corridor, which had once been a boot room. It had a long row of pegs along one wall and a cast-iron umbrella rack by the door, but had been turned over to her desk and typewriter so that the noise of her typing would not disturb Charles's concentration.

Charles was also a fast writer, and his desk drawers were stuffed with piles of short stories and even a couple of novels, ready to meet any deadline, while he was already working several months ahead. All Florence had to do was type up in duplicate the piece he selected to fulfil his commission. He seldom revised old copy he'd chosen from this archive: he knew what his readership wanted and he never disappointed.

Florence thought working for Charles Summers was a dream of a job. The only downside was his sister, Connie, who lived with him and who, although she was in her late fifties, seemed not to have found her place in life. She had no husband, no occupation, no particular talents and no charm, so far as Florence could see. She was, however, extremely bad-tempered and liked to tell Charles what to do. She tried to tell Florence what to do, too, but Florence politely declined to follow Connie's orders and answered only to Charles.

Charles had a daily help called Mrs Vera Mayhew, who lived in Clitheroe and to whom Florence gave a lift home if they were leaving at the same time. Florence and Vera got on very well from the off, and Vera was soon bending Florence's ear about the hard time Connie Summers gave her.

'Honestly, love, that one's got nowt to do with her life, that's her trouble. It's a shame she never married and had half a dozen children, as I did. That'd give her summat to occupy her time with. I have my routine and on Tuesdays it's the kitchen what gets cleaned. The dining room is Wednesdays and the shopping at the market is Thursdays. I don't need Miss Connie Summers to tell me what I should be doing, or that I'm doing it wrong.'

'Is that what she said — that it wasn't right?' asked Florence gently, pulling up outside Vera's home. Charles's home, what Florence had seen of it, was spotlessly clean, and this criticism of Vera's efficiency sounded unfair.

'Eh, I can do nowt right for that one. Just you beware, love. Stand firm or she'll undermine you and you'll come to think your efforts are worth nowt. That's what she did with the last one. Sarah Strong, she was called — nice girl, about your age — but she weren't strong enough, if you get my meaning. In the end she ran off in tears and wouldn't come back. Her father had to come and tell Mr Summers that she'd left. And now you're here in her place. Don't let that Connie drive you away, too, Florence.'

'Thanks for the warning, Vera. No, I have every intention of staying,' Florence said. She waited until she saw Vera had her front door safely open and then drove off with a merry wave goodbye.

At first Connie Summers' bullying manifested itself as minor and rather pathetic attempts to put Florence in her place.

'Mrs Percival, please will you not leave the boot-room door open when you're typing? That noise goes right through my head,' said Connie, who was reading a magazine in the sitting room when Florence passed by the open door.

'Of course, Miss Summers,' said Florence, pulling the sitting-room door quietly shut as she moved on with her pile of papers.

Another day it was: 'Mrs Percival, I'd like you to take my letters to the post this afternoon, please.'

'Certainly, Miss Summers. Do you have them ready?'

'No, I might be a couple of hours yet.'

'Well,' said Florence, 'I'm going at three o'clock to catch the post for Mr Summers. If you leave anything to be posted on the hall table I shall take it with me then.'

'Well, can't you just wait while I finish?' The woman sounded affronted.

'No, I'm taking Mr Summers' letters at three, when I stop work for the day,' Florence said with a charming smile.

'You're very disobliging,' snapped Connie.

'Oh dear, I fear I probably am,' said Florence without a trace of regret.

Another day Connie implied that Florence was a slow worker.

'Is that all you've managed this morning? Heavens, I would hardly have thought you were qualified for the job,' she sneered.

'Wouldn't you?' said Florence, and carried on typing, making it clear her work was nothing to do with Connie.

'I think I'll have to have a word with Charles about your laziness,' Connie said nastily.

'Do,' said Florence, not even looking up. She'd already left a pile of typed pages on the side of Charles's desk that morning but she wasn't going to defend herself to Connie.

If anything was said, Florence heard nothing about it. Charles was delighted with her work and her efficiency.

At the end of every week, Charles and Florence did his correspondence together. He received much fan mail, many of the letters forwarded by his publisher, and he made a point of replying to every one of them.

'Good grief!' said Florence, the first time she had been handed a sackful of letters by the postman. 'How on earth are you to answer all of these?'

'With your help, of course, Florence. They've all taken the trouble to write and I owe each one a proper reply. But I certainly need your help. If we get behind we'll be overwhelmed so it's important to keep up and not risk disappointing kind people.'

'I understand,' said Florence. 'Let's get going . . .'

They smiled at each other. They were already a team.

They sat in the armchairs in Charles's study, side by side, and went through the letters together. Florence soon got the hang of the kind of reply Charles liked to send and she even suggested a line or two that picked up something in the fan's letter and added even more of a personal touch. Some of the fans requested photographs, which Charles said he never sent.

'They would only be disappointed, Florence. I was never a good-looking man and at sixty-four I can see I've not improved with age.'

'You could always send them a photo of Robert Donat instead,' Florence joked.

'Don't be ridiculous.' It was Connie, at the door listening to her brother and his secretary laughing together. 'If they wanted a picture of

Robert Donat they'd write to *him* for one, not Charles.'

'Hello, Connie. We were just having a joke,' said Charles. 'You know, a bit of a laugh?'

"A bit of a laugh' indeed,' said Connie heavily. 'How common you're getting to sound, Charles. I can't think where you get it from.' She looked straight at Florence, who met her eyes and did not look away.

'Can't you?' said Charles, not smiling now. 'Well, you and I were brought up in the same house in Blackburn, so if you don't know I reckon you've forgotten. And I'm blessed if I know what's making you so high and mighty. If I've pulled myself up with hard work and education then I've taken you with me 'cos I don't see hard work or education where I'm looking.' He gave Connie a very hard stare. 'Did you want owt, our lass, or did you just come in to be rude to Florence?'

Connie had no answer to this, of course, and went away looking humiliated.

After that a couple of letters disappeared from Florence's desk, and once, a whole typed short story, ready to send to a magazine, went missing. At first Florence thought she had mislaid them or made some kind of absent-minded mistake. She apologised to Charles and did the work again very quickly, but she knew she wasn't a careless worker and she had her suspicions.

One day Connie was grumbling that Florence's footsteps on the hard floor were resounding throughout the house.

'You're that heavy on those great feet of yours,' she said rudely.

It was true that Florence's heels did tap loudly in the largely silent house. 'I'm sorry to have disturbed you, Miss Summers,' she said. 'I shall do summat about it.'

Connie looked pleased at her victory. It was, Florence had long since realised, her dearest wish in life to score points off people and put them in their place.

The next day Florence brought in a pair of slippers that Lily had chosen for Lucy to give her as a Christmas present. They were red felt, with soft white fur trimming and pompoms on the front like rabbits' tails, which had amused the little girl very much. They were very beautiful and, with their soft soles, totally silent.

How glad of them Florence was when, one day, she padded silently in the lovely slippers into her boot-room office and found Connie Summers grabbing pages out of the typescript Florence had been working on.

'Miss Summers, may I ask what you're doing?' asked Florence, who had been able to get very close to Connie and observe her vandalism before she spoke quite loudly.

Connie leaped in the air — literally, her feet left the ground — and she turned to Florence with guilt written all over her face.

'I was . . . that is, I just . . . It's not your place to question me,' she finally settled on.

'No, and that is not my work really, is it, Miss Summers? It's your brother, Charles's.'

'Don't you mean 'Mr Summers'?' spat Connie. 'You are just his secretary and you'd better know your place.'

241

'Or what, Miss Summers?' asked Florence quietly, looking pointedly at the pages Connie was grasping, taking the exchange back to the essential situation.

'I was just . . . just looking for something and . . .'

'And?'

'Mrs Percival, you are a very annoying woman,' said Connie, slapping the pages down on top of the typescript.

'Oh, yes, I suppose I must be, to you,' said Florence. 'But then I don't work for you, Miss Summers, so it doesn't matter in the slightest, does it? Now, if you've quite finished I have rather a lot to do . . . and I expect you have too,' she added, knowing full well that Connie had nothing to do whatsoever.

Connie sidled towards the door.

'Don't worry, I shan't tell Charles that I saw you trying to steal pages from his typescript,' Florence added. 'Unless I have to.' She raised an eyebrow at Connie, who turned and hurried from the room.

After that Florence asked Charles if he had a key to the boot room. 'I think if we keep a key each, just the two of us, and keep the door locked when I'm not here, then if anyone breaks into the house at least your work will be safe.'

'Quite right, Florence,' Charles said. 'Good thinking. I would hate to have to do all that again.'

'So would I,' said Florence.

★ ★ ★

'I'm glad you got the better of that awful woman, Florence,' said Violet, continuing to stir her pan, her face looking heated in the steam. 'What was wrong with her that she was so unpleasant? It can't be just that she had nothing to do.'

'Well, that was a part of it, but I gather she had been disappointed in her youth. Something to do with her fiancé running off with someone much prettier and, I gather, much nicer. It seems Connie Summers had always been a bit envious, and when Charles got to be successful she sort of rode on his coattails while resenting him for it. She liked to live in the famous author's comfortable home, but at the same time she was jealous of his success. They had, after all, come from the same parents, although I think, being a boy, Charles had advantages of education that were denied Connie. After all, why go to grammar school if you're destined to be a wife and mother? If a family can only afford for one child to stay on at school and be educated while any others have to go out to work at the earliest opportunity, it's always going to be the first clever one, isn't it?'

'I guess you're right. Poor Connie.'

'She could have taken a different view, even learned to type and been Charles's secretary herself, played her part and shared in their joint success, but she preferred to live her life on the verge of a permanent sulk, hard done by, and bullying those she could. It was a sort of power thing: a little amount of power in her little life over the people she regarded as littler than herself.'

'Very sad.'

'Anyway, here I am, bending your ear, Violet,

and I really should be thinking about going to read to the Kendals. I'll take a few of those jars from yesterday with me and bring out the rest of the blackberry jelly to go to Nicolson & Filbert later this week. But thank you for listening.'

'Oh, but you haven't finished,' said Violet. 'You've already told me that you married Charles Summers, but now I'm worried that you had a miserable time at the hands of his sister. Please tell me that awful woman didn't get the upper hand in the end.'

Florence's mouth was twisted in an ironic little smile. 'I'll tell you about it another time, when it's just us two again. It's quite . . . a difficult story and, to be honest, Violet, I haven't ever told anyone, not even Lucy — especially not Lucy — and I'll be glad to get it off my chest.'

'Well, you tell me when you're ready, Florence. And if there's anything I can do to help you, in any way, you know I will.'

'You're a good friend, Violet.'

When Florence set out for the Kendals, she was thinking about Charlie, the love of her life. What a dear, good, kind man he'd been. They had been so happy together . . . in the end.

★   ★   ★

It was late on a Sunday evening and Florence, having gone to bed early, was fast asleep.

Suddenly there was a knocking sound from outside and she was awake in a moment. What was that noise? Had she dreamed it? No, she had no recollection of any part of a dream just now.

244

She listened. There it was again, thumping, as if someone was hammering at the door, and now Scamper, downstairs in her basket in the sitting room, was barking loudly.

Frank Stanville? Surely not. Yet, why not?

In the weeks since Lucy had alerted Florence about Frank's visit to her home and the letter disappearing, Florence had, after fixing the extra bolts to the doors, been especially vigilant at first. With the passing of time, though, she had almost given up thinking about the possibility of his turning up, although she was still careful to bolt the doors. Now she thanked God for that.

There was the loud knocking again and then the doorbell ringing. She had to go down and see who it was; she had to go to Scamper, who was, from the sound of it, now beside the front door, barking her head off.

Florence switched on her bedside light, quickly put back on her clothes from earlier and went to the landing. She wondered about using the torch she kept to hand in case of a power cut, but what was the point of keeping the house in darkness with whoever it was hammering at the door like that? She didn't want this person even thinking about breaking in. No, she decided, the thing to do was to make the maximum amount of show and noise. Certainly Scamper was doing her very best to provide the latter. Florence switched on her bedroom light, the landing light, the light downstairs in the hall on its two-way switch, then went down.

'Scamper, here,' she called loudly. 'Good girl. Mum's here, love. Who is it?' She lowered her voice. 'Shall we take a look? Shush now, Scamper, shush. *Good* girl . . . '

Florence went into the sitting room, not switching on the light there, and carefully lifted a corner of the curtain so she could see the front doorstep. There was a man there, wearing a coat and a hat that shaded his face. She peered out but it was impossible to tell who he was, or even if she might know him. One thing was certain, however: it wasn't Frank Stanville, not unless he'd grown taller in the years since she'd last set eyes on him.

The man banged on the door and rang the bell again, then tilted his head back to try to see through the little fanlight at the top of the door. The light from the hall fell on his face.

Good heavens!

It was Anthony Bird. Florence remembered how easily he'd almost knocked her over and she felt a pang of fear. She needed reinforcements and she thanked God she'd had her telephone installed.

'I know you're in there, Florensh Shtanville,' Anthony Bird shouted, then hammered his fist on the door again. 'Come out and tell me why you stole my workersh.' He sounded full of the kind of bravado and swagger that came out of a bottle.

Right, so now she knew why he was here, the stupid man. Really, this was too bad. What on earth could he hope to achieve, except to wake folk up and make a holy show of himself? It wasn't as if Violet and Carmen were ever going to work for him again. Florence quickly checked the telephone number, listed at the back of the parish magazine, then telephoned Constable Paige, the Guisethorpe policeman, who, she thought, had

246

probably never been called out in his life before. Well, she was giving him something to do at last. She hurriedly explained where she was, that she was alone but for her dog, and that a man she thought was Anthony Bird was shouting in a threatening way on her doorstep.

'Don't open the door to him in case he's dangerous, Mrs Stanville,' advised the policeman. 'I'm on my way now, don't you worry.'

'I *knew* it was you took my workersh,' yelled Anthony, outside the front door, unaware that Florence was listening just four feet from him to his right. 'I just *knew* it. Interfering in my café and trying to take over. Then taking my staff away.' He thumped the front door and rang the bell insistently again. 'Come out and answer for yourself. There's a law against shtealing people's workersh.'

'What's all this noise?'

It was Jim, who had evidently not yet gone to bed. He had his coat on and was holding up a lamp. He was standing at Florence's front gate, which Anthony Bird had left open.

'Mr Bird, isn't it?' said Jim, calmly. 'What are you doing here making a row at this hour?'

Anthony turned. 'Who are you? Where's Florensh Shtanville?'

'Mr Bird, it's Jim Yateman — you know me; been in the café a few times. Now, whatever the matter is, I think you'd better go home until you've sobered up; see things from a more . . . rational perspective.'

'I want to speak to that Florensh Shtanville and I want that . . . that thieving woman to explain to me why she's shtolen . . . stolen my staff from

247

under my very nose.'

'You can't steal people, Mr Bird. You can't make them go — or stay — if they don't want to.' It was Florence, glad of Jim's backing but unable to allow him to fight her battle for her.

Anthony turned to her, fury in his face. 'So you've dared to show yourself,' he snarled. 'You should be ashamed, shtealing people's workersh. You took Violet and whatshername . . . Carmen from me and so I had to close the café. You shtole them and now I'm out of business.'

Jim had come down the path and firmly took Anthony by the arm. 'Come away, Mr Bird. You can't stand here shouting about on a Sunday evening.'

'Why not? I'd have come shooner if I'd known it was her that shtole my cook.' He turned to jab his finger in Florence's direction. 'I shuspected but now I know. People need to know that Florence Stanville is not to be trusted. She shteals people.' His voice grew louder so that he was yelling by the time he'd had his say.

Scamper came out to stand directly in front of Florence, a low growl starting in her throat and growing louder. She bared her teeth and her eyes were fixed on Anthony. She looked as if she was thinking of going for his leg at any moment. Anthony took a step away and Scamper advanced menacingly. Florence pulled her back by her collar.

'Sit, Scamper, *sit.*'

'Call your dog off,' said Anthony, unable to take his eyes off Scamper.

'She's all right, Mr Bird, which is more than

you are, shouting about in that disgraceful way. Scamper won't hurt you unless you're a threat to me. Now I suggest you go home and calm down — '

'I *am* calm. I just need to know why you shtole my shtaff from me. What have you got against me? Why have you come here, to this little place, to deshtroy me?' He dashed his hand clumsily over his eyes, his truculence beginning to evaporate. 'What did I ever do to you to deserve this?'

Florence exchanged looks with Jim over Anthony's shoulder and gave a little shrug. She had no idea where he had got such ideas from. Jim, understanding her, shook his head in reply: *Me neither.*

'Now, then, what's all this, Mr Bird?' It was Constable Paige, wearing his police uniform, including a helmet, and boots that gleamed in the light of Jim's lamp. Impressive, thought Florence. He must have dressed in seconds. Or maybe he wore his uniform all the time, just in case he was ever called out. 'Come along now, sir, and leave the lady in peace.'

'But I need to know why she's deshtroying me,' wailed Anthony.

'You have no business disturbing Mrs Stanville in the night and behaving in a threatening manner — ' began the constable.

'Is that what she told you? That I was threatening her? It'sh her who has reduced me to . . . nothing.' He flung a hand out drunkenly. 'If only she'd threatened me, I could have dealt with that, but she gave me no warning. She has shtuck . . . stuck . . . struck me a fatal blow and I didn't even see it coming.'

249

'She struck you, sir?' Constable Paige looked alarmed and his eyes went questioningly to Florence.

'Well, no, but her actions have defeated me as surely as if she'd physically ashault . . . assaulted me.' Anthony gave a hiccup. He sounded almost tearful now. It was also perfectly obvious to the other three that he'd drunk quite a lot of what smelled like whisky but he was sobering up fast.

There was a short silence while the constable, Jim and Florence all looked at each other, nonplussed.

'Oh, for goodness' sake, let's go inside before we catch our deaths,' Florence said. 'I refuse to stand outside arguing. Constable Paige, I'm grateful for your presence so we can clear up Mr Bird's misunderstanding to everyone's satisfaction. Then we can draw a line under the matter. Jim, thank you for your help, and I'm sorry you've been disturbed on a Sunday evening, but it's late and if you want to go home now, and Constable Paige agrees, that's fine.'

'I'll not go until I've seen Mr Bird has left first, Florence,' said Jim, and followed Florence inside, the policeman escorting Anthony firmly by the arm behind them and Scamper bringing up the rear, giving a naughty little snap at Anthony's heels.

Florence showed them into the sitting room, where she offered Jim an armchair and the others perched on upright chairs. She went to close the front door and then came back in.

'Right, Mr Bird. Let's have it from the beginning,' she said, taking charge. 'The first time I ever saw you was in August, when I stopped at your café and bought a pot of tea. Me and Scamper were at an outside table.'

'That's right. I'd seen you on the beach before that and I recognised you. I wanted to know who you were.'

Florence said nothing. She remembered Anthony crowding her, being a bit of a nuisance so that she'd wished he would go away.

'So Mrs Stanville bought a pot of tea and left?' asked Constable Paige.

'Oh, no, she took over!' said Anthony. 'She came straight into the kitchen as if she owned the place.' He went on to say what had happened when Carmen dropped a large pile of crockery.

'Sounds like you needed the help, lad,' said Jim when he'd finished. 'What did Violet Peasall say afterwards?'

'That she was glad of the help,' said Anthony, in a small voice. 'But *I* wasn't. We were managing all right.'

'Well, you were there when Violet agreed to my helping,' said Florence. 'You could have told me you didn't need me then.'

'Is that so?' asked the constable.

Anthony nodded.

'So why didn't you say so then?'

Anthony looked at his hands. 'I don't know. It seemed easier if you cleared up the mess, as you were offering.'

'And it was, especially easier for you,' said Florence, 'so we're in agreement so far.'

'So what happened next?' asked Constable Paige.

Anthony racked his fuddled brain. 'Oh, yes, the next time she came to the café she — Mrs Stanville — had some tea at the outside table and when she'd finished she put the crockery on a tray and brought it inside, like she worked there, like it was *her* café.'

'And then what happened?'

'That was it. I . . . I told her I didn't want her pretending she worked there and then I couldn't find the bill and she told me what she'd had. Cleared the table and then itemised the bill! Again, it was just like she owned the place. I think she was planning even then on driving me out of business. Maybe she wanted to reopen the place with herself in charge. After all, she has my staff. Stole them, she did.' He voice was getting louder again and he thrust out his jaw in an aggressive way.

'Is this true, Mrs Stanville?'

'It's quite true I cleared the table because Carmen was busy. I asked her and she agreed as she had a lot of clearing up to do and the café was about to close. It was that time we had tea together, Jim, do you remember? And it's true Mr Bird couldn't find the bill.'

'And what did Violet and Carmen Peasall say about that, Mr Bird?' asked Jim. 'I'm sure you made your feelings very clear to them so they must have said something.'

Anthony sighed, his shoulders slumping. 'Violet said she was embarrassed and it was no wonder no one came in the café.'

'It was well known in the village that Bird's Café didn't have many customers and you'd likely have to close before long,' said Jim.

Constable Paige was nodding. 'So the rumours were true weeks ago, Mr Bird?'

'We might have kept going . . .'

'How?' asked Florence.

'We'd have kept going if you hadn't poached my cook and my waitress to work for you.'

'Would you, though?' Florence asked reasonably. 'Did the café close because you hadn't any staff or did it close because you hadn't any customers, Mr Bird? I already knew the answer to that, and when I saw that situation coming I offered jobs to Violet and Carmen because I knew they needed to work, knew they were good workers who would be an asset to my business, whereas they were entirely taken for granted in yours, which was about to go bust anyway.'

'But I needed them! They worked for me!' Anthony said furiously, sounding like a child protesting how unfair everything was.

'And they could have told me if they'd wanted to continue working at the café. But they chose to leave.'

There was a brief silence during which everyone turned to Anthony Bird. He had nothing left to say, though he was looking very cross.

'I'm sorry for you, Mr Bird,' Florence said, 'but I reckon you must face it: the end of Bird's Café was brought about by you, not by me. I merely saved Violet and Carmen from going down with you.'

'Now listen here — ' said Anthony, rising to his feet belligerently.

'No, you listen,' said Jim. 'What Mrs Stanville

253

says is true. It's time you grew up, lad, and took some responsibility. I remember your father and how he ran the café, how he worked so hard to make a success of it, worked every hour he could. He and your mother did without so that you had everything you wanted. Maybe in the end they did you no favours, spoiling you like that, because what they didn't give you was any idea that it doesn't always just fall into your lap; that sometimes you really have to work, and work hard, for what's worth having. Life isn't always easy. And now you know that.'

Anthony looked away angrily.

'Well,' said Constable Paige, 'no doubt Mrs Violet Peasall and Miss Carmen Peasall can give me their version of the events that led to their leaving the café. But it's unlikely I shall need to speak to them. I think this should be the end of the matter now. Mr Bird, I shall escort you safely back to your home and if Mrs Stanville, who is the injured party in this evening's disturbance, agrees, no action will be taken against you. I shall caution you, however, against committing any further breach of the peace. Let us call this a misjudgement brought on by intoxication, and you'll no doubt regret it all in the morning. Mrs Stanville, are you willing that this should be taken no further?'

'I am, provided there is no repeat of this or any other aggression towards me or towards Violet and Carmen Peasall,' said Florence, looking hard at Anthony.

Constable Paige had taken Anthony by the arm, but Anthony shrugged him off. 'I'm going,' he said, 'and I don't need an escort home.' He elbowed his way to the sitting-room door then turned to look at Florence. 'Mrs Stanville, I've learned something this evening and it's a lesson I won't forget.' He stared at her grimly for a moment, then barged his way down the narrow hallway. The front door slammed and there was a brief silence.

'I'll go after him; make sure he goes straight home and doesn't get into any more trouble,' said Constable Paige. 'If you have another unwanted visit from him you just telephone me, Mrs Stanville. Now, I'll show myself out. Good night to you. Good night, Mr Yateman.'

'Good grief, Jim,' said Florence when the constable had left. 'How could that have blown up from nowt?'

'Search me, Florence. The café had been struggling for a long time, it was common knowledge, and if Anthony Bird is pretending otherwise then he's deluding only himself. You've done the right thing by Violet and Carmen. I saw Mrs Peasall in the lane the other morning and she looks years younger already. It's as if a weight has been lifted from her since she came to work with you. And young Carmen has a smile on her face these days, too. She's barely more than a child and she needs her confidence building and a future she can look forward to. You've given her something to do that she's good at and it's made a difference.'

'Oh, I hope you're right, Jim. I did poach Anthony's staff — of course I did — and not entirely to make their lives better, but mine, too. I like Violet and Carmen, I knew I could work with them but

255

I saw also that they would be useful to me.' She laughed. 'Or at least Violet would be. Carmen has turned out to be an unexpected bonus. I'm sorry for Anthony but, as you say, the end of the café was already in sight. From what I've seen he's not one to put in an effort to help himself. I certainly wouldn't want to employ him, even if there was owt for him to do.'

'Good heavens, Florence, you're not running a charity. He's a ne'er-do-well and you should leave him to sink or swim as he chooses, especially after his behaviour this evening. It's time for him to make that choice and you may even have done him a favour. Perhaps this'll be the making of him.'

'Mm, mebbe . . . '

'Now, just to remind you — as if you needed it — this is Guisethorpe and tonight's little drama will be all round the village by breakfast time. I'm going to deny all knowledge of it.'

Florence smiled. 'I might even do the same myself; see if I can get away with that.'

She saw Jim out, Scamper coming to the door to wish him good night, too, and then locked up doubly carefully. But when she went back up to bed she lay awake a long time, thinking of Anthony's parting words: 'I've learned something this evening and it's a lesson I won't forget.'

This, she thought, was probably not the end of the matter.

13

Florence hadn't had a letter from Lucy for a few days. Maybe Lucy was busy, what with the Christmas season approaching and Judy being in such a whirlwind of activity at the shop, always thinking up new ways to entice in the customers. Florence had met Judy on several occasions, not least at Lucy's wedding to Denis, and liked her style, her energy and her cheerful can-do spirit. When she'd decided to move to the seaside Florence had been glad to know that Lucy was happy in her work with such a good employer. Still, if she didn't hear from Lucy soon she'd ring the shop and make sure everything was all right. It was a shame Lucy and Denis hadn't got a telephone, but that wasn't unusual.

When she was walking Scamper or out shopping, some of the bolder and more curious villagers asked Florence about the disturbance at Paradise Cottage the previous Sunday evening, but she batted away their questions by saying she'd put it right out of her mind and hadn't anything interesting to say about it. Florence had, of course, apprised Violet and Carmen of the whole wretched incident, since it concerned them. Violet shook her head sadly and said she was sorry Florence had been troubled by 'that good-for-nothing layabout', and Carmen just said, 'Horrible man,' and left it at that. Anthony Bird was no longer their concern. Florence liked to think he wasn't

257

her concern either, but he had given every impression of having unfinished business with her, which was a slight worry.

However, she had far too much to do to be bothering overly about Anthony Bird. Most days, the kitchen was steamy with boiling pans, condensation running down the windows, and the orders for special Christmas preserves were keeping all three of them busy.

'We really could do with some more space, a proper commercial kitchen like the one at the café,' said Violet one day, moving aside some jars to make room for her chopping board.

'We could,' Florence agreed, 'but there's no chance I could afford to rent the café kitchen. What makes those premises viable is the shop part and I don't want to open a shop.'

'Not even if it was a Florence Lily shop?' asked Carmen, drying more jars and looking for somewhere to put them down.

'No, we'd never be able to make enough to supply an entire shop, Carmen, and I'd have to bear all the costs. We'd be working like navvies and it would take all the fun out of it. And anyway, I don't want a shop or a kitchen below where Anthony Bird lives.'

'No, of course not. But you have to admit, bigger premises would make our lives easier, and you'd be able to reclaim your home from the smell of pickling.'

'Aye, I'd be glad of that, true enough,' said Florence. 'I'll have a proper look at what's on the market when Christmas is over.'

Lucy was feeling terrible. She lay in bed shivering, pulling the covers up to her chin and clutching her hot-water bottle. Then, a few minutes later, she would be hot and sweaty, weakly kicking away the blankets and pushing the bottle over the side of the bed, where she could reach it easily when she grew cold again. She lost all track of the days. Going to the shop every morning, working cheerfully alongside Judy, seemed a lovely distant dream compared to the nightmare of rumpled, stale sheets, her raw throat, the barking cough that hurt her chest, and the miserable feeling that everyone had abandoned her.

She was so restless and coughed so loudly during the night that Denis had taken to sleeping downstairs in the comfy chair. Then he left early in the morning without coming to say goodbye because, he said, he didn't want to wake her, so she saw him for only a few minutes a day in the evening. Her sole 'companion' in the meantime was Mrs Walden, although Lucy might have thought 'gaoler' was more appropriate.

Denis's mother was now happily accommodated in Denis and Lucy's spare room. Lucy sometimes heard her going downstairs in the morning, cooking Denis's breakfast, calling goodbye to him and moving around, putting on the wireless . . . If she remembered to bring Lucy a cup of tea eventually, it was stewed and only just warm, obviously the dregs of her own pot of tea. If Lucy was asleep she'd find the tea later, cold on her bedside cabinet. There was seldom any food left with it.

Often Mrs Walden didn't come up to see if Lucy needed anything for hours, and Lucy's throat was too sore for her to call out that she'd like a drink of water to wash down her aspirins. Once Lucy got up to go down to the bathroom and on the way back to bed she tripped on the stairs, fell heavily against one of the higher steps and bruised her face. She'd heard Mrs Walden going out what seemed like hours before, and she lay there, cold and exhausted, wanting Denis to rescue her. She wanted his strong arms to help lift her up and tuck her safely back in bed, replenish her hot-water bottle and make her a soothing honey and lemon drink.

She lay on the stairs for a while, hoping for Denis but realistically expecting Mrs Walden to come back from wherever it was she'd gone. But no one came. Eventually Lucy crawled back to bed unaided. It was all she could do to manage that, and she collapsed into her bed shivering and weeping. She wanted Denis to come home but now, even more than him, she wanted her own mother.

Her face hurt where she'd hit the step but no one even noticed her bruised cheekbone, or if they did they didn't say anything about it. Maybe she now looked so awful that a bruise wasn't even noticeable, she thought.

One afternoon she heard a knock on the door. Mrs Walden answered it and Lucy could hear voices. Then the door was firmly closed and whoever it was had clearly gone away. Lucy was too weak to get out of bed and go to the window to see.

Later, Mrs Walden appeared with a bottle of cough mixture.

'Your cough is fairly going through my head, young woman,' she said. 'Here, get some of this down you and perhaps we can all get some peace.' She left the bottle, which had its metal cap still sealed, and a teaspoon.

'Who was that who came to the door?' asked Lucy, huskily.

'Oh, just some girl to see you. Said her name was Betty. I told her you were too ill for visitors and not to come again.'

Tears sprang to Lucy's eyes. Betty was her friend with whom she had lived for a few months before she married Denis. She was a cheery sort, full of funny stories, just the kind of tonic Lucy needed to lift her spirits. She certainly got no entertainment from Mrs Walden.

'I wish you'd let her in,' said Lucy sorrowfully.

'Oh, don't start your maundering on,' snapped Mrs Walden. 'You're that spoiled, you think only of what you want. Be grateful I've got you your medicine and shut up your moaning.'

She stomped out and Lucy was left with her disappointment. How she'd have loved to have seen Betty, even for a minute or two. She wept a little but that made her sore throat worse, which exacerbated her cough. She leaned over to get the cough medicine but the new bottle cap was sealed to the neck and she was too weak to break it open.

She lay back in her rumpled bed, with her cold hot-water bottle and her inaccessible medicine and cried herself to sleep.

Violet was eager to hear the next part of Florence's story of how she came to marry Charlie Summers. Violet had heard of Desmond Dashwood, the name under which Charlie wrote, and was very impressed that Florence had had two fairly well-known husbands.

'A film director and a writer, Florence. You do seem to move on the most interesting circles,' she said one morning when Carmen was at home with her great-grandmother again and the two women could talk over the quiet industry of stirring simmering pans.

'Ha, Violet, have I not already told you that the famous film director was a very ordinary adulterer? There's nothing grand about betrayal. He was every bit as grubby a character as Frank Stanville — and no one would be impressed by *him*. I have to admit, I think I must have lost my marbles when I married Frank.'

'Or maybe you were just lonely, love,' said Violet, gently. 'I know when I was widowed I found it hard to think I'd face the rest of my life without the love and companionship of a good man. Don't blame yourself for your mistake over Frank Stanville. But tell me about Charlie. I'd like to hear more about the wonderful man you fell in love with. You remember, you told me you were his secretary and that he had a very difficult sister who wanted to keep everyone else out of his life.'

'That's exactly right, Violet. I was puzzled at first why she should do anything to hurt Charlie, like vandalising his work. Of course, it was hurting me as I'd have to do it again, which I took to be her motive, but it was also hindering Charlie, whose work supported them both. Mebbe she was angry with him for employing me and because we got on well. I think she was a bit mad, but in the end it was me, I'm afraid, that was insane.'

'I can't believe that, Florence. She must have driven you to it, whatever you did, if you were.'

'Well, I'll tell you what happened . . .'

★ ★ ★

1936

Florence soon came to realise what a good, kind man Charlie Summers was. He had always been good-humoured and friendly but, after she'd been working for him for a few months, he began to try to make her job more fun by proposing little treats as respite from sitting at her typewriter, such as visits to a teashop, or a short walk around the town for a change of scene, or, if they were going through the letters, sitting outside on the lawn in the sun if the weather was warm. Then he started asking Florence if she'd like to accompany him to a concert in the evening, or to some local event if she was free at the weekend, which she was very pleased to do, sometimes bringing Lucy with her. Her liking of Charlie was growing into love and she took every opportunity to be in his company. It seemed to Florence that Charlie had acquired the entire share of thoughtfulness and good temper of both Summers siblings, while Connie had merely been dealt the hand of meanness of spirit, envy and ill temper.

Eventually Charlie told Florence he was in love with her and wanted to marry her. He had been married before, in his twenties, but his young wife had died of TB and he'd never met anyone else he'd wanted to make a life with. Until now.

'I wonder if I'm being ridiculous at my age, looking to marry again? I've made a life already, but it could be so much happier, Florence, with you and Lucille in it.'

Florence had already taken Charlie to meet Lily at her cottage, and both Lucy and her grandmother were charmed by him. Lily was even a little star-struck at first. She'd never met a real-life author before, she said later, and was amazed he was 'quite an ordinary sort of fella, not at all stuck up'.

'Just someone who works at one sort of job, Mum,' said Florence. 'He's good at what he does because he makes an effort to do it well; he's organised.'

'Oh, you and being organised,' laughed Lily. 'But, from what you say, I doubt you'll organise that sister of his. She sounds a right tartar.'

'She's not a kind person, Mum, and I wish . . . I just wish she wasn't there. I keep expecting her to spring out from behind a door and confront me with some invented failing.'

'Jealous,' said Lily tersely. 'Not just of a beautiful younger woman but of anyone in her brother's life. She wants him all to herself, I reckon.'

'I'll not be defeated by her, Mum,' said Florence. 'Vera Mayhew said she bullied the previous secretary out of the job, but I'm determined she's met her match.'

'Well, just you be careful, love,' Lily warned. 'That kind can play dirty.'

Florence had to consider carefully whether she could live with Connie as well as Charlie. After all, Charlie's house was also Connie's home and she had no other. Florence didn't want to give an ultimatum — 'Either Connie goes or I won't marry you' — but she didn't fancy her married life having constant behind-the-scenes skirmishes with her sister-in-law through no fault of her own.

'Charlie, of course I want to marry you, but I know Connie wouldn't like it if we were married. She's lived with you for many years and I fear she'd feel . . . ousted from her position as mistress of the house.'

'I've seen how Connie behaves towards you, Florence, and I don't like it. I've raised the subject of her rudeness and her temper before now and it pains me that she seems not to have taken the slightest notice. I'm going to have to make it clear, if I haven't already done so, that if she wishes to live any longer under my roof she must mend her ways. I mean it, too. She behaves herself or she goes: her choice.'

'Thank you, Charlie. I wish Connie would be friendlier. I can't seem to get the right side of her and I'd very much like to be welcomed as your wife by your only sister.'

'I know, Florence. You've done nowt wrong. But can anyone get the right side of her when she's that side out all the time?' said Charles, shaking his head sadly. 'I'm tired of her snapping her head off at everyone and everything, awkward atmospheres if I invite folk here. I'm starting to believe she wouldn't be satisfied unless I never left the house, never met my friends, and employed neither you nor Mrs Mayhew.'

'Mebbe when you've had another word she'll think again,' said Florence, but she didn't hold out much hope. On the other hand, why should the path to her future happiness be decided by Connie Summers?

Florence chose to do as she wanted despite the presence of Connie in her new husband's house and she married Charlie in the summer of that year. They enjoyed a honeymoon in Cornwall, where Charlie said he'd never been happier. He'd also drafted the plots of his next two novels. Florence must be his muse as well as his wife.

'I'm not sure how to take that, Charlie,' she said with a smile. 'I'm glad you feel inspired but am I really the muse for a couple of murder mysteries?'

When they arrived back home to the house in Clitheroe, Connie was in bed with what she described as a migraine, and she stayed there for several days. In the meantime, Florence went to collect Lucy from Lily's home to bring her to her new home, with cheerful promises to visit Grandma often.

Florence and Charlie settled into a new routine as parents as well as newlyweds and colleagues, setting up a swing in the garden for Lucy to play on and making one of the spare rooms downstairs into a playroom. They let Lucy play largely by herself in the mornings, when they were working, although sometimes Mrs Mayhew, with her vast experience of motherhood, let the little girl 'help' with baking. Then in the afternoons Florence would take her daughter for a walk, play with her in the garden or the playroom, and then go back to work in the early evening to catch up.

'Do you think this is working, Charlie?' Florence asked. 'I don't have time to do as much as I used to, though I think I'm keeping up fairly well. But if I'm getting behind and you want to get a new secretary, I think you'd better sack me now, not keep me on out of loyalty.'

Charlie laughed long and hard. 'I only worked so hard all these years because I had nowt else in my life, Flo,' he said. 'I didn't need to keep so busy. I can see now that it's a habit and it's time for me to break it. My desk drawers are full of stories and novels I've long since finished. I think we should step back a bit from the pressure of work and enjoy having little Lucy with us before she goes to school. How about we begin tomorrow *not* doing any work and just enjoy ourselves? The only thing we really must do is keep up with the fan mail. If folk are kind enough to write, then they deserve a prompt reply.'

Connie recovered from her migraine sufficiently to leave her room, but she just lay on the sofa downstairs with the curtains drawn, so everyone felt they had to tiptoe around. Mrs Mayhew found this particularly infuriating because she wanted to get on with the housework, which she couldn't do silently.

'Mummy, is that lady very ill?' asked Lucy, round-eyed with anxiety after two days of this. 'Is she going to die?'

'I doubt it,' said Florence. 'Don't worry about her, love. Just don't go disturbing her, that's all. She'll get better soon.'

That afternoon Charlie and Florence decided to take Lucy for a walk up to the castle. They had gone only as far as the end of the road when Charlie suddenly said he'd left his wallet at home; he'd need some money if Lucy was to have an ice cream.

'It's all right, love. I've got my purse,' said Florence.

'No, I'll nip home now. I won't be more than three minutes,' he insisted, and set off back while Florence waited and Lucy skipped on the spot excitedly at the mention of ice cream.

Later — much later, long after it mattered — he told Florence exactly what had happened and the details did not surprise her.

Charlie had opened the front door very quietly and, hearing music and the sound of activity in the kitchen, tiptoed along to see. There was Connie, busily making herself a pot of tea and a sandwich, having insisted at lunchtime that she felt too ill to face any food, while the wireless was on in the sitting room, where she had claimed that her head was splitting.

'I'm delighted to see you've recovered at last, Connie,' said Charlie, from the doorway. 'And so suddenly in the end.'

Connie's face was an almost comical picture of guilt mixed with anger at being caught out.

'I told you we're going to the castle. Come with us, if you like,' he said, ignoring her reaction. 'Florence and Lucy would like that.' It was a blatant lie, but a kind one to Connie.

'I bet they wouldn't,' said Connie. 'Why would they? They don't want me here. *You* don't want me here. I'm superfluous, like leftovers.'

'Rubbish, Connie. If you'd make yourself pleasant you could be a good friend to Florence and a much-loved aunt to little Lucy.'

'Why should I? These people have been foisted on me. I didn't choose to have them in the house. They're nowt to do with me.'

'But it's my house, Connie, and *these people* are both very much the ones I have chosen to live here. Just remember what I said to you before Florence and I were married. You put one foot out of line and you're no longer welcome here.'

When Charlie rejoined Florence and Lucy, his wallet in his pocket, as it had been all along and he looked rather fierce.

'Is summat wrong, love?' asked Florence in a low voice.

'Just a little word with Connie, Flo. Nowt more than that.'

For a while there was a kind of truce. Connie went about at a constant simmer of resentment, but it didn't boil over into mean-minded acts of sabotage or open argument, and Florence did her best to avoid her sister-in-law, which wasn't too difficult as they didn't live under each other's feet, and to concentrate on her husband and daughter.

At the end of summer, Lucy had her fourth birthday and Charlie, with Florence's approval, bought her a kitten. Much was made of the importance of the little girl taking responsibility to entertain the pet and remember to put out food and water, even though Florence knew it would be she who would be doing this in reality. Then there was the big event of a trip to a nearby farm where there was a litter of kittens for sale, and the ritual of Lucy being allowed to hold each one and then make her choice.

'I want them all, Mummy,' she whispered, over-awed at the knowledge that she must choose only one.

'I know you do, Lucy, but you know what we agreed.'

In the end she chose a very pretty black-and-white kitten, which the farmer's daughter told her was a girl.

Florence drove them home with the kitten in a cardboard box and Lucy kicking her legs in excitement and calling out possible names as she thought of them.

Lily was invited to come to a birthday tea party at which the kitten, now named Mitten, was the centre of attention.

As Florence was bringing in the tea tray from the kitchen, she could see Connie in the corridor, standing at the sitting-room door, a look of pure hatred on her face. She moved away when she heard Florence approaching. At the door Florence paused and saw what Connie must have seen: Lily and Lucy sitting close together on the sofa, Mitten asleep on Lily's lap while Lucy very gently stroked her baby-soft fur. Florence felt a rush of love for her mother and daughter and a flutter of alarm at Connie's reaction. It was clear, if clarity were even needed, that Connie was still brimming with resentment that other people were sharing her brother's life.

Charlie came in with his Brownie box camera and Florence stood behind her mother and daughter while he photographed them.

'Did you get Mitten in the photograph, Daddy?' asked Lucy.

'I got in all my best girls, Lucy,' said Charlie.

It seemed as if the novelty of having a little pet of her very own would never wear off for Lucy. She and Mitten played endlessly in the playroom, and that became the little cat's home. Florence declared that Mitten should not be allowed to wander just anywhere in the house and the playroom door was to be kept closed for the time being.

'I value your nice curtains too much, Charlie,' she said. 'Those sharp little claws could rip them to shreds. Lucy is old enough to learn there are rules, even for kittens.'

One morning Mitten could not be found. Lucy had been playing with her in the playroom and had gone to have the drink and biscuit that Mrs Mayhew always made ready mid-morning. When she got back, the playroom door was open and the kitten gone.

'Mummy, I'm *sure* I closed the door. I did, I *did*,' she howled.

Everyone joined the hunt for the missing kitten. Even Connie made a show of looking, although she had never taken an interest.

Eventually it was clear that Mitten must somehow have left the house, and the search was repeated in the garden and then up and down the road. Charlie knocked on doors and asked the neighbours to keep a lookout, while Lucy flung herself on her bed and cried hysterically, Florence stroking her hair and trying to keep her own tears at bay.

The following day, when there was still no sign of Mitten, the house was like a place of mourning. Only Connie was unaffected.

'I expect Lucille just let the silly creature out by mistake,' she said. 'She's far too young to take responsibility for a pet of her own anyway. I don't know what you thought you were doing buying it for her,' she chastised Charlie.

Later that day, as Connie reached up to open the top latch on the French doors, Florence saw for a few seconds a narrow row of sharp scratches on her right forearm as her sleeve shifted. She gave a gasp of shock and jumped to her feet.

'What's matter with you now?' asked Connie, her face contorted in a sneer.

Keep calm, Flo . . . keep calm . . .

Florence struggled to swallow down her fury and address Connie as if she were concerned for her welfare. She must not jump to conclusions.

'Connie, what have you done to your arm?' She could hear her voice trembling; she sounded far from casual.

'My arm? Nowt. Why do you ask?' said Connie, holding out her left arm and pushing up her sleeve to reveal unblemished skin on her forearm.

To Florence that was proof enough that Connie knew exactly what she was talking about. 'Your right arm, Connie. But same place. As you know full well.'

'What can you mean?' said Connie, taking a step away. 'Silly girl, there's nothing the matter with me.'

'Yes there is,' said Florence, grabbing Connie's right arm, holding it aloft and pushing her sleeve up to reveal the scratches. 'There's an awful lot the matter with you, Connie Summers. And I don't just mean that the kitten scratched you when you were getting rid of her, however you did that. I mean there's summat wrong in your head. You vile creature, I can't believe you could be so cruel, not just to Mitten but to Lucy.'

'It's you who's soft in the head, Florence Percival.

Making daft accusations — '

'I'll give you daft accusations,' snarled Florence. 'I think you've murdered Lucy's kitten, just out of spite. These scratches are recent and they're obviously made by tiny claws.'

'You're talking rubbish. 'Murdered', indeed. You're as hysterical as your daughter. Why don't you go and lie down until you've regained some sense?'

'I'm going nowhere, Connie, until you tell me how you came by these cat scratches.'

'I don't have to answer to you.'

'No, you don't *have* to, but why wouldn't you unless you have summat to hide?'

'Oh, go away, you silly girl. You don't frighten me.'

'Well, I should,' said Florence, burning her boats, 'because I only have to say the word and you're out on your ear. And I shall. I've had enough. I can't believe you would start on a little girl and her kitten with your bullying.'

'What's all this?' said Charlie, standing in the

273

doorway. 'Florence, Connie, please!'

'Look,' said Florence, and she grabbed Connie's arm again and, though Connie struggled, held on to her wrist and yanked up her dress sleeve. 'Cat scratches. Recent ones. She's got rid of poor little Mitten and broken my Lucy's heart.'

Charlie came over to see, looking very severe. 'Florence, be calm. Let Connie explain. She's a right to answer.'

'But she won't. She's refused to answer me and I know what she's done, I just *know* it.'

'Florence! Please, darling. Let Connie speak. Connie, please tell us how you came by these scratches.'

'They were made by that cat, yesterday morning, early. It was in that room that's now the playroom, drinking its milk, and I tried to pick it up but it's an ill-tempered thing and it hissed at me and scratched my arm. That's all that happened.'

'Why didn't you mention it at the time?' asked Charlie.

'Because there was nowt to say that mattered,' said Connie. 'Contrary to what you might think, there's more going on in life than that blessed cat.'

Florence was looking daggers at Connie. It was possible that she had received the scratches if she'd tried to pick up the kitten, but Florence just didn't believe the story. She'd never seen Connie pick up Mitten, or even show any interest in her. Why should Connie even have gone to the play-room when she disliked both Lucy and the kitten? She did, however, have a right to go there if she wanted. Florence could see Charlie was wavering too. But they had no evidence Connie's story

274

wasn't true.

'You'd better be telling the truth, Connie,' said Charlie heavily. 'Not only would it be the most disgusting act of cruelty against an innocent creature and little Lucy, but I can't live any longer with this kind of unpleasantness between you and Florence.'

'It's her — '

'No! It's you. This is your last chance, Connie. Any more — anything at all — and you're out. I'll find you lodgings somewhere, mebbe not round here, and you can clear off.'

Connie didn't say anything, but she didn't look concerned either. Charles had given her a last chance before and now she had another. She'd never be forced to leave.

As Florence turned to leave the room she saw Connie's look of triumph and she knew, whatever anyone said, that Connie was there to stay.

★ ★ ★

'Poor little Lucy,' said Violet. 'Do you think that Connie woman really did get rid of the kitten? Did you find out for sure in the end?'

'No, I never found any proof, but I still think it was her,' said Florence.

There was the rattle of the letterbox and Florence rinsed her hands and went to see what had been delivered.

On the mat was a letter, the envelope addressed in handwriting she didn't recognise. She went into the sitting room and slit the envelope and extracted a single sheet. It was from Denis and her eyes flew over the page in a panic to see why Lucy hadn't written.

Dear Florence,

I'm writing cos our Lucy isn't well and I don't want you to wonder why she hasn't written to you. The doctor says she's got flu. She's been in bed for days and so I think maybe she's getting a bit better. My mum is looking after her cos I have to go to work. I have been to the shoe shop to tell Judy not to expect Lucy back soon. Lucy said I was not to worry you but I thought you should know.

With best wishes from
Denis

Flu! Oh dear God, it was flu that killed Dad and Rosa.

But that was a terrible disease, the Spanish flu, far worse than any flu usually is. Lots of people have flu and aren't very poorly. It needn't be fatal . . .

These thoughts raced through Florence's mind.

Florence paced the sitting room, holding the letter and then stopping to reread it, to look for hidden messages in the simple sentences. 'I think maybe she's getting a bit better' only addressed the possibility; it wasn't a fact. But 'my mum is looking after her' wasn't good news at all. Florence had not taken to Mrs Walden, and she knew Lucy didn't like her either, although she was so starry-eyed about Denis that she had thought that didn't matter. The poor girl, in bed, feeling her very worst, and having to rely on a woman she disliked to look after her. Florence suspected Mrs

276

Walden wasn't someone who'd put herself out for anyone else if it didn't suit her, but on the other hand she had raised a child of her own. She surely couldn't be entirely selfish.

It had been good of Denis to go to tell Judy that her assistant was ill, but 'not to expect Lucy back soon' might be a subtle way of saying she was gravely ill. No, that was silly: Denis wasn't subtle that way, and he'd have said if Lucy was in danger. But then: 'Lucy said I was not to worry you' — did that mean that there was something to worry about?

'Florence?' It was Violet.

'In here, Violet. Come on in. I've had a letter from my son-in-law. My daughter, Lucille, has flu.'

'I'm sorry to hear that. I hope she's feeling better soon,' said Violet. Then she looked closely at Florence. 'What is it? She's got it badly?'

'I don't know, Violet. Thing is, I think I told you about my father and . . . and my sister . . . ' Florence heard her voice shaking.

'And now your daughter has flu and you're fearful for her,' said Violet.

'Yes. Here, Violet, please read Denis's letter and tell me what you think. Is she terribly ill?'

Florence handed over the letter.

Violet read it in seconds and then handed it back to Florence. 'Nice of him to write, otherwise you *would* have been wondering. And he does say he thinks she's getting better. And his mother is looking after Lucy while he's at work, so that's all good.'

'Oh, but it isn't, Violet. Poor Lucy can't stand

the woman. She's a good girl and tries to smooth things over but she's been hinting in her letters for some time now that Mrs Walden is riding rough-shod, always there, never lends a hand, nothing suits her. I told Lucy to get Denis to help her deal with his mother and, to be honest, I'd have shown the woman the door long since. But Lucy was determined to keep the peace as she feared it would sour her marriage if she stood up to Mrs Walden. I should have taken her worries more seriously. Mebbe I should have visited and tack-led Mrs Walden myself. Now my lass is poorly and in bed, and someone she dislikes and who seems to dislike her is supposed to be taking care of her. What if she's gravely ill and Kathleen Walden nei-ther knows nor cares?'

'You don't know that, Florence, though I can see why you're worried.'

'I think I should go to her,' Florence said. 'Yes, it's no use dithering and wondering and doing nowt to find out for sure. I should go to Blackburn today . . . now. Will you be all right? I reckon you can manage fine without me for today . . . mebbe tomorrow if I have to stay over.'

'Course, love. That sounds like a good idea. Then you'll know just how your daughter is and you can do what you have to and stop worrying,' said Violet. 'I'll take Scamper home with me this afternoon in case you're not back tonight and then you won't have to worry about her either. Carmen will be pleased about that.'

'Thank you, Violet. I don't want to take her on a long journey.'

'Get yourself together, don't forget to telephone

the Kendals if you need to, and then off you go,' said Violet. 'I'll tell Jim to keep an eye on Paradise in case you stay over and it's empty tonight.'

'Thank you. Thank you so much.'

'What friends are for,' smiled Violet, and went back to the kitchen to recommence stirring the simmering pans.

★ ★ ★

It was afternoon and the light was already dimming on this overcast day when Florence arrived at Lucy's house. Her back was so stiff by then that she thought she'd never stand up straight again. It would have been an uncomfortable journey for Scamper, too, and Florence was glad Violet had offered to look after her, but she had missed the company of her little dog on the long journey. She parked in the street directly outside Lucy and Denis's terraced house and, clutching the small of her back to try to ease the stiffness, she knocked on the door.

She waited a minute or two but no one came. She knocked again. Mrs Walden was far from light on her feet and it could be taking her a while to come down if she was keeping Lucy company upstairs while she was in bed.

Florence tried to look in at the front window but Lucy had net curtains and Florence could see nothing.

'Hello, can I help you, love?' It was Lucy's neighbour, standing at her front door. Florence didn't know the woman's name.

'Hello. Yes, mebbe you can. I'm Lucille's mum.

279

Denis tells me Lucille's not well and so I've come to see her. I gather Denis's mother is here looking after my lass but I haven't been able to raise her.'

'Yes, Mrs Walden is staying there but I saw her going out earlier. I haven't seen Lucille for a few days and Denis tells me she has the flu.'

'I wonder when Mrs Walden will be back. I don't want to keep trying to attract Lucille's attention; she may be asleep, or too ill to get up to answer the door and anxious about who's knocking.'

'I've got a key, love. I can let you in,' said the woman. 'You've told me enough for me to know you really are Lucille's mother, even if I didn't know by looking.' She glanced at Florence's hair.

'Oh, thank you. That'd be a help. It's been quite a drive and I don't want to have to wait for Mrs Walden to return before I see Lucille.'

The neighbour went back inside her house and came out directly with the key. 'I'll let you in, love, and just wait to see if all's fine, if you like?'

'Thank you. That's good of you,' said Florence.

The woman came and unlocked Lucy's door and Florence went in and called up the stairs, 'Lucy? Lucy, love, it's Mum.'

'Mum? Oh, Mum. I'm up here,' said a wobbly little voice. 'I'm not well.'

'I'll be there in a moment, love.'

Florence turned to the kind neighbour. 'You've been grand. I'm glad Lucy has such a good neighbour. I expect Mrs Walden will be back in a minute but if I miss her I'll pull the door to when I go. Thank you for your help.'

'Lucille'll be pleased to see her mum, I reckon,' said the woman. 'Safe journey home, love,' and she went back to her own house.

Florence ran upstairs as fast as her stiff back would allow.

'Lucy? Oh, my darling . . .'

Lucy lay in bed, her face drained of all colour, shadows under her eyes. Florence could see immediately that she was thinner — much thinner, her arms like pale sticks, her cheekbones prominent — and her hair was lank and tangled. She looked terrible.

'Oh, Mum, I feel awful,' she said huskily. 'It's flu . . .' She coughed loudly and Florence could see her whole body was racked with the effort.

'Denis wrote to tell me and that's why I've come.'

'Oh, Mum . . .' Lucy looked as though she wanted to cry but hadn't the strength. 'I thought you were an angel. Such a long way . . . Did you bring Scamper?'

'No, love, but she's in good hands at home. How long has Mrs Walden been out? Has she just popped out to the shops?'

'What time is it?' Lucy propped herself up on her elbow and looked at the little bedside alarm clock. 'Heavens, I must have been asleep. She went after she'd eaten her dinner — she goes to Bingo on Thursdays.'

'What did she give you to eat, love? Have you eaten?'

'She didn't offer owt. I haven't been able to face food for a while, Mum.'

'Too ill to want to eat, not even offered owt to ease your throat, and that woman's gone to Bingo and left you! I'll make us a cup of tea, love, and

281

while it's brewing we'll think about getting your things together.'

'My things . . . ?'

'You're coming home with me. I'll not leave you here. You need proper looking after, not left with nowt to eat or drink. We'll put you in the car, all wrapped up snuggly. You can lie on the back seat, and there's a nice clean bed waiting for you in my spare room at Paradise.'

Lucy's bottom lip trembled. 'Oh, Mum . . . I'm so pleased you're here,' she said.

★ ★ ★

Florence drove home through the long dark evening, having had the tank filled with petrol on the outskirts of Blackburn before she set off. She very much hoped not to have to stop in the dark on the journey back to Guisethorpe. She'd left a note addressed to Denis on the kitchen table. His mother would probably open it and read it first, when she got back from Bingo, but Florence had deliberately omitted all mention of that woman.

Dear Denis,

Thank you for your letter. I came here straight away and I can see that Lucy is very poorly so I'm taking her home with me to recuperate at the seaside, where I can look after her properly.

I'm sorry to miss you but I know you're working hard and I'm afraid we need to set off now and not wait for you to come home as it's such a long journey.

Lucy sends her love and will be in touch very soon.
With love,
Florence

Lucy was wrapped in a blanket and curled up asleep on the back seat with her pillow and a hot-water bottle. Florence had made up a flask of tea, too, in case she was thirsty, and there was a bar of chocolate to eat. Florence herself had not eaten all day but she didn't care. She was sustained by her anger at Mrs Walden's selfishness and her neglect of Lucy. How could she just go out and leave her like that? And for nothing but a game of Bingo?

While she drove, her headlights making a yellow tunnel through the dark, the roads growing quieter as she went south and east, into the countryside, Florence thought about her life in Guisethorpe and she wondered what her daughter would make of it.

Paradise Cottage was a pretty home but it was also, now, a tiny pickle kitchen, and it smelled like one, too. What if Lucy couldn't bear the smell? Guisethorpe was a blissful seaside place, in Florence's opinion, but very, very quiet out of season. Maybe Lucy would be bored once she was well enough to leave her bed. Perhaps she'd hate the little village — and worse, make no secret of her dislike — and be looking to return home as soon as she raised her head from her sick-bed.

Florence had good friends in Violet and Carmen, Jim, the Kendal sisters and Becca, even Mary Davis, Mavis Farlowe and Derek Clough at the produce market, but what of Anthony Bird, who had caused a disturbance outside only last weekend? Florence remembered his final words to her before he left, closely followed by Constable Paige: 'Mrs Stanville, I've learned something this evening and it's a lesson I won't forget.' It sounded like a threat. Could the man actually be dangerous or was he just a pathetic drunken failure?

No, Anthony Bird was not her immediate worry, and at least she'd rescued Lucy from Kathleen Walden.

But at the back of her mind was a nagging, selfish little worry. Up until now she had been able to do almost entirely as she wanted. She lived alone and she liked it. What if she were now incapable of accommodating anyone else in her daily life? Would she be able to live with another person again, or in a week or two's time would she be glad to see the back of her own daughter?

No, that was silly. She was a mother and it was a mother's instinct that had led her to rescue Lucy from the selfish neglect of Denis's mother. Still, life at Paradise Cottage was going to be a little different in the near future.

Come on, Flo, you daft thing. It's going to be even better. There is nothing to worry about ...

14

'I was right to go,' said Florence to Violet the following morning as they worked together in the kitchen. 'It was a long journey and I don't like driving in the dark, but when I saw my lass lying there, all poorly, and not even a hot drink or any food left for her to pick at, I didn't hesitate.'

'Awful,' Carmen muttered, up to her elbows in suds, washing jars.

'Poor Lucille. Still, safe and sound here now,' said Violet. 'She'll soon get well with her mum looking after her.'

'I'm hoping so. She's got it badly but she's staying upstairs until she's feeling better. I don't want to find she has passed on the flu to you. I reckon it's better I keep away from the Kendals for a few days, too, and not risk spreading it there.'

'Good idea, but as for me and Carmen, there's no sense in us worrying. I understand why *you're* anxious, after what happened to your dad and your sister, but to be that ill is rare now. The pandemic was quite an unusual event. Let's just get on and see what happens,' said Violet, stirring a large pan. 'I reckon the smell of boiling vinegar is enough to defeat any virus.'

Florence gave a crooked smile, pulling herself out of her immediate worries. 'It's nearly defeating me. I didn't realise until we got back last night how it hangs around. I think we've all got a bit used to it.'

'Mm, it would be nicer for you if your whole house wasn't pickled,' Violet replied.

'Great-Grandma says we smell of pickles,' said Carmen. 'But she also says she's pleased we're looking more cheerful now we work for you. She was asking about you.'

'Was she?' said Florence, measuring out spices. 'Well, it would be grand to meet her.'

'We'll have to arrange that,' Violet said. 'Now, Florence, shall I carry on with this while you go and telephone the Kendal sisters . . . ?'

★ ★ ★

Florence knew she needed to do something about finding a professional kitchen for her little business before long, and when she went to Fleming St Clair to get some cough mixture for Lucy, she took the time to enquire at some letting agents, but this only confirmed what she feared: decent commercial premises were too costly for her to rent. She saw the details of the former Bird's Café, and the kitchen certainly looked suitable, but she simply couldn't afford it, even if she had needed the shop part, which she didn't.

In the meantime, Lucy was slowly recovering from the flu. By the beginning of the following week she was able to come downstairs for a short time without feeling faint or dizzy, though she soon tired and couldn't raise the energy to put on some daytime clothes and go for a walk or, indeed, do very much at all. Florence encouraged her to telephone Judy at the shop and Judy set Lucy's mind at rest about her job and even made her laugh. Florence, searching through a pile of recipe books, could hear Lucy's side of the conversation.

'Four pairs! Oh, Judy, that's lovely. She's such a nice lady . . . ' Lucy broke off to cough. 'No, no, I'm all right . . . Do you remember, she used to come in and look at all the nicest shoes, and enquire the prices, and then her choice got less ambitious, and less and less until she found some she could afford? . . . Yes, it was sad, but she always tried to make the best of it, though you could tell she really wanted the others . . . Thank you, Judy. I should try to get dressed tomorrow and mebbe even walk as far as the sea in a day or two . . . I'll let you know . . . Thank you, I'll tell her you said. Great news about Mrs Coleman, though . . . '

Lucy put the phone down and turned to Florence. 'Mum, Judy sends her regards. She says she's 'just about managing' without me, and I'm not to worry about going back just yet.'

'I should think not. You haven't even got dressed since you arrived, love, and you're hardly eating a thing. We'll have to build you up before you're ready to go back home.'

She saw Lucy's face fall and was unsure how to interpret that. But the truth would come out when Lucy was ready, she thought, so she changed the subject.

'What's this 'great news about Mrs Coleman' then, Lucy? Isn't she the nice old lady who wants to buy the best and has to come away with the cheapest? I believe they call that 'champagne taste and beer money', and it's a pity for those that have it, though good taste and money don't always go

287

hand in hand anyway.'

'Not a pity for Mrs Coleman any more, though, Mum. I'm that cheered by the news: her Premium Bond came up and she can afford to buy summat nice for herself at last. So the first thing she does is to go to Ruby Slipper. She told Judy that she'd always made her most welcome, even though she hadn't a lot to spend, and now she could choose she was going to buy the shoes she really wanted. Then she bought four of the most expensive pairs and Judy said they both couldn't stop smiling, it was so nice.'

'Ah, love, I'm glad for Mrs Coleman and for Judy.'

'I wish I'd been there to share that moment.' Lucy, who was still fragile, suddenly looked tearful. 'Oh, I'm such a cry-baby just now. Sorry, Mum.'

'It's only 'cos you're not well, Lucy. You'll soon be ready for anything, but I'm right glad to have you here with me until you're feeling better.'

'I know, Mum, and I'm so glad to be here.' Lucy took a long breath. 'The thing is, Mum . . .' She frowned and hesitated.

'What, love? Come on, you can tell me.'

Lucy sighed. 'It's Mrs Walden . . .'

'I thought it might be. You said in your letters that she was being difficult and I'm sorry but I should have paid more attention. I've been that busy with the business and I thought you and Denis would sort her out between you. I didn't realise things had got so bad. Thank goodness I went to fetch you when I did.'

'It's like I'm the least important person in my

288

own home,' Lucy said, 'her servant. She makes it clear I can do nowt right, in her opinion, yet she does nowt at all, and when Denis is there he . . . well, it feels like he defers to her and simply ignores what I might want or think or do. I sometimes reckon he'd prefer it if he still lived with his mum; that . . . that he hadn't married me at all.' She dissolved into tears, sobbing into her hands and then into Florence's shoulder when she went to hug her.

'Oh, love, I'm so sorry. I'm sure that isn't so about Denis. He loves you very much. There, Lucy, my darling . . . don't cry. It's all right . . . it's all right, love . . .'

Eventually Lucy's weeping subsided and Florence smoothed her hair and mopped her face for her.

'Why don't you go up and run yourself a really deep bubble bath — not too hot, mind — and I'll bring you some lemon and honey? Things always look bad when you're feeling fragile, but we'll sort this one out, love, I promise.'

'I think it's summat I have to do for myself, Mum,'

said Lucy sadly, standing up carefully and holding on to the chair, 'but I don't know how to do it.'

Florence summoned an encouraging smile. 'We'll work summat out, a strategy. After all, it's your home, not hers, and she has no right to just move in and take over. Don't worry, you'll feel up to dealing with her when you've got your strength back. Now, off you go, sweetheart, and think about nice Mrs Coleman, who's got some good luck at last. And I've found what I was looking for in those books so at least summat's right about the afternoon.'

Lucy slowly dragged herself off upstairs to do as Florence suggested.

Florence went into the kitchen to see how Violet was getting on, and showed her the recipe she'd found. While they were discussing it the doorbell jangled, and Scamper, as usual, gave a little bark in case her mistress hadn't heard it. Violet looked out of the kitchen front window.

'Nice car parked outside,' she remarked as Florence went to answer the door.

'Mr Kendal, what a surprise. Is everything all right with your aunts?'

'Yes, they're fine, thank you, Mrs Stanville. Aunt Jane and Aunt Bea sent these for your daughter.' Matthew Kendal held up a bouquet of pink roses. 'When you telephoned to say she was staying with you while she recuperates from the flu, they wondered what they could do to help. They soon concluded they could do nothing so they've sent me round with these instead.'

'Oh, thank you, Mr Kendal. Lucy will be so pleased. She's still feeling poorly and hasn't really been up properly since I brought her here, but she'll be cheered by your aunts' kindness. I'll telephone to thank them and Lucy will do so herself in a few days. It really is so thoughtful of them.' Florence took the flowers from him. 'Would you like to come in for a cup of tea? I'm afraid I don't know if we're a house of disease, so to speak, but I haven't caught the flu and the ladies who work with me are quite well, too.'

'Thank you, Mrs Stanville. I'd better not risk it as I have to think of my aunts, but maybe I could visit again another time? No hurry, but I'm really interested in what you're doing.'

'Doing?'

'Yes, the pickles, the jam.'

'Er, yes, of course. I didn't know you had an interest in preserving, Mr Kendal,' she said, puzzled.

'Ah, I have an interest in a lot of things, Mrs Stanville. Now, I hope your daughter is feeling better soon and you all escape the infection. Goodbye for now.' He turned and limped up the path, smiling briefly from the gate before he got into his car.

Mm, bit friendlier than last time . . . and the flowers are beautiful . . .

Carmen came in through the back door, her eyes wide. She'd been working in the garden and had seen the visitor arriving, though she'd remained shyly out of sight.

'Mrs Stanville, was that actually Cary Grant?' she asked.

'Oh, Carmen, don't be ridiculous,' laughed Violet.

'No, Carmen, it was Miss Bea and Miss Jane Kendal's nephew, and he brought some flowers for Lucy. Wasn't that kind and aren't they pretty?'

'I wish a handsome man would come round and bring me roses,' said Carmen, grinning.

'Good heavens, child, you're only fifteen,' said Violet with pretend shock.

'The flowers are from the Miss Kendals, not from Mr Kendal himself. He only brought them over from Fleming in his car.'

'Lucky Lucy,' said Carmen. 'Cary Grant . . . flowers . . . a lovely little sports car . . .' She sighed dramatically.

Violet shook her head. 'Get away with you, Carmen. I've half a mind to send you back to school; keep you out of mischief.'

'Oh, Grandma, you know school didn't suit me. I'm much better finding my own way than following direction; you said so yourself, remember?'

'Well, I think you should find the direction of that back garden and tidy away those tools before we go home.'

'Yes, Grandma.' Carmen disappeared outside again.

Florence was smiling as she put the flowers in a vase to take up to Lucy's room. 'She's such a love, and she's done wonders with the garden already. It's going to look grand come springtime.'

'Yes, she's good at the things she's good at,' conceded Carmen's doting grandmother. 'Fifteen can be a difficult age, but I think my duckling might grow into a swan by the time she's seventeen. Every girl looks her best at seventeen. Even I did . . . for a week or two.' She burst out laughing and Florence couldn't help but join in.

It was good to have Violet and Carmen here working alongside her, Florence thought later as she sipped a cup of tea, Scamper peaceful in her basket and Lucy wrapped up, snug and warm, asleep in bed and, at last, beginning to feel a little better. During the daytime now, busy working with the Peasalls, and with Lucy to take care of, Florence almost forgot the bad dreams, the occasional momentary half-glimpses of her dead sister,

Rosa, even the heavy burden of her bereavement. Maybe eventually these happier times would banish away all of that. Maybe . . .

★   ★   ★

Kathleen Walden looked up from her copy of *Home Chat* and noticed that time was getting on. Denis would be home soon. She'd bought a loop of black pudding, which she thought she'd fry and serve with beetroot from a jar and some sliced bread.

She rose stiffly to her feet and looked around, tutting under her breath. Oh, but this room was a mess. Lucille never seemed to do any dusting or vacuuming, and even the armchair cushions were sagging and creased with the imprint of people's backs. No time to vacuum or dust now before she had to go to make the tea, but at least she'd plump the cushions . . .

Kathleen was pleased Lucille had gone. That girl was far too much trouble when she was feeling ill, and was showing signs of growing bossy like her mother when she was well. And Kathleen was doubly pleased she'd missed the mother, who'd written a very cold letter to Denis saying she'd had to set off back home and wasn't for waiting to say goodbye, and making no reference at all to the trouble she, Kathleen, had taken to nurse the wretched girl through the flu without a care for her own health. No, not a thank you, nor even a mention. Completely taken for granted! Ungrateful bunch, those Stanvilles.

Clearly it would be better all round if Lucille

decided to stay at the seaside with her ill-mannered mother, and left Denis to the proper care of *his* mother. After all, she and Denis had been together for years — just the two of them — and, really, Lucille was superfluous to their domestic lives. Denis had given Kathleen a key to the house with very little persuasion, so it ought to be easy enough, now Lucille had gone, to persuade him to let his lonely old mother come to live here permanently. Soon it would be like old times, but in this nicer house with a proper downstairs bathroom. It wouldn't be difficult to build a case against Lucille and her slovenly ways as a housewife ...

Kathleen ran her hand across the mantelpiece, wrinkling her nose. Filthy dirty, and all this rubbish lying behind the clock and the ornament: a couple of invitations to parties, if you please — that Lucille was far too fond of a good time and had her mind on frivolity and flightiness; you could tell by the way she dressed for work, all high heels and the kind of showily narrow skirts skinny women wore, which couldn't be comfortable — and a couple of bills, still in their envelopes. Kathleen looked to see if they'd been paid: they had. She placed them back behind the clock and pulled forward and central the cat ornament she'd given Denis and Lucille as a wedding present, sliding the clock and the envelopes across out of the way.

Right, cushions ... She thumped the back cushion and then lifted the seat pad to reshape the wide basin shape in it from where she'd been sitting. Underneath were crumbs and dust — disgusting — and an envelope addressed to Lucille in bold handwriting and black ink.

For a moment Kathleen couldn't think how it had got there, and then it dawned on her that she had put it there herself. She had completely forgotten about it. It was that evening when Frank Stanville had come round and made himself comfortable, and then Lucille had got upset and shouted a lot about his behaviour and Denis had arrived and thrown the awful man out. Lucille's handbag had been on the table when she went to answer the door and, quick as a flash, Kathleen had grabbed the letter from where it lay beside it and shoved it under the chair seat. Lucille was getting very careless and absent-minded . . . If the letter came to light in that unlikely place Kathleen would just say she had put it there for safety because she thought it was the kind of thing a man like Frank Stanville would filch, and it might well cause trouble if he read it and found out things about Lucille's mother now she'd run away to the seaside to live by herself.

Kathleen had known the letter addressed to Lucille was from her mother because she'd just happened to see one lying about one time. The stationery was posh — crisp and thick; Florence Stanville must have money to waste — and the handwriting was quite distinctive and easy to recognise, especially since she'd read the letter.

She read this one now. It was amusing and affectionate, full of news about people who, Kathleen thought, must live in the village, and about what Florence was doing, which seemed to involve selling pickles. Could that possibly be so? It sounded so unlikely.

The letter had been under the seat pad for weeks now and Kathleen was sure everyone would have forgotten about it, as she had herself. She was about to throw it on the fire when she had a thought that it might come in useful. It would serve Florence Stanville and her daughter right if that spivvy former husband of Florence's *did* find out where she was. That would give her summat more than pickles to think about. Let her direct her bossiness towards her own affairs and leave Denis and Kathleen in peace. Florence thought herself so high and mighty, the way she grabbed everyone's attention when she came into a room, with her height and her hair, accepting compliments in her confident way, as if they were her due. No doubt she'd be giving herself airs and graces in this new place where she'd gone to live. Well, her neighbours would soon learn all about Frank Stanville when he turned up on her doorstep. He hadn't been her only husband, and mebbe she had gone to live at the seaside to find another, where no one knew her . . . no one knew what she was really like: outspoken, rude and ungrateful . . . Mebbe Frank himself ought to go to this Guisethorpe place and tell folk all about that . . . that *divorcée* . . .

Kathleen hurried upstairs, so far as it was possible for her to hurry, and put the letter in her handbag, zipping it into the side pocket. She'd seen Frank Stanville in the street once or twice since he'd come to the house, around the market, and she thought it not unlikely that one day soon she'd see him again. She'd have the letter ready to hand over. She only wished she could see Florence and Lucille's faces when that man turned up on their doorstep.

★ ★ ★

It was a cold day, damp in the air, but Florence thought Lucy had been moping around inside long enough and should take a walk. Lucy had been at Paradise Cottage for a week and was feeling better but still very weak.

'We'll take Scamper, and we'll walk on the beach, just a short distance. I'll drive us down the road to the seafront. That way you won't have to face the uphill walk home along the lane,' suggested Florence. 'There comes a point when staying inside is worse for your health than going out and taking some exercise. Come on, Lucy, you're quite well enough now to make a bit of an effort.'

'Yes, all right, Mum. I'll get my coat. Please may I borrow a hat and scarf? I haven't got my own and it does look quite cold out.'

'Borrow what you like, love. Do you want my big coat, too? And there's a pair of mohair mittens somewhere that I knitted. I'll look them out. You can have them and take them home when you go, if you want.'

'Thank you. I'd love them. You are the best mother I could possibly wish for,' Lucy grinned.

'Don't be daft.'

Florence drove them down to the seafront road and parked overlooking the beach. They got out, and as Lucy retrieved Scamper from the back seat, Florence glanced across the road to what had been Bird's Café. It now looked desolate, shabbier than ever, with a garish 'To Let' sign taking up most of the window, the name of the letting agent displayed boldly in red. She wondered what Anthony Bird was doing these days and whether he still lived in the flat above. When she glanced up at the huge picture window, she thought she saw a shadowy figure move away further into the room, but she wasn't sure.

Florence and Lucy walked Scamper along the beach. For once there wasn't a biting wind blowing in from the east, just heavy damp air and greyness everywhere.

'It's nicer in summer,' said Florence when she'd watched Lucy, looking unimpressed, staring out at the sullen, charcoal-grey sea, 'but I love it any time of year. It's the sound and the smell of it as much as the sight.'

'Is that why you came back here, Mum, just for the seaside? Only it's such a long time since you lived here when you were little, and I was worried that you might not find what you were looking for . . . whatever that is. That everything might have changed and you'd be disappointed.'

Florence was silent for a minute or two, gazing out to the far horizon. 'What I'm looking for . . . ' she said then. 'D'you know, love, before I came here I thought mostly that it was just a beautiful, peaceful place with happy memories, and where I'd like to spend the rest of my life, but as soon as I arrived — the very first night I spent at Paradise — I started having such strange and vivid dreams. It's as if some long-hidden secrets are trying to come to light. I think mebbe it started with summat your grandma said to me when . . . when she was dying . . . '

'Oh, Mum . . . '

'She said there were a lot of widows at the time we came here together — it was just after the First War — and it didn't matter what the truth was. Summat like that. She said she was running away and that she was unable to forgive, and now it was too late.'

'Oh, that sounds very sad. I wonder what she meant. I'd hate to think she had regrets. Mebbe she was just a bit confused.'

'I wonder . . . I thought she was happy here in the end, but now I suspect she just made me think so by making *me* happy. She certainly worked at that. She was such a dear mother. I hate to think she was enduring silent misery, which never went away, and keeping uncomfortable secrets all those years.'

'Tell me about these dreams, then, Mum.'

'Well, it's always the same one. I'm in a long dim corridor and my sister, Rosa, is running away down it, getting further and further out of reach, though I'm trying as hard as I can to catch up. But I'm just Little Flo, the child who came here in 1919, and my big sister can run faster. Then she kind of disappears and I just know something awful has happened, but I have no alternative but to turn back, all alone and frightened. Then I see Mum, your grandma, looking as she was then, too, and she's crying. Really crying, as though the very worst thing has happened, which of course it had. Rosa and my father had both died of the Spanish flu, as you know.'

'You haven't spoken of that for years.' Lucy

linked her arm through Florence's and leaned in to her. 'Poor Mum. It doesn't sound very restful.'

'What's so strange is that Mum and Rosa are in my dreams, but never my father.'

'Do you think you might be able to find out what Grandma meant about the truth and being unable to forgive? I don't know how you'd even begin to do that after all this time.'

'Yes, it's like the past is pulling at my arm,' Florence clutched her coat sleeve to demonstrate, 'saying, 'C'mon, there's important family history here waiting to be uncovered,' but I don't know anyone who can help. Jane and Beatrice Kendal thought they remembered seeing Mum when she was a young widow, and I think I may have found the house where we lived, but the woman there knew nothing, was a bit suspicious and didn't invite me in to look, and I seem to have reached a dead end.'

'So frustrating. What about Mr Yateman and Violet? They're both quite old.'

'Well, Jim and Mildred have been here years, but not that long, and Violet was married and living elsewhere at that time.'

'Maybe the dreams are really about Grandma dying,' suggested Lucy, her voice wobbling. 'You're still sad about Grandma, but you can't help that, Mum. It's inside you and you take it with you wherever you go. You'd mebbe feel just the same, have the same dreams, if you hadn't come back here.'

'Yes, love, you're right. I've got to give it time. Most days I'm all right and then suddenly I can be just driving along, or walking Scamper, or even in the shops, and the sadness — the sudden, sharp, unexpected assault of it — it's like a stab to the heart.'

'Oh, Mum . . . '

Florence pulled at Scamper's lead and she and Lucy strolled slowly along.

Florence remembered one time when she'd been queuing at the butcher's shop just across the road and the woman in front had asked for a pound of minced beef and two pork chops. The utter certainty of the recall of her mother's voice asking for exactly the same thing in the same words had drenched Florence in a sudden tidal wave of misery for Lily's death and she'd had to leave the shop to hide the rush of tears, and go and walk on the beach to recover.

She decided she needn't tell Lucy about this. She was supposed to be a grown-up; pretending to be strong was an act you practised until you assumed it for real. It was a life lesson that competent adults were supposed to have learned.

'I'll cope,' was all she said.

'And what about the business?' asked Lucy, pulling the long hand-knitted mittens further up her arms under the coat sleeves. 'You and Violet and Carmen seem to be working hard at the preserves. Are you a real business, Mum?'

'Nearly. I don't want a factory, a vast workforce, hundreds of jars delivered across the country by lorry. I just want to use Grandma's recipes so that they aren't forgotten, make them available so that other folk can enjoy them. It makes me happy to think I've achieved that, starting from scratch, that I am self-reliant, independent, making my own way. I admit I'm not making much of a profit yet — my market is still too small, and I pay Violet and Carmen now — but I'm fortunate to have enough money so I need not worry too much about that, so long as my overheads don't run out of control. At the moment I'm doing it all for next to nothing from my own kitchen, so the costs are not too high.'

'But wouldn't you prefer to go home to Paradise and find it smelled of roses rather than vinegar?' asked Lucy. 'I didn't notice at first because of the flu, but now I'm getting better I have to say it's becoming a bit much.'

'Yes, love, I would prefer the scent of roses. I hadn't really anticipated the smell and it's starting to get to me too.'

Lucy put her nose to the sleeve of Florence's coat that she was wearing. 'Even your nice coat smells of pickles a bit. The smell is stronger downstairs, of course, in the kitchen, but the cushions and curtains in the sitting room are beginning to be vinegary, have you noticed?'

'I haven't. I'm sure you're right, though. Oh dear, perhaps people can smell me coming and they're too polite to say owt. 'Watch out, I can smell Mrs Stanville's just round the corner!"

Lucy laughed, then coughed and turned up the collar of the coat. 'It's not that bad but you're stuck with it until you find somewhere else to cook the pickles. In the meantime, it's only going to get worse.'

Florence looked at her daughter. 'Yes, you're right. I should get a move on finding new premises.'

'I love what you're doing, Mum, and understand

why you're so proud of it being all your own work, but you've been independent for years, of course.'

'Yes, I've been very lucky. I've made all my own choices since I divorced your father. Some of them were good, some were bad and some were downright ridiculous, but they were all mine. Now I suppose what I really mean is, I have a new sense of purpose. Grandma is dead, you're married and I have the rest of my life to do exactly what I want. I'm only forty-five; I'm not going to waste my time sitting in a chair reading silly magazines. I need to have something to show for the last third of my life.'

'Well, you certainly have that already. I've seen how professional your jars look and it's a grand tribute to Grandma that her name is on those smart labels. You should be proper proud of them. You're like Judy is with Ruby Slipper, except you're Florence Lily. Can you even imagine Judy without thinking of the shop and all she's put into it?'

'No, I can't. But Judy doesn't live at the shop and the shoes don't smell like the vinegar does.'

'Well then, you *have* to find somewhere else to make the pickles.'

'I've been to a couple of rental agents and the premises they've got on their books are too dear for me. I can't let it be a stupid vanity project: I have to break even at least for it to make sense ... What's Scamper doing with that piece of wood? Come on, my girl, give it to me. Good girl ... Are you getting cold, Lucy? Shall we turn back now?'

'If you don't mind, Mum. My legs are getting

tired and it is a bit murky today.'

They turned north again and strolled slowly back in the direction of home, the sea on their right and the raised promenade of shops high up on the left.

'Someone's waving at you, Mum. Who's this coming?'

'It's Jim Yateman, love, Jim who lives opposite and sells me lots of vegetables. Jim, hello! Not much of a day for a walk but Lucy and I thought we'd take Scamper out for a bit of air. This is my daughter, Lucille, who's staying a little while.'

Jim and Lucy shook hands.

'I thought I was seeing double,' said Jim. 'You look just like Florence.'

'Except twenty years younger,' Florence said.

'Very alike,' said Jim. 'I hope you're on the mend, Lucille. Your mum told me you've had the flu.'

'Much better now, thank you, Mr Yateman. I'll stay for a bit longer, though. Mum and I were just talking about the pickles and how Paradise smells of them. We've concluded Mum needs a separate kitchen where she, Violet and Carmen can work; have more room and give the poor old cottage a bit of an airing.'

'Neatly summed up, Lucy,' said Florence drily.

'It's a good idea if you can manage it, Florence,' said Jim.

Lucy looked up to the seafront shops and there was the bold notice in the window of the former Bird's Café.

'How about there? Very convenient, being so close to home.'

'No!' Florence was sharper than she'd meant to

be. 'I mean, I know how much they want for that place and it's too dear.'

Lucy, puzzled, risked a glance at Jim and saw from his face that he knew something more but wasn't going to say.

Just then two people approached along the sand, smiling and waving.

'It's Miss Bea and her nephew, Matthew Kendal,' said Florence. 'Hello! Miss Bea, what a nice surprise. It's not like you to brave the cold sea air.'

'I hope I haven't been foolish. Jane says I'm quite mad but I did fancy a little walk and Matthew brought me down in the car. I think we've parked just behind you. I recognised yours straight away. And you must be Lucille?'

Florence introduced her daughter to the Kendals, and Jim to Matthew, and then Lucy thanked Beatrice for the roses and Matthew for bringing them. They chatted briefly and Florence and Beatrice agreed a date to resume the reading sessions.

'Time to get the invalid home,' said Florence, seeing Lucy's face was looking pinched with the cold. She said goodbye to everyone and pointed Lucy and Scamper towards the steps up to the road.

'What a lot of nice people,' said Lucy, getting into the car, having put Scamper on her rug in the back. 'It's almost like our little corner of Blackburn, where everyone knows each other and we can leave our doors open if we're in so's folk can come round for a cuppa.'

'Mm, I met your kind neighbour when I went to fetch you,' Florence said absently. She was thinking that yes, she did know some nice people, but

305

she certainly wouldn't be leaving her door open for folk to drop in. Anthony Bird, for a start. And she still wondered if Frank Stanville would be showing his face.

She drove home, pondering the kitchen problem. Lucy had made her see it clearly and there was no way she could continue for much longer pickling at Paradise Cottage. She'd just have to look harder for kitchen premises to rent. One thing was certain, though: there was no way she would be renting Bird's Café, even if she could afford it. Not with Anthony Bird living over the shop.

15

Kathleen Walden was feeling disgruntled. It was Saturday afternoon and she was shopping in Blackburn Market.

It was typical November weather for Lancashire, and Kathleen pulled her flowerpot hat down and shrugged her coat up to her ears against the damp, sooty air. She didn't fancy anything much for sale in the market. Tripe was a speciality, and black pudding, but somehow they didn't appeal today. She felt on edge, as if she was waiting for something but she didn't know what.

Earlier she'd been wondering whether to treat herself to some new shoes from Ruby Slipper for the coming winter months, but when she'd gone that way to look, the shoes in the window were the kind you might buy for a Christmas party. Kathleen didn't buy fancy shoes or go to parties. It all seemed such a frivolous waste. The whole shop looked frivolous, too, with that smiley Judy Hutchinson charming the customers into opening their purses and parting with their hard-earned money or their pensions. Well, they could fall for her smooth talk, but Kathleen was not taken in.

She sighed: nothing was right today. She emerged from the market, her plaid shopping bag empty but for four apples and two ballpoint pens. She stood in the shelter of the Market Tower to think where to go next or whether to give up on the day and return home to Denis, whom she'd left with his feet up, reading the newspaper , when a familiar face came towards her down past the town hall. She realised straight away that this was what she'd been hoping for. She was prepared just in case, but without any real expectation that she'd encounter Lucille's stepfather this afternoon.

'Frank Stanville? It is you, isn't it?'

The man stopped and looked, puzzled.

'I'm sorry, madam, I don't reckon I've had the pleasure,' he said, raising his hat — a hat with a crown and a brim, not a flat cap, though it looked a little greasy and had clearly seen better days.

'Kathleen Walden. You came to my house — ooh, it must have been the end of September.'

Now he looked even more puzzled. 'I doubt it, missis,' he said. 'I think I'd have remembered,' he added, which Kathleen took as a compliment. 'I'm afraid I don't know who you are or where you live, though you seem to know me.'

'Well, it wasn't my house, exactly. It was more . . . well, it's my son's house. Denis.'

'No, missis, you've got me there. I don't know a Denis.'

'Walden. My Denis is married to your Lucille.'

Light dawned. 'Lucille. Yes, though she's not my Lucille. I was her stepfather once; now I'm not even that. She doesn't want to know me and I can understand it.'

'Too cruel,' said Kathleen, sighing. 'But mebbe I can do summat about that.' She opened the large plain black handbag she carried over one arm and produced an envelope. 'I'm thinking you might want to see this,' she said, holding out the letter she'd hidden under Lucy and Denis's armchair seat and forgotten about. 'It's to Lucille from her mother, Florence Stanville.'

Frank Stanville's face was completely unreadable as he looked at the, by now, slightly dog-eared and scruffy envelope with Florence's unmistakable handwriting on the front.

'Where did you get this?' he asked in a neutral kind of voice, as if enquiring out of mild interest.

'Lucille left it lying around. She didn't seem bothered about it. I wondered if you would find it useful . . . that mebbe you'd like to be in touch with Florence again. And if you visited, you'd find your stepdaughter there now, too.'

'Oh, did you? That's very interesting,' said Frank, still not taking the envelope.

'Yes. Lucille was so rude to you when you came round. She didn't give you the chance to say what you'd come for, but I guessed it was about her mother, now she's moved away from Lancashire — that you might want her address — and so I thought if I gave you this old letter then you'd have it.'

'Did you indeed,' said Frank softly.

Kathleen held out the letter, her little eyes blinking expectantly in her round face.

Seconds passed and neither of them moved. Then Frank reached out slowly and took the letter, holding one corner, avoiding touching Kathleen's hand.

'Kathleen Walden, did you say your name was? Lucille's mother-in-law?' he asked.

'That's right, Mr Stanville,' she nodded. 'I do hope you find that letter useful.'

'Oh, yes,' he said, looking her straight in the eye

but not smiling. 'I'm sure of it.'

He pocketed the letter, turned and walked away without saying goodbye. Kathleen watched him go, slightly puzzled that he hadn't heaped thanks on her, but then maybe he wasn't that kind of man, and soon he was lost to sight in the afternoon crowd.

Well, Florence and Lucille had a surprise coming. Kathleen was only sorry she wouldn't be there to witness the scene when Frank turned up.

★ ★ ★

Early the following week, Florence went to the Kendal sisters' house to read. She had very much been looking forward to a change of scene, the gentle kindness of Beatrice and Jane, Becca's quiet attention to everyone's comfort, the novel itself — they were halfway through *The Pickwick Papers*; 'It will get us in the mood for *A Christmas Carol* in keeping with the season,' said Jane — and she'd be able to collect some Florence Lily produce from the storeroom and take it straight over to Nicolson & Filbert afterwards.

That afternoon she'd left Scamper with Lucy, who was now feeling well enough to say she'd walk her when Violet and Carmen had left for the day. Lucy was also helping to try out the recipe Florence had found and adapted a few days before. It often took several attempts to get something just right . . .

★ ★ ★

310

'Good,' said Violet, 'that's all done now. Let's see how it turns out in a couple of weeks.'

'We could have one of those tasting sessions like Mrs Stanville says they have at Nicolson & Filbert when they test the pickles,' said Carmen. 'Cheese or some nice ham or a pie to try it with.'

'Sounds lovely. I should have gone with Mum. I'm curious to see this fancy grocer,' Lucy said.

'You know, it's not a bad idea, testing the chutney with what customers might eat it with. I'll bring some Cheddar from Blake's and we'll give it a go when it's ready,' Violet offered.

Lucy could see why her mother enjoyed working with Violet and Carmen. They knew how to make the everyday fun, rather as Judy did at Ruby Slipper. The afternoon had whizzed by.

'Now, Carmen, get your things together and we'll set off home. It's hardly got light today so I hope you've changed that failing battery in your rear light.'

'My rear will be lit up like a beacon,' said Carmen solemnly, and Violet pretend-boxed her ears.

After they'd gone, the cottage seemed very quiet. Lucy hadn't been there by herself before and for the first time she was noticing how few people there were in the countryside compared to the terraced street in Blackburn where she lived. She'd been quite wrong to think Guisethorpe resembled Blackburn. At home, there was always a van or a cart passing along the cobbles, or the sound of people's footsteps, some of them wearing clogs, even these days, which clattered loudly. Folk would be calling greetings, and children played in the street so there would be piping voices singing

311

skipping rhymes, and the thud of footballs and boys shouting out to each other. The countryside had none of that.

She looked from the sitting room out of the back window onto the little garden Carmen was working so hard to improve. Without the presence of Carmen in her dungarees, bright headscarf and hand-knitted cardigan, it looked no more than a dark tidy space sadly waiting to come back to life in springtime.

'Come on, Scamper. I promised you a walk and it'll do us both good. We won't go too far,' said Lucy bracingly. She didn't really want to go out but she had promised to take Scamper. She borrowed Florence's coat again, her hat and mittens, looking in the mirror over the sitting-room fireplace and adjusting the hat brim to a better angle over her long red hair. She'd never be as elegant as her mother — Mum had the looks, and she'd also got the knack of wearing everything with style, which came from having been a model, Lucy supposed — but the adjustment was an improvement. There might not even be anyone around to see her anyway, though Lucy hoped she'd see Mr Yateman or Mr Kendal again. It had been fun, meeting those nice folk on the beach.

They set off, Lucy locking the front door carefully and testing it was secure. The front garden also looked as if it was asleep, the earth turned over, the roses pruned into vicious-looking barbed prongs, bare of leaves and flowers. It lacked colour and light. Over the road, Mr Yateman had already gathered in his unsold vegetables and the table was empty. There was no one in sight.

'Now I can't really understand what Mum sees in all this, Scamper,' said Lucy, walking towards the sea end of the lane. 'It's not very lively, is it? I'm glad she likes it, but without friendly people to chat with like we did the other day it seems a bit . . . creepy. I don't think I'd want to live here myself. Still, the sea is always worth looking at . . . '

They went along to the seafront road and then Scamper, being a creature of habit, led Lucy down the usual steep steps to the deserted beach. The sea was iron grey, relentlessly pounding the shore and then pulling away with a great *shush*, the clouds were low, the breeze from the east was picking up. The view — leaden sky, murky sea, dull brown sand and shingle — was desolate and forbidding.

'All right, Scamper. We'll go on beside the sea a bit and then up and back by the road where it'll be less windy,' said Lucy, turning up the coat collar, overcoming her wish to head back at once and curtail the walk.

They set off south and there still wasn't a soul in sight. Lucy thought she would have met at least ten people she knew by name and three she regarded as friends by now, if this were Blackburn. She pursed her lips as she surveyed the dismal scene: today, this place and Blackburn seemed as if they were on different planets.

She wondered how Denis was getting on at home with his mother. She did miss him but, like the landscape, she seemed a world away from him. They hadn't spoken on the telephone. There wasn't a phone at their home, of course, and phone boxes weren't for chatting; they were for emergencies only. She was due a letter and she hoped to learn that Mrs Walden had taken herself off home by now. Lucy would have to think about going back soon, too; Judy had been generous and thoughtful when they spoke, but she really needed Lucy in the shop. Lucy knew she must decide what she was going to say to Mrs Walden and Denis if she found that woman in her sitting room, still holding forth from the only comfy chair.

It's my home, not hers. I'll just ask her to go. I'll say I'm quite better, thank you, and I don't need any help. I'll say I'll get summat nice in for tea one day next week ... next month ... and invite her over and would she please leave the spare key because we need it, but we'll see her soon ... or mebbe later.

No, I don't have to coat it in sugar. I'll just say thanks for looking after our Denis, but I'm back now, I'm better and I don't want your help. Please leave the spare key when you go 'cos you won't be needing it.

Lucy imagined various scenarios in which she pointed Mrs Walden towards the door, or even helped her through it. It might be a good idea to practise a few polite but firm phrases so there'd be no hesitation, no dithering or distraction, no unfortunate slip into letting rip with what she really wanted to say, which might sour relations for ever. Mum was a great one for practising things, making sure she was prepared. She'd told Lucy how she'd even practised reading aloud before she went to meet the Kendal sisters for the first time.

That sounded like an odd kind of job, but a nice one. Miss Bea Kendal had been so lovely when they met the other day, and her nephew,

314

Matthew, well, he was very dashing. To think he'd gone to the trouble of bringing those beautiful roses round in his car! Maybe he was in love with Mum! He had certainly looked at her with admiration that afternoon they met on the beach — round about here, in fact — though he was a bit younger than Mum. Perhaps they were just friends, like Mum and Jim, who also gazed at her as if he thought she was beautiful. And Mum had said, after Frank, that she wouldn't marry again. She seemed to be getting on fine without a man in her life. She had been all right before Frank appeared on the scene, just in need of more fun. If only Frank had brought her fun and none of the downsides. Mum had called him 'a deviation' — no, that wasn't quite right — 'an aberration', which Lucy took to mean a lapse of taste.

What had happened to that letter that disappeared? It was very odd that it had never turned up. Maybe it never would, now. If Frank had taken it he hadn't done anything about it, which was a relief. Or perhaps he had, and Mum had seen him off and was keeping quiet about it. No, she'd have said, if only to draw a line under the matter, knowing the worry the missing letter had caused.

Lucy wandered along slowly, Scamper continually running ahead and then back to collect her.

It was good that Mum had so many friends in the village, though people didn't live almost on top of each other as they did in Blackburn and must take more seeking out and getting to know. And there was more variety of people here, too. Mr Yateman was an ordinary sort of old fella, so nice and friendly and easy to like. Violet was like any normal old lady and would fit in in Blackburn as well as she did in Guisethorpe. There was something about Carmen that was a bit unusual: she didn't seem as worldly, as tough, as the girls of about her age at home, but she could be very funny, and she knew lots of things, even though she had told Lucy that her time at school hadn't been a success. And what about Miss Bea and Mr Kendal? They were not at all like Blackburn folk Lucy knew, and yet they couldn't be kinder and were certainly not stuck up, for all that they clearly came from a different world from the ordinary run of folk. Lucy supposed it took all sorts ... But those she had met here so far were very friendly. None of them was on the beach this afternoon, though.

By now she was getting cold and ready to turn back.

'OK, Scamper, let's go up the top and walk back by the shops,' she said, and Scamper gave a last long look at the waves sweeping the shore and then turned with a kind of doggy sigh towards the steps, submitting to having her lead reattached.

Lucy hadn't brought her watch with her from home so she didn't know what time it was now, but the shops were closing. The grocer was locking up and the sweet-shop was already shuttered. The shoppers, if there had been any, had gone home. Lucy came to the place that had been a café, but now was closed all the time and had the letting agent's sign in the window. She peered through the glass of the door, trying to see how big the place was and what it might contain to recommend it.

Mum could really do with a place like this to make the pickles, and it's so close to home. I wonder what she's got against it. She was a bit snappy when I suggested it, and Mr Yateman seemed to know what she was thinking. It looks sad but it could be made lovely.

She stood back to assess the view from the pavement, imagining Florence, Violet and Carmen in matching pinnies, with the smart Florence Lily-style writing embroidered on the bibs, smiling out from the front of the premises, with the same beautiful curly style of lettering in the name on the window.

'Come to gloat, have you?' It was a man's voice, right next to her, right in her ear.

Lucy gasped in shock at the hateful tone and at finding a strange man breathing what smelled like strong drink down her neck.

She stepped away, turning to see who he was. 'W-What do you mean? Who are you?' She backed off, but Scamper had started up an ear-splitting barking, pulling on her lead to get at the man.

The man, slightly behind Lucy so she stood between him and Scamper, suddenly grabbed Lucy by the elbow and held on to her tightly, pinching her arm painfully. 'Aren't you ever satisfied?' he spat. 'Isn't it enough that you've destroyed me?'

'What? Get *off!*' Lucy said, struggling to release her arm. 'Let go of me.' She tried to pull away but he held on, his large hand almost circling her thin arm, even though she had on Florence's thick coat. She couldn't shake him off and she felt the strength of his grip and was suddenly very frightened. Scamper was growling loudly now, baring her teeth.

317

'Shut up!' the man snarled at her and, as the dog went for his leg, kicked out at her, sending her sprawling. Lucy dropped the lead in distress, wanting to pick up Scamper, but the man held on to her.

'No! Stop it, stop it!' she yelled, trying to pull her arm free, trying to push him away with her other arm, but he held on tighter so that she felt as if she was being held by pincers. 'Help! Help me!' she screamed to the empty street.

'And you can shut up, too,' he said, raised his hand and gave her a sharp clout around the head.

Lucy would have fallen if he hadn't been holding her arm, but he pulled her upright again and delivered another blow, which sent Florence's hat sailing onto the pavement.

Lucy's screams died in her throat and she felt herself gasping for breath with shock and fear. Her ear was throbbing but the man still held her arm and she could not get away as he raised his fist.

'It's time you paid for what you did,' snarled the man.

Rather than pull away, Lucy quickly stepped towards him and kicked his knee as hard as she possibly could. She had hurt her foot but she knew she'd hurt his leg more. As he bent to his injured leg she raised her free arm and gave him the hardest punch she could manage right in the eye. The mohair mittens cushioned the blow, and saved Lucy's knuckles, but the punch was hard enough for her assailant to drop her arm and clutch his face and then his knee.

Lucy needed no second chance. She scooped up Scamper in her arms, the lead dangling, and ran as fast as she could up towards the lane and Paradise Cottage.

'Oh, Scamper, oh, my darling,' she gasped. She didn't dare turn to see if the madman was pursuing her. He might be right behind and she had to get away. She didn't think she had the strength to fight him off again and Scamper was hurt. All she could hear was her own rasping breath and Scamper's increasingly faint whining.

It was all uphill from where the lane joined the seafront road, but Lucy kept on running as fast as she could, which became slower and slower, even though she willed her legs on, and her tired arms not to drop the little dog.

At last she had to give in to her exhaustion and stop, her lungs burning, her breath coming in wheezy gasps. She turned ready to kick out at the man again with what strength she could muster but he wasn't in sight. The twilit lane was empty.

Oh, thank God, thank God . . .

'Scamper, my darling, let me look . . . let me see where you're hurt,' she said, but her shock and exhaustion overwhelmed her, and she sank onto the high verge that ran along the lane, sobbing and shaking, holding the injured dog close.

After a while Lucy had regained her breath and she raised her tear-stained face to look up and down the lane. There were no houses along this part, just a field sloping up on the inland side and a patch of scrubby, untamed land on the sea side. There was a house with a big garden in the distance, but Florence hadn't mentioned these neighbours to Lucy at all. They might be anyone . . . maybe even the madman himself! She couldn't rely on the kindness of strangers. She had to go where she knew she was safe.

She got up and, in an exhausted shambling run, carried Scamper up the lane, crooning to her tearfully all the way. Paradise Cottage was in darkness and Florence's car wasn't round the side so she wasn't back from Burton Barrow yet. Lucy turned towards Sea View and opened the little garden gate with one hand, resting Scamper on her shoulder now. Then, gasping and weeping, she wove her way up the straight front path.

As if by magic the front door opened and an old lady, whom Lucy thought must be Jim's wife, said, 'Good heavens, what on earth has happened?' and helped Lucy inside, where she sank to the floor, clutching Scamper and crying as if she would never stop.

★ ★ ★

Florence had had a very enjoyable afternoon, reading to the Kendals. There had been much laughter over *The Pickwick Papers* and then Florence asked if Becca would take her to the storeroom so she could load up a boxful of preserves for Nicolson & Filbert.

Florence carried out the required box, thanked the sisters and Becca, and drove happily away towards Burton Barrow.

Soon, however, the drive started to feel lonely. The afternoon was gloomy, the vast sky over this flat land blank, for once, with uniformly grey cloud. It wasn't raining, it was just miserable. Florence had become used to the company of

Lucy, or having Scamper on the seat next to her or in the back, and she felt their absence, as if she had left something vital behind that worried at the edge of her mind.

She parked in front of Nicolson & Filbert, the shop's golden lights shining through the big windows and lighting up that end of the pretty village street, and took the box of jars from the boot. Harry Nicolson had the shop door open for her before she reached it.

'By, it looks grand in here,' said Florence, glancing round. She put the box down.

The shop was like a beautiful Christmas grotto, with shelves laden with festive-wrapped biscuits and fruitcakes in boxes tied with bows, bottles of fancy drinks with special shiny labels, chocolates and glacé fruits, dates and bowls of nuts, all in addition to fine cheeses and hams displayed in a fridge.

'Just the usual Christmas display,' said Harry nonchalantly. 'We do it every year.'

Sandra Filbert came out of the back. 'Hello, Florence. The good news is that our customers dismantle it for us by taking it all away piece by piece.'

'It's amazing.' Florence, eyes wide, looked round, slowly taking it all in.

The Florence Lily preserves and pickles had a whole display shelf and Florence thought she would die of pride when she saw them lined up prominently in their Christmas finery. The beautiful jars she, Violet and Carmen had worked so hard to produce now seemed to be nothing to do with them. It was difficult to think that these goods had been boiled up in the kitchen of Paradise Cottage. They'd taken on the glamour of

Nicolson & Filbert.

'I'll leave you these, let you get on,' she said eventually. 'I've put in a jar of summat new I've been working on for you both to try. I'm keen to see what you think.'

'We'll let you know,' said Harry, deadpan as always.

She went out with a goodbye and a wave. Sandra called goodbye. Harry said nothing.

Florence drove home, smiling.

Oh, but Harry Nicolson is piece of work, pretending the Christmas display is nowt special. He knows damn well it's a work of art, of course. Just as he pretended he couldn't quite decide if my mincemeat was up to his standards, then ordered three dozen jars to be going on with . . .

★ ★ ★

When she got within sight of Paradise Cottage, Florence could tell that something was happening. The cottage lights were all on, the front door ajar. The lights were on at Sea View, too, and Jim's garden gate was open. Florence pulled up in front of the cottage behind a big Wolseley: a police car.

She leaped out, slammed her car door and rushed into the cottage.

'Lucy! Lucy! What's going on, love?'

'Mum!' Lucy called from the sitting room.

Florence was there in an instant. She saw Constable Paige and another policeman, standing up, taking up a lot of room, and Lucy, who was sitting in a chair, looking pale and ill, holding a flannel to her ear. Jim was sitting on an upright chair beside her, holding her hand, and Scamper was lying in her basket with her eyes closed.

'What?' said Florence, looking at each of them in turn, panic roiling in her stomach. 'Tell me.'

★ ★ ★

When the policemen had gone, Florence sank into a chair. She was furious. She wanted to take the fireside poker, get in her car, drive down to the seafront and beat the hell out of Anthony Bird. There was absolutely no doubt that it was he who had attacked Lucy and Scamper, mistaking Lucy for Florence. The description was exact enough. Sergeant Knowles and Constable Paige had written at length in their notebooks, and of course the constable remembered escorting Anthony home after he came here causing a disturbance little more than a fortnight previously, when Florence had said she was prepared to draw a line under the matter.

Scamper, meanwhile, was well enough to drink a little water, but she was whiney and subdued, and soon went to lie in her basket again.

'I can't see or feel anything but I think she might be bruised,' said Florence. 'I'll take her to the vet in Fleming first thing tomorrow. Disgusting cowardly man: Scamper's just a little scrap compared to him.'

'Now, are you sure you'll be all right here tonight?' asked Jim. 'You can always come across to Sea View if you'd rather. We've got room for you, and Scamper too, of course.'

'Thank you, Jim, but we'll be fine. I reckon Anthony Bird will be spending the night in the cells at Fleming police station so we've nowt to be frightened of now. And I'll be sure to lock up securely, as I do every night. Thank you for everything you've done. It's right good of you and I'm sorry your evening's been ruined.'

'Ah, Florence, I was glad to help. And Mildred, too, of course.'

'Yes, Mrs Yateman was very kind,' said Lucy. She still sounded shaky.

'I'm lucky to have such good neighbours,' said Florence. 'I seem to have brought trouble to Nightingale Lane of late, and I'm sorry for that. I wouldn't wish it on you.'

'And we wouldn't wish it on you either,' said Jim gently. 'It's not your fault Anthony Bird has lost his sanity.'

'I thought he was a madman,' said Lucy, 'appearing like that, saying I'd ruined his life.'

'Oh, love . . . He's a sad, angry person who . . . well, I don't know . . . has no purpose. I haven't told you about what happened the other week — I'll fill you in later; Jim doesn't want to relive it — but I reckon you're right, Jim, Anthony's completely lost his marbles. Mebbe things have got worse for him this week, but, if so, it's nowt to do with me.'

'I expect the police will get to the bottom of it when they interview him,' said Jim. 'I'll wish you good night, both, and I'll come over early tomorrow, if that's all right, just to see how things are.' He cast an anxious glance in the direction of Scamper, who was lying still with her eyes closed but breathing calmly. 'I hope Scamper is feeling better then.'

Florence showed Jim out, waiting with the front door open to light him up the path to the lane, where he picked up the light from his own wide front windows to see him home. In any case, Mildred had the door open before he had closed his gate.

When she'd locked up and drawn all the curtains, Florence went to tell Lucy what had happened when Anthony had come round, protesting that she'd stolen his workers, and how he had nearly pushed her over in the street before that.

'I wasn't going to say owt about it, love. But now you know why I won't be renting out the old Bird's Café premises, even if Anthony Bird wanted me to, which I can't think he ever would.'

'Yes, I do see, Mum,' said Lucy, 'and I wish I'd never stopped to look in the window. I was imagining how nice you could make it and how suitable it would be for your business, but obviously that's not the case.'

Florence sighed. 'Now, show me where else you're hurt, love, beside your poor little bruised face. If I take a photograph of it, that may come in useful if Anthony tries to deny anything.'

Lucy took off her cardigan. She had a short-sleeved jumper underneath and Florence immediately saw the purple of a large bruise just above her elbow where Anthony had held her arm.

'I'll just get my camera. I'll take one of your face and your arm now and another tomorrow morning in daylight, when they might look worse. Anthony Bird is pathetic and stupid, Lucy, and

I'll not let him get away with this. I can't draw a line and pretend it doesn't matter this time. He'll be punished for what he's done.'

16

Early the following morning, as he had promised, Jim came round to Paradise Cottage to see how Lucy and Scamper were.

Lucy's arm now showed a bigger, darker bruise and the side of her face was purplish, too. Florence had photographed the injuries in all their sombre glory. They weren't serious enough to need a doctor to treat them, but Florence felt infuriated that they'd been deliberately inflicted on her daughter by someone who was totally unknown to her.

'My arm really hurts,' Lucy said. 'Honestly, Mum, I've been dreaming all night that some madman was grabbing me and I couldn't get away.'

'I'm not surprised, Lucy. An upset like that takes some getting over — more than the bruises themselves. Thank goodness it was no worse, but when you go home to Denis I reckon you'll quickly put the whole nasty business behind you. You'll forget all about it.'

Florence was already aware of Lucy's disturbed night because she had been sleeping in her armchair next to Scamper's basket — which meant hardly sleeping at all in reality, listening for any change in the little dog's breathing — and she'd heard Lucy calling out in her dreams. This morning Florence's eyes felt gritty, and her stomach heavy and out of sorts.

'I didn't want Scamper to need me and find I

wasn't there,' she said to Jim. 'I'm going to take her to the vet now.'

'You do that, Florence. The sooner you go, the sooner the vet can put your mind at rest. I think Anthony Bird will have spent the night in police custody and won't be around today. In any case, I doubt he'd come here, but I'll wait with you until Florence is back if that would make you feel safer, Lucille?'

'Thank you, that's good of you, Mr Yateman,' said Lucy, 'but I shall be all right. I can't let that awful man fill me with fear and spoil my stay with Mum.'

Florence nodded approvingly. 'You're right, Lucy,' she said. 'I've been thinking the same. We will have to be careful we don't allow him to spoil anything. Jim, I'd appreciate it if you'd be extra-careful not to mention owt of last night to anyone. Least said, and all that.'

'Course not, Florence. I'll be sure not to speak of Anthony Bird at all. I understand what you're saying. Let the police do their job and deprive gossip and rumour of oxygen lest you some-how become associated with him and his bad behaviour in people's minds. I've already warned Mildred that — as it's a police matter — she'd better not be circulating her own accounts of events or she could be in serious trouble.' He sounded very strict when he said this and Florence thought Mildred would have got the message.

★   ★   ★

328

Anthony Bird had not spent the night in police custody. Far from it: the police had been unable to find him.

He hadn't been at his flat when Sergeant Knowles and Constable Paige went there and, receiving no answer to their ring on the doorbell, forced open the front door. What they found was the flat in a shambolic state, furniture turned over, papers strewn about, broken glass, cigarette burns and various stains on the carpet, unwashed dishes mouldering in the kitchen sink and, most sinister of all, a bloody handprint on the staircase wall. It was impossible to tell whether Anthony had fled with any of his belongings as his bedroom was in similar chaos.

Constable Paige had known Trudie Symons all her life and he was aware that she had been Anthony Bird's girlfriend until recently. Maybe she could throw some light on what had happened and where he might be. He and Sergeant Knowles drove to the house where Trudie lived with her mother.

'I'm glad you've come,' said Mrs Symons, showing them in. 'It's about Anthony Bird, isn't it? I was going to call you but Trudie said I wasn't to. Now she can tell you what you should know.'

Trudie was sitting on the sofa in the back room, clutching a hot-water bottle and holding a flannel to a very black eye. She also had a split lip.

'Tell them, Trudie,' said Mrs Symons. 'Too late to hide it now.'

The policemen sat down and Constable Paige brought out his notebook, writing down Trudie's account of how she'd gone round to see Anthony

Bird the previous afternoon with a job advertisement she'd seen in the *Fleming and Guisethorpe Courier*. He had not taken it well.

'It was the first time I'd seen him since I walked out on him. I'd tried to help in the café and it was a disaster and he had to close,' she explained to the two men. 'I lost all patience with him then and I've stayed away. We used to have fun together when I first got to know him but since the summer he's become . . . well, he's changed. He's always been lazy and selfish — I realise that now — but recently he started to get frightening. Breaking stuff and trashing the place, sketching horrible pictures. I didn't like him throwing things, smashing up the furniture. Once or twice he hit me, but not very hard and he said he was very sorry afterwards. But I decided to stay away from him. I was getting scared he might beat me up.'

'And now he has,' said Mrs Symons. 'Tell them, love.'

'Yes, Anthony did this. I only wanted to be kind. I thought he was probably feeling bad about the café still, and moping about in his flat alone; that he needed a bit of incentive to make an effort. I showed him the job advertisement and he just went completely mad. Started shouting he wasn't going to do some tuppenny manual job. He'd run his own business and he wasn't prepared to answer to anyone else. Did I think that was all he was worth? He went on a lot, swearing and shouting, and kicking the chairs. Then he kicked me, here.' She showed them a nasty bruise on her ankle, which was swollen and blue-looking. 'Then I tried to get out but he grabbed me and punched my face, and . . . and then he sort of threw me against the wall and stormed out.' She started to cry.

'There, there, my brave girl,' said Trudie's mother, rubbing her back.

'He left you lying there hurt?' asked the sergeant.

'Yes.' Trudie nodded and blew her nose. 'I was winded and lay there for a bit. When I was sure the coast was clear and I felt OK to stand, I left. My mouth was bleeding — I had blood dripping onto my hand — but I just went downstairs and out of the front door and ran away. It was afternoon but very quiet and I didn't want anyone to see me so I ran all the way home to Mum as best I could with my ankle.'

Trudie's mother reached out and squeezed her hand.

'Did he say where he was going when he stormed out, Trudie?' asked Sergeant Knowles.

'He's got a view of the beach and can see who's passing,' said Trudie. 'He'd caught sight of someone, I think, because he said, 'That damned woman,' and then he left, slamming the door. I don't know who he meant. He seems to hate most people these days.'

'Show them the cartoons, love,' prompted Mrs Symons.

Trudie got up and limped out to the hall. She came back in with a paper carrier bag in which were a jumble of pieces of paper, dog-eared, with bloodstains on a couple of them.

'I took these this afternoon, after Anthony left. I don't know why, except that I thought maybe someone should know about them — the kind of thing that's in his head.' She handed them to the policemen, who looked through them grimly. Many were drawings of people they recognised, even knew and liked, enduring terrible punishments.

'Wait, there's another upstairs,' said Trudie.

'I'll get it, love, if you tell me where it is.'

'No, it's all right, Mum. I've hidden it.'

They heard her going slowly upstairs and then returning.

'I took this one a few weeks ago. Anthony had screwed it up and thrown it away but left it on the floor by the bin. I think it's a lady who annoyed him in the café.'

She handed the sergeant the drawing of Florence Stanville. He recognised her straight away: like all good cartoons it had an element of truth at the heart of the exaggeration.

The sergeant and constable exchanged looks and then explained that they were seeking to question Anthony in connection with another assault that afternoon.

Trudie was unable to offer any idea as to where Anthony Bird had gone, but she answered as best she could, and when they'd exhausted their questions they left, taking the drawings with them. Constable Paige called in at home and asked his wife, who was the district nurse, to go round and see what she could do to soothe Trudie's injuries.

'It looks to me as if the folding of his business has upset Anthony Bird mentally in a way no one realised,' said Constable Paige to his sergeant as they drove to Fleming St Clair police station.

'Well, if he wasn't unstable before, he certainly

is now,' said Knowles. 'What kind of a mind is behind drawings like these? We need to find him before he attacks anyone else.'

★ ★ ★

The good news was that Scamper was not badly injured. The vet advised the application of a cold compress to her shoulder at frequent intervals and slow, short walks only for a few days. She would soon get better. Florence felt her tiredness evaporate at the good news and she drove home as fast as the speed limit would allow to share the glad tidings with Lucy.

Violet and Carmen turned up to work and heard the shocking news that Anthony Bird had attacked Lucy in the street, mistaking her for Florence. Everyone felt upset but they carried on as best they could, subdued and disinclined to talk and laugh over their work as they usually did.

Towards the end of the morning the telephone rang. When Florence answered, Constable Paige told her that Anthony Bird seemed to have disappeared. Lucy listened, growing anxious.

'Yes . . . Yes . . . No, she'll probably want to go home soon. She has to go to work . . . Blackburn . . . Yes, of course. But you will let me know straight away if he turns up? . . . Thank you. Goodbye, Constable.'

'What, Mum? I can tell it's not good news.'

Florence told Lucy that the police had been to Anthony Bird's flat and he was not there. Anthony's former girlfriend had been very helpful but she didn't know where he had gone.

333

'You heard me tell the constable that you had to go home to Blackburn. They can always be in touch with you there, should they need to.'

'I'll be pleased to be away from here if that man is still at large,' said Lucy, 'but at the same time I want to stay and keep an eye on you and know you're safe.'

'I'm quite old enough to take care of myself, love, and don't forget, I've got the telephone, I've got stout locks on the doors and I've got Jim across the road. Look how good he and Mildred were with you yesterday. Tomorrow, if you're up to it, I'll take you home. Judy will be needing you at the shop and Denis will be overjoyed to see you. Does that sound all right?'

'I suppose so,' said Lucy, not sounding all right about it at all.

'What, love?'

'You *know* what, Mum. I've already told you. What if Denis is all comfy at home with his mum spoiling him and fussing over him at every turn, and she's moved herself into the spare room for good? For ever! How will I bear it?'

'You won't, Lucy,' said Florence seriously. 'I've told you before, you won't put up with owt you don't want in your own home. *Your* home, not *hers*. And if you think that woman has got her feet under your table and is trying to reclaim her boy in your absence, then the sooner you turn up and put her right the easier it will be for her to accept it.'

'Yes, Mum. You're right, of course,' Lucy agreed in a small voice.

'Oh, for goodness' sake, love, you and Denis

don't half deserve each other! He's a mummy's boy and you're behaving like a mummy's girl. Well, I'll tell you summat, Lucy. You *are* my girl and that means you won't be putting up with non-sense from the likes of Kathleen Walden. Didn't you show Frank Stanville the door? Well, then, dish out the same to Mrs Walden. She needs to get the message. I can do it for you but if I do, as soon as I'm out of the way she'll be back and you'll be stuck with her. But do it yourself and I reckon you won't have to repeat the exercise.'

'Yes. I know you're right, Mum. It's just that she's Denis's mum . . . '

'What's that got to do with it? It's him you're married to, not her. I know she comes as part of the package but you never agreed to have her living full time in your lovely new home. She's got her own place and she can stay in it.'

'Yes . . . ' Lucy pulled herself up. 'Denis can always go round to hers if he wants to see her. I shall tell him that.'

Florence laughed then. 'Actually, love, I think you're probably worrying about nowt. I've met Mrs Walden, don't forget, and I reckon she could get on anyone's nerves. By the time you get home, you may well find Denis has had quite enough of his mother. He'll be only too glad to see the back of her. Better be prepared for the worst, just in case, but don't be too surprised if it all turns out far better than that.'

★ ★ ★

Florence and Lucy rose early next morning. Florence wanted to start out in good time to make the most of the daylight. She didn't fancy driving the whole way home from Blackburn in the dark.

They had had a lovely last afternoon together the day before, with a trip to Fleming St Clair, where Florence had bought them fish and chips to eat on the beach for lunch, and then she had taken Lucy, whose face was made up to cover the bruise, to choose some wool for a new scarf.

'Here, love, I knitted up that wool last night after you'd gone to bed.' Florence now handed Lucy the scarf she'd stayed up late working on, for all she had hardly slept the previous night. 'Put it on. Let's see . . .'

Lucy did so, looking in the sitting-room mirror to arrange it nicely. 'Perfect,' she beamed. 'Thank you, Mum.'

'You chose the colour, love. Never be afraid to wear red just 'cos you've red hair. You just need to get the right shade. Now, make sure you've got all your bits and pieces while I take Scamper across to Jim. Take a couple of those jars of chutney, if you want, but not the ones Carmen has labelled already.'

'Thanks, Mum. I wish Scamper could come with us. She'd be all right on the back seat and you'd be glad of the company on the way home.'

'You're right about the second part, but she wouldn't be comfy all the way there and back. No, Jim said he'd take her and she can have a little explore of his garden if she's up to it. We know she's in good hands.'

Lucy made a big fuss of saying goodbye to

Scamper, and when Florence got back from Jim's they had one last look round, Florence locked up and they set off on the long journey north and west.

It was well after lunchtime by the time Florence drew up in front of Lucy and Denis's neat little house.

'Got your key, love?'

'In my bag.'

Lucy opened the door while Florence busied herself unloading Lucy's things from the boot. Lucy peered into the sitting room, hoping and praying she wouldn't see Mrs Walden there asleep in the one comfy chair. But no, the place was deserted. Denis would be at work still, of course. Oh, thank goodness. It must be as Florence had said: Denis had got fed up of his mother and she'd gone back to her own home where she belonged. Lucy felt herself relax as if she'd been holding her breath. *Oh, such a relief.*

Florence came in with the bags.

'Thanks, Mum. Just leave them in the hall and I'll sort them out later.'

Florence left them at the foot of the stairs and looked tentatively into the sitting room just as Lucy had done.

'She's gone?'

'Looks like it, Mum.' A huge beaming smile lit up Lucy's face and they both laughed in delight.

'Told you it would be OK,' said Florence. 'Right, let's have a cup of tea and I'll just get my back straight and then I'll be off . . . '

Within an hour Florence was stepping back out

of the door, hoping to make at least part of the journey home in daylight.

'Darling Lucy, it's been so lovely having you to stay.

Scamper and I will miss you.'

'And I'll miss you both, too.'

'Ah, as soon as Denis gets home from work you'll forget all about your old mum. He'll be overjoyed to have you home, my darling.'

'Course I won't forget you, Mum. I wish we had a telephone so I could ring you up.'

'It can be arranged.'

'We'll see. I'll ask Den what he thinks.'

'And don't go fretting about Anthony Bird, love. You're quite safe from him here and the police will soon round him up. I'll tell you when he's behind bars.'

'Yes, I'll be pleased to learn that. Now, give my thanks and best wishes to Mr and Mrs Yateman, and best regards to the Kendal sisters and Mr Kendal, and love to Violet and Carmen . . . '

'I'll put up a notice at the hall sending best wishes from you to the entire village,' laughed Florence, getting into the car. 'Bye, Lucy. Love to Denis.'

'Bye, Mum . . . bye.'

Lucy waved her mother off and then went back inside. She decided to take her little suit-case upstairs, then sort out what she needed to put away downstairs.

She'd just got it unpacked and her clothes hung up when she heard a key in the door.

'Denis! Oh, Denis, love, I'm home,' she cried, and rushed down to meet him.

But there, removing her little boots on the door-mat, was Kathleen Walden.

'Lucille? What, back already? I thought you'd gone for good. You might have written to warn me. I've got a bit of tripe for tea and I doubt it will split three ways,' she said.

17

'You'll be missing Lucy,' said Violet, at the end of that week. 'I'm missing her myself. She did fit in well, didn't she, and Carmen liked her being here, too.'

'Yes, it was lovely to have her here, but she's got her own home and her own life with her lovely husband — although I'm hoping not with his troublesome mother.'

'Indeed . . . Well, we're on the home run for this batch and there's just the two of us to finish it off and maybe get on with a second. It's good of you to give Carmen a day off to help Mum with her Christmas shopping. Carmen's so gentle and patient with her.

They've taken the bus into Fleming and I think they'll make a day of it: tea breaks in cafés, a little snack lunch somewhere, the lot.'

'Quite right, too. Good idea to start early and do it all in one day. Sensible girl, Carmen.'

'In some ways, yes,' said Violet drily. 'And while I've got you to myself, Florence, please, would you like to tell me what happened next in the story of your marriage to Charles Summers? I keep thinking about poor little Lucy and her lost kitten, and that awful Connie. I hate to think you had to put up with that woman for years and years.'

'I'm not really one to put up with anything I don't like for very long, Violet,' said Florence. 'Yes, I seem to remember I left off with Connie

340

probably triumphant about getting rid of the kitten, though I never did prove what I suspected. Anyway, there we were: Charlie and I married and also working together, Lucy fitting in perfectly with her new father's life —Charlie was so good to her and they grew genuinely to love each other — and Connie just about tolerating me and Lucy most of the time. She and I tended to avoid each other and that suited me just fine. Lucy sensed her hostility, of course, and instinctively avoided her too, which suited Connie. As the months went by she probably found it difficult to keep up her ill temper and criticism, alternating with sulking about us being there at all, because she seemed to back off a bit. Charlie remarked on it once. He said he was glad she had accepted me and mebbe we would become friends. Charlie was such a dear man. He always hoped for the best and I reckon he thought by the power of wishful thinking that all would be well. Course, I couldn't ever forget what I suspected about the kitten, having caught Connie sabotaging my work, and there were a few other occasions when I didn't find things as I'd left them or she told me I was so stupid, doing this or that wrong — some simple thing — so I could never entirely let down my guard with her. So far as I was concerned, we'd never be friends.'

'Am I right in thinking it all came to a head?' asked Violet gently.

'You could say so, Violet. And so suddenly, too.'

* * *

After he'd been married to Florence for a year, Charlie thought a summer holiday would be a treat for them all and he booked them into a hotel in the Lake District.

'Doesn't it rain a lot there?' asked Connie, when Charlie proposed the trip.

'Keeps the lakes topped up,' he replied. 'We'll take our mackintoshes.'

'And Lucy can have some new wellies,' promised Florence.

'Red ones, please, Mummy?'

'Whatever you want, Luce. We'll be fine if it rains, as long as we're properly organised.'

The hotel in Keswick was very comfortable, not grand, but friendly, warm and welcoming, and they managed some very enjoyable days out, driving around the lakes, or walking and admiring the stunningly beautiful scenery. Even Connie joined in and seemed to enjoy herself enough to be pleasant.

One afternoon Charlie said he'd got a good idea for a story and he'd go back to the hotel early and get it down on paper while he felt inspired. Florence had bought Lucy a new jigsaw to do in case bad weather set in and the little girl said she'd go back with Charlie and do her puzzle: 'And I promise to be very, very quiet.'

So Florence and Connie were left to keep each other company for the afternoon. Florence didn't really mind now that Connie seemed to be trying to get into the holiday spirit.

'Shall we go on a boat trip?' Connie suggested.

'I noticed at the landing stage that there's a pleasure boat that takes trips around a couple of the islands.'

'Sounds fun,' said Florence. 'The weather looks on the turn but we've both got our waterproofs. You never know, it could be sunny again before we get back.'

Florence paid for the tickets and the women were handed down with care by the boatman into his little pleasure cruiser. There were just two other sightseers on board, a young couple, from somewhere in the south by the sound of them. They smiled but didn't introduce themselves to Florence and Connie, in the way that folk from the south tended not to be chatty with strangers, in Florence's experience.

The boatman waited as long as he could to see if anyone else was going to turn up for the trip, but the jetty remained empty and he started out with only the four passengers. As the boat chugged away, the crewman
— whom the boatman said was his son — started to describe the scenery and the islands for which Derwentwater was well known. He had to raise his voice above the sound of the engine and the wind, which was gathering strength.

The hills around loomed massive and grey. Florence could appreciate their majestic beauty, but that afternoon they looked forbidding and hostile, harbingers of stormy weather.

The boat was just rounding Derwent Isle, with its views of an imposing house, when the wind started gusting in sudden squalls and the lake water broke all around in waves like the sea. The waters were getting choppier by the minute and Florence began to feel queasy.

'It's just a little rough water along this side,' the young crewman reassured his passengers loudly. 'When we get round the other, the wind will be at our backs and we'll speed along. If it gets too rough, don't worry, my dad will get us back safely.'

'It's looking at the horizon going up and down that's making me feel sick,' whispered Florence to Connie. 'I think I'm going to have to lean over the side.'

'Yes, you do that,' Connie agreed. 'Go to the back, away from the others. I'll come with you.'

'Thanks, Connie.'

Florence kneeled on the wooden bench towards the stern, leaning over the side of the boat, where splashes of lively water occasionally leaped up to catch her face, but she didn't mind. She felt a little better. Suddenly she felt a strong shove at her back and her head went down low over the side so she was looking straight into the depths of the lake. Any moment she knew she would go overboard and she grasped the edge of the boat, which was polished wood and difficult to hang on to, and tried to pull herself back. Then her coat was grabbed from behind between her shoulders. Florence kicked out with all her strength with one leg and turned to see Connie stumbling back onto the deck. In a second, Connie was up and rushing towards Florence, both her arms up to push Florence over the side. Florence, still on her knees on the bench, managed to roll away to the side just as Connie would have made contact with her. At exactly that moment the boat rose up on the opposite side with a sudden massive swell, the lake water spilling in over Florence as Connie went straight over the side and into the lake.

Florence could feel herself going over too, and clung on to the slippery woodwork, grabbing onto a fixed rope, desperate to save herself, but a second later the boat settled and she fell forward onto the wet deck, her heart hammering. It had all happened so quickly that she questioned whether she had imagined it — a seasickness nightmare — but she did not hurry to get up. She waited one, two, three seconds — she counted them — and then she got to her knees and shakily rose to look over the side.

The waves were tossing furiously, with white caps and grey murk beneath. There was no sign of Connie.

'Help! Help!' Florence shouted, running forward as best she could on the shifting boat to lift down a lifebelt from outside the little cabin and cast it into the lake somewhere near to where she thought Connie had gone overboard.

The young crewman and his father went immediately into an emergency drill, but it was too late. Florence didn't know whether Connie could swim, but even if she could she was unlikely to be a strong enough swimmer to stay above the deep and rough lake waters in that weather. She had disappeared without trace.

★ ★ ★

For a few moments Violet said nothing. She set down her knife and covered her mouth with her fingers, speechless with shock.

'Well . . . ' she said eventually.

Florence didn't prompt her.

'Goodness, Florence. What an awful thing to happen. I'm tempted to say it served her right. If she hadn't been trying to tip you into the lake, she would never have gone over herself, would she?'

'True, Violet. But the fact is I wanted her to drown. In those three seconds, all I could think was that if Connie Summers was dead, my life with Charlie would be so much better. I thought: you've just tried to kill me, you got rid of Lucy's little kitten, and now I'll make you pay. And yes, I thought it served her right. Yet what a price to pay! Many might ask who I was to be judge and executioner of the woman. It was three seconds of moral insanity, I know. It was a bad thing I did, but I thought it for the best then and it turned out to be so.'

Violet had no answer for this.

Florence went to put the kettle on to make a pot of tea while she waited to see what else Violet had to say.

Eventually Violet said, 'You know, it's possible she sank straight to the bottom and she could never have been saved anyway, even if you'd tried to help her sooner.'

'I don't know that, Violet, though it's kind of you to suggest it, but, you see, I wanted her dead and she was, so it's always felt to me that I killed her. I chose to do that.'

'Do you think if you'd gone overboard she'd

346

have thrown you a lifebelt? I don't, because she was trying to tip you in when *she* fell in and drowned. Connie Summers got herself in that position through her own wickedness. As I say, you don't even know if you could have saved her had you acted immediately.'

'But I *didn't*, Violet. Yes, she *might* have drowned, but I damned well made sure that she did.'

They stood silently, thinking about this.

'Oh, Florence,' said Violet, 'it sounds to me as if she was an awful woman, and the world was surely a better place without her. In the end she brought about her own death. Let that be the end of it, love. If your conscience has been prodding you about this over the years then I think you should ignore it. What's done is done, and no innocent person was hurt, were they?' She reached out and squeezed Florence's hand briefly.

'Mm . . . Thank you, Violet.'

'So what happened afterwards?'

'Well, it was the boatmen I felt sorry for. It wasn't their fault. It looked like a freak accident. That's what the coroner judged it to be, and the police were very kind of me. Of course, I didn't say she'd fallen over the side while trying to push me in. No one thought it was my fault.'

'Because it wasn't. Not really.'

'Charlie was upset, of course, but he got over it. I don't think Connie was ever an easy person to live with. He told me she had lived with their parents as she'd never married, just stayed at home, working at first and, when Charlie could afford to help them out, not really doing anything with her life, though she did look after their parents when they grew old and frail. Then, when both of them had died, she was alone and cast adrift, and Charlie, who was widowed by then, gave her a home with him. He once confided to me that he suspected she must have made their parents' final years miserable with her bullying; he hadn't realised what a bully she had grown to be until she came to live with him. He said he wished he'd known and done summat about it.'

'Well, there you are, then. I know that it's a big thing for you to have told me, but you've shared your secret and I've told you what I think. Now, put it behind you. There's nothing you can do about it anyway, can you, love?'

'You're right, of course.'

Florence poured them each a cup of tea.

'So you and Lucy and Charles Summers lived together happily, once he'd got over his sister's death?'

'Very. But he was much older than me and after we'd been married a little while, not long before the war, he had a heart attack, which left him very ill. He never recovered completely and then a second killed him. Lucy and I were very sad as we both loved him dearly. He really was a very good, kind, generous man, a thoroughly nice man, a wonderful husband and stepfather.'

'I'm sorry, Florence. That must have been hard.'

'It was. I miss him still. Charlie, I told you, was a hard worker and had left some unpublished stories and a novel in his desk at the time of his death, so his legacy lived on for a while and provided some money for me and Lucy. I sold the house in Clitheroe eventually, and bought another on the outskirts of Blackburn, not far from my mother. Mum had lots of friends in her village and didn't need us for company, so I set up home near to her, but where I could send Lucy to a good school and work for the WVS in the war. I missed Charlie terribly and I was quite down for a long time. A few years after the war ended Lucy thought I needed a bit of fun and she was pleased when I met Frank Stanville. I was pleased myself, but what a disaster he turned out to be as a husband: a chancer, a drinker, a cheat. Well, I gave him the benefit of the doubt so many times — I must have been a lunatic — but one day I decided I'd simply had enough. That's when I booted him out, then sold up and moved back to Mum's cottage. I should have gone straight there after Charlie died, but I didn't want to crowd my mother, impose on her life, and I thought I'd be more useful to the war effort in Blackburn. Of course, Mum welcomed Lucy and me with open arms and I lived with her after that until she died nearly a year ago. Then I came here.'

'Wasn't Frank Stanville the reason you went and bought those extra locks for your doors?'

'He was, Violet, but I don't think he'll turn up now. If he'd been going to come and make a nuisance of himself, he'd have done so as soon as he found out my address.'

'And you bought Paradise Cottage because you wanted to settle here after your mother died?'

'I did, and now I have this wonderful new life, with good friends around me. If I can just find out more about my mother, what she meant by some things she said at the end, then I reckon I shall be

349

entirely settled at last.'

'So difficult when you don't know where to look for the answers. I'd help if I could . . . '

'Violet, you're already more help than I could have dreamed you'd be,' said Florence. 'Now we'll finish off here, get another batch on and you can tell me all about your Christmas plans . . . '

★ ★ ★

Lucy loved working at Ruby Slipper, especially at this time of year, when the shop was decorated with a little Christmas tree. Judy always let her imagination run riot, so far as her budget allowed, with the Christmas-themed window, and some of the regular customers brought in cards or even little presents, like a couple of mince pies for Judy and Lucy to eat if they had a brief break. Slippers and party shoes were selling well and, of course, wet-weather gear, so the shop was lively with friendly chat and busy with sales.

Lucy wasn't looking forward wholeheartedly to her Christmas holiday. As the days went by she was beginning to dread two extra days at home with Mrs Walden lording it over her. The prospect of Christmas loomed with Lucy as cook and skivvy, and the butt of Mrs Walden's snide remarks, point-scoring and meanness of spirit, not as a joyful celebration.

'So trying to manage Mrs W isn't working?' said Judy, when Lucy had been noticeably quiet one Saturday morning soon after her return to work.

'She can't be managed, Judy. I've tried.'

'So what did your mum say? I can't imagine

350

your mother putting up with owt she doesn't like.'

'She said I was to show Mrs Walden the door. She said if she did it for me, Mrs Walden would only be back when the coast was clear. So I've just got to do it myself, the sooner the better.'

'Oh, Lucy, what are you waiting for? You've got to get rid of her before she ruins your first Christmas with Denis. You know, love, I reckon Denis might well be feeling the same, but that woman's got you both dancing to her tune. When you're grown up and have your own home, it's a wise mother who keeps her visits short and knows not to outstay her welcome. No man with any backbone wants his mother suffocating him, especially when he's got a beautiful new wife.'

'Yes, you're right, of course, Judy.'

'Well, have a serious word with Denis. Do it this afternoon. I think you'll be amazed what can be done when you've been straight with each other and know you're on the same side.'

Lucy nodded, pulling herself up and smoothing down her skirt. 'Yes, you're right. I'll do that.'

'You know it's for the best, and come tomorrow morning, it'll be done and your home will be your own again.'

'Yes!'

When the shop closed for the afternoon, Lucy hurried home, determined to do what she must.

She opened her front door and saw Mrs Walden's coat on a peg in the hallway and her little boots on the floor beneath. Oh dear, it would have been easier to tackle Denis if his mother had gone out shopping, but Lucy was determined not to weaken.

351

'Hello, love,' called Denis, from upstairs. 'I'll be down in a minute. Just trying to fix this curtain rail.'

'Eh, Lucille, you're back a bit late. My lad and I will be ready for our dinner,' said Mrs Walden, of course occupying the only comfy chair in the sitting room.

'Excuse me, Mrs Walden,' said Lucy, and went straight off upstairs.

'Denis, what are you doing?' she said, seeing him sitting on their bed reading his newspaper.

'Shush, love, keep your voice down. I just came up for a bit of peace. Mum doesn't half go on sometimes about folk at Bingo, things she's heard on the wireless, stuff she's read in her magazine . . .'

'Yes, Denis, I *know*,' hissed Lucy. 'And I know summat else, too. She's got to go.'

'Well, I've been thinking about that. It's been nice having her here — '

'No it hasn't!'

'And she *is* my mum, Luce. She's only got me. She lives all alone — '

'Denis, you know as well as I do that she's *this close* to moving in permanently, and I'm not prepared to share my home with her another day. She's spinning you a yarn about being all alone. She's got her social life at Bingo, she's got neighbours she knows, she doesn't have to live here. With us. With me running around after her trying to please her while she's determined never to be pleased. She's making my life a misery and you don't seem even to have noticed.'

'Well, I've been thinking about that, too — '

352

'D'you know, Den, I'm even beginning to regret marrying you — be quiet; I'm speaking — not because I don't love you, because I do, but because I didn't realise when I married you that I'd be taking on your mother like a life sentence. Well, I've had enough. Either she goes or I do.'

Denis looked at Lucy in shocked silence, his mouth slightly open.

'You can speak now,' said Lucy.

Denis gaped at her for a few seconds longer. 'Oh, Lucy, I'm sorry, but I've just been trying to say — '

He was interrupted by a very loud knock at the door.

Oh, good grief, now what?

Fired up, Lucy stomped downstairs, knowing full well Mrs Walden would not have moved from her chair. She flung the front door open.

'Frank!'

'Lucille — '

'It's not a good time, Frank. I thought I made it clear before — you're not welcome here.'

'You did, and I won't be bothering you again. I've brought this for you.' He held out a grubby-looking envelope addressed to Lucy herself, in Florence's handwriting.

'What? Where . . . ?'

'Your mother-in-law, Kathleen Walden, gave it to me. She thought I might find it useful to know where your mother now lives. It's a private letter to you from Florence and I promise you I haven't read it.'

Lucy took the letter and looked carefully at the envelope. She noted the date of the postmark and remembered the missing letter that had caused such a panic two months before.

'Thank you, Frank,' she said quietly. 'You'd better come in.' She held the door wide and Frank stepped inside and removed his rather greasy hat. 'Come on through,' said Lucy, leading him into the sitting room. Denis was halfway down the stairs and followed them in.

'Do sit down, Frank,' said Lucy with great dignity, 'and please tell me how you came by this letter and why you've brought it to me now.'

Mrs Walden was sitting up properly in the armchair and looking furtive, but she kept quiet.

'It was about a fortnight ago. I was round by the market and this lady' — he indicated Mrs Walden — 'saw me and pulled this letter out of her bag. Of course, I recognised Florence's handwriting straight away. She said she thought I might find it useful to know where Florence was now living. I took the letter, not because I wanted to use it to cause mischief to Florence but to make amends to you, Lucille.'

'What do you mean, Frank?'

'Well, it seems to me that there's a viper in the nest, Lucille, and you need to know that. This lady may be your mother-in-law, but she's certainly no friend to you. She had that letter in her bag, planned ahead to give it to me should she see me, plotted mischief and troublemaking. She thought I'd go off to wherever it is Florence lives and stir things up for her. Isn't that so, missis?'

Everyone turned to look at Kathleen, but for once she had nothing to say. She sat there, trapped in the corner of the room under the gaze of three furious people.

'When I came here before, Lucille, it was only to try to apologise. I let your mother down badly. Florence Stanville is an amazing woman — as generous, clever and brave as she is beautiful — and it is the regret of my life that I didn't value her as I should. I was a fool and, worse, a cheating, lying fool, and I got what I deserved. I came to tell you that and say how sorry I am for everything I did. I shall never be able to say that to Florence because I'm not worthy to set eyes on her again. She made it clear she's done with me, I'm out of her life and I respect that.'

'Goodness,' breathed Lucy. 'Well, Frank, er, thank you for coming to tell me. Thank you for returning the letter.'

'A marriage should be built on trust, Lucille. Being untrustworthy was my big mistake. Don't let any element of betrayal into your marriage, love.' He turned to give Mrs Walden a very hard stare. 'And now I'll wish you every happiness, you and Denis, and I'll be off and I won't bother you again.'

He stood up and sidled out of the room, just as he had done on his first visit, but this time to stunned silence.

Lucy heard the front door closing gently behind him and then the heavy silence stretched to a further minute.

'Mum?' said Denis eventually.

'I—I didn't mean any harm. I just thought . . .' She trailed off. There were no excuses.

'I think it's time you got your things together and went home,' said Denis. 'Off you go and pack your bag and I'll take you home in the van.'

Lucy said nothing. She was shocked that her mother-in-law should have plotted such mischief. She was disappointed to discover the depth to which this selfish woman could sink, but — and she had to compose her face a little as the thought ran through her mind — Kathleen Walden would not be round here again in a hurry, and Lucy's heart was singing about that. The Christmas holiday was suddenly looking as if it was going to be a lot more festive.

18

'Such a long month, January, and so little day-light,' grumbled Violet, carefully pouring chutney through a funnel into a hot sterilised jar.

'I think it's the contrast with the run-up to Christmas,' said Florence, ladling more into the jug. 'There's so much to do then that the time flies by, whereas January has so little to look forward to, not even the first signs of spring.'

'Still, it's nice to have got Christmas out of the way, with all those jars we filled,' Violet said. 'It's not that I'm frightened of a bit of work, but it was relentless when Florence Lily mincemeat was selling so well at Nicolson & Filbert that they kept wanting more.'

'We certainly cleared the shelves in the Kendal sisters' storeroom,' Florence agreed. 'I thought the suspension of the Morris was in danger of collapse on the way to Burton Barrow with so many boxes in the back.'

'Ah, but you're properly established there now. Christmas was the test, and you passed with flying colours. Harry Nicolson won't be looking to buy from any other supplier, for all he likes to play it cool and keep you guessing. You're quite safe as the golden girl of pickles.'

'Mm, I doubt it,' said Florence, thoughtfully. 'We've got to be inventive. If someone new comes up with a winner and we're just supplying the same old recipes, we'll be quickly relegated to second spot.'

Violet heaved a sigh. 'Just when I was thinking we could put our feet up for a well-earned rest.'

'A what?' asked Florence, deadpan. 'I've never heard of one of those.'

They both laughed as Carmen came through the back door, Scamper following muddily at her heels.

'Stay there until you've washed Scamper's paws and taken your boots off, my girl,' ordered Violet.

'Yes, all right, Grandma. I've planted those snowdrops I brought from home in a few clumps at the back and also at the front, Mrs . . . Florence,' she said. It was taking some getting used to, addressing Florence by her first name, as she'd been invited to do. 'They're best planted now, when they're green. They look brilliant: nothing this morning, flowers now.'

'I'll come and admire them when we've finished here, Carmen.'

'It's getting foggy,' Carmen said. 'Don't be too long 'cos you'll never see white flowers in a fog.'

When Florence and Violet had finished the potting-up a few minutes later, they went to inspect the snowdrops.

'I was wrong,' said Florence. 'We *do* have the first signs of spring, even though we're only halfway through January. Thank you, Carmen. They look so hopeful and brave there, all delicate in the winter weather. Such a boost to the spirits when there's nowt else to make us feel better. Flowers in the garden already, the first of many.'

A foghorn sounded distantly, a mournful sound. The fog was swirling around, the moisture so thick in the air that it was visible in the fading light.

'I hate that sound,' said Violet with a shudder, going back inside. 'I know it's about keeping people safe at sea but it always sounds to me like a lament, like lost souls moaning.'

'Ooh, Grandma, do you think it's Anthony Bird calling out from the depths of the sea?' said Carmen. She waved her fingers in the air like someone trying helplessly to swim up to the surface of deep water, but her eyes were full of laughter.

'That's not funny, Carmen. Behave yourself and show a bit of decency,' Violet snapped. 'We don't know that he drowned. All we know for sure is that some clothes the police said were his were found on the beach soon after he disappeared. Now make sure you've put all the gardening tools away and clean up while you can still see to do it. This fog is coming in fast.'

When Carmen had gone to do as she was told, Florence said quietly, 'It's odd that Anthony's body has not been washed up. You'd have thought someone out at sea or on shore would have seen summat in all these weeks.'

'You would, wouldn't you?' said Violet pointedly. 'I wonder whether he ever went into the sea at all. No money, those assaults on your Lucy and on Trudie hanging over his head . . . better to disappear, leaving a false trail on the beach. He's probably loafing about somewhere he's not known, doing as little as possible, scraping along under a false name.'

'D'you think? It seems such a big decision: throw away everything you've got — perhaps even your name — and start all over again. I reckon it would take more effort than Anthony Bird, from the little I know of him, would be prepared to make.'

'But why not? Easiest way, to give the police the slip, and put any debts and his former reputation as a hopeless failure behind him.' There was the sound of Carmen talking to Scamper just outside the door. 'Carmen's getting quite a morbid curiosity. I'm trying not to encourage it,' Violet added, lowering her voice.

Florence put her finger to her lips and nodded. She hadn't thought about the clothes found on the beach being a con; she was just sorry about the whole wretched Anthony Bird business and how it had impacted on her and Lucy. Still, whatever the truth was, it was a sad tale of failure, the only good part being that she was unlikely ever to encounter the man again.

'Right,' said Violet, as Carmen came in, Scamper, with clean paws now, at her heels, 'let's get on those bikes and be off before it gets worse.'

'It's already worse, Grandma. Even since you came to see the snowdrops.'

Florence went to the front kitchen window. Outside the fog shifted in thick white waves.

'Oh, no, you can't go home on your bikes in this. No one would see your lights. I tell you what: leave the bikes here and I'll run you home in the car.'

'If you're sure . . . '

'Come on, let's go before it gets even thicker. I'll leave Scamper here — I won't be long. And as you'll be without your bikes in the morning, I'll come and collect you then.'

'Oh, Florence, you're a treasure. I don't fancy cycling,' said Violet.

They set off, Carmen in the back, Violet in the front passenger seat leaning forward to peer through the windscreen, looking for the turning inland from the seafront road.

'Just here . . . no, I'm wrong, a bit further on . . . here. Turn right here, Florence.'

'Heck, but this is bad. Tell me where to turn next, Violet.'

'Go up here a bit yet.'

Florence looked in the rear-view mirror. 'Luckily there's nowt coming up behind, so far as I can see. I'm going to have to go even slower. How far am I off the kerb at your side, Violet?'

'You're all right . . . no, you're drifting towards the other side . . . That's better. Now, it's a left here somewhere, going up.'

'Here! Here!' called Carmen. 'By the pillar box. I can just make it out.'

Florence turned left and engaged first gear. It was quite a steep hill and she was driving very slowly, though she could see nothing of what houses or land there was along the sides of the road.

'We're just here somewhere on the right,' said Violet. 'Number forty-one. You'll need to remember that for tomorrow. But just drop us here, love, and then if you take the next left it'll lead you straight down to the front again, but further on. That might be easier than turning round.'

Violet climbed out and Carmen clambered from the back seat.

'Thank you for the lift . . . Go carefully . . . See

you tomorrow,' they called.

As soon as Florence had pulled away, they were invisible in her rear-view mirror. She was surrounded by white. It felt as though the chill fog had entered the car, too, in the brief time it had taken Violet and Carmen to get out.

Oh heavens, what have I let myself in for? C'mon, Flo, you can do this. OK, next left . . .

She drove slowly — ludicrously slowly, it felt — and the turning on the left suddenly loomed out of the fog. There was still no one behind, thank goodness, as she signalled, turned the large steering wheel and tried to position the car on the left of the road while completely unable to see the sides or any central line.

The road sloped down steeply and Florence dared to gather speed slightly, if only because she felt she was hardly moving and was worried about being rammed from behind by another car, though she had yet to see anyone else on the road. Possibly only she was foolish enough to go out in this fog. No need to look for a turning: it was straight on until this road met the seafront one, Violet had told her.

Suddenly: 'Aaah!' She stepped on the brake and the car jerked to a stop, throwing her forward into the steering wheel then back in her seat. A figure had appeared briefly in the headlights, coming from her right as if crossing the road directly in front of her.

Oh good grief, did I hit him?

She was panting, her heart racing. She had to get out and see if she'd hurt someone. He — she thought it was a man but she wasn't sure — had come from nowhere, not even hesitating. She didn't think she'd felt an impact, but then the emergency stop had hardly been the smoothest.

Swallowing down her panic, she opened the car door.

'Hello? Is anyone there?' Her voice sounded little and frightened, like a child's, and muffled in the fog.

No sound. The whiteness swirled wetly all around.

Florence glanced behind to make sure the road was clear, so far as she could see, then sidled out and rushed round to the front of the Morris. She half expected to see a figure lying under her front wheels but there was no one. She went to the side and looked up and down and underneath, but there was not a soul in sight. The foghorn sounded again then, that doleful warning. Florence shivered with cold and fear. She was *sure* there had been someone there . . . a man.

Have to look right round . . . have to.

She went round to the back of the car where the wet road was lit by her fog lamps. No one.

'Are you lost?'

'Huuh!' Florence leaped in surprise, gasping in fear.

'Oh . . . oh, my goodness. I didn't hear anyone coming.'

'Can we help?'

It was a tall couple, standing arm in arm, wrapped in long black coats, hats pulled down, the brims obscuring their faces.

'Are you lost?'

'No . . . thank you.' Florence heard her voice

trembling — the air was so cold suddenly — and she made an effort to pull herself together. This was ridiculous. She was a grown-up woman driving home on a foggy evening and it was just tricky to see the road, that was all. She'd hit no one; she'd imagined the figure. 'I thought I might have hit someone . . . what with the fog, but . . . Oh!'

Where had they gone? The couple seemed to have dissolved into the fog even as she was speaking. But then it was thick enough to swallow up anyone, and who'd stick around dealing with a daft motorist on an evening like this? She didn't recognise them, for all Guisethorpe was such a small place, but then she hadn't seen their faces under the dark brims of their hats. They left no sound of retreating footsteps.

Suddenly, in the absolute silence, she was overcome with fear. She felt as if a strange dread had entered her soul, leaving her more afraid than she had ever been before. She rushed back into the car and slammed the door, locking herself in. The inside of the car was no warmer but at least she was alone. Was she . . . ? She dared to glance in the rear-view mirror at the back seat. Empty, thank goodness.

All right, Flo, it's all right . . . She was breathless, trembling, unable to think for a moment how to drive on. *C'mon, Flo, think* . . .

She engaged first gear . . . Suddenly a face loomed at her side window, a wild, angry, mad face. It was Anthony Bird. His hand, dirty and unkempt, banged on the window.

'Aaah!' Florence's hand flew over to make doubly sure her door was locked. She pressed the accelerator and pulled away, Anthony running beside her, pulling at the door handle. She changed into second gear and accelerated again, unable to see where she was heading with the fog all around, just hoping she wasn't about to drive straight over the kerb and into a tree or a garden wall.

Her breath was coming in sharp gasps, her hands were cold and clammy on the steering wheel as she tried to see what was ahead, tried to outrun the madman snarling in at her. She thought she would never outpace him, but eventually she saw he was no longer beside her. She kept going, gasping out a prayer of sorts — '. . . please, please, please . . . ' — and tried to gather herself to reach the bottom of the road safely, where she would join the seafront road and turn for home.

She almost overshot the road end, but luckily no one else was out driving on such a foggy evening. At least there were streetlights along the front, though smothered by the fog they had become fuzzy globes of opaque yellow. Still, they helped Florence to find the turn-off to Nightingale Lane and then it was a crawl uphill home, Paradise Cottage lit by all the lights she'd thought to switch on before she left.

She parked at the side — it didn't matter if it wasn't neatly — and ran to let herself in, slamming the front door behind her. Scamper gave her the usual joyful welcome home and Florence held her warm little dog gratefully.

'Oh, Scamper, such a terrible thing in the fog. Oh, thank goodness I've got you here with me.'

Quickly she went to the telephone, called

Constable Paige and, swallowing and stuttering, told him about her encounter with Anthony Bird. For some reason she did not want to say anything about the other figures she thought she had seen. They didn't seem to make sense.

The constable told her to stay inside, make sure she locked the doors and to telephone 999 if she had the slightest suspicion Anthony Bird was outside her cottage.

All evening Florence felt unsettled, pacing about her sitting room, peering outside, trying to work out what had happened, even thinking she might have imagined the whole terrifying incident. Was it just a few moments of madness, a weird sort of waking nightmare brought on by her fear of driving in the fog? She tried not to think of it, yet couldn't help re-examining what she'd seen . . . or what she'd thought she'd seen: maybe someone in the road, then those two strange black, silent figures and then Anthony Bird.

Scamper caught her mood and kept getting up and wandering around aimlessly.

When she went up to bed, having checked the doors and windows three times, she peered out before drawing the curtains, hoping to see the lights of Sea View, but the fog was an impenetrable shroud and Paradise Cottage felt completely isolated as the foghorn sounded mournfully along the coast. She did not sleep soundly that night.

★ ★ ★

'What was that about, Scamper, eh, my darling?' said Florence, next morning.

366

She'd brought the dog basket upstairs. She had never done this before and rather despised her weakness, knowing it would be confusing for Scamper, who wasn't usually allowed to sleep upstairs, but, she told herself, it was her house and her dog, she'd do as she liked, never mind being sensible.

The fog had lifted, dispersed by a stiff breeze. There was a weak winter sun low on the horizon. The frightening events of last evening had lost their edge, though Florence still felt unnerved by what she had seen.

'Come on, Scamper, a little walk and then we'll go and fetch Violet and Carmen.'

Scamper knew their names and grinned in anticipation. Carmen in particular had enhanced Scamper's days with her child's energy for a regular mad five minutes and her constant chat.

Half an hour later, Florence set out for Violet's house, Scamper on the front seat. Yesterday's night-marish journey seemed vaguely absurd now she could see the road, the fields, the sea stretching away on her left, yet at first she kept glancing in the mirror, looking for some unnamed thing behind her.

There were people out, opening up the shops, waiting to catch the bus . . . Mr Blake from the grocer's shop recognised Florence's car and waved as he polished his front windows. It was a normal day and this helped to calm her nerves.

'Right, Scamper, I reckon the turning is this one,' said Florence, having driven past most of the shops.

She turned right and felt that the uphill drive was at about the right gradient. There were a few pretty cottages and Victorian villas at first, painted white and pink, long gardens and privet hedges before them. Then the houses were more widely spaced and varied in style. There was something familiar about it. Hadn't she come up here before, to see Mavis Farlowe, and another time to find her old home?

'Now, a turning by a pillar box, Carmen said . . . ' Florence slowed, looking for the left turn, found it and drove up the hill. Parts of the road she didn't recognise at all, but then she spotted a house that she thought she'd seen before: one with distinctive ornate brickwork along the front, then another with a very tall tree in the garden.

Number 41, on the right, she remembered Violet telling her. There . . . the number set into the brickwork of the garden wall was prominent.

She drove in and parked on the gravel in front of the house, which was old-fashioned but looked very clean and neat. She got out of the car, bringing out Scamper on her lead, and saw there was a border of neatly pruned shrubs and the shoots of bulbs peeping among them, and some pots in which the tiny green shoots of what Florence thought might be daffodils were just beginning to show: Carmen's work. Then her attention was caught by the house next door, with its distinctive turret at one corner. There was a hedge between the two gardens and Florence went across to see more of the neighbouring place. She pulled a couple of bricks from a small pile at the side of Violet's garden and stood on them to peer over the hedge. Yes, there it was, the red-brick Victorian house with high gables, bay windows and chimneys: Tempest House.

Of course . . .

'Florence, what on earth are you doing?' It was Violet, standing at her open front door, looking amused.

Florence stepped down. 'Hello, Violet. Such a nice surprise: I recognise the house next door. I couldn't see it in the fog yesterday, of course, and now I find you live next door. It's where my mother and I used to live when we were here. I remembered the turret as soon as I saw it some weeks ago.'

'You lived at Tempest House? Good heavens. I wonder if my mother remembers you when you were little.'

'Your mother? She lived here then? What, all that time ago?'

'Yes. Why not? She brought me up in this house but, of course, I married and moved away, as I think I told you. Then when my dad died, my husband, Will, and I came to live here so Mum wouldn't be alone. When our son was killed in the war his wife, Priscilla, and their baby daughter, Carmen, came to live here, and now it's just Mum and Carmen and me.'

'Yes, I remember you telling me there were the three of you. But of course I had no idea your mother was once my mother's next-door neighbour.'

'Come on in, Florence. It was good of you to bring us home yesterday. We'd never have made it on the bikes,' said Violet, leading the way inside. 'Did you get home all right? We were a bit worried.'

'Not really. I'll tell you in a minute. At the time it was, well, very frightening and I still feel a bit unnerved.'

'That fog *was* frightening. We get a few bad ones every winter but that was especially awful.'

'It wasn't the fog, Violet. It was something really strange.'

'Come and sit down, and tell us. Mother will be so pleased to meet you and see Scamper again.' Violet led the way into a pretty, old-fashioned sitting room, with a sofa and some armchairs, the cushion of which were covered in faded floral fabric. Nothing was new or smart in the room; it might once have been beautiful, but now it all looked well used and worn.

'Mother, this is Florence Stanville. Florence, this is my mother, Frances Marchant.'

'How do you do, Mrs Marchant?'

Florence shook hands with the lady who sat in one of the armchairs near the window. Florence thought Violet's mother was a bit like her surroundings: once beautiful but now very old. Her clothes were outmoded: a pretty dress that looked as if it dated from the thirties, over which she wore two cardigans, both shapeless with age. Her hair was white and thin, her face and neck very wrinkled, but her dark eyes were still bright and shone with intelligence.

'I'm very pleased to meet you,' said Frances. 'I hear a lot about you, and of course your little dog has been here before to stay the night. We all love Scamper. No wonder Carmen is always so full of what this dear little dog is up to,' she smiled.

'I'll get Carmen to make us a pot of tea while

370

Florence tells us her adventure in the fog and then I think I might have a surprise for you, Mother.'

'Tell Carmen to be careful, dear. You know what she's like.'

Violet went to call Carmen, who put her head round the door to say hello to Florence and Scamper.

'Now, tell us what frightened you in the fog, Florence. I'm pleased to say you look unscathed.'

'Anthony Bird.'

'No! Good heavens. What happened? Tell us from the beginning.'

So Florence told them how, after dropping off Violet and Carmen, she'd turned down the road towards the seafront and had been convinced she'd seen a figure passing directly in front of her car.

'I can't think how I avoided hitting him, but when I got out to look there was no one. I was so sure, though . . . and then two people suddenly appeared out of nowhere — I didn't even hear their footsteps and they startled me — and asked if I was all right.'

Violet and Frances exchanged looks.

'What exactly did they say?' asked Violet.

Florence thought hard. 'One said, 'Are you lost?' and the other, or it might have been the same one, said, 'Can we help?' What? I can see you know summat.'

'I won't fob you off, Florence. Some people refer to that road as Haunted Hill, though it isn't its real name, of course. Few have seen them, or at least have said so, though if you ask around maybe you'll find out different, but there is a story

371

of a couple dressed all in black who appear asking people if they're lost.'

'You mean they're ghosts?'

'What did they look like, dear?' asked Frances.

'It's hard to say. Tall, thin, wearing long dark coats, but I can't really describe them. I can't think of any details, except they wore hats with brims. I didn't see their faces — oh, thank goodness I didn't see their faces!'

'Maybe they have no faces,' said Frances.

'Mother!'

'Who can say? What you have described, Florence, is what I have heard before. Tell us what happened then.'

'I started to say I'd been looking to make sure I hadn't hit someone in the fog, and while I was speaking they sort of went . . . disappeared. I thought they'd just moved away in the fog but I didn't hear them go. The air felt very cold, icy suddenly, and I was frightened. I rushed back into the car and locked the door. And thank goodness I did. Next thing I know, Anthony Bird's got his face pressed against the window and is trying to get in.'

'What?' Violet's hands flew up in shock. 'But he didn't? Please tell me he didn't hurt you?'

'No, I managed to drive away and left him behind, but of course I couldn't go too fast in case I ran into anything.' Even recounting the event made Florence feel anxious all over again. 'I got home, rushed inside and locked the door and then telephoned the police. I hardly slept last night, thinking about the weird figures and then that madman leering and snarling through the car window.'

'So he didn't go into the sea after all?'

'He looked wild and mad, as if he had been living rough, gone feral.'

'How terrifying,' said Frances. 'At least the police are alerted now. They'll search and find him.'

'Oh, I hope so. I don't want another encounter like that. It was bad enough with the strange couple. What are they all about? Do they just appear and then go?'

'Something like that,' said Violet, quickly. 'I wouldn't have told you to go down that way if I'd thought for one moment you were going to stop and get out of the car.'

'Well, I wouldn't have done out of choice. What was so strange to start with was that I was certain — completely convinced — I'd seen someone cross the road right in front of me and there was no one there at all.'

'Possibly that was just the swirling of the fog making pictures,' said Violet. 'I've never heard of that being part of the old story.'

Frances agreed and looked hard at Violet, who shook her head slightly.

Then Carmen was at the sitting-room door, precariously balancing a tray of tea, and Violet hurried to take it from her and place it safely on a side table before she spilled anything.

'Would Scamper like a drink?' Carmen asked. She laughed. 'It feels a bit like being back at Bird's Café.'

'It does not,' said Violet snappily.

'I'm sure she would, please, Carmen, but not in

here where she'll make a mess.'

'I'll find a bowl for her in the kitchen. Come on, Scamper . . . '

'Now, Mother,' said Violet, 'you'll never guess what Florence told me outside.'

'Probably not, dear.'

'I used to live in the house next door, Tempest House, with my mother. Violet thinks you might remember her.'

Florence unclasped the chain of the locket she always wore, with the photographs of 'Little Flo' and 'Lily' in it. She opened it and passed it to Frances.

'Ah, Lily Townsend, of course. Who else could it be? As soon as I saw your red hair, I thought of Lily. And I remember you, too, from this photograph. Your mother was a nice young woman. Is she still alive, Florence, dear?'

'No, I'm afraid she died a year ago, in Lancashire, where I lived with her. I sold her house and came here. We were very happy here so, when I was ready to start a new life, I chose this place with its good associations.'

'I'm sorry to hear she's died. But happy, you say? Strange, I always remember Lily had such a sad life. When she inherited the house from Mr Carswell, I hoped her luck had changed and she was setting a course for happier days.'

'Mr Carswell. I had completely forgotten the name and I can't picture his face. Carswell . . . Carswell. Am I right, he had a very quiet voice, so we'd be whispering all the time, taking our voices down to his level?'

'Ah, yes, a very quiet man altogether. Everything

about him was 'less than', if you know what I mean: small, pale, very thin hair, little tiny voice. But kind, very kind indeed.'

'I don't really remember,' said Florence. 'I wish I did. I just know we lived there after my father and my sister died of the Spanish flu, but I don't quite know why there, and then Mr Carswell must have died and then, at some point, we moved away.'

'Spanish flu?' asked Frances carefully. 'Is that what your mother told you, Florence, dear?'

'Mother, I really don't think — '

'Yes, she told me that, Mrs Marchant. Wasn't that the truth?'

'It's nothing to do with us, Florence. It's your family, not ours,' said Violet, looking crossly at her mother.

'But now that my mother's dead, there's only me and my lass, Lucy, and I'd like to be told if I'm mistaken in my past. Mebbe it's my misunderstanding, or I've forgotten something, but I'm sure my father and Rosa died of the flu. I told you, didn't I, Violet? That was why I was so worried when Lucy had flu before Christmas. Why would my mother have told me that if it wasn't true?'

'I remember, of course. Now, Mother, if you think that isn't so, do you also think there might be a good reason why Florence's mother told her something different?'

'I'm sorry, Florence, I was just so surprised that, even now, you still think it was the flu that killed your father and sister. I never thought Lily would have taken the truth to the grave with her.'

'Well, she didn't really,' said Florence. 'She said something at the end that made me think

375

there was more to her time here than she'd let on, some secret she thought it was too late to impart, mebbe because she hadn't the strength to tell it. She said she'd been running away, that she hadn't been able to forgive, and something about it didn't matter what the truth was. You seem aware of whatever it is she kept from me, Mrs Marchant, and you've already implied you think it's summat I should rightly know, so, please, I'd like you to tell me. What exactly happened to my father and my sister, Rosa?'

19

'I don't know what happened to your father in the end, Florence, but I can tell you about Rosa,' said Frances. 'Your mother was heartbroken when she died and she invented the story about the flu because she thought it would spare you.'

'Spare me what? Mrs Marchant, I'm imagining all sorts now.'

'Mother, I really don't think — ' began Violet.

'What's Great-Grandma saying? Am I allowed to stay?' said Carmen, coming back in with Scamper.

'No — ' began Violet.

'Carmen, I don't mind you hearing if your great-grandmother thinks it suitable for young ears.'

Frances nodded and Violet looked resigned.

'Come and sit here, love, and Scamper can sit between our feet,' said Florence, patting the seat on the sofa next to her. 'Now, Mrs Marchant, *please*, tell me about Rosa.'

'She didn't die of the Spanish flu, Florence. Neither of them did. Rosa died in an accident in the street, Lily told me. She was run over and killed.'

'What! Oh, no! Oh, poor Rosa. What an awful thing to happen.' For a moment Florence was stunned with surprise and shock. 'But I don't understand. Why would my mother lie to me about it? Rosa was still dead — how was it any better to tell me that she died of the flu?'

'Because your sister was out with your father when she was killed. They'd gone to get some shopping together or something — I don't know the details — and he went into a pub to get a jug of beer and left Rosa waiting outside. Then she saw someone she knew — a friend from school, I think Lily told me — across the road and made to go to her without looking, and . . . well, you can guess what happened. I'm so sorry. Lily blamed Robert, your father. She said she could never forgive him, that he was too selfish and irresponsible to be bothered to look after Rosa properly. He'd sacrificed his daughter for a jug of beer. Lily had lost her firstborn daughter because of him, as she saw it, and so she took her other daughter — you — away with her 'to be safe from him because he's a bad father', she said. He wasn't to be trusted with her little girl. She'd never trust him again and she'd never forgive him. Oh, Florence, she was distraught when she told me.'

Florence sat quite still, trying to take all this in. She felt as if her whole life had shifted, as if on dangerous quicksand; that what she'd thought was safe and true was suddenly neither. Yet this fitted in with her mother's words, which had puzzled her all these months.

She cleared her throat. 'How did she come to tell you, Mrs Marchant?' she asked, and her voice came out very small, as if the essential Florence had been blown away by this revelation.

'We were friends. Lily brought you to Guisethorpe, I think to get right away from Robert, and she took up a job looking after Mr Carswell, the old man who lived alone in the house next door, Tempest House. It was a live-in job and so you both lived in that big place, with all its twisty stairways and endless long corridors. I thought it rather a creepy kind of house, full of echoes and loneliness — I wouldn't want to be wandering around there in the dead of night — but your mother took to it, and to Mr Carswell. She was very good to him and for a while his poor health improved with her care. It was touching to see her gentleness and thoughtfulness. Lily and I used to see each other over the hedge, or in the street when she was doing the shopping, or taking you down to play on the beach or to school, and we became friends, even though I was quite a bit older — Violet was already married by then.

'Lily passed herself off as a widow. It saved people asking questions, I suppose. So many people knew of someone who had died of the Spanish flu around that time and it was perfectly plausible that the poor woman had lost her husband in the pandemic. She told you the same, I suppose so you wouldn't tell a different story, or to protect you, perhaps — you were only a little thing, after all — and she clearly never told you different. Maybe it became the reality, a story told so often that it became believed over time. It would have got increasingly difficult to give you a different version as time went on.'

'Poor Mum . . . So what changed? She could have gone on for ever pretending to be a widow, couldn't she? Why did she tell you the truth when she never told it to me?'

'Mr Carswell wanted to marry her. He was a

great deal older than she was and he had no family that he knew of. He wanted to leave his house to Lily, all his things and all his money. He was quite a wealthy man. But he didn't want some distant cousin he'd never heard of turning up and staking a claim of kinship. He reckoned that Lily had been the only person to care for him when his health was failing, so he thought that if he married her then her inheritance would be secure.'

'You hear of this,' said Violet, 'carers putting in all the effort, all the kindness to help a person in their last years and then some relation emerges from the woodwork to lay claim to the fortune or overturn the will when they never spared their dying relative five minutes of their time.'

'Selfish,' muttered Carmen.

'Of course, Lily couldn't marry him because she was still married to your father, Florence. She'd cut herself off from him completely. She didn't even know where he was, but her anger at what she said he had done was still simmering. She was faced with a dilemma: whether to seek out Robert and divorce him so she could marry Mr Carswell, as the kind old man wanted, or to tell Mr Carswell that she couldn't marry him, even if she didn't reveal why, thereby disappointing him. That's when she told me the truth. Her original deception was done with the best intention, which was to protect you, but in the end she was worried that it could potentially cost you both a great deal in terms of material wealth.'

'Poor Mum. But I know she didn't marry Mr Carswell, so I guess she either told him the truth or mebbe summat that passed for it.'

'She thought about it a lot. I couldn't really advise her and I could see it was wearing her down. But finally, because of what happened to Rosa, she decided to risk losing the inheritance to any relative of Mr Carswell's with a familial claim. She told me she had vowed never to seek out Robert, speak to him or set eyes on him again, even though it meant she couldn't marry Mr Carswell.'

'Was she in love with Mr Carswell? Did she want to marry him?' asked Florence. 'Was she cutting off a second chance of happiness because she could never forgive my father? I can't think she was so filled with anger. I just *can't* believe it. She wasn't an angry person.

She was gentle and kind. We were as close as any mother and daughter could be and I don't recognise her as a woman simmering with hatred, living with this awful tragedy and all its fall-out.'

Carmen patted Florence's hand comfortingly, while Frances and Violet were silent.

Florence stood up, wringing her hands, turning this way and that, then sat down again.

'Oh, I don't know . . . ' she said helplessly. 'How can I even take in the truth now, after believing a lie for nearly forty years? I thought I knew that my father and sister had died in the pandemic, but I knew nowt in reality, and all the while my father was dead to my mother in an altogether different way. My poor darling ma . . . Such a brave step she took, bringing me up by herself because she thought it was for the best. And yet, she lied to me, too.'

'It's possible she wanted to tell you the truth,

Florence, but maybe as time went on she was worried you might think she'd done the wrong thing, that you'd think less of her if you knew,' said Violet. 'I hope you don't think less of her now.' She shot a severe look at Frances.

'No, I loved her so much. She was the best mother I could ever have had. I understand now she believed my father was not a good father and so she cut him out of our lives. After all, what sort of relationship would they have had, my parents, if Mum was unable to forgive him? How could they have lived together? Impossible . . . '

Violet shook her head sadly.

'Well, she didn't marry Mr Carswell,' sighed Florence. 'She told me an old employer died and left her his house which she then sold and lived on the money. If a distant relative did turn up to try to claim it, I know nowt about that and they didn't succeed.' She smiled a crooked smile. 'It must be partly Mr Carswell's fortune that's enabled me to set up the pickle business. After she sold Tempest House, Mum was able to live doing exactly as she wanted without the need to 'make ends meet', which snuffs out many a woman's creative talents. She took up painting and became rather good at it, and she travelled about a bit with another widow, with whom she'd struck up a friendship after I left home. She lived quite modestly — no one would have guessed she had money — though she knew it was a privilege not to have to work. She wasn't an educated woman, having left school without sitting any exams, but she educated herself in later life, reading what interested her, which was a great deal. I thought she'd made the best of her life after being left a young widow, but now I learn that so-called widowhood was underpinned by a completely different reality.'

'Such a sad story,' Violet said quietly. She stood up and came to put her arms around Florence. 'But it need make no difference to you unless you let it. Your mother acted for the best when she could no longer trust your father. There's no doubt that she loved you dearly.'

'Yes,' sighed Florence. 'Thank you for telling me, Mrs Marchant. It's the truth and it's right that it should emerge eventually. It's just such a shock, especially after I thought we were both so happy when we lived here. Mebbe it was only me who was happy, too taken up with myself to see that my mother was suffering.'

'I don't know, Florence,' said Violet. 'But *you* were happy, and it's your memories of that time that brought you back here. Don't let this spoil how you see your life now. You're settled here, aren't you? I hope you are.'

'Yes, I am, thanks to you and Carmen, thanks to Jim and the Kendal sisters and Becca, the little community at the produce market, a good relationship with Harry Nicolson and Sandra Filbert ...'

'Then don't go worrying about what you thought, love, just go with how it *is*,' Violet advised. 'You can't change anything of your mother's life now. You loved Guisethorpe when you lived next door, at Tempest House, and you love it now you're at Paradise Cottage.'

'Except for the pickle smell,' Carmen added solemnly.

Florence laughed loudly, a relief from the tension. 'Aye, you're right about that. I *must* find new premises so I can reclaim my home from the pickles. I'll make a proper effort to do it now that Christmas is over, and then we'll be all set for Jim's new and ambitious crops, come the better weather.'

'Hurray,' said Carmen quietly, smiling at Florence.

Florence got up and rubbed her eyes. 'I think, if you don't mind, Violet and Carmen, I might just go home and forget about the pickles for the rest of the day. I've got quite a bit to think about.'

'Of course you have, love,' said Violet. 'Try not to blame your ma, though. Who knows what any of us would have done in similar circumstances?'

Florence attached Scamper's lead and led her to the hall and the front door, Violet following. On the doorstep Florence turned.

'Well, that wasn't in my plan for the morning.'

'I'm sorry, I had no idea about it and certainly can't think why my mother should have just embarked on 'the truth' like some evangelist. It wasn't her truth to tell you. I wish she'd kept quiet.'

'Oh, but I don't really, Violet. I've been wondering about the things my mother said to me at the end and now the mystery is solved. It's not a comfortable truth, that's for sure, but the alternative is just a lie. A long-established lie planted firmly in my life like a deep-rooted weed in a flowerbed, but a lie nonetheless. I haven't decided yet which is better. I just need time to think it all through.'

'Course you do, Florence. But you know where

I am if you need me. And you've got Jim if you want another pair of listening ears. He's a good man and I know he's fond of you.'

'Thank you, Violet. But it's not just the lie I have to come to terms with, is it? You see, if my father didn't die of the Spanish flu, it's possible that he is still alive.'

Violet was taken aback. 'Heavens, that hadn't occurred to me. You're right, of course.'

They looked at each other and then Violet patted Florence's shoulder and Florence led Scamper out to the car.

★ ★ ★

'Well, Mother, you certainly caused an upset there,' said Violet, back in the sitting room after Carmen had gone to amuse herself outside in the weak winter sunshine, taking advantage of her unexpected day off. 'She didn't have to know. You could have kept quiet.'

'But she wanted to know, Vi. She asked me to tell her. Florence Stanville obviously agrees with me: I think we must always seek the truth, even if it's unpalatable.'

'Do you indeed? Well, I'm not sure I agree. Poor Florence. Really, Mother, I can only thank goodness you managed to keep quiet about what legend has it happens when a person has seen the ghostly figures. I'm surprised you didn't tell her that, too.'

'Ah, now, that's different. We've only been told that their appearance foretells a death; we don't know that for sure.'

'Then I suggest you keep your mouth firmly

shut on the subject. Poor woman's got enough to think about, thanks to you and Anthony Bird. Still, so far as I'm aware, Carmen doesn't know that part of the story, so at least she isn't going to blurt out something stupid . . . '

★ ★ ★

Florence drove slowly home, her mind on what she had learned. Could Frances Marchant possibly be wrong? It was unlikely, given that she said Lily had told her all this. The part of the story about Lily being left some money and a big house and selling it was exactly what Florence already knew, so why shouldn't the rest of it be correct? And Frances would have no motive to lie.

'Oh, Scamper, I just can't settle with thinking about it,' she said, parking at the side of Paradise Cottage. She couldn't remember any of the journey from Violet's house, although she had retraced her route from earlier that morning, avoiding going on to the next turning and down Haunted Hill again. The ghostly and terrifying experiences of the previous evening had lost their edge and faded in her mind now, supplanted by this morning's revelations.

She got herself something to eat, but afterwards she couldn't decide what she wanted to do and walked about the cottage aimlessly, wasting time, for which she reproved herself.

'Right, better have a walk, Scamper,' she said. 'At least we'll have achieved that.'

They set off down the lane, then on to the seafront road and down the first set of steps to the

386

sand in the usual way, Scamper leading, her tail waving like a furry flag in the breeze.

Florence sauntered along, letting Scamper run ahead and have some fun while her own thoughts could only be on what she had learned that morning. Eventually she sat down on the shingle, not caring about her coat getting damp, and Scamper nosed around the shallows in front of her, knowing not to wander too far.

Could Robert Townsend be alive? How old would he be now? She wasn't sure — all parents seem old to their small children — but he would certainly be in his seventies, perhaps older. Yet it was possible he lived still. He would not know that Lily was dead. Who knew what kind of life he might have had since Lily cast him out from hers. He could be anywhere — abroad, even. Perhaps he had another family. Just because Lily had been truthful about the fact that she was married, it did not follow that Robert had been. What if he had married bigamously and had a whole family of grown-up children, and then Florence turned up, claiming to be his daughter, upsetting people where there was no need? After all, it would be illegal for him to be married to a second wife, but it would not be the fault of the woman or any children if he hadn't told them. One read about such families in the newspapers and no one was a winner in those situations.

She gazed out at the grey North Sea. It was exactly the same as it had been all those years ago; this sand and shingle just the same, too. Little Flo and Lily had sat in this exact same place, quietly enjoying each other's company, being everything to each other. Yet what underpinned that wonderful time was now so different from what Florence had thought.

She hugged her knees, resting her chin on them, and let what memories come that would, like brief snapshots of her partially forgotten childhood.

★ ★ ★

1919

A woman and a child were standing in front of the large house, their bags at their feet. The little girl looked up at the front, seeing a huge wooden front door within a handsome porch, vast windows and, unusually, a little tower in one corner like in a fairy story.

'Are we really going to live here, Mummy?'

'We are, my darling, at least to start with. Let's see how it works out, shall we?'

Lily knocked on the door and after a very long time an old man came and opened it.

'Mrs Townsend, come in. I am Arthur Carswell. I'm delighted to meet you. And this little one. Remind me of your name, please, child.'

'Florence Elizabeth Townsend, sir.'

'Come in, Florence Elizabeth Townsend,' he smiled. He had a very quiet voice, as if he'd been so used to living alone and in silence that an ordinary level of sound would be like a blast of harsh noise, a rude intrusion.

Florence was invited to explore the house, which took many weeks, as she gathered her courage and ventured further into the tall rooms, along the lofty corridors, up into numerous unoccupied bedrooms and attic rooms. There was endless space to play — to play by herself.

Lily settled into cooking and cleaning for Mr Carswell, washing and dressing him, taking him for walks, which took a long time as he moved so slowly. He was very kind, always thoughtful, grateful for the care Lily showed him, though he paid her generously to do so.

What a summer that was: Florence's first sight of the sea, sparkling every day under a hot sun and cloudless sky. And what a seaside! Not the crowded beaches and tawdry attractions of seaside resorts popular with day trippers that were promised in places like Blackpool, but a pretty village, a peaceful place — almost a secret one — where voices were never raised, where the only visitor attractions were the long beach and the very cold sea, brisk walks along the sand and shingle against a stiff easterly breeze.

Mr Carswell liked to have a sleep downstairs in the afternoons, and once Lily had settled him on the shady terrace at the back of his house, or inside with the French windows propped open if it was especially hot, she would take Florence down to the beach and they'd sit on the sand drawing pictures in it with pointed stones, or build sand-castles together, or paddle in the cold shallows. The beach had a special clean-dirty, salty, sea-weedy smell that they both loved, and sometimes they just sat on the sand and breathed in that wonderful seaside scent.

'Let's just sit and be,' Lily would say, and she'd close her eyes and breathe calmly, and Florence would do the same. It took a while to learn to do it, to be still and not fill her mind with questions and ideas about what else to do that afternoon, but eventually Florence acquired the skill just to empty her mind, just to be. To enjoy just being together, the two of them: Little Flo and her mother, sitting on the sand.

The weather grew colder as autumn set in, but Lily and Florence just wore more clothes on their visits to the beach and dug their castles with more energy, and took fewer paddles and more brisk walks, then sat higher up wrapped in their coats and emptied their minds in the shelter of the sea-front wall. The last of the visitors went home, and the beach was quieter, which suited Lily and Florence. Living with Mr Carswell, they were becoming accustomed to quiet; they preferred it.

Once Florence said, looking at the vast sky, the setting sun casting reflections of gold on the grey sea, 'I don't want to go back and live in a town again. I want to stay here for ever,' and Lily replied, 'We don't live in a town. We live here. I don't think of the town now. That's all quite forgotten. This is a lovely place, Mr Carswell is very kind, and we are so lucky to be here, just you and me.'

Florence went to school in Guisethorpe and made friends, although she could not invite them to come to play at Tempest House. It wasn't her home to invite them to, and Mr Carswell liked to live his life in near silence. He wouldn't want noisy children running about the place, Lily told Florence. But that didn't matter because Florence had her friends to play with at school, and at home it was just her and Lily, living quietly in the big house belonging to Mr Carswell. Mr Carswell himself was so silent and moved so slowly, and Tempest House was so large that Florence sometimes forgot he lived there at all. She'd go whole days and not even see him.

Once, brushing her hair at the mirror, Florence realised how like Rosa she was growing. It could almost be Rosa's face reflected back at her. For a fraction of a second she had even thought it was, and had given a little gasp of fright. Rosa had died very suddenly of the terrible flu that had killed so many people, and that had killed Florence's father equally swiftly. One day they were there and then they weren't, and she never saw them again. Florence tended not to think of her father much because there was nothing in her life to remind her of him now — Lily had no photographs of him — but her own face reminded her of Rosa every day, which was something she couldn't help.

'Do you ever think about Rosa, Mummy?' she asked once, as they sat having breakfast in the big echoey kitchen with the very high ceiling.

Lily's eyes immediately reddened with unshed tears. 'Of course I do, love, but she's gone now. We hold her in a special place in our hearts so she's always with us, but it's just us — Lily and Little Flo — now, and we're so lucky to have each other and to be here together, aren't we?'

Then she wiped her eyes and lifted the teapot with its blue-and-white knitted tea cosy with a pompom on top and poured Florence a cup of tea into 'her' special cup with the pink flowers, which was the one she chose to use herself from among Mr Carswell's pretty things.

★ ★ ★

Florence lifted her face and looked out at the sea again. Those little memories were probably of events months apart, all the days in between forgotten for ever with the passing of time. Now, in the light of what Frances Marchant knew, they had come to light again and acquired a different emphasis, a heart-rending subplot.

'Oh dear . . .'

'That was heartfelt, Florence.'

It was Jim, wrapped up in a coat that had seen many winters, and an ancient-looking scarf. Scamper came over straight away, wagging her tail enthusiastically.

Florence stood up, knowing Jim found it difficult to sit on the ground and then get up again, his knees beginning to feel their age.

'Oh, Jim, it's grand to see you. Ah, it's just summat I have to think through . . . bit of a downturn, but I'll manage. I thought a good walk on the beach would straighten my thoughts.'

Jim frowned. 'Looks like the only one enjoying the walk was young Scamper here.'

'Don't flatter her, Jim, it'll only go to her head. She's seven, you know, quite a middle-aged woman, for all she's as daft as a puppy.'

'Not working this afternoon, then?'

'No, I got distracted and gave Violet and Carmen the day off.'

'I wondered if I'd find you down here, love.

Mildred saw you going out earlier and shortly afterwards Constable Paige turned up at Paradise.'

'Oh, he'll have come about Anthony Bird, I expect. I had a bit of an encounter with him in the fog yesterday evening and it was all rather frightening. Thing is, now it's clear he didn't go into the sea, as the police thought he had when they found those clothes on the beach.'

'So I gather. Rodney Paige saw no harm in imparting his information to me, so I'll tell you. Anthony Bird will not be bothering you or Trudie or anyone else again, Florence. He was involved in an accident late last night. A motorist on the road to Fleming ran over him in the fog and killed him.'

'Oh . . . ! I was nearly going to say 'Oh, thank God', but that isn't really what I mean, although I'll be more than pleased never to see the wretched man again. I mean, what an awful waste. I think Violet and Carmen will be shocked to hear that, and Trudie Symons, too, though I've never met the girl. I think Anthony Bird descended into lunacy, or maybe he was always mad and that's why he couldn't seem to apply himself to anything, but I'm afraid in the end he was a troublesome and violent lunatic.'

'Yes, it's a sad tale right enough: all those opportunities missed, lovely little business handed to him on a plate and he squandered it all. Such a shame.'

'I can't say I won't miss looking over my shoulder to see if he's pursuing me in the street, but I just wish . . . Oh, I don't know, Jim. Lots to think about, that's all.'

'Let me know if I can do anything to help.'

'Thanks. But these are mostly things I have to sort out myself. Anyway,' she brightened, 'unless you're off somewhere particular, why don't you come home with me and we'll have a cup of tea?'

'Only came along to find you, Florence. Thank you. Tea's a good idea: fortify us in the face of sad news.'

Florence gathered herself to make the generous gesture. 'Ask Mildred to join us, why don't you?'

20

The next morning Florence collected Violet and Carmen from their home and brought them back to Paradise Cottage, as she had intended to do the day before. There wasn't much to pickle in January so they moved on to marmalade making. At least the cottage now smelled of hot sugar and oranges instead of vinegar, although the kitchen became strangely tacky, however careful everyone was not to spill anything. Carmen was found to be the sticky culprit. One side of her apron had several patches of marmalade spilled on it, which she had transferred to the sides of the table and the cupboards as she passed, and which had then got transferred to Florence and Violet's fronts.

'Never mind, Carmen,' said Florence. 'I've never made marmalade yet without having to clean the entire kitchen afterwards. Just, whatever you do, don't walk it into the sitting room. That's all I ask. And please try not to get it on Scamper, either.'

'Rinse your pinny out, please, Carmen, and then go and hang it on the line outside,' said Violet, rolling her eyes at Carmen for her carelessness. 'It's good that the marmalade is ready to eat now. If these test jars are a success we can get going on a huge amount straight away.'

'I'll take a jar to Miss Bea and Miss Jane this afternoon and solicit their opinion,' said Florence. 'And you can take some home to Mrs Marchant, if you like, Violet.'

Carmen was outside dealing with her pinafore, so Violet felt she could give vent to her opinion about Frances. 'No, I shan't bother, Florence, love. She doesn't deserve any after the way she just blurted out what your mother told her yesterday.'

Florence sighed. 'I have to say, it was a big thing to learn, but I'm certain it was what my mother was alluding to at the end of her life. I'm just finding it hard to take in the fact that what she told me, and what I believed all my life up to now, was untrue. She could have revised her story any time over many years.'

'So difficult for you, Florence. I do understand. But it's the way my mother told you that gets my goat: not asking if you might like to ... I don't know ... consider learning what she had heard first, before she launched in.'

'Oh, Violet, I think my stars must be aligned for surprises or summat, what with that, the ghosts and the awful business about Anthony Bird. I telephoned Constable Paige and he said he'd been to see you at home, and also Trudie, who was very upset.' She sighed. 'I hope you and Carmen are OK.'

'We're all right, Florence, thank you. We're sad, of course — who wouldn't be when it's all such a tragedy — but we've both got mixed feelings about Anthony. He wasn't a kind man or a good employer. Shame; his father was widely liked ... Anyway,' she changed the subject, 'you said it was time to think about new premises now Christmas is behind us.'

'It's hopeless, Violet. I've been looking around for weeks and there's nothing suitable that's affordable.'

'So what will happen if we can't find a place?'

'I don't know. I might have to think about whether to continue. Or mebbe just stick to making the other preserves, though it's the pickles that sell best. But don't worry, I'm not defeated yet. There must be somewhere.'

★ ★ ★

Beatrice and Jane were delighted with the marmalade that afternoon.

'Ooh, the jar is still warm,' said Beatrice.

'Pass it over, Bea dear, and I'll warm my hands on it,' joked Jane.

The sisters were wrapped up in two cardigans each, little hand-knitted scarves knotted at their necks. 'Becca knitted them. Isn't she a dear?'

'Come and sit by the fire, Mrs Stanville . . . '

'. . . and get yourself warm after the journey.'

'We have Scamper's basket waiting for her, too.'

Florence wasn't really cold but she did as they asked, politely accepting their hospitality. Scamper, of course, greeted the sisters like long-lost friends and then settled into her basket. Becca came in with the tea tray and then Jane said it was her turn to choose a new book, and would Florence mind reading *Emma*?

'Just what I would have chosen myself,' declared Beatrice.

'I know, dear,' murmured Jane.

So they sat around the library fire, the glass-shaded lamps on the walls at either side of the chimney breast and suspended from the ceiling giving off a pink glow, and Florence began reading aloud the much-loved novel.

Just as she was finishing for the afternoon — and very much feeling the calming effects of the witty and elegant prose — Matthew came in.

'Good afternoon, Aunt Jane and Aunt Bea, and Mrs Stanville.'

'Matthew, how lovely of you to visit . . .'

'. . . dear boy.'

'Mrs Stanville, I am very pleased to find you here this afternoon. I was thinking of going over to see you and you've saved me the journey. I have a proposal to make to you.'

'I do remember you saying you had an interest in what I was making, Mr Kendal. It must be a couple of months ago now, when my daughter was staying and Miss Bea and Miss Jane sent over some lovely flowers to cheer her recovery from the flu.'

'Yes, time moves on, and of course we've had Christmas since then.'

'Matthew, dear, why don't you take Mrs Stanville into the sitting room . . .'

'. . . there is a fire in there so you won't be chilled . . .'

'. . . and then you can discuss your business in private?'

'Thank you, Aunts. Good idea.' Matthew stood back to let Florence go first.

'So, Mr Kendal,' said Florence, perching on one of the armchairs, as Matthew closed the door,

'I am all ears to know what interest you have in the Florence Lily business.'

'Well, Mrs Stanville, when I came round with the flowers for Lucille, I couldn't help noticing the aroma of pickling vinegar at your home, and I think you might have mentioned to Becca that you're beginning to find the smell rather overwhelming, is that right?'

'Mr Kendal, the whole place stinks of vinegar. Even Scamper smells of it. I was daft not to realise it was inevitable. I've been looking about for a kitchen to rent at a price the business can afford, but I've not found anywhere. Luckily, we're on to marmalade this month so the lingering vinegar smell is overlaid by oranges, but I'm dreading the smell in summer with a full menu of pickles to cook. I've made a vow to find somewhere before spring.'

'Maybe I can help you there, Mrs Stanville. I have recently acquired a bit of land and on it are some huts that housed Land Girls during the war. The farmers hereabouts needed the labour but some hadn't the accommodation, so they got together and had these huts built. They're very basic and they need a lot of renovation, of course, but they do have water and electricity already. I'm thinking of doing them up and renting them out as business units. I shall need the necessary permissions, of course, but I don't envisage any problems there.' He smiled like a man who had some special foreknowledge. 'There will be only half a dozen units, and all for small local businesses such as yours, so no one could possibly raise objections about the volume of traffic coming and going or anything of that nature.'

'Good heavens! But where is this land and these huts?'

'Here, in Fleming St Clair. Turn right at the top of the hill instead of left for Long Barrow Lane and there you are.'

'Have you drawn up any plans that I can see?' asked Florence, her heart lifting at this possible good news but trying to be sensible and professional. 'I'd need just a big kitchen with a pantry and storeroom, with plenty of ventilation. Is that a possibility?'

'You can have what you like, within reason, if you agree in advance to rent it from me. I can have a kitchen built to your specs.'

'But I'm anxious that I might not be able to afford it.'

'We'll need to discuss what would be fair to both of us, of course . . . '

Florence was relieved to hear that. 'I do hope we can agree. This could be the answer, the difference between me carrying on with the pickles and giving up. Thank you, Mr Kendal.'

'Well, it's a start for me if I get you on board. I'm sure a smart label like Florence Lily will attract other businesses of the right sort.'

As Florence set out for home, Scamper on the front seat beside her, she couldn't help smiling, despite all the drama of the past couple of days. Never in her whole life had she thought of herself as 'the right sort', an asset to attract others of the same kind. She told herself not to get too excited: there was a long way to go and Matthew Kendal wouldn't rent out his business space cheaply to do her a favour. Still, it was a beginning.

At the end of the lane, instead of turning down the hill, she drove straight on and pulled up outside the field she thought must be the place Matthew had described. She got out of the car and peered in the gathering gloom over an ugly metal gate, chained and padlocked, at a muddy field with a row of dismal, rundown huts to one side of it.

Good grief, could this really be the place? But there was a sale board up by the gate with a 'Sold' sign stuck over the top, so it must be. Oh dear, this looked awful. What on earth was Matthew Kendal playing at? Was this all a con? Surely not — he was Miss Bea and Miss Jane's adored and adoring nephew — but how could this rubbishy old row of huts ever be a professional kitchen where she, Violet and Carmen could all work with light and space?

'Scamper, I don't think we should get our hopes up,' she said, getting back into the car. 'I'm going to have to discuss this further with Matthew Kendal.'

Feeling low again, she drove home, thinking about the ghostly figures who had planted their creepy presence into the back of her mind and would not leave. Then she began mulling over everything Frances Marchant had told her again. She wondered whether her father was still alive and, if so, how she would ever find him . . . and whether she really wanted to.

★ ★ ★

401

Many jars of marmalade were produced at Paradise Cottage in the long dark month of January. Florence's recipe was very popular at Nicolson & Filbert, while a few plainly labelled jars made a welcome bright display on the windowsill behind Jim's rather utilitarian offering of seasonal root vegetables and cabbages at the St Jude's Hall produce market.

'Your jars look like a sunrise, Florence, all red-gold and shiny,' said Jim.

Doreen Potter came over, looking furious, as Florence and Jim were setting up.

'Have you cleared that display with Mary?' she snapped. 'It seems, Mrs Stanville, that you're deliberately trying to usurp my long-established position as preserve maker at this event.'

'Ask Mary if you like,' said Florence, who already had, 'but with your 'long-established position', surely you're the first person customers will seek out? Jim and I don't greatly mind whether my marmalade sells or not. It's just a little sideline, so far as I'm concerned.'

Doreen didn't look very pacified but she turned to go. Then suddenly she spun back and asked Florence abruptly, 'How do you get yours so clear and bright?'

'I reckon it may just have been luck this time,' said Florence, trying to look as if she hadn't a clue. 'I haven't your experience and I really know nowt about it.'

Jim laughed as Doreen stomped off, the scowl on her face certain to frighten off her first potential customers.

Mavis Farlowe, who had completely got the

hang of making eye-catching displays of her cakes these days, and was managing without Florence's help, came over from her table next to Jim's.

'Florence, love, I wonder if I might buy a jar of yours with a view to including it in a cake recipe I want to try. If it works out well, I could buy quite a few jars, if you have them?'

Florence thought of the shelves of jars in the Kendal sisters' storeroom and her own pantry. It had been a very sticky month at Paradise, and the kitchen had had to be cleaned countless times, but the result of all the hard work was so satisfying.

'Of course, Mavis. Thank you, I'd love to sell you a jar, and I can manage a few more if your cake comes out well and you want them.'

'The thing is, dear, it's not 'a few' so much as 'quite a few'. Maybe, if the cake is a success, I'd need several dozen. I know it's a lot but I'd rather buy from you than anyone else.'

'Good heavens, are you sure?'

'Well, I bake cakes for the two bakeries in Fleming — they're actually owned by the same person — and if they like them they do sell rather a lot of cake.'

'I'd no idea, Mavis.'

'Well, I don't make a big fuss about it, love. I don't suppose many people know. Though I'm thinking of setting up my own shop, with my granddaughter, who's also a baker. I thought about the old café premises on the seafront.'

'Well, that would be wonderful. Guisethorpe needs a bakery,' said Florence. 'Good luck for that. I shan't be telling anyone what your plans are, though.'

'Jim knows, of course. I can rely on his discretion.' She beamed at Jim, who was carefully placing a cabbage with a circumference of over two foot to one side of his display.

'Here, Mavis, take a jar, never mind about the money, and if you like it we can discuss where to go from there.'

'Oh, thank you, Florence. You are a sweetheart.' She took the jar of marmalade and shuffled off back to her table.

Later, she came over with a cake in a paper bag. 'A little Eccles for your tea, love,' she said, handing it to Florence.

You certainly saw all sorts in Guisethorpe, Florence thought, as she helped fold up the tables at the end of the morning. The folk in this little village were as varied as those in Blackburn or Southport, though possibly not London. She was so fortunate to have made such good, kind friends. When she'd first arrived she had been so wary of everyone, in case they turned out to be the kind of person she'd rather not know, and she still thought rather shame-facedly of her suspicions about dear old Jim when she'd first encountered him and his little welcoming gift of beans. If you just took your time and let people's characters unfold, you might well be pleasantly surprised, she reflected. Mavis Farlowe was a case in point: on the face of it a rather timid old lady, easy to underestimate, who, Florence had thought, made a few batches of traditional cakes for the produce sale. In fact, she was in so many ways a woman after Florence's own heart:

enterprising and hard-working, determined to make her own way. How good it would be if she did expand her business and move into the old Bird's Café and give the place a new purpose. The premises had been sad and abandoned for far too long.

★ ★ ★

On the way home, with Jim's few remaining vegetables in a box in the boot, the marmalade all sold, Florence was unusually quiet.

'You all right, Florence?' Jim asked. 'Only these last few days you've looked a bit . . . thoughtful, and I'm hoping you're not worried about anything. Anthony Bird's gone now, so it can't be that bothersome blighter.'

Florence smiled at the description. 'No, not him. Truth be told, Jim, I've been thinking a lot about what brought me here in the first place: my mother.'

'But she's been dead for only a year, Florence love, so of course you think about her still. I imagine you always will.'

'Yes. I miss her so much. Not as much as I did at the beginning, but there's not a day that I don't think of her. We lived together so happily here after . . . oh, I keep forgetting! I was going to say 'after my father and my sister, Rosa, died of the Spanish flu', but they didn't. I'm so used to thinking that, I'm finding it hard to acknowledge the truth. It hasn't quite sunk in.'

'It sounds like you've only just found out something different.'

'Yes, Jim, and quite by chance, from Frances Marchant.'

'Violet's mother? How extraordinary!'

'Well, not really. It wouldn't be so strange to find someone who might have known my mother when we lived in Tempest House, up the hill, and Mrs Marchant lived next door then and still does. She was friends with my mother . . . '

Florence told Jim what she had learned from Frances about her father and Rosa.

'Such a tragedy,' said Jim, shaking his head sadly. 'No wonder Lily tried to hide it from you.'

'Yes, I can't blame her for doing so when I was little, but I wonder if she might have told me the truth later. I think she tried to tell me at the end but it was too late: she hadn't the strength or the words. You know, Jim, I've been having some very strange dreams about my mother and my sister and I even thought for a short while that Paradise was haunted by them. Ridiculous, of course. Now I wonder if it was just the truth trying somehow to break through: my mother's unhappiness, from which she tried to shield me, succeeding so well that it's only my unconscious mind that recalls it, and perhaps Rosa, who I do know to be dead, trying to tell me summat.'

Jim looked puzzled. 'That's a very fanciful idea, Florence. What do you imagine it might be?'

'Ah, Jim, I think you've already guessed.'

'You did say, 'Rosa, who I do know to be dead'.'

'Exactly. I can't help wondering if my father is still alive. He was dead only to my mother after she blamed him for Rosa's accident, and she made him dead to me, too. I think mebbe that's the reason she never told me the truth. Now, however, it needn't be so. He'd be quite old — in his seventies,' she smiled an apology at Jim, 'but he may still be living.'

'He could well be. Some of us have attained that great age and have yet to be called to our Maker.' Jim smiled back. 'If you don't do anything about finding him, it will be as if what Lily told you was true. But if you do try to find him, that's when Frances Marchant's story will make a difference.'

'Yes . . . and I just don't know what to do. I don't want to seek him out and stir up trouble. I can't blame him for Rosa's death now when I never have done in the past. That was my mother's action, not mine. On the other hand, perhaps he'd be glad to see me again. How can I know?'

'I can't advise you, Florence,' Jim said. 'I don't even know what I would do if I were in your position. The decision must be yours. All I can advise you is to tread carefully. The only other thing to consider is, if you are going to look for your dad, love, it might be better to get on with it rather than delay.'

'I think you're right, Jim. There must be no more messing about, one way or the other: either I look for him now or I decide to forget all about it and honour Lily's version of events as if that's all I know.'

Florence drove up Nightingale Lane and drew up outside Sea View.

'Feels bitter now, like snow,' Jim remarked, getting out of the car.

'Oh, I hope not. Always such a nuisance, and

I don't fancy those long country roads to Burton Barrow in the snow.' Florence lifted the boot and handed out the box of remaining vegetables to him.

'I forbid you to even try it!' said Jim. 'I'm sure the Morris is a handy little car, but I don't want to read in the newspaper about you being found upside down in a ditch.'

'Nor do I,' said Florence. 'I was brought up to believe it was vulgar to appear in the newspapers.'

Jim laughed.

'There is one thing I'd like to ask you, Jim, in confidence if you don't mind. Matthew Kendal — you know, you met him on the beach when I had Lucy staying — has bought some old wartime huts up above Fleming St Clair and wants to do them up for local small businesses to rent. He's offered to rent me one as a kitchen for the pickles. I went to look at the site and it was a right mess. I was a bit shocked, truth be told. I thought he was a genuine kind, what with him seeming so plausible and being the Miss Kendals' nephew, but I can't believe the place would ever come to anything. It couldn't be a swizz, could it?'

'I'd be amazed if it was. Matthew Kendal has done a lot of property deals round here and the villages are better for them. St Jude's Hall was privately owned and all falling down at one time, and he bought that, did it up and now the parish rents it from him — and not for very much, either. There's a café in Fleming that he did up and sold on, which is flourishing in smart premises, and several more besides . . . '

'So you reckon it'll be all right?'

'I think you should be drawing up plans for your new kitchen, Florence. I hadn't heard of these huts, and nor shall I be saying anything, but when word gets out you can be sure there'll be stiff competition to get in there.'

'Well, if you're sure . . . '

'I am. I know you've been looking round for somewhere new and you'd really regret it if you missed out on this place.'

★ ★ ★

It was a Thursday evening in late February and Lucy came in from work looking more than usually tired. The house was warm, the fire blazing merrily in the sitting room and she could hear Denis busy in the kitchen already.

'A letter from Mum this morning, Denis,' said Lucy. 'Do you want to have a read?'

'Aye, I'll just peel these spuds for our tea and then take a look,' said Denis.

Lucy had been amazed at the transformation in her husband since his mother's vindictive nature had been revealed and she'd been asked to leave. Tellingly, they had heard very little from Kathleen Walden since she'd departed under a cloud of shame. She had spent Christmas with her spinster sister, whom she'd always professed to find difficult.

Consequently, Lucy and Denis had enjoyed a wonderfully romantic Christmas together, just the two of them, with all bad feelings, resentments and misunderstandings buried and forgotten. Typically, Denis hadn't said much about his mother since then, but Lucy recognised that he'd understood he'd not been fair on his wife at all — allowing Mrs Walden to invite herself in to be waited on, and he himself not helping at all with the cooking and cleaning. Now Mrs Walden was pretty much off the scene, he seemed to be seeing his domestic life in a sharper focus, and he had said rather shame-facedly that he'd resolved to treat Lucy with all the care and devotion she deserved.

'Mum's got some unusual news. See what you think . . .'

Denis set the potatoes to boil, dried his hands and picked up Florence's letter to Lucy.

. . . I heard from someone who knew Grandma all those years ago that it's possible your granddad is still alive. I'll tell you how this came about next time I see you. It seems such a strange thing to learn after all this time, and at first I thought it would be better to leave things be, which is why I haven't told you before. He wouldn't expect me to be turning up, would he, so he wouldn't be missing me at all. And then I thought: well, he is my dad and it would be a shame not to find out, so I've engaged someone (a private inquiry agent, he's called) to find out if he's still alive and where he is. Then, when I know the answer to that, I can decide what to do. I don't want to go making trouble so I can always back off without him ever knowing I tried. I'll tell you when I learn more.

The other news I have is that I'm to move the pickles out of Paradise and to a new kitchen. I know you'll be pleased for me, having got your nose turned up about the smell! Matthew, who brought you the flowers from Beatrice and Jane, is doing up some old wartime huts to rent out to small local businesses. I even get to decide on the kitchen layout so I can be sure it will suit. This will make a huge difference to me, Violet and Carmen, and also to Jim, who's intending to grow all sorts of new things I can use and will want to be sure I have the room to deal with them, and also to Beatrice and Jane, who have lent me their storeroom and can now have it back. Honestly, Lucy, I was worried I'd have to give up the pickles, they were so stinking me out, and it didn't seem fair to Scamper either, but now it will all be wonderful . . .

'So much news Florence has got. Does she ever stand still?' said Denis. 'A pickle factory!'

'It's not a pickle factory, you daft thing, it's a preserves kitchen. I'm just glad she'll be able to reclaim her cottage from the vinegar smell.'

'I can see why she's going a bit carefully about your granddad, though. Who knows what she'll discover there?'

'Yes, but it's her choice. I know she'll do the right thing by everyone. If I never get to meet him, I'll know it's because she's decided that's for the best.'

'And if you do . . .'

'Then I can tell him he'll be a great-granddad before the year's out, can't I? Mum's not the only one with exciting news. I should write and tell her now I'm really certain about the baby.'

'She'll be made up, Lucy love.'

'Yes, Den, she will. I'll write after tea, if I can stay awake long enough. Can't tell anyone else until we've told Mum.'

'What about my mum? Do you think we should invite her over one Sunday for dinner and tell her about the baby then?'

'Why not?' said Lucy, generously. 'She'll be the baby's other grandma.'

'When would suit you best, love?' asked Denis, solic-itously. 'I don't want you taking on too much.'

'No, it's all right, Den. I'll manage with your help. How about a fortnight next Sunday? Say, about half past twelve?'

'I'll ask her. And I'll take her home around four so you can put your feet up for the rest of the day.'

They smiled, confident in their love for each other, the prospect of a long and happy marriage — blessed with children — stretching ahead of them.

21

The lakeside town of Bowness was quiet in March, with very few visitors braving the rain. The Lake District peaks were still capped with snow and the roads had been wet all the way from Guisethorpe to Blackburn the previous day, where Florence had stayed the night at Lucille and Denis's, and now on into Westmorland today. Florence hadn't been to the Lake District since that holiday nearly twenty-one years ago when Connie Summers had drowned. When the choppy waves and grey water of Windermere came into view, against her will her eyes were drawn to the vast, bleak, cold water, and that memory was stirred up afresh. Connie's body has never been recovered from Derwentwater. But, Florence told herself, that was all in the past; this was nothing to do with then. She had come for a purpose, she had arrived now, and she would see this visit through.

She felt no optimism about seeing her father, just a vague feeling of sadness mixed with a little dread. Her spirits were low, despite the excitement of visiting Lucille and Denis. The news about the baby was wonderful but, even so, Florence felt as if the dark days of winter had entered her soul and spring wasn't yet in sight. The troubles of her past life, the bad dreams, those ghosts . . .

The weather had been bleak in Guisethorpe towards the end of winter, as in much of the country, with deep snowdrifts, so that daily life in the village had largely ground to a halt. The bulbs Carmen had planted in Florence's garden were trying to push their green shoots up into the light, but what showed of them had been bowed under snow for days and they had yet to reveal any cheerful spring colour. It wasn't a good time to make a journey, but Florence was mindful of what Jim had advised about not delaying if she were going to do this at all, and Mr Sharp, the private inquiry agent, had reinforced this with the news that her father was ill.

She found the house — Mr Sharp had given her very clear directions — and parked in the street right outside.

The heater on the Morris seemed to be failing and was hardly giving out any warmth at all, so Florence was stiff with cold as she stepped out of the car, wearing her hat and coat.

How she wished Scamper was with her, but Scamper had gone to stay with Jim and Mildred, with strict instructions that she was not to be over-fed. Mildred had taken a liking to the little dog, which Jim thought was a way of Mildred properly making friends with Florence without actually apologising, and which suited Florence just fine.

Such a long journey to think it all through, this meeting with her father, but now she was here at last, standing outside his house, she still didn't know what to say.

Better just say hello, tell him who you are and see what happens . . .

She went up the short front path to the modest house with a half-timbered front and knocked on the door.

After a couple of minutes she could hear bolts being drawn back and then the heavy front door opened. A woman stood there, which was not what Florence had been expecting. She took a step back. Maybe this was the wrong house.

'Yes? Can I help you?'

'I'm not sure. I'm looking for Robert Townsend.'

'Then you've come to the right place.'

Florence had to ask. Mr Sharp might have got his details wrong, after all, and there would be no back-tracking if Florence's visit was a particularly unwelcome surprise. 'Are you Mrs Townsend?'

The woman, who looked to be about Florence's age, smiled. 'No, I'm here looking after Mr Townsend. My name is Mrs Plowden. But come in. Mr Townsend is here. Who shall I say . . . ?'

'Er, say a face from the past, please, a friendly one,' said Florence. She tried to adopt a bright smile to match her words, but her stomach was dancing and her mouth felt trembly with nerves.

'Ah, one of Mr Townsend's pupils,' assumed Mrs Plowden, and went into a room on the right of the little hall.

Florence knew from Mr Sharp that her father had been a teacher at one of the Westmorland grammar schools. She didn't know what his job had been before then. Now he was retired and lived here in this town, popular with summer visitors, overlooking Lake Windermere.

Mrs Plowden came back almost straight away. 'Please, go through,' she said. 'He's always glad to have a visit from a former pupil, though he tires easily, I must warn you. Best not stay too long.'

Florence almost held her breath as she pushed

415

the room door open wide and saw her father for the first time in almost forty years. She stepped in and looked curiously at him.

He was very thin and very old-looking, as if he was wizened and dried out. His hair was sparse and faded to white and his skin was so white it was almost blue. He did not look a well man and he made no attempt to rise from his chair. There was a narrow bed in one corner and it was clear he lived in this one room.

'Hello, Dad,' Florence said, and took off her felt hat so that he could see her hair.

For a long moment the old man said nothing at all, just looked and looked at her, at her face and her hair.

'Florence . . . ?' His voice was quiet and thin with the whispery quality of tissue paper.

'Yes, Dad.' Florence swallowed. 'Little Flo.'

His eyes roamed her face again, searching intently. 'Florence? Is it really Florence?' His face was now lit by a smile, though his eyes were bright with unshed tears. 'Oh . . . oh, my darling . . . my darling child . . . You have come back to me.' He held out shaking arms. 'I never thought . . . I have dreamed of this moment for over half my life.'

Florence sank to her knees beside his chair, and he raised a thin white hand to stroke her hair.

'Yes, it is you, it *is*. I can see that now. Only my darling girls have such red hair.'

'Oh, Dad,' she wept, 'I didn't know where to find you. I would have come sooner if I'd known. I was told . . . that is, I thought . . . '

'Well, Little Flo, you *have* found me. My clever girl. You have found me at last and I was never so

416

glad of anything as I am to see you now.'

They held each other and Florence felt her father's bones beneath his woollens. He's dying, she thought, and I have found him only just in time.

★   ★   ★

Florence stayed at a guesthouse in the town that night and came to visit her father again the next day. He tired easily, as Mrs Plowden had said, and yet he wanted to hear all about Florence's life, just as she wanted to know about his.

He told her he had lived 'an exemplary life of sobriety' since Rosa had been killed, which Florence, with a crooked smile, said was a perfect schoolmaster's phrase.

'I wasn't a teacher then, Flo. I was a manager at a cotton mill, but when I saw what I had lost I knew the path I was taking would lead me to hell. So I gave up the drink and trained to be a teacher. I tried to be a new person, a better man, and I took Lily's utter rejection of me as my due. I did not deserve her, or you. How I wished I'd seen the light sooner and not lost you all. Poor Rosa, gone for ever, my fault . . . and now you say Lily is dead, too.'

'A year ago, Dad. More — fourteen months. She told me you and Rosa had died of the Spanish flu and I had no reason to disbelieve her until I learned different, quite by chance.'

Florence went on to explain to her father how she had found him with professional help.

'I worried so much that I might not be welcome,

that you might have a new life with no room for me — your old family — in it.'

'Never, love. Never! You are all I have. You're the answer to my prayers.'

Florence told him about Lucy, that there was a new baby to look forward to in the early autumn, but he hardly seemed to take in the news.

'Now I have seen you again I can die happy,' he said. 'I'm glad for you, but I shan't see the autumn.'

'How long do you think you have?' she asked. There was no point denying what they both knew. She had seen the bottles of liquid medicine and tablets on a shelf just out of reach. It looked like a lot of medication.

'Mebbe days, Rosa, love. Mebbe less.'

Florence was shocked that he was expecting to die so soon, and yet she could see how frail he was. She didn't correct him over her name. Already she'd learned the medicine sometimes made him confused Mrs Plowden wasn't a daily help; she was a nurse.

'I'm so very grateful to have you back. I'm glad now that I've clung on to life for so long. I was waiting for you, love, and I didn't even know it.'

'Oh, Dad . . . ' Florence swallowed down her tears. She seemed to have been weeping most of the time since she'd arrived here.

'Ah, lass, don't take on so. We all have to go one day. So much better now . . . I am so very lucky in the end . . . more than I deserve to be.'

That afternoon he was too tired to sit up and had to lie down in his bed. Florence thought if she left that night she wouldn't see her father alive again. He was ready to die. She slept in a chair in the other room downstairs, taking it in turns with Mrs Plowden to sit beside him. It was four o'clock in the morning when she heard his breathing begin to change and she took his hand for the last time.

'Ah, Lily, lass,' he whispered. Those were his last words.

★ ★ ★

Over a week afterwards, late in the afternoon, Florence arrived back at Paradise Cottage. She had been away less than a fortnight but it seemed far longer. Her father was now buried in the churchyard of St Martin's Church, Bowness, and Florence had been pleased to meet many of his former pupils, and a lot of friends, at the funeral she had arranged. It seemed her father had not lived a lonely life all these years, although he had been without family, and nothing could make up to him for that.

She felt very tired as she got out of the car and let herself into the cottage, but also lost, as if she had no purpose. What day was it? What was she meant to be doing tomorrow? Did any of it matter anyway?

Paradise smelled faintly vinegary, though nothing like as bad as Florence remembered, and also damp. She went to the sitting room first, leaving her bags in the hallway. She should at least light a fire and then collect Scamper. In the sitting-room hearth the fire was neatly laid with kindling and logs, and there were extra logs and newspapers

419

stacked in the coal scuttle.

Jim's work, or Violet's. So kind . . .

The post and circulars were neatly piled on the little table next to the telephone and the cushions were plumped, the rug vacuumed.

Florence lit the fire, drawing it up with a spread of newspaper, then put the guard in front and went to see how she'd left the kitchen what seemed like half a lifetime ago.

Good grief! It's as if the fairy folk have been in!

The kitchen was spotlessly clean, and tidier than it had ever been since the day Florence made her first batch of pickles there. Nothing was lying about; every surface was cleared and the range was also clean and shiny. The only exception was the kitchen table, where a vase of daffodils stood on a mat in the centre. Tears sprang to Florence's eyes to see their delicate brightness, their optimism, when she felt so gloomy.

Violet and Carmen . . . I am so lucky to have them.

Florence opened the pantry and was astonished to find it empty of preserves. There was a loaf of bread in the bread bin and a pint of fresh milk sitting on the marble slab. What had happened to all the jars of pickles and jam? She tried to remember how she'd left it, how many jars there had been, though most were stored at the Kendal sisters' house. Violet had evidently moved them, though how she had managed it on her bicycle was a mystery, but it would be for a sensible reason so there was no need to worry.

Having checked the fire was safe to leave, Florence went across to Sea View to collect Scamper. She now noticed as she went along her front path that there were daffodils and primroses flowering, and shoots peeping above the soil, which might be the red tulips Carmen had planted in November.

Jim answered the door, but there was no sign of Scamper.

'Hello, Florence. I got your letter and Violet passed round the news after you telephoned her. I'm sorry for your loss, love.'

'Thank you, Jim. And thank you for all you've done at the cottage for me.' Florence pursed her lips to stop herself blubbing. She'd been brave and practical while she'd put the funeral arrangements in hand, but now she felt drained and vulnerable, and kindness was likely to make her cry.

'Is Scamper . . . ?'

'Mildred's just drying her off. She's been bathing her.'

'Good heavens.'

'Quite.'

Mildred came into the hallway then, Scamper leading her, barking with delight and with her coat looking unusually curly. Rather like Mildred's hair, really, Florence thought.

There was the joyful reunion and Florence thanked Mildred for her efforts.

'And here's some stew for your tea,' said Mildred, having fetched a Pyrex bowl from her kitchen. 'Enough for you and there'll be some leftover for Scamper, too. I left some bread and milk but you'll need a hot meal after all that driving. I said to my Jim — '

'Let Florence get on, Mil. She must be tired.' Jim gave a little wink and Florence thanked them again and took Scamper home.

That night, as she climbed into bed, Scamper tucked up in her basket downstairs, Florence felt a huge sense of relief that she'd found her father, that it hadn't been too late to tell him what she'd wanted to, and let him say what he had to. She had given him a good funeral, well attended. She could have done no more. Now she was home, in her own little Paradise, with her darling dog settled safe and warm, and looking only slightly fatter for her stay at Sea View. There was the sale of her father's house to see to, but that was in hand and could be completed by letter. Already his effects had been given away and an auction house had collected some of the furniture. There had been nothing Florence wanted except for a photograph of her parents on their wedding day, which she'd found in a drawer. It was framed a little fussily, not to Florence's taste, and had been wrapped in a pillowcase; now it sat beside her bed on her little chest of drawers.

That night, despite all the turmoil, all the revelations and sadness, Florence slept more soundly than she had done for many months. There were no more unquiet dreams.

★ ★ ★

The following day Florence forced herself to be up early, although the comfort of her own bed in her own home tempted her to a day of idleness. But people who run small businesses seldom get a day off, and Florence was long overdue to return to normal life. Time to get organised before everything got out of hand.

While she fed Scamper and made some toast for her breakfast, she tried to pick up in her mind where she'd left off when she'd gone to find her father. There was a delivery due at Nicolson & Filbert, and also at the other retailers she supplied with Florence Lily jars, and she must get on with making some fresh pickles. Jim had promised very early baby vegetables he'd been nurturing, and Harry Nicolson was keen to get his hands on those. So much to do . . . And where was she with Miss Bea and Miss Jane and the reading? She could barely remember what it was they had been enjoying . . .

Get the bowls out for salting, take Scamper for a quick walk and then it would be over to Jim and the baby vegetables . . .

But where were the bowls? And what had happened to the big preserving pans? Where was the salt, for that matter? She searched the cupboards and found them empty of all her preserving utensils and supplies.

Now what?

'Florence?' It was Violet, calling out as she let herself and Carmen in, Scamper going to greet them. 'Ah, Florence, love, it's so good to see you back safely. We're all so sorry about your dad. Big thing for you to face, up there by yourself . . . He'd have been so comforted by your being there, though.'

'Thank you, Violet. And thank you and Carmen for everything. I seem to have mislaid a few things but I can see your hand in all this cleaning and tidying.'

'No bother. When we knew to expect you back we just got on with it. Carmen was a whirlwind.'

'I broke a jug — I'm sorry,' Carmen confessed, 'but I'll get you a new one.'

Florence sat down then and was laughing and crying at the same time.

'Oh dear, I didn't mean to,' Carmen began, looking stricken.

'Don't be daft, Carmen. Doesn't matter about the jug. I'm only being silly because everyone's been so kind and I've got such good friends.'

'No need to cry about it,' said Violet. 'In fact, better go and put on some nice clothes while Carmen runs Scamper up the lane and back . . .'

'. . . If she can go that far. I'm sure she's fatter.'

'Shush, Carmen . . . and then we've got somewhere to be at ten o'clock.'

'Who? Not me? Sorry, Violet, but I'm a bit slow this morning. What exactly is going on? Is this summat to do with my pans and bowls disappearing? And where are all the jars from the pantry?'

'All will be revealed,' said Violet, tapping her nose like a ham actress. 'Carmen and I are saying nothing for the minute.'

Carmen mimed zipping her lip. 'And Scamper's not saying either,' she laughed, going to fetch the dog lead.

★　★　★

'I'm guessing it's summat to do with the huts,' said Florence as Violet directed her to turn right at the top of the hill above Fleming St Clair, 'but they must be weeks off being ready yet. I gave Matthew my layout for the kitchen only a few days before I had to go away.'

424

'Turn in here on the left,' said Violet. She shot a look over her shoulder at Carmen, on the back seat of the Morris, as if she just knew she was about to speak.

'Oh, this has all been cleared and flattened so I can drive right up. That's good. The outside looks smart, too. Someone's been working hard to have got those windows in, and to do that new paintwork. And there's Matthew's car, if I'm not mistaken. And Miss Jane and Miss Bea with him! What are the Kendal ladies doing here? And Becca. And, good grief, Jim and Mildred. And Mary Davis and Mavis Farlowe. And isn't that Sandra Filbert? I don't believe it.'

'What time is it, Carmen?'

'One minute to ten, Grandma.'

'Just right. Come along then, Florence. Right on time.'

'Violet . . . ?'

'Don't just sit there, love. People are waiting.'

Florence got out of her car and went round to help out Violet, Carmen and Scamper. Then she straightened her hat in the wing mirror and smoothed down her red jacket.

'Good morning,' called Matthew, and his aunts came hurrying across to kiss Florence and express their condolences.

'Are you ready to do the honours?' said Matthew. He took Florence's arm and led her to one of the huts. Sandra Filbert stood aside to reveal that the door was painted bright red with 'Florence Lily' in the same smart copperplate style as it appeared on Florence's jar labels.

'Hah . . . ' gasped Florence. 'So beautiful. I can't

425

believe it. Thank you, Matthew. We didn't really talk about the outside and I reckon you thought this up yourself.'

'Well, I did have the labels to refer to in my aunts' storeroom,' he laughed, 'and a lot of suggestions from Mr Yateman and Mrs Peasall, too. Now, would you care to look inside?'

He gave Florence a key and she fitted it into the lock and opened the door.

She had been expecting to find the unit empty; cleared and painted, at best. What she saw was a beautiful professional kitchen, exactly as she had drawn it for Matthew in her layout. It was all fitted and finished, and her bowls, pans and jars were neatly stacked on shelves. There were two big modern cookers, sinks, and shelves for storing the finished products. A door led to a large pantry with marble slabs and there was even a refrigerator for storing the vegetables.

Florence walked all round, looking and smiling and looking again, speechless with surprise and joy.

'Oh, it's wonderful,' she breathed at last. 'It's exactly what I wanted.'

'I'm glad we got it right,' said Matthew modestly.

'It's beyond right. It's perfect,' smiled Florence. 'I know an awful lot of people — some of them here now — have helped to do all this for me. Thank you. Thank you all.'

Everyone bustled round, admiring the kitchen.

'It's lovely,' said Becca shyly, stroking the beautiful smooth worktop and looking at Matthew.

'Marvellous . . . ' said Jane.

'. . . but don't think you have to move the

pickles from our storeroom . . . '

'. . . in a rush. Better just to take them when you need to.'

'Oh, but we did laugh to see all your pans trans-ported in the back of Matthew's car,' added Beatrice.

'As Harry's representative on earth, I thought I ought to take a look at the new premises of our most popular supplier,' said Sandra Filbert mischievously. 'He'll be sorry to have missed this. He and I have been discussing expanding our order. Now you've got the capacity, we can talk about that seriously.'

'So you think we've answered the brief?' asked Matthew.

'Better than I dreamed,' said Florence. 'Thank you for making it ready so quickly. It's just what I need: a proper preserves kitchen so I can get on with all that I'm planning, all my hopes for the future of the business. I really appreciate your kindness and everyone's effort.'

Matthew laughed then. 'I've heard that you're a great one for getting on and getting things done,' he said, 'so, as this was for you, I took a leaf out of your book. It was just a case of being organised.'

'Aye, you're right,' said Florence, as Carmen circulated with a tray of sherry glasses for a toast without spilling a single drop.

'To Florence Lily,' said Matthew, raising his glass, and the company all echoed the toast.

'Thank you, Matthew. And I'll raise my glass in turn to all of you. It's no use being organised if you haven't got good people watching your back.

Where would I be without you all? So here's to the kindness of dear friends.'

'The kindness of friends.'

Epilogue

Florence decided it was high time to change the frame around the photograph of her parents. She tended to notice the fussy, gold-painted scrolls of the frame more than the picture itself, and she wanted something simple and elegant to enhance the photograph.

She decided the easiest way to choose the right size would be to take the old frame and the surround, which was a little foxed with age, to the shop to use as reference.

It was easy enough to unclip the frame on the kitchen table, but when she pulled off the cardboard back, there was a small oval scrap of paper lying on top of the photograph of her parents. She picked it up and turned it over. It was a photograph of Rosa.

Florence sat looking at her sister for a long time. She hadn't seen any real image of her since she had died, only in her dreams, in a long corridor in Tempest House, and the wraith that sometimes flickered at the corner of her eye. Rosa looked so like Little Flo in the locket, but a year or two older when the photo was taken, with a confident little smile on her beautiful face and a very direct look. The image was in black and white, but Florence knew the exact colour of Rosa's hair: red, and just a little darker than her own. 'Only my darling girls have such red hair,' Dad had said.

Eventually Florence looked again in the hope

of finding another layer of backing and more photographs, but there was none. Just Rosa.

Slowly Florence went upstairs and took the locket with the pictures of her mother and herself from her drawer and brought it down. With the end of a teaspoon she eased the photograph of her mother carefully from the locket and smoothed it flat — there would be a second frame to buy for this — then pressed Rosa's picture into the locket in its place. It was so tiny it fitted without need of trimming.

Now she had her whole family. They had been divided by death, by foolishness, by heartbreak, by falsehood, and by being unable to forgive, but they were all here at last, in the hands of the only one still alive. The Townsend family, parents and children: Robert and Lily, Rosa and Florence.

Dear Reader,

Josephine Cox has been such a huge part of our publishing for many years. We shared so many moments together, whether it was singing carols at Christmas, sorting her bags of fan mail, library tours around Blackburn or celebrating her countless Number 1 bestsellers.

More than anything, her readers meant the world to her, and she was as loyal to you as you were to her, writing a reply to every single fan letter that she received.

Josephine was an inspiration, forging a path from humble beginnings to the top of the bestseller lists, and through her stories that continue to touch the hearts of millions. She really was the 'Nation's Favourite', touching so many of us with her writing and will be greatly missed by one and all.

Kimberley Young
Executive Publisher

Remembering Josephine Cox

by Gilly Middleton

Josephine Cox was a great writer of popular fiction, the queen of family drama. She didn't write her first novel until she was in her forties, and yet she managed to produce over sixty bestsellers in the second half of her life. Who wouldn't admire that amazing work ethic, and the talent to give her vast readership exactly what they loved?

This, of course, was the secret of Jo's success. She took what we all know — the family — and wove through her timeless tales of love and loss, tragedy and heartbreak, triumph and disaster. The appeal of her characters is that we can all recognise something of them from real life, though Jo made them always wonderfully larger than life, more vivid, more dramatic, more fun to read about. For a co-author, this legacy is a very special gift.

When Jo dreamed up the idea of a woman who leaves her old life to start afresh in a place where she knows no one, there already was the basis for a classic Josephine Cox novel. A woman who no one knows is a woman with a past waiting to be revealed, someone with Jo's favourite subject, secrets. Fate has bestowed on Florence Stanville beauty and courage, but she hasn't had life all her own way. Florence is a strong character but, like all Jo's heroines, she isn't flawless. In the sleepy seaside village of Guisethorpe, where she has chosen to begin her life anew, she cannot escape the hidden dramas of her childhood, nor the antagonism a strong woman can evoke when she won't sit down and shut up. Readers may well recognise the wonderful community spirit such as thrives in Guisethorpe, a place where everyone knows each other and people look out for their neighbours and lend a helping hand. This year, of all years, people have valued this in their home towns. However, this would not be a Josephine Cox novel if, behind the quiet, picturesque seafront, turbulent emotions didn't threaten to erupt.

In contrast, Florence's sweet-natured daughter, Lucy, is settling down in Blackburn, the noisy, crowded, friendly city of Jo's birth and the backdrop to so many of her stories. Lucy is just starting out on married life to a man she adores, but when she takes on the man she doesn't envisage she has to take on his far-from-lovable mother, too. That's family life in all its glory; turbulence, the falling out and making up, the misunderstanding and understanding all too well. It was a privilege to work with Jo on a novel so deeply rooted in the topic she made very much her own and for which she was much-loved.

When Jo died in July 2020, it was a very sad day for her loved ones and for those who worked with her. We all admired her clear-sightedness about what she wanted to say and why it was right for her book. She has been described as 'a force of nature', and that sums up the astonishing energy Jo possessed, without which she would not have written a fraction of the wonderful stories that made her a household name and a top favourite in lending libraries over many years. We are lucky to have the legacy of this timeless fiction, and I count myself beyond fortunate to have worked with her.

Gilly Middleton, November 2020

Jo knew what it was like to grow up in poverty. Barnardo's was one of her favourite charities — here is what she said about the power of kindness.

Even in this affluent age, we are all constantly made aware of families, including the young and the old, who in silence, continue to suffer the agony of being cold and shivering; without any form of heating to relieve the pain and the slicing bitterness that robs them of content and comfort.

As a child in the fifties, alongside my siblings, we knew what it was like to lie in bed at night and shiver uncon-trollably when the cold bit hard. We rarely had the comfort of the thick, fleecy warmth of a blanket to wrap ourselves in, or a hot water bottle, or electric blankets. There was no relied from the cold with the cheery warmth of a fire burning in the hearth. Instead, the dampness glistened down the bedroom walls, and no matter how hard you tried to keep warm, there was little relief form the biting misery of coldness stealing over you.

For some of us, it was a way of life, and we quietly accepted it, because that's the way it was. Back then, times were hard and money was short, and the families did the best they could, with what they had. Being cold was simply a fact of so many people's lives back then. Now though, we live in a more affluent society, where we are made to believe there is more work to be had, and more money to be earned, and neighbours who care, and that might be true for many, but not for everyone.

Right now, someone else may be shivering not far from you. Someone else who is bitterly cold and suffering in silence because they don't like to talk about it. They have a sense of pride and an idea that to ask for help, or to talk about it is not done. Or maybe they believe that no-one will care.

But those of us who are warm at night and have never know what it's like to cry with cold. Right now, someone somewhere is bitterly cold inside and out; often tears because they don't know what to do, or who to turn to. Someone out there is too proud or too ashamed to ask for the help they badly need.

And then there are the ones who are more fortunate and want to help. Those of us who ache with the idea that in this day and age, a person can be inside their own home, shivering, so cold and miserable they become unable to get out of the chair. So they sit still, believing no-one has the time or patience, or even care. Instead, they may feel abandoned and so impossibly lonely, they are in danger of sinking into oblivion, because they either don't know who to turn to, or maybe their pride won't let them reach out.

And so, it must be us who reaches out to them; gently, kindly … not in a condescending manner but with gentleness and humanity; making them feel as though they have a friend who truly wants to help, and will never make judgements.

To donate to Barnardo's, visit their website https://donate.barnardos.org.uk/